Prais

Best La

"Grimdark on the High Seas!" - **BiblioSanctum**

"...Piratical grimdark mastery, superbly written, with utterly engaging characters." - **Fantasy Book Review**

"... a fantasy story not to be missed." - **Bookwraiths**

"Rob J. Hayes has crafted one of the most entertaining duologies I've ever read in Where Loyalties Lie and The Fifth Empire of Man." - **Booknest.eu**

"... the perfect fusion of Grimdark and epic nautical fantasy that you never thought possible." - **Fantasy Book Critic**

Rob J. Hayes

The Fifth Empire of Man
(Book 2 of Best Laid Plans)

by

Rob J. Hayes

For everyone who waited.

And for rum!

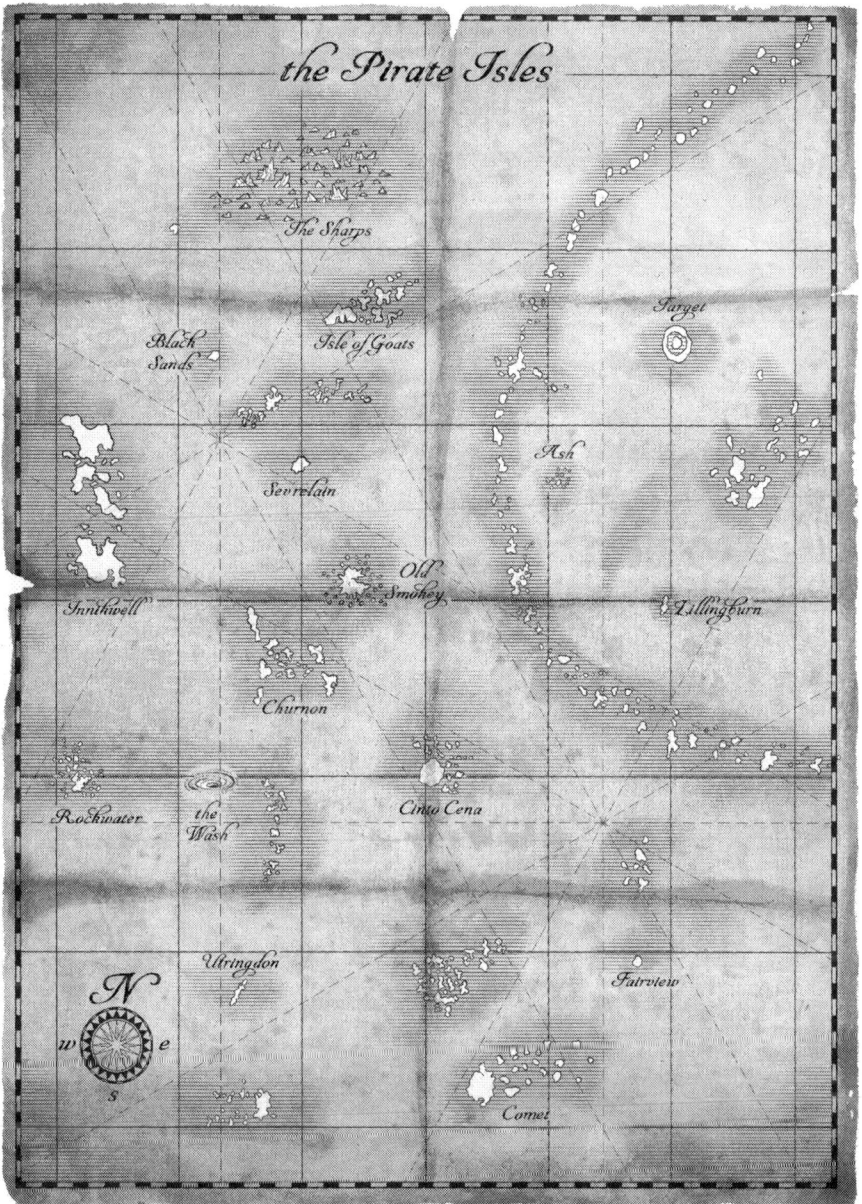

the Pirate Isles

The Sharps

Target

Black Sands

Isle of Goats

Ash

Sevrelain

Old Smokey

Innihwell

Lillingburn

Churnon

Rockwater

the Wash

Cinto Cena

Utringdon

Fairview

N

W · E

S

Comet

Part 1 - Batten Down the Hatches

They will come at you again and again said the Oracle
We'll be ready said Drake
You will lose people said the Oracle

Starry Dawn

"What about the decorations?" Elaina said, thumbing towards the stocks.

Three men and one woman were locked into the wood-and-metal contraptions, where they faced both the heat of the day and the cold of the night without food or water, nor clothing on their backs. All four of them looked to be in a truly sorry state, and it seemed one of the men was already long past dead. There's a certain smell that only corpses can produce, and it was strong in the air.

The little woman in the big cavalier hat snorted, and Elaina caught a glimpse of a sneer underneath the broad brim. "Ambassadors from the blooded, those of the bastards that still breathe anyway. They said something 'bout Thorn's direct manner an' Rose took exception to it. Don't reckon we'll be gettin' no more ambassadors any time soon."

Elaina grimaced. She was no stranger to pain or brutality and had caused more than her fair share of death, but a slow one was very different to a quick one.

"Say." The little woman tilted her head so that her eyes were visible underneath her hat, and Elaina found a pair of shit-coloured browns twinkling at her. "You're pretty much an ambassador, ain't ya?"

Elaina fixed the smaller woman with a hard stare, but her tormentor simply cackled and started up the steps to the yellow-stone building.

Feeling at the mercy of others was something Elaina hated. Back home in Fango she was one of those in charge, respected and feared in equal measure for her skill and savagery as a pirate as much as for being the daughter of Tanner Black. Everywhere and anywhere you could sail in the Pirate Isles, Elaina Black was a name known and known well. Here in Chade she was just another person, a captain of her own ship but no one important. A large part of her wanted to run back to *Starry Dawn* and sail away, but her father had given her a job to do and it would be a long time before it brought her back to the Pirate Isles.

She wandered behind the little woman in a sort of daze, staring at the pillars to either side of the steps leading up to the doorway. The pillars held up an awning a good ten feet above them that provided welcome shade from the sun. Two guards stood either side of the waiting doorway, and both looked at Elaina with cold eyes behind metal helmets.

"Henry," one of the guards said, with a nod to the little woman. "This the pirate?"

The cavalier hat bobbed. "She even came alone."

Elaina had the feeling she was being mocked. She swallowed her pride and followed the woman past the two guards and through the door into the mansion.

"You're Henry the Red, ain't you?" she said.

"Aye."

"Heard lots about the Black Thorn," Elaina continued, hoping to get a rise out of her. "Heard you were with him for much of it. That's about all they say of you."

Henry the Red laughed, a harsh sound that echoed around the largely empty hallway. "Sounds like most of what ya heard is shit, girl." She stopped in front of a door and turned to face Elaina. "They're in there. See yaself in."

Elaina started towards the door, but stopped when she realised her sword was still buckled to her belt. "Should I be leaving this with you?"

Again Henry the Red laughed. "Keep it. You're walkin' into a room with the Black Thorn an' his Rose. Ya'd have ta be some special kind of dumb cunt ta draw steel in there." With that last laugh, she turned and walked away, leaving Elaina standing alone inside the Lord and Lady of Chade's home.

Elaina realised she had no idea whether she should knock or not. She imagined how she would feel if someone entered her cabin without knocking, and knew it would put her in very much a murderous state of mind. Of course, she also had to admit it would make for a much stronger and more confident entrance. Elaina shook her head with a growl and stopped procrastinating. She put her hand to the door and threw it open, stepping into the room beyond without pausing to take it in.

Perhaps it was the size of the room, or the grandeur of the furnishings – the rugs, bookshelves, and tapestries. Maybe it was the smell, clean but lived-in with just a hint of something flowery. Whatever it was, something made Elaina falter, and she stopped short of a loud announcement of her presence, instead standing motionless as her eyes swept across the room.

"Oh, the manners of pirates," said a woman standing at the window. She was stunning, with perfect white skin, hair even darker than Elaina's, and a sleek black dress that hugged her curves – including the fairly obvious bump of pregnancy. The woman turned fiercely intelligent eyes on Elaina. "It's polite to introduce yourself upon entry, Captain Black."

Elaina glanced around the room; it appeared they were alone. "Ya already know who I am. Seems a bit pointless to introduce myself."

"We're trying to civilise the Wilds," the woman countered. "Manners are important."

"You're Rose?" Elaina said, taking a couple of steps forward.

The door slammed behind her and Elaina startled, hating herself for it. Looking back, she saw a big man, one of the ugliest she'd ever seen, lying on a padded sofa next to the door. A big-booted foot dangled off the edge of the sofa and a large axe lay on the floor nearby.
"Must you kick the door, Betrim?" Rose said.

He pushed himself into a sitting position and yawned through his patchy beard. The horrific scars on the left side of his face tugged his visage into a ghastly picture that made Elaina want to look away.

"Door gets closed no matter which way I close it," he complained.

"Scuff marks." Rose let the accusation hang.

The man leaned closer and looked at the door with his one eye. "Gives it a lived-in feel, I reckon."

"You're the Black Thorn?" Elaina said, trying to pull the attention back to herself before the two of them got into an argument over the décor.

"Aye," Thorn said, standing and picking up his big axe. He walked past Elaina towards the desk at the far end of the room. He glanced at Rose. "She's definitely a Black. Got her da's eyes."

"You've met my father?" Elaina said.

The Black Thorn nodded as he reached the far side of the room and leaned against the wall. "Unfortunately. Never liked the bastard though. Always had this… feel about him. Big man who thought he was bigger. Met another like him once, Never Never Jago. Dumb shit used to say 'never' all the time. Never killed a goat, never eaten horse, never fucked a woman at the same time as her sister.

"One day old Never Never decided to break one of his nevers and attack me. Came at me with a spear." The Black Thorn paused and Elaina glanced towards Rose, but the woman was staring out of the window again. "Wanted to make a bigger name fer himself, I reckon. Fuckin' fool. Sure knew how to bleed though."

"That's the first time I've heard that one, dear," Rose said sweetly.

"Aye," the Black Thorn said with a laugh. "Well, the list of folk tried or tryin' ta kill me seems ta be growin' daily. If I told ya every single one we'd never never get the bloody Wilds under control." He turned his one-eyed gaze back to Elaina. "So, why are you here?"

Elaina took a step forward and glanced once more at Rose before addressing the Black Thorn. "My da wants an alliance with Chade."

The Black Thorn let out a groan, rolled his eye, and scratched at the burnt side of his face all at the same time.

"You'll have to forgive my husband," Rose said. She made her way from the window to the desk, cradling the bulge in her midsection. "I'm afraid he detests peace talks. Much more suited to putting axes in things, really."

Elaina eyed the man's axe and wagered it had been put into a great many things. "Which one of you's in charge?"

"I am."

"She is."

Elaina focused on Rose as the woman perched on the desk, and darkened the room with a radiant smile. "Tanner's willing to let your ships pass through the isles untouched. Any of them bearing your endorsement. It's the same deal as the Guild gets."

"So it is, and an excellent deal at that. There's a reason those Acanthian merchants are so fat, and at least part of it is their permission to sail through the isles unmolested." Rose fell silent, looking Elaina up and down.

Elaina was starting to feel impatient. She wasn't built for negotiations and treating with folk. She was built for action, for piracy. She hated to admit it, but her father would have been better off sending Blu.

"Do you want to know the terms?" she said.

"His terms?" Rose said.

"Aye."

"Not particularly." There was something in the woman's eyes that gave Elaina the impression Chade had been a safer place when it was ruled by thieves and corrupt politicians. "But I'll take a guess at ships, crew, and weapons. The same things Drake Morrass recently asked from us."

The Black Thorn snorted. "That man is a fucking demon, and I should know. I fought a bloody army of them."

"A very handsome demon." Rose grinned at her husband.

"Don't matter what Morrass offered," Elaina spat. "Bastard is dead."

That made both Rose and her Thorn pause, and Elaina felt the weight of all three of their eyes pressing down on her. It seemed both of them could give a glare when they wanted to. Elaina shifted her footing, but under such scrutiny she couldn't find a comfortable spot.

"Did ya see his body?" the Black Thorn said.

"No," Elaina's voice broke a little. She realised her mouth was as dry as a desert.

The Black Thorn snorted. "Then he ain't dead. Fucker is harder ta kill than… uh, me."

Rose picked up a bottle from a silver drinks tray and poured dark red liquid into a cup before sliding off the desk – gracefully, given her swollen belly – and approaching Elaina.

"We've been horribly rude, haven't we?" Rose handed the cup to Elaina. "Come, sit down." She took Elaina's spare hand and guided her to one of the sofas lining the walls. She sat without a hint of effort and pulled Elaina down next to her.

"It's ice wine, Captain Black," she said. "You sounded thirsty."

Elaina sniffed the cup and wrinkled her nose at the acrid smell, but she supposed that if they wanted her dead then poison would be the last method they would use. With that thought in mind, she raised the cup to her lips and took a deep swallow. It was a pleasant taste, some sort of fruit she couldn't name, cool and refreshing on her tongue and throat.

"Thank you," she said. It dawned on her that she was more than a little out of her depth. "Morrass is dead. I set it up myself."

Rose's dark eyes bored into her own blues. "Do explain."

"I set up a meet between Morrass and my da," Elaina continued, ignoring the worry in her gut over the fate of Keelin Stillwater, whom she'd also sent to the meeting. "My da ain't about to let Morrass walk out of that one. He's been wanting the bastard dead for somewhere close to forever."

"A very bold statement, given you have no idea of our affiliation with Captain Morrass." Rose's voice was so sweet it was almost a purr. "Are you aware my husband has worked for him in the past?"

"Hey," the Black Thorn said, wearing a look that might have been affront. It was hard to tell underneath all the scarring. "I didn't know I was workin' fer him. You knew it was him when you were fuckin' him."

Boldness had always been one of Elaina's strengths, and she decided to stick to it. "Doesn't matter a drop what happened in the past. Right now Tanner Black is offering an alliance, and that's all that matters."

"I will not ally Chade, nor the Wilds, to Tanner Black," Rose said.

Elaina snorted out a laugh. "Siding with Drake then? Seems a poor choice to ally with a dead man."

"Let her finish," the Black Thorn said. "She gets this look in her eyes when she's got more to say."

Elaina looked back at Rose to find her smiling. "I will not ally ourselves with Tanner Black or with Drake Morrass. I will, however, form an alliance with Elaina Black."

"What?" Elaina said, more than a little shocked.

The Black Thorn let out a rasping laugh.

"I have no intention of allying myself with Tanner or with Drake," Rose continued. "One is evil and the other… well, we all know what sort of a man Drake Morrass truly is, alive or dead. The Pirate Isles will have what ships and soldiers I can spare them as long as you are part of it, Captain Black. They will sail for you and fight for you, but not for your father. Do you understand?"

Elaina barked out a laugh. "No."

Rose sighed. "Men have no idea how to rule, dear."

Elaina glanced at the Black Thorn to find him nodding.

"Whoever moulds your Pirate Isles into a throne will need either a queen or an heir, and you can be both."

Elaina had a vision of being Drake Morrass' queen, and it was not a pleasant one. "Morrass is dead and Blu is Tanner's heir, not me."

Rose shrugged. "Accidents happen."

"I…" Elaina started, but realised she had no idea what she was going to say. "Uh…"

Again Rose laughed, and the sound echoed around the large room. "You need some time to come to terms with the idea. I understand. It will take time for me to assemble the ships and crew." Rose stood and pulled Elaina to her feet, guiding her towards the door.

"Take a few days to think about it, and when you come to terms with the offer and realise how much you truly want it, return and we will make it official."

Rose opened the door. The little woman in the cavalier hat was standing outside again, a sneer plastered to her face.

Elaina turned to find Rose smiling at her. "I do hope ours will be a long and fruitful relationship, Captain Black." The woman stepped close and kissed Elaina before ushering her out through the door and shutting it behind her.

Elaina stood in the corridor like a mute fool, wondering at the offer that had just been laid before her.

"She has that effect on most folk," said Henry the Red. "Ya should see her negotiate with men." An ugly laugh escaped the woman's lips. "Come on. Fancy a drink?"

Elaina followed her down the corridor, paying no attention to where she was being led. Her mind was awhirl with the possibilities.

"She offer you the world?" said Henry.

Elaina shook her head. "Just a part of it."

North Gale

T'ruck marched along the corridor with two soldiers in front of him and three behind. He towered over all five men, but he was under no illusions; should he so much as step out of line he would be skewered, and there was only so much even he could take.

His wounds had been patched up by a competent priest of the Five Kingdoms. Priests were good for tending wounds and making folk feel guilty, and little else. T'ruck had killed a few of them in his time; they infested the Five Kingdoms like ticks on a mange-ridden dog. Eight gods the Five Kingdomers worshipped, and each one needed more priests than the last.

For two days now he'd languished in a cell, alone. The brig on board *Storm Herald* was large, and T'ruck had heard other voices, other members of his crew, but they were kept away from him, and any attempt to raise his voice was met with the threat of beatings. T'ruck wasn't afraid of beatings, but if he was to escape – and he intended to – he would need to be as whole as possible.

His escorts stopped and opened a heavy wooden door, standing aside and motioning him in. T'ruck ducked under the frame and walked into the room. The door shut behind him. He'd been wondering how long it would take for the cowards to start the torture.

It was a large cabin, spacious enough for a good number of folk, with two chairs and a single table. T'ruck eyed it and decided it was likely to be where the torturer would put his devices, lay them out for all to see. The anticipation of torture was said to be even worse than the ordeal itself. T'ruck plucked the table from the floor, unhindered by his manacled hands, and turned it to kindling against the far wall, grinning at the petty destruction. Whoever came for him would have to put their precious knives and clamps on the floor. He paced the room, searching for a way out. There was nothing. The cabin had no windows, and while shattering the small storm lantern would allow him to start a fire, he would no doubt be the first to die from it. It did seem strange that they would leave a lantern unguarded with him. At the very least he could use it as a weapon and bludgeon the first man through the door when they came for him.

When the door did finally open, a chill ran down T'ruck's spine and all thoughts of assault by lantern fled. The man who entered was tall and muscular, with long brown hair and cold grey eyes. He wore bleached-bone trousers, a shirt to match, and a yellow tabard over the top, cinched at the waist with a red sash. The man wore no armour, and his only visible weapon was a longsword buckled to a belt underneath the tabard. T'ruck swallowed and backed up further into the cabin.

The Sword of the North smiled as he stepped into the room, briefly glancing around before slowly walking past T'ruck to the far corner. T'ruck was watching him so warily he didn't notice a second man enter until he spoke.

"You appear to know Sir Derran," said Admiral Verit, the man who had beaten T'ruck, scuttled his ship, and captured or killed his entire crew.

T'ruck glanced at the admiral before turning his attention back to the Sword of the North. "He killed my brother."

The swordsman squatted down and stared at T'ruck with eyes like cold steel. "I've killed a lot of brothers and a lot of clansmen."

"My brother was at Snake Pass," T'ruck spat.

"Oh. Then he died well. They all died well at the pass."

"What does it matter how some long-dead barbarian died?" the admiral said with a sigh.

"It matters," the Sword of the North hissed.

T'ruck nodded to him, acknowledging his respect. It was the first time he'd ever met the Blademaster, but every man, woman, and child of the northern clans had heard of the knight and knew how many of their kin he'd killed. They called him a warrior without equal and, standing in front of him now, T'ruck could believe it. Here was a man who could give T'ruck a glorious end, and if he was to have one, he wanted it to be glorious.

"I would challenge you," T'ruck rumbled, standing to his full height and rolling back his shoulders to show off his size.

The Sword of the North smiled; it was the smile of the Reaper, not one of friendship. "And I would accept, but the admiral has your death claimed already, so it cannot belong to me. Besides, I didn't come to this shit hole to fight you. I came for someone else."

"Enough," said the admiral. "I didn't bring you here to exchange pleasantries, Sir Derran."

"Careful, Admiral. Unless you've inherited a golden crown recently, I don't answer to you. I'll keep you safe from the giant, but if you insult me again I'll kill you myself."

The admiral held Sir Derran's stare for a few seconds longer before turning to T'ruck. "You are T'ruck Khan from the Herasow clan of the World's Edge mountains?"

"No," T'ruck rumbled. "That clan is long dead. I am Captain T'ruck Khan of the *North Gale*."

"Your ship is wreckage, and your crew – those who didn't drown – are my prisoners. You are captain of nothing, Khan." The admiral pulled a chair over and sat down. "I was going to order some refreshments brought, but I see you took offence to the table."

"Five Kingdoms trash," T'ruck spat, pacing behind the second chair. "It broke as easily as your men aboard the ship we took."

Admiral Verit sighed. "I am offering you the chance at a civilised conversation, barbarian. I suggest you take it. It is the only chance you have of saving your neck."

T'ruck stopped pacing and fixed the admiral with a stare, leaning over the back of the chair. "And my crew?"

"Will be hanged for their crimes."

T'ruck said nothing.

"We already have the location of New Sev'relain," the admiral continued. "Sir Derran will be leading a force to take the island soon enough. What we would like to know from you is its current defences, how many troops are stationed there, and the best method of attacking the settlement."

T'ruck said nothing.

"In return we can offer you special consideration. Cooperate and your case will be brought to the attention of His Majesty King Jackt himself. He will personally officiate over your hearing – and the king has been known to be merciful, even to barbarians like you."

T'ruck said nothing.

"I would advise you not to squander this opportunity. It will not be offered again. Once I leave this room, if you have provided no useful information you will be transported to Land's End with the rest of your crew, where you will be hanged and your body displayed to warn others from the course of piracy."

T'ruck looked over towards the Sword of the North. The Blademaster was still squatting in the corner of the cabin, watching T'ruck's every move. No doubt the man could spring to life and gut T'ruck before he could even strike the admiral.

"You follow orders," T'ruck said. "Go where you're told to go. Kill who you're told to kill. Men like him" – T'ruck pointed at the admiral – "give orders. Tell others to kill for them."

T'ruck glared at Verit. "Men like you killed my wives, killed my children. I would see you all opened." He pointed at his crotch and drew the finger up to his neck. "I would dance on your guts and feed your heart to my dogs."

The admiral sighed. "Men like me will see you hanged."

T'ruck reached into his trousers, pulled out his cock, and pissed on the deck, aiming for the admiral's shiny boots. The man launched himself backwards, knocking over his chair and stumbling towards the doorway, all to the laughter of the Sword of the North.

"Savage!" Verit shouted as he pulled open the door. "I will watch you stretch for this."

The Blademaster, still laughing, stood up and walked after the admiral, making sure to avoid the expanding puddle of piss. He nodded once to T'ruck and left, pulling the door shut behind him.

T'ruck put his cock away and waited. They would come for him before long and put him back in his cell, and the admiral would no doubt make good on his threat. The Five Kingdoms was a long way away, though, and there was plenty of time for him to either escape or force the crew of the behemoth to kill him in battle.

Starry Dawn

Three days Elaina whiled away in Chade. She toured the city and witnessed the things Rose and the Black Thorn had done with it. Chade had once been a dark, grimy city full of thieves, murderers, and those corrupt and rich enough to call themselves politicians. Elaina remembered the city as dangerous even for a pirate to travel alone, and more than one had ended up in a slave's iron collar for no crime other than being in the wrong place at the wrong time.

Then Chade had become a war zone, and that had been Drake Morrass' doing. For months upon months folk had fled the city, many of them taking to ships and crossing the Pirate Isles. Elaina remembered seizing more than one boat only to find it brimming with passengers instead of loot. Some folk called it a shadow war, but there was nothing shadowy about it. Gangs, guards, and pirates had walked the streets, slaughtering each other and causing chaos. As always, the good folk of Chade had been the ones to suffer most. The city had burned day and night until the Black Thorn murdered the man opposing Drake.

Out of the conflict and the war and the mindless death, Rose had appeared, taking the city in hand and restoring order. Elaina wasn't clear how Rose had taken control, but once she did, peace quickly followed. Now the free city of Chade was larger, safer, and more prosperous than it had ever been. Everyone agreed the change was Rose's doing, not her more famous husband's. But the Black Thorn commanded Chade's army, and considering they now had almost half the Wilds under their rule, he was apparently doing a fairly good job of it.

"What would you do?" Elaina asked the little woman in the cavalier hat. She'd met with Henry twice now, and both encounters had ended in a tavern with plenty of booze and plenty of stories. It was a friendship, of sorts, but now she was once again being escorted to Rose's mansion, to make her decision.

"Me?" Henry said, tilting her head so Elaina could just see the sneer on her lips. "I'd fuckin' run. Jump back on that little boat of yours an' see what the other side of the world looks like. Take it from someone who accidentally started a rebellion once. Power ain't what ya reckon it'll be. Don't mean ya get ta do what ya want all the time; means ya gotta do what every other fucker wants. Much better bein' the knife in the darkness than waitin' fer it ta come for you." Henry finished with a cackling laugh.

"Did Rose mean it?" Elaina said. It was the question she'd been wanting to ask Henry for the past three days. "Is her offer legitimate?"

Henry sniffed and spat into the street. "Aye, she'll make you a queen if she can. She'll hold it over you fer as long as she can too. Bitch is smart."

Elaina glanced down at her. "Doesn't sound like you like her much."

Henry laughed. "I don't. I reckon she's a treacherous little whore."

"Then…"

"'Cos he does," Henry interrupted. "Thorn's earned more than his share of trust. Reckon ya know the way from here."

They were standing outside Rose's mansion. The guards at the stop of the steps watched them, but at a nod from Henry they stepped aside to allow entry.

"You're not coming?" Elaina said.

Henry's cavalier hat shook. "Got my own place ta be. Part of her plan too, I reckon. Don't let her haggle ya down. Anything she's offerin' is because she needs somethin' from it. You're the one with the shit ta offer, not her." Henry spat once more into the dusty street and turned away, leaving Elaina alone.

Trepidation seemed as good a word as any. Elaina was nervous, and that was because she was inclined to accept Rose's proposal. The terms seemed good, but before she committed herself she needed to know just what the woman wanted from her in return.

Raising her chin and putting purpose in her stride, Elaina climbed the steps and proceeded into the refreshing shade of Rose's home. She hammered on the same door as before and waited for a response.

The door opened, revealing a tall man in long white robes. He had short brown hair and bright yellow eyes that set Elaina's skin crawling. He stared at her, a slow smile spreading across his face.

19

"Reckon ya wanna be staring elsewhere, before I make you," Elaina snarled.

"I apologise, Captain Black," the man said in a Sarth accent. He slipped out of the room. "Good day."

Elaina watched him walk away and felt a shiver travel up her spine.

"Are you coming in, Elaina?" Rose called from inside the room, and Elaina turned and walked through the doorway, still feeling uneasy from the encounter with the robed man.

"Have you come to a decision yet, my dear?"

Rose was sitting behind her desk, fanning herself with a large paper triangle and looking very uncomfortable. Despite the obvious discomfort, she was still beautiful in a composed, powdered sort of way.

"Not yet. Reckon we need to talk over a few points first."

Rose smiled and beckoned Elaina to the chair opposite the desk. "Do sit down, dear. We have water or wine if you would like. I always find negotiations go so much better with refreshments. I take it these are negotiations."

Elaina approached the chair and nodded. "Aye."

"Excellent. Then we're already all but agreed."

"Where's the Black Thorn?" Elaina said as she sat.

"He has some business a bit further north. Besides, he hates negotiations like this. Not nearly enough stabbing for his tastes."

"Mine either," Elaina said with a crooked grin.

"I'm sure." Rose shifted in her seat. She looked distinctly uncomfortable in her own skin. "I'm very sorry if I seem unsettled. It appears my daughter has her father's restless spirit."

"This alliance," Elaina prompted.

"Yes," Rose said. "With you. Not your father, and not with Drake Morrass. Just you."

"In the hope that I'll be queen of the isles one day. What do you get out of it?"

"A powerful ally," Rose said with a genuine smile.

Elaina laughed. None of the Blacks would claim to be the smartest folk on the ocean, but Elaina was as wily as her father and she recognised a bum deal when she saw one. She doubted the future queen of the Wilds would make an alliance without some immediate gain.

"It could be years before my da shuffles off…"

"Plenty of time to see your brother fall foul of a bad storm or an angry serpent."

"Or me."

"We wouldn't want that. I'm sure you'll survive us all, Elaina."

Elaina shook her head. "Life on the water is dangerous for even the most timid, and I ain't that. No guarantee I'll outlast Tanner, and your alliance with me means you get nothing 'til I'm the one on the throne. So what else is there? What else do you want?"

Rose shifted in her seat, taking her glass and sipping rosy-coloured liquid from it. "An advance upon our alliance."

"Eh?"

"My empire is in a dangerous period, Captain Black. I am fighting wars on more fronts than most people realise exist. Do you believe you pirates are the only ones experiencing pressure from Sarth or the Five Kingdoms?"

Rose's smile slipped, and for just a moment Elaina saw past the perfumed composure. In that moment Rose looked tired, worn thin by the rigours of building a kingdom, fighting for that kingdom, and pregnancy. But with just one deep breath Rose's smile was back, and its viciousness was matched by the flashing danger in her eyes.

"We have them feeling threatened, Captain," Rose continued. "Their two empires have stood on top for too long. They believe themselves to be the peacekeepers of our world, controlling those weaker than themselves. For years they have hunted you pirates, keeping you small and scared of them with their purges. Hanging those they catch."

"Aye, well, we are outlaws," Elaina conceded. "We do steal from them."

"Steal from them?" Rose said. "Is that what they would call confiscating a neighbouring empire's wares for travelling through their lands without paying for the privilege?"

"Huh?"

"They sail your waters and give you nothing for the use. You don't rob from them – you just take what you're owed."

Elaina wasn't sure that was the right of it, but it certainly painted the pirates in a much less damning light.

"They have done us a similar injustice, Captain Black," Rose continued. "For generations they have fuelled the hatred between the blooded families, supplying each of them with weapons, horses, even soldiers."

"Why?"

"To keep them fighting. To keep the Wilds in turmoil and to stop us uniting under one banner. They are scared, Captain. Scared of us becoming another power in the world and realising we don't need them. Just like Acanthia doesn't need them. Just like the Dragon Empire doesn't need them. There are four great empires of man in the world, and the last thing either Sarth or the Five Kingdoms wants is another."

"You want us to keep fighting," Elaina said, sure of herself now. "We're taking the heat away from you."

"Yes. You pirates are, on the surface, a much greater threat than I am. Every ship they throw at you makes it all the less likely they'll sail up here and put another army on my field. Or even worse, give their support to that blooded arse, Niles Brekovich.

"At the same time, every ship I do not lose to you pirates makes me that bit stronger." Rose leaned forwards and fixed Elaina with a dark stare. "I need you to stop pirating my ships, and I need you to fight the bastards who are trying to kill you. If possible, I would like you to win."

"So why me? Why not my da, or Morrass?"

"Because you are a woman, and because you are young, and because I can see ambition in you. I make no apologies for opinions. Drake may well be better suited to rule, but I do not trust what he might do with such power. All he has ever wanted was the crown and for others to call him king. All your father wants is to stop Drake from having whatever he wants. In you, I see someone unburdened by such pettiness."

Elaina licked her lips. She was certain she now knew the truth of it. "We needs ships, fighters, and food."

"Done," Rose said without hesitation. "Ten ships, fully crewed and carrying stores of food. All sailing for you and no one else. I will need sixty days to prepare them. I presume you can hold out that long?"

"Aye, though best make it ninety. I got another stop before home. My da wants a similar alliance from the guilds of Larkos."

Rose laughed. "Good luck. The guilds give nothing without payment up front."

"Aye, well I'm better off trying than not, with my da."

A long silence blanketed the room. Rose narrowed her eyes and gave Elaina a queer stare. Eventually the Lady of Chade poured herself another glass of rosy liquid, and then a second for Elaina.

"To our new alliance, Captain Black, and to both our empires."

Elaina took the glass and drank deeply. It was hard to believe, but she'd just secured herself a fleet of ships along with the crews to sail them and she'd offered so very little in return. There was no way her father could be disappointed in her now.

"He won't hang," Elaina said. "My da. Come what may, he won't hang."

Rose smiled, fanning herself again. "We'll see."

North Gale

Days passed without any sort of indication as to what was happening above decks. The brig was secured tighter than a virgin's arse, and the only light came from the lanterns the guards carried when they fed and mocked the prisoners. For much of each day T'ruck was in near complete darkness, with only the scurrying of mice and the distant sounds of his own crew, to keep him company.

He talked to his crew and learned that only twenty-two of them had survived the sinking of their ship. Three-quarters of them either died on the end of Five Kingdoms steel or drowned in the waters of the isles when *Storm Herald* ploughed through *North Gale*, splitting it right down the midsection.

The door to the brig opened and light spilled in. A moment later a storm lantern poked through the opening, followed by the squat-faced guard whose uniform was slightly too short for him. T'ruck didn't know the man's name. He didn't need to know the names of all the men he would kill. The guard sniffed the air and sighed.

"Buckets need emptying again."

"It's your turn," someone else growled.

"I say we just let them stew in it for a few days." The squat-faced one laughed.

T'ruck approached the bars, grabbing hold of them and flexing his muscles, once again testing his own strength against that of the tempered metal. For the hundredth time the bars proved to be the stronger of the two. The squat-faced guard watched him with a sneer on his squat face.

"Big bastard is trying to break free again."

"Starve him again," said the other voice. "Fuck it, starve all of them. More food for us. Get precious bloody little as it is without feeding criminals."

The guard laughed and closed the door, once again bathing T'ruck and his surviving crew in darkness.

The next time the door to the brig opened it was the squat-faced guard and his storm lantern once again, but this time he looked far from comfortable. His back was straighter, and his uniform, though still slightly too small, looked as though he'd recently fussed about smoothing it down.

T'ruck was lounging against the bars to his cell, but rose when the door opened. No matter what was sent into the brig, he would meet it on his feet.

"The admiral said to put her in with the others," said a new voice, one with an air of command. "And I'm to make sure it's done personally."

There was some grumbling, and T'ruck thought he heard mention of the admiral's mother, but there seemed to be an agreement to follow the orders and the guard started into the brig, followed leisurely by a beautiful woman with raven hair and an iron collar. A tall man in an officer's coat followed her in and shut the door behind them. He stayed there at rigid attention, standing guard.

As the guard walked past T'ruck's cell, the woman tapped him on the shoulder. He turned to face her, his eyes going wide as they met hers.

T'ruck leaned into the bars and caught a glimpse of the woman's eyes. They were a swirling mass, almost like a bag of snakes writhing against each other. T'ruck found himself being drawn in, unable to look away.

"Please control yourself, Captain Khan," the witch said in a voice like an ice bath. "It is hard enough to keep these two under my sway without your attempt to subjugate yourself."

T'ruck shook himself free of her spell and dragged his eyes away from hers.

"Open the door to this cell," the witch said sweetly, and the squat-faced guard began fumbling for his keys.

T'ruck noticed the officer standing at the door to the brig stumble and shake his head. The witch snapped her head around and locked her evil eyes onto the officer's. "I would be very grateful, my dear, if you would just wait there for now."

T'ruck looked at the witch again. He'd transported Lady Tsokei halfway across the world in the bowels of his ship, and not once had he seen her look so dishevelled. Her black hair was dull and greasy. Her skin was dirty, coated with a sheen of grime. Her black dress was heavily ripped and stained, hanging loose and tattered upon her small body. Sweat dripped down from the witch's forehead, running down her cheek and chin and disappearing beneath the iron collar.

"Quickly, please," Lady Tsokei hissed at the guard. She was shaking a little, as if cold despite the warmth and closeness of the brig.

The guard slid a key into the lock and the door to T'ruck's little cell squealed open. T'ruck had to duck as he wasted no time in exiting his prison, the doorway clearly designed for smaller men – but then, most men were smaller than him. Squat-face stood by with a curiously expressionless face as T'ruck pushed past him.

"Please kill one of these men," Lady Tsokei said, steadying herself against the bars to T'ruck's former cell. "I cannot keep them both bound to me much longer."

T'ruck wasted no time in choosing. The officer would likely be more useful, and the guard had already proven himself to be unworthy of life. He wrapped his giant hands around the smaller man's throat and began to squeeze. At first there was no resistance, but soon the man's eyes lit up as the witch released her control – T'ruck saw her collapse against the bars at the same time that the guard began to struggle – but he was no match for an angry giant. T'ruck watched the life fade from the guard's eyes before he let the corpse drop to the decking. The officer didn't so much as blink at the death of his crewmate.

"I will be glad when that one is dead too," Lady Tsokei hissed, nodding towards the officer. "The fool tried to claim me as any man might an errant slave. I will teach him the error of his ways. I will make him watch as I burn his ship and force him to kill his own friends. I will drag the knowledge of his family from his mind and release him just long enough to realise he has condemned them all to death."

T'ruck ignored the vengeful witch and scooped the squat-faced guard's keys from where they'd fallen. He decided right then it would probably be a bad idea to ever look into her eyes again. The iron collar she wore was supposed to stop her using her magic.

"Release me, Captain Khan," Lady Tsokei said, "and I shall send this monstrosity of metal and wood to Rin's court."

T'ruck stopped, the keys in his hand and vengeance within his grasp. "I told you before, Lady Tsokei," he said, not looking into her eyes out of both fear and pride, "I do not want this ship sunk. I want it taken. I want to sail it against my enemies. Against the Five Kingdoms. Against the bastards who murdered my family. I would use this monstrosity to break them and help carve out the new home Drake Morrass dreams of." He laughed. "T'ruck Khan, once mightiest leader of the clans, displaced and driven from his home, again sitting in a position of power. I believe that would taste bitter to even…"

"Spare me your speech, Captain," the witch said with a sigh as she pushed away from the bars. "I do not care one bit about your new home. I wish only to stay one step in front of the Inquisition's dogs."

T'ruck grinned and risked a look at her, hoping she wouldn't have the strength left to take control of him. "And what makes you think the Pirate Isles and Drake aren't also your best chance?"

"What?"

"The free cities stand up to the Inquisition. They grant the witch hunters no power within their walls. We are carving out a new kingdom here, and we can set the same restriction. You would be safe, protected."

"If you believe my kind are safe from the Inquisition while in the free cities, you are very much mistaken, Captain Khan. The Inquisition hunt us no matter."

T'ruck raged inside at the witch's stubbornness. He spat on the deck in frustration. "Then you would sink this ship and die along with your captors, taking us all down to Rin with you. You may not feel it, but we have been sailing for days. Like as not, we are far from friendly lands, and if we do not take this ship then we sink with it."

That seemed to bring her up short. No matter how powerful she might be – and T'ruck was fairly certain she was powerful – she would die here with the rest of them if she couldn't find land to live off.

"Help me take this ship," T'ruck continued, "and I will drown that collar. Never again will you be leashed."

Lady Tsokei smiled, and when she spoke her voice was like silk. "You will offer me a permanent position aboard the ship for as long as I wish to remain on board. My identity will remain secret and you will guarantee your crew's silence. And I will not take on any of the ship's duties."

"No bewitching any of my crew."

"I'll need a bigger cabin."

"You can take your pick of any but the biggest."

For a moment T'ruck and the witch stared at each other.

"Good?" T'ruck said eventually.

"Good," Lady Tsokei said.

"Rest of the crew are just down here," T'ruck said. "I'll get 'em freed while you figure out how you're gonna help us take this ship." He turned towards his crew's cells, keys in hand.

"Captain Khan," the witch said, a hint of humour in her voice. "The collar."

T'ruck looked back, ambition warring in his head with what he assumed was probably better judgement. He towered over the small woman and yet she showed no fear, even with her powers limited. A memory flashed through his mind of Lady Tsokei before she'd willingly donned the collar and bound it to T'ruck. She was terror given flesh, fear pulsing off her in waves that had terrified men and women alike, even though they didn't know why.

With a greedy smile, T'ruck reached out towards the witch's neck and placed his thumb on a flat panel on one side of the iron band. There was a click, and the collar opened up and fell away. T'ruck winced, expecting to feel the same fear he'd experienced when he first met the woman, but it didn't come.

Lady Tsokei rolled her head around and stretched out her shoulders as though a great weight had been lifted. She glanced at T'ruck and laughed.

"Do not look so surprised, Captain Khan. I would not have eluded the Inquisition for so long had I not been able to control my aura. Before, it served my purpose to keep you and your crew scared. Now, I believe it to be otherwise. Release your crew and let us lay waste to our enemies."

With the lantern in one hand and the keys in the other, it didn't take T'ruck long to find his imprisoned crew. They were crowded together, twenty-one living bodies and one dead, in just four cells. Some of them were in fine shape, with only a few scratches and bruises from the fight, whereas others had obviously been the victims of beatings and bore more serious wounds. Yu'truda had survived, though she now walked with a painful-looking limp, but her husband, Zole, had drowned when *North Gale* went down. The grief was plain in Yu'truda's eyes, but she was a clansman the same as T'ruck, and they were well used to the death of loved ones.

After a few words of caution to his surviving crew members, and some assurances that freeing the witch was in all of their best interests, T'ruck gathered them near Lady Tsokei and they prepared to leave the brig. There were just twenty-three of them in total, and T'ruck wagered they faced nearly a thousand.

North Gale

With wooden cosh in hand, T'ruck burst through the doorway and out of the brig. He'd been escorted through the guard room twice and knew the layout well. There were three men inside, two sitting around a table playing dice while the third was bent over a desk, writing something on a sheet of parchment. T'ruck leapt towards the table and the first soldier went down with a cracked skull before he could even gain his feet. T'ruck swung at the second just as the man launched out of his chair. The doomed guard managed to get his hands up, but they only delayed his fate, and T'ruck rained down blow after blow until the man collapsed into a quivering, bloody heap.

Turning to the third guard, T'ruck found four members of his crew had rushed in behind him and pulled the man down. They were busy giving him the last beating of his life as more of *North Gale*'s crew squeezed into the room and finished off the two guards T'ruck had left unconscious.

The witch pushed past a few of T'ruck's pirates with her enslaved officer in tow. She glanced at the three bodies only momentarily, taking more interest in the parchment the guard had been writing on.

"A poem," she said with a wry smile. "To his wife. A shame it will never reach her – the man appeared to have some skill with words." She stepped over the corpse of the soldier she'd just praised and approached the door that led to the rest of the ship.

"We will need weapons. Where are we likely to find the armoury?" the witch asked her minion.

"There is a store of weapons two decks down, my lady," the officer said in a voice as blank as his face.

"Are we likely to encounter any of your crewmates?" T'ruck squeezed past a couple of his crew, wondering why they seemed so determined to fill the small room.

"Yes," the officer said. "Just below us are the quarters assigned to the knights."

T'ruck felt his blood go cold. "Is the Sword of the North down there?" He heard Yu'truda gasp.

"No," said the officer. "Sir Derran left a few days ago aboard *Gold Glitter*."

"Thank fuck," Yu'truda muttered. She'd witnessed the man's ability to deal death first-hand, and was lucky to have escaped herself.

T'ruck inched open the door and glanced through. The hallway beyond was empty for now, but there was no telling where the other soldiers might be. "We need those weapons," he said.

"Stealth is our strongest ally." Lady Tsokei lingered nearby. "I can weave illusions to keep us hidden for a short time, but we must move quickly and be ready to kill anyone who spots us. Some are curiously resistant to such magic."

They exited the guardroom quickly, with the enslaved officer leading the way and Lady Tsokei just behind him. T'ruck followed, leaving his crew to jostle for spots in the procession. They set a brisk pace, only briefly checking interconnecting hallways before moving on. They encountered no soldiers or sailors until they came to the ladder leading to the lower decks.

Just as the officer reached the ladder, a head poked up from below – a sailor by the looks of him, with crooked teeth and a sunburnt complexion. He nodded to the officer before noticing the line of pirates behind.

"The prisoners…" the man said, looking utterly confused, before T'ruck barged past the witch and her minion, grabbed him under the arm and hauled him up, clamping a meaty hand over his mouth.

Pain blossomed in T'ruck's side, and he looked down to see a small knife sticking out of his flesh very close to a barely healed wound he'd received during the battle aboard *North Gale*. With a grunt, T'ruck tossed the man to his crew, who proceeded to quietly beat the poor fool to death. He pulled the knife from his side and handed it to Yu'truda.

"How bad is it?" said Lady Tsokei.

"A scratch," T'ruck bragged, wincing at the pain. It didn't appear to have hit any vital spots, but the wound was bleeding and hurt like fire on his skin.

Lady Tsokei narrowed her eyes at him, and T'ruck did his best not to let the pain show.

"We should keep moving," he said.

The witch spoke in a language T'ruck didn't recognise and tapped a finger on his new wound. Pain erupted in T'ruck's side and he stumbled, collapsing against the wall, his vision swimming. He bit down, squeezing his teeth together as hard as he could to stop himself screaming as the pain in his side grew and grew until he was certain someone was cutting him open from the inside.

The pain started to lessen, dwindling down until it was no more than a dull ache, and T'ruck realised his eyes were squeezed shut. He opened them and saw Yu'truda standing over him with an expression caught between terror and anger.

"What did she do?" Yu'truda said.

T'ruck looked down at the wound. It had closed, and was now little more than a small, angry red line on his bronzed skin.

"She healed you?"

T'ruck looked over towards the ladder, where the witch was waiting patiently. He wasn't sure whether to dash her head against the decking or thank her.

"I did not heal you," Lady Tsokei said. "That ability is far rarer than you might imagine. I simply sped up your natural healing at great cost to yourself. You may find yourself weaker than normal for a few days, but it is better than having you collapse from loss of blood before this night's work is finished. Are we ready to continue?"

T'ruck pushed himself back to his feet and ignored the slight wobble in his legs. "Aye. We've not even started yet."

The enslaved officer set his feet on the ladder and started down, followed closely by Lady Tsokei, who chanted as she went. T'ruck waited a few seconds, then set his own feet to the ladder and started to descend. Before long he found himself passing through a large, open area of the ship with bunks lining either side, each complete with a bulky chest and an armour stand. Of particular concern was the number of men in the room, most of whom had a distinct warrior feel about them, both in the way they moved and the way they smelled.

T'ruck froze, unsure whether to continue down or head back up before any of the men saw him. It was a wonder they hadn't already, given his size and how conspicuous the ladder was. He spotted the witch standing just at the foot of the ladder, waving frantically at T'ruck in a downwards motion. She was holding one hand out towards the knights and appeared to be chanting. Whatever magic she was using, it was hiding him from sight, and with one last glance at the knights as they joked and drank and gambled, he resumed his descent at a faster pace.

At the bottom of the ladder was another hallway, where the enslaved officer was waiting silently. T'ruck felt more than a little uneasy with the witch above him maintaining her illusion; if any soldiers discovered him and his crew while they waited, he might have a hard time stopping them before they raised the alarm.

His crew climbed down quickly, one at a time and full of hushed panic. When Yu'truda hit the deck she pulled T'ruck aside and whispered in his ear.

"What are we gonna do, Cap'n? There must be fifty knights up there, and a fuck load more soldiers throughout the ship. We're twenty. We can't…"

"Trust in the witch," T'ruck grumbled, silencing his quartermaster. "She's as much stake in this as the rest of us, and she can get us through it."

T'ruck didn't wait for her reply. The last of his crew hit the deck and stood aside as the witch followed them down. Her face was coated in sweat and her hands were shaking.

"That's some useful magic," T'ruck whispered.

Lady Tsokei froze him with a stare. "If only you knew the cost," she said in a haunted voice before turning to her enslaved officer. "Lead the way to the armoury."

There were two soldiers guarding the door to the armoury, and both were carrying sharpened steel. They would be no match for twenty-two angry pirates, but T'ruck doubted they would fall without a fight, and he couldn't afford to lose even one of his surviving crew. Lady Tsokei had a different plan in mind.

Dropping any attempt at stealth, the witch marched towards the two guards with T'ruck and his crew following along behind her. T'ruck felt the hairs stand up on his skin, and a sudden, unnatural fear fell upon him. It took every drop of willpower he had not to run from the woman and find the nearest dark corner to hide in. The soldiers didn't fare so well.

As Lady Tsokei closed on them, both men dropped the steel in their hands and their shouts died in their throats. One of the guards collapsed onto the deck, curling into a ball and sobbing quietly, while the other began to claw at the wall, trying to escape the horror bearing down upon him.

The enslaved officer barged past T'ruck, running past the witch and picking up one of the dropped swords. The man first stabbed the soldier on the deck before cleaving the other guard's head in two. As swiftly as it had begun, the oppressive fear emanating from the witch disappeared. T'ruck realised he was frozen in place, his entire crew similarly caught.

"I suggest you arm yourselves," Lady Tsokei said without turning to look at the pirates. "Not all will die as easily as these two."

"Fetch me a sword and shield," T'ruck ordered Brendin, one of the youngest surviving members of his crew. He stepped closer to the witch. "That magic affects us too."

"It is difficult to control," the witch said, turning her dark gaze on T'ruck. "Those in front of me are most affected, but everyone around me will experience a similar fear."

"We can't fight like that," T'ruck snapped. "I could barely bring myself to move."

The witch nodded. "I will try something different. But Captain Khan, those above and below me will also have experienced that fear."

T'ruck glanced upwards. "The knights?"

Another nod.

"Then we deal with them first," T'ruck growled, taking a sword and shield from Brendin. He turned and stormed back towards the ladder, a grin spreading across his face. It had been years since he'd last had a chance to kill a knight of the Five Kingdoms. Not since he'd been driven from his home, leaving his murdered family behind. He was going to enjoy the night's activities.

Nerine Tsokei was angry. It was the type of anger that boils over and quickly turns from a hot, burning rage into a cold, calculated fury. She knew the limits of her magic, and she knew the limits of her ability to channel power from the Void, but she would push past those limits to strip away everything these Five Kingdoms pigs held dear. The despair of her enslaved officer was a balm to her soul. He could do nothing but serve her now, his will no longer his own, hers until she released him. And she had no intention of doing that until the man witnessed just what his fervour had cost him.

The fools had plucked her out of the water, soaked through and shivering, on the verge of drowning as she struggled to hold on to the wreckage that had been *North Gale*. They saw her iron collar and assumed she was a slave serving the pirates, and they put her to use accordingly, giving her to the chef to work her way back to the Five Kingdoms. For days and days she'd scrubbed floors, stirred broth, and cleaned pots until her fingers bled.

Her anger built daily. Nobody had ever treated Nerine Tsokei, lady of the red ice, Keeper of Shadows, that way. She endured the disgrace, willing to put up with a little indignity if it allowed her survival. She'd eluded the Inquisition for decades – she would survive this too. Nerine had already set her mind upon sinking the ship and escaping as soon as it made port somewhere with a civilised population. Preferably somewhere not allied to Sarth. One witch hunter she could deal with, but the six that chased her included an Inquisitor, and she needed to evade them at all costs.

Her plan, and all resolve to suffer the undignified treatment the crew showed her, disappeared the moment the fool of an officer decided he wanted what was beneath her dress. Nerine had let him take her back to his quarters before she took control of him and turned him into her slave using nothing but her will and the barest hint of magic. She'd long ago learned that lusting men were the easiest to dominate.

Once Nerine had enslaved the man, she no longer had a choice. She couldn't continue to control him while she slept, and she would need to sleep eventually. It was at that point that she decided to release Captain Khan, so he could in turn release her from the infernal collar that kept her powers constrained.

Setting a foot to the ladder, Nerine began to climb, Captain Khan's call to wait falling on deaf ears. Before long she reached the level where the knights they'd passed earlier were quartered. But this time she didn't bother to hide her presence.

The casual atmosphere on the deck had disappeared. Some of the knights were busy encasing themselves in armour while others stood guard with drawn steel. Three men approached Nerine as she finished her climb. The first was tall and muscular with a perfectly groomed moustache in the shape of a horseshoe; he held out a hand to Nerine.

"You're the cook's slave. Away from there, wench, and tell us what you've seen," he said in a voice as pompous as his facial hair.

Nerine opened herself up to the icy call of the Void, sending out a request for power. She didn't bother to ask the name of the being who answered her – she didn't care. Nerine never cared; she just hoped whichever creature answered opposed Volmar and his Inquisition.

With power flowing through her and the spell whispering out from between her lips like an invisible serpent, Nerine knelt down and tore at her shadow. It ripped in two, and one half shattered into thirty shards that slithered away along the deck, seeking out living targets.

The three knights in front of Nerine stumbled backwards, attempting to jump out of the way of her snake-like shadows, but the spell wasn't targeting them; she had very little control over whom they would attack.

The first man to die did so with barely a sound as a shard latched onto his own shadow, distorting and growing until it reached up from the deck behind him and tore open his throat. The knights around him didn't die so quietly. Before long there were plenty of screams.

"Witch!" the man with the moustache shouted. A shadow in the shape of a monstrous dog leapt out from a dark corner and pounced on one of his comrades, bearing him to the ground and savaging him.

The knight charged at Nerine, followed closely by his surviving companion. As the moustached knight swung his sword, Nerine stepped sideways into the attack, the blade skimming past her stomach, and quickly slammed her shoulder into the man's chest. Despite weighing twice what she did, he flew away from her, and she plucked the sword from his hand as he went. The second knight attempted to catch her off guard, but Nerine was never off guard. She parried the strike as smoothly as water flows and stepped past him, leaving the moustached knight's sword in his companion's chest.

As his comrade dropped to the deck, the first knight regained his feet and leapt at Nerine, this time without the protection of a weapon. Waiting until the last moment, Nerine sidestepped the knight's bullish charge, catching his flailing arm and dragging him about with his own momentum. Then she wrenched, dislocating the arm and sending the man to the floor once more. All the while, Nerine's shadow creatures continued their gruesome work, each one finding a single victim and slaughtering them before vanishing like mist.

Captain Khan gained the deck from the ladder and wasted no time in stabbing the downed knight through the neck. He took in the sight in front of him with a curl of his lip and then looked at Nerine.

"You know how to fight," the captain said as more of his crew scrambled up the ladder.

"Better, I would imagine, than you," Nerine said. "I have sown the seeds of death and chaos, Captain Khan. I suggest your crew capitalise on that distraction."

The giant pirate grinned and charged off to join the battle. There were precious few of Nerine's shadow creatures left, and the pirates still had plenty of killing to do. She could have killed them all, but she needed to preserve her strength.

It didn't take long for T'ruck and his crew to finish off the knights, distracted as they were by the shadows. Not a single one of the fools escaped, but the battle had made more than enough noise and Nerine was certain the alarm had been raised. The rest of the night wouldn't go nearly so easily.

North Gale

T'ruck slumped against the wall, looking up at the ladder that led to the main deck of the ship. He could hear the creak of rope and canvas, the shuffling feet of nervous men, and the occasional shout from those in charge to keep steady. He looked back at his own crew, all as weary as him and all spattered with blood both fresh and long since dried.

One of his pirates, Pocket, a younger lad with a crooked nose and heavy jaw, had collapsed onto the deck and was leaning against a wall, sobbing quietly into his hands. T'ruck would have loved to leave the man to his sorrow. They all needed time to come to terms with the things they'd done, but there were precious few of his crew left now. Of the twenty-two pirates who had escaped the brig, only twelve remained in any sort of fighting condition, and they were lucky that many of them had survived.

"On your feet, lad," T'ruck said, walking over to his grieving pirate and trying to hide how much effort just that small feat took.

Pocket didn't respond.

T'ruck glanced around at the rest of his crew, who were all watching the exchange. He knew that if he let just one of his crew break now, they would all follow suit – and there was still plenty of slaughter left to do. Even Yu'truda looked on the verge of giving up.

"Get up, Pocket," he said again, in a voice that sounded weary even to his own ears.

Still the lad just wept into his hands.

T'ruck leaned his blood-soaked sword against the wall and reached down, grabbing hold of Pocket's shirt and wrenching the man to his feet. He pinned him against the wall and gave him the full force of his captain's stare.

"I'm a monster," Pocket said with a sob, his eyes crazed and red with tears. "We're all monsters. So much blood. So much… I… I lost count."

T'ruck cuffed the lad on the side of the head. "Aye, you're a monster. Tonight we all are. We're monsters 'cos monsters is what we need to be."

T'ruck dropped the lad back to his feet. Pocket stayed standing, his eyes blank. T'ruck had seen it before, warriors on the battlefield coming out of the bloodlust and realising just what atrocities they'd committed. Every one of his crew had killed during the night, and every one had killed again and again. With the help of the demons Lady Tsokei had been summoning, they'd murdered hundreds of men. What they'd accomplished so far was nothing short of a miracle, a bloody miracle that would likely see them all damned in the eyes of whichever god they believed in. Unfortunately, what they'd accomplished so far wasn't the end of it.

T'ruck and his crew had moved from deck to deck, room to room, ambushing soldiers with steel and monsters formed of shadow. Hundreds upon hundreds of men had fallen, and blood washed every deck of the ship except one. The last of *Storm Herald*'s resistance were gathered above decks under the command of Admiral Peter Verit, and there they waited, no doubt with bows ready to ambush the surviving members of T'ruck's crew. T'ruck himself could barely lift his sword, his arm aching like fire in his veins, but unless they stormed the deck and finished off the admiral and his soldiers, they would surely die just as if they'd stayed in their cells.

"We need to be monsters for just a little bit longer," T'ruck said. "Up there are the last bastards standing between us and freedom. We kill them, and we've done the impossible, so I need you to be strong. We either finish them off now or we all die when they come for us, so I... *we* need you all to be strong for just a while longer."

Pocket looked up at his captain and nodded slowly.

"Pick up your sword, lad," T'ruck said.

The witch was standing apart from his crew. Her back was straight, but she was swaying on her feet and her eyes looked distant. Her skin was pale and her hair was plastered to her head with sweat. They all looked terrible, exhausted and speckled with blood, but Lady Tsokei looked like she had nothing left to give. She'd joined each battle with the rest of the crew and had tipped the scales of each encounter in their favour with her magic. T'ruck worried she wouldn't have the strength to complete the taking of the ship, and he knew they would fail without her.

"Are you…" he started.

"I am fine, Captain Khan," Lady Tsokei said. Her voice lacked its usual iron and ice. "This much contact with the Void… I feel raw, used up."

"I have a plan," T'ruck said. "Can you summon any more of those… um… shadow monsters?"

The witch nodded, and a sigh escaped her lips. "I believe I can do that once more, Captain Khan. But that will be all the magic I can…" She trailed off, tears in her eyes.

"Aye, it'll be enough. Stay here with Yu'truda and Connel. They're gonna make some noise, make it sound like we got an army down here. I'll take the rest of us to the aft deck ladder. Give us a few minutes, then release your monsters. We'll wait until the chaos is good and started and then we'll charge up the ladder, take the bastards from the rear."

Lady Tsokei nodded, saying nothing, her eyes fixed on the ladder. Without another word, T'ruck turned to his crew.

"Make plenty of noise, Yu'truda," he said with a forced grin. "The more of those fuckers looking this way, the less likely any will be pointing bows at us. Once the fight is on, you pop up the ladder yourselves. We'll need you."

"Aye, Cap'n," Yu'truda said without a hint of emotion. Between the loss of her husband and the death she'd seen over the last few hours, T'ruck wondered if the last surviving member of his clan would ever be the same.

T'ruck and nine of his crew jogged quickly to the aft of the ship, not even bothering to check the rooms they passed. They'd been this way earlier and cleared it of soldiers and sailors alike, and there were plenty of bodies both in the corridors and in the otherwise empty rooms. T'ruck ignored the dead, concentrating instead on not slipping on the pooling blood left behind.

The ship was sitting still in the water, no doubt stopped while the crew dealt with the escaped prisoners, but there was still a slight sway as her massive frame moved with the waves. T'ruck prayed a storm would rise up out of somewhere; it would provide them with an extra distraction and some protection from the archers. Aiming with a bow was next to impossible when standing on a deck that couldn't decide which way was up.

They slowed their pace as they came close to their destination, attempting to keep as quiet as possible so the men up on the aft deck wouldn't know they were there. T'ruck waved for everyone to stay silent and approached the ladder at a crouch. He could hear a dull, rhythmic banging, and guessed it was the noise he'd asked for. He crept closer to the ladder and waited for the witch to do her final part.

It didn't take long for the shouting and screaming to start.

T'ruck held up a hand to his crew, making them wait a bit longer. He wanted as many of the folk up on deck distracted as possible, and a few extra seconds of staring into the face of a rampaging shadow monster was fairly distracting.

After a tortuously long count of ten, T'ruck grabbed hold of the ladder and started to climb as quickly as he could with a sword in one hand and a shield in the other. The hatch to the deck was open and T'ruck rushed up through it. Something struck his shield with a solid thud, and pain erupted in his chest, near his right shoulder. T'ruck ignored it – he needed to get up out of the hatch and out of the way so the rest of his crew could follow him.

The sky was a dirty orange dotted with clouds, obscured by giant masts stretching up to greet them. There was a small group of soldiers watching the hatch, two busy reloading crossbows while another two were armed with swords. They charged at T'ruck even as he got a knee onto the deck.

With a roar of fury T'ruck swung his shield, swatting away the first soldier's attack while he blocked the other with his sword, swallowing down the agony in his shoulder. He pushed off from the foot he had on the deck and launched himself at the two men, barrelling into both of them at once and bearing them down with his weight. The world twisted beneath him and the pain from his shoulder reduced his vision to a tunnel. T'ruck had no idea where he was, let alone where the soldiers were. He surged back onto his knees and began to lay about himself with his sword, the pain in his shoulder fuelling his rage.

"Cap'n! Cap'n!" one of his sailors shouted, and T'ruck stopped his wild flailing and opened his eyes. His own crew were gathered in front of him. The two soldiers with the crossbows and their guards were down, dead or dying. The two men he'd dragged to the deck with him had died where they fell, plenty of bloody gashes in each from T'ruck's wild sword-swinging.

"We need to get into the fight, Cap'n," said Pocket, a numb sorrow in his eyes.

T'ruck glanced down and saw a bolt sticking out of his flesh. Only a finger's width still showed. He knew it would need removing and that his body would need time to heal, but time was something he didn't have. He would have to ignore the wooden intruder for now and hope one of his surviving crew would know how to patch him up later.

Struggling to his feet, T'ruck limped forwards and stared down at the main deck, where the majority of the fighting was taking place. Soldiers were everywhere, struggling with the witch's shadow monsters. T'ruck saw a giant, four-legged shadow lumber out from the darkness cast by the main mast. The creature scooped up the first soldier it came across and dashed the man into the deck, before turning to face a knot of men who had started hacking at it with swords. Whether or not the steel had any effect, T'ruck couldn't tell, but it certainly seemed to enrage the beast, and soon it was slamming two more soldiers into the deck with its massive paws.

More and more shadows were pouring from one of the hatches on the main deck, each one like a snake slithering across the wood to find a larger patch of darkness to feed it. Everywhere T'ruck looked, soldiers were dying to the witch's magic, and he could only wonder how she had the strength to manage it in her state of exhaustion.

"*You!*" someone shouted, and T'ruck looked sideways to see Admiral Peter Verit climbing the stairs to the aft deck, guards swarming around him. "You did this!"

T'ruck plastered a weary grin to his face and turned towards Verit, noticing for the first time how close they were to *Storm Herald*'s dinghies. The admiral was attempting to abandon his ship, giving it up for lost. T'ruck's own depleted crew moved to his side, each of them as weary as he was, but each one just as determined to survive and to pay back the admiral for destroying their ship and murdering their friends.

One of the witch's creatures slithered its way up onto the aft deck and angled towards T'ruck, disappearing into the large shadows cast by his crew. A moment later T'ruck felt a chill as a small monkey-like shape brushed past him. The monster seemed to have no head and no eyes, just a body and legs that looked like black smoke. He shuffled out of its way, but it didn't seem interested in either him or his crew. It broke their ranks and charged at the admiral and his guards.

T'ruck bellowed out a laugh that set all his wounds to aching, and rushed in after the shadow monster. The admiral's guards moved to meet him even as his own crew followed him in, and a moment later the battle was joined and the world became wood and steel and sweat and blood.

Blocking the first strike with his shield, T'ruck struck back with his own sword only to have it deflected. As the remainder of his crew joined him, forming a loose shield wall, the first of the admiral's soldiers went down. The little shadow monster was attached to his chest, tearing into it with bloody talons.

Two of the downed soldier's comrades turned on the shadow and hacked at it. The little beast ceased its attack and started to fade, soon leaving no evidence that it had ever existed except for the ruined mess of a man dying on the deck. T'ruck and another of his crew, Owan, locked shields and started to push as one, driving a wedge into the loose enemy line, protecting each other and forcing the soldiers to turn so that the rest of his men could attack their flanks.

T'ruck felt a cut open up on his left side and roared in pain. Rage filled every part of him, and new strength flowed into his limbs as he broke free of the two-man wall, swinging his stolen sword about him in wild, powerful strokes that shattered defences and sent men crashing to the deck with horrific injuries. His crew surged in his wake, taking advantage of the distraction to murder their enemies. They were all veterans of T'ruck's crew, and every one was used to his berserker strength. They knew just how much it terrified their foes and how to make the most of it.

Admiral Verit came out of nowhere, leaping at T'ruck with well-timed, perfectly aimed blows that T'ruck struggled to turn aside despite his greater strength. The man was obviously well trained, but if he could just hold the bastard up for long enough the odds would turn in the pirate's favour.

Strike after strike after strike and the admiral kept his composure, not a hair out of place on either his head or his chin. His eyes were cold steel. T'ruck decided he didn't want his crew's help to defeat the man – he wanted the royal bastard's death all to himself.

T'ruck waited for his moment, blocking blow after blow, then catching the admiral's sword on his shield and pushing forwards to catch him off balance. The admiral sidestepped at the last moment, dancing to the side.

New pain blossomed in T'ruck's right leg and he stumbled to the ground, flailing with his sword and catching the admiral with a glancing blow of the flat of his blade.

T'ruck tried to stand, but his injured leg collapsed underneath him and a glance down told him the admiral had cut a deep gash in his ankle, probably severing a tendon. The pain was intense, but not as bad as the bolt still in his chest. He struggled to his knees and looked up just in time to see the admiral dance in and impale him.

T'ruck had experienced more wounds than he cared to count, and he had the scars to prove each one, but this was the first time he'd ever been run through. In truth he would have expected it to hurt more. He felt cold and detached, watching the battle being fought around him. His own crew were slaughtering the admiral's guards, and soon they would turn and deal with the bastard himself. By then it would be too late. It was already too late.

The sun was rising over the admiral's shoulder, and it was a brilliant orange-gold that lit the ocean and the sky like fire.

"Barbarian filth," Verit hissed, leaning into his sword to drive it deeper into T'ruck's chest. The pain rushed in and shattered the calm cold that had settled over him. He gasped, tasting blood.

"I may die here," the admiral continued, "but I will see you dead first."

T'ruck lifted an arm to stop him. But he had no strength left, and the man easily batted it away and changed his grip on his sword to pull it free of T'ruck's chest.

Something large and angry crashed into the admiral from the side, sending him to the deck. T'ruck toppled sideways, too weak to stop himself falling. He saw the admiral struggling with Pocket, only for the young pirate to smash his head again and again with the edge of a wooden shield.

As the world started to go dark, the last thing T'ruck saw was Admiral Peter Verit's head battered to a pulp, his perfectly groomed facial hair finally ruined.

North Gale

Nerine climbed up onto a deck awash with blood. The sun was rising low in the east, giving everything a warm feel and casting deep shadows across the pools of red spreading over the planks. As she stood still, taking in the carnage, one of the puddles spread to her feet and seeped in around her bare soles.

Yu'truda had come up on deck first, and she stood still as stone, her mouth hanging open at the sight before her. All of Nerine's shadows were gone, but the massacre they'd left was nothing short of sickening even to the witch, and she'd witnessed more than one massacre in her years. Some of the soldiers were still alive, clinging to what little strength they had left and calling for help, but most were as dead as they could be. Some were little more than parts sitting in their own congealing blood.

Nerine heard retching and glanced sideways to see Yu'truda emptying her stomach. It was the smell that offended Nerine more than the blood. She'd seen rivers of red before, but death had a peculiar smell about it that couldn't be denied, almost as though human flesh rotted the moment it ceased to live. It was acrid and foul, and Nerine felt her lip curl.

Her skin felt raw and exposed, and her legs shook from the effort of keeping her upright. It was a side effect of extensive contact with the Void. So much power and magic had been channelled through her, it had left her feeling stripped away. Her own reserves of strength were almost depleted, and only her iron will was keeping her going. She would need to rest soon, and rest long. Any more attempts to channel magic could leave her with permanent damage.

Not bothering to step around the pools of gore, Nerine headed aft towards where she believed the captain's cabin might be. Captain Khan may have claimed it for himself, but Nerine needed to rest before her strength gave out completely, and she doubted she would find a more comfortable sanctuary than the cabin the admiral had been sleeping in. She went to step over a body and recognised the face. It was the officer she'd enslaved.

Kneeling down in the man's blood, Nerine turned his head towards her. To her surprise, she found him clinging to life, stubbornly refusing to admit that he was dead. She'd expected him to die when she sent him up the ladder with her shadows, and it now appeared that his own crewmates had cut him down and left him for dead.

"Do you recognise me?" Nerine said softly.

The officer didn't say anything, but Nerine thought she saw recognition in his eyes.

"All this is your fault," she continued, holding the man's chin in her hand so his head couldn't flop away. "I would have let you all return to your backwards kingdom and hang the pirates if not for your fervour. You thought me a slave, and thought to use me for your desire. I am a terror beyond your understanding, and I would never consent to be touched by your filthy hands."

There was no comprehension in the man's eyes. Nerine wagered he was long past anything but the barest slip of consciousness. He would die soon, of that there was no mistake, and she would let him.

"Yu," someone shouted from the deck above. "Yu, Cap'n's in a bad way."

Yu'truda broke into a run, ignoring the treacherous footing and rushing past Nerine, taking the steps up to the next deck two at a time. Nerine stood slowly, marvelling at how much blood had soaked into her tattered dress, and followed at a more leisurely pace.

At the top of the steps she saw more bodies – mostly soldiers, but a couple of Captain Khan's crew also lay there. Those pirates who remained – Nerine counted only eight of them – were gathered around a giant body that could only belong to Captain Khan himself.

Nerine approached slowly, her feet leaving bloody prints on the deck behind her. As she moved closer, she saw that the captain had a number of shallow wounds and one that wasn't so shallow. A sword was buried deep in his gut, almost up to the hilt, and blood leaked slowly from his mouth. He wasn't showing any signs of life that Nerine could see. She would have to strike a deal with Yu'truda now, and hope the woman was as amiable as her deceased captain. Now was not the time though. Nerine turned away from the funeral.

"Can you help him?" Yu'truda said in a voice that barely carried over the lapping of the waves and the creaking of the hull.

Nerine glanced back at the hulk of a corpse and felt a twinge of sadness. "I cannot bring back the dead. And even if I could, you would not like what came back."

"He's not dead," Yu'truda said urgently. "Not yet."

Nerine approached the circle of pirates slowly, and they parted to let her through. She knelt down by the giant body of T'ruck Khan and placed two fingers on his neck. It was very faint, but there was the barest beat of a pulse. With the wounds that he'd suffered, she doubted he would last for long.

"Can you heal him? Like you did before?" Yu'truda said.

Nerine sighed. "As I have said, I cannot heal, only speed the natural process. There is no natural process that can heal him now."

"Isn't there something you can do, anything to save his life?" Huge tears were rolling down Yu'truda's cheeks.

Nerine shook her head slowly. "I cannot save his life. But I can give him yours."

The Phoenix

Keelin watched the ship's boy as she dangled precariously over the side of *The Phoenix*, attempting to reach the jelly that had attached itself to the hull. Aimi had a rope tied around her waist, and Feather was attached to the other end. Feather wasn't exactly the largest or strongest of lads, but Aimi wasn't exactly the largest or heaviest of women, and the boy was just about managing to keep hold of her. Aimi had walked down the side of the hull and was reaching for the jelly with one hand while keeping the other firmly on the rope.

The Phoenix cut through another wave and the force of the spray knocked Aimi to her knees. Feather grunted, but held on tight all the same. Keelin smiled at the scene, enjoying the sight of Aimi soaked through.

"Don't you have captain things to do, Cap'n?" Smithe said, having sneaked up behind Keelin.

Fighting the urge to turn on his treacherous quartermaster and thanking the sea goddess Rin that the man hadn't taken the opportunity to throw his captain overboard, Keelin waited just long enough before replying for Smithe to bristle.

"The safety and well-being of the crew are captain things, Smithe." Keelin pushed away from the railing and turned on his quartermaster, cursing that he had to look up at the man. "But that's something you'll never need to know."

Smithe's jaw clenched and veins popped out on the man's neck. He was just over six feet of bronzed muscle with close-cropped hair, muddy eyes, and a burning desire to see *The Phoenix* in his own hands. He was a dangerous man, and even more dangerous since being voted into the position of quartermaster, but no matter how much Keelin would like to rid himself of the surly bastard, he couldn't. Smithe had many allies among the crew, and they wouldn't be pleased should the man disappear. For now the two were stuck in a dangerous dance, but Keelin was under no illusions that, should the opportunity present itself, he would find a knife in his back and Smithe attached to the handle.

"Crew want paying, Cap'n," Smithe said, the sun lending extra menace to his eyes. Which, Keelin had to admit, were normally more than menacing enough.

"Right now?" Keelin said. "What are they intending to spend it on, Smithe? Rat racing? Or are you bending over and taking payment these days?" It was a petty insult not really worthy of a captain, but Smithe had a way of making Keelin want to hurt him.

Smithe's eyes boggled, practically popping out of his skull. "We ain't pirated nothing in a long while, Cap'n. Crew need paying once we get back to Sev'relain, and the ship's coffers ain't exactly bursting."

"With you in charge, I'm surprised they're not dwindling."

"You calling me a thief?" Smithe took a step forward, looking down at his captain. Keelin stood his ground.

"We're all thieves, Smithe. Stealing shit is our trade, and there ain't been a quartermaster who didn't take a little extra for themselves." It was a blatant lie, but if Smithe could be caught stealing from the ship and crew it would be all the excuse Keelin needed.

"We need to take a ship," Smithe said.

Keelin sighed. "Were you unconscious during our escape from Ash? There are Five Kingdoms navy ships behind us, Smithe. Do you see our escort? There" – Keelin pointed over the port side of the ship – "*The Black Death*, and there" – he pointed over the starboard side – "the *Fortune*. Even if we did spot something to take, both those ships are faster and would get there first."

"Then we should leave," Smithe protested.

"No." Keelin stared down his quartermaster. "Right now we should run for home and regroup, and that's exactly what we are doing. We no longer have the liberty of operating out on our own. We all stick together or we all die alone. Is that clear?"

An ugly grin spread across Smithe's face. "Aye, Cap'n. No pay it is. Again." He turned and walked away, and Keelin realised that more than a few members of the crew were close by and had been listening in.

"Shit," he muttered, turning back to face the sea just as a jelly leapt over the railing and landed with a splat at his feet, thin tendrils flopping about on the deck.

Keelin put his hands on the railing and stared out across the sparkling blue waters of the Pirate Isles. If he concentrated really hard he could even pretend *The Black Death* wasn't sailing alongside him, obscuring his view and reminding him that Tanner Black was now working with them rather than trying to kill them.

"You heard all that?" Keelin said.

"Every word, more or less."

Keelin looked down to see Aimi holding onto the railing with both hands, a sympathetic look on her face. She still had a rope tied to her waist, and Feather was still nearby, holding on to the other end, trying desperately not to garner his captain's attention.

"Well, you're not the only one. Everyone on the ship will have heard by tonight, and I'm sure Smithe will make it sound like I don't want to pay the crew."

"Actually, you did a pretty good job of that yourself, Cap'n."

"Please call me Keelin."

"Not on duty, Cap'n," Aimi said with a grin. "Those are the rules. Your rules, if ya remember."

Keelin nodded, and silently wished he'd never imposed rules upon their relationship, but somehow he didn't think Aimi would be comfortable without them.

Reaching down, Keelin grabbed hold of Aimi's hand and helped her up and over the railing. He didn't let go of her hand.

"I could take you off duty," he said with a smile.

"No doubt we'd have a lot of fun," Aimi said. "But that would be along the lines of preferential treatment, which we also covered in your rules."

Keelin released her hand and stepped aside, motioning to the jelly lying on the deck. "Back to work then, boy." He finished the order with a slap on her arse and turned away before she could turn her glare on him.

Kebble Salt was standing at the bow, staring out into the blue. It was rare to see the man down from the nest, and even rarer to see him without the rifle that he was known to be so deadly with. Keelin approached quietly, leaning on the railing and waiting for the man to speak. He found himself waiting for some time.

"Do you see the mist on the horizon?" Kebble said eventually.

Keelin squinted, but saw nothing resembling a mist. In fact, it was a gloriously sunny day with plenty of wind and barely a cloud in the sky. Still, Kebble had proven his sight to be greater than that of most men. Of course, the sharpshooter also believed himself to be immortal, so Keelin had cause to question his sanity.

"I see nothing but clear skies and clearer waters," Keelin said with false cheer.

"Perhaps it is just me," Kebble said. "The mists herald the coming of *Cold Fire*, the wraith ship. It would not be the first time they have come for me."

Keelin glanced sideways at him. "So, this immortality of yours…" It was a subject he'd always tried to stay away from, and Kebble seemed disinclined to share. "How did you come about it?"

Kebble let out a bitter laugh. "I am cursed, Captain Stillwater. A god whose powers deal with life as much as your goddess' deals with water. A demon's power is the power to change fate. The Dread Lords hold death in their sway. It seems any of those powers could make a man immortal."

It was a vague answer at best. "What about Reowyn?" Keelin decided that if they were simply naming creatures of vast, unimaginable power, he might as well throw the bogeyman into the list.

Kebble's mouth twitched into a smile. "You believe Reowyn to be a myth. A tale of a monster told to scare children. You should be glad you do not know the things I know."

Keelin let out a ragged sigh. He was more than happy believing Reowyn to be nothing but a myth. "So what did you do to earn the curse?"

"I murdered an entire civilisation."

Keelin opened his mouth to speak, but quickly shut it and shook his head. He was more certain than ever that Kebble was indeed a madman, but sane or no, he was also a very useful man to have around.

"And you still think I may be able to find some god to take pity on you and kill you?" he said.

"I hope so," Kebble replied, still staring out at the ocean.

"Well, if you see any gods or ghost ships, let me know." Keelin turned and started away.

"I see land," Kebble said.

"Aye, that'll be Cinto Cena. Looks like we're home." Keelin squinted, but he couldn't make out the telltale line on the horizon that would indicate an island. "This is where the fun starts."

Keelin knew that before long they would be standing back on the dry land of New Sev'relain, and not long after that Tanner Black and Drake would be arguing. Given Keelin's history with both captains, he was more than sure he would be arguing too.

Fortune

Beck waited, watching Drake out of the corner of her eye while trying to seem uninterested. He was a mystery to her despite the amount of time they spent together, and every time she thought she'd unravelled a part of that mystery, two more questions sprang up to take its place. It was beyond maddening.

Drake's resistance to her compulsion, her magic that forced the truth from people, was as enticing as it was irritating. Of course, it helped that the pirate captain was handsome, and even more so that he knew his stuff between the sheets. Beck had been with a number of men in her time – some Arbiters, some not – but rarely had they left her feeling satisfied afterwards. Drake was different, and the fact that he knew it was insufferable.

For months they'd been stuck together. An order from Inquisitor Vance had driven Beck to the Pirate Isles, an order to protect Captain Drake Morrass, for reasons unknown to her. Since then she'd learned that there was a Drurr matriarch after Drake, and she could only conclude that that was the reason for her orders.

The Drurr were malevolent and evil on a scale that the Inquisition could not allow. There were some few exceptions who were allowed to live in a peaceful community in the northern reaches of Acanthia, and then there was the Queen of Blades in the free city of Larkos. But most of the Drurr haunted the places where humanity, even the agents of the Inquisition, feared to tread.

Beck had been able to glean some information about Drake and the Drurr from her time with him. He'd been a prisoner, a slave if the tattoos he wore were any indication, and for years he'd been held deep underground, tortured and likely worse at the hands of the Drurr – a matriarch no less. Beck had never heard of anyone escaping from the Drurr before, and that was yet another mystery she desperately wanted to solve.

New Sev'relain had grown again in the time they'd been away. New buildings, new ships, and new faces. Already the fledgling town had become a true settlement in its own right, and if it continued to expand it would soon match some of the smaller towns in Sarth for size. The Five Kingdoms' attempt to purge the isles had failed to wipe out the pirates, but it had funnelled them into one place and united them under one flag. Drake's flag.

Already Beck could see the evidence of industry. Smoke rose from the town, maybe from a bakery, maybe from a blacksmith – she didn't know, but its mere existence was sign that New Sev'relain was on its way to becoming a living city.

Folk crowded the docks, waiting for the *Fortune* to secure its berth and its captain to depart. Beck spotted many of the people who had been elected as representatives for the townsfolk, those who weren't pirates but were now living under Drake's rule all the same. She saw Riverlanders too, dirty and dishevelled with their tattooed faces. She'd never seen so many of the vagrants before.

The Riverlanders tended to be secretive and violent towards outsiders. They mostly travelled the riverways in the densely packed jungles south of Sarth, living off the land and whatever they could trade with those they didn't attack and eat.

Beck counted eight ships floating in the bay, and that was more than she'd ever seen in one place in the Pirate Isles. Judging by the whispered talk of the crew, it was as rare as Beck thought it to be. With the *Fortune*, *The Phoenix*, and *The Black Death*, that took the count up to eleven, and the docks looked crowded. As they approached, one of the ships at berth was towed away by dinghies, and the *Fortune* made for the free spot right away, leaving the other ships to wait in the bay.

"You coming?" Drake said as the *Fortune* came to a stop and its crew started to secure the lines.

Beck waited for a few moments, gazing out into New Sev'relain. "No," she said eventually.

Drake stared at Beck for a while longer before snorting out a laugh and turning away. "Suit yourself, Arbiter."

The pirate captain mounted the gangplank and swaggered down it, greeting those waiting for him at the bottom with open arms, a warm smile, and plenty of reassuring words. He glanced back towards Beck once, but she made certain she was looking elsewhere. Once Drake was off the docks and heading towards the town, Beck turned and walked towards his cabin.

"Can I help you, Arbiter?" Princess, Drake's first mate, said just as she reached the door. He was loyal as a dog where his captain was concerned, and Beck was in no doubt that Drake would hear of her attempt to enter his cabin.

"Actually, yes, Princess, you can," she said with a predatory smile. "I need to clean my pistols and I've run out of metal oil. You can fetch me some."

"To the captain's cabin?" Princess persisted.

"My cabin used to be yours," Beck said. "Do you believe there's enough room in there to perform the proper maintenance?"

Beck's compulsion locked onto Princess' will and forced the truth out of him. "No," Princess said, and let out a shiver. It was unlikely he would have lied, but Beck found using her compulsion to dominate folk from time to time reminded them of their place. "I bloody wish you wouldn't do that, Arbiter. I'll fetch ya oil, just… don't go magicking me any more, eh."

As Princess hurried away, Beck put her hand to the door handle and twisted. The door didn't budge. Drake rarely bothered locking it when he was aboard ship, but at times like this it didn't surprise Beck that he had. She was starting to understand bits of Drake, and it was obvious his circle of trust was small.

Beck whispered two words into her hand and then placed that hand against the lock. There was an immediate click as the bolt slid back, and she tried the handle again. The door opened and she stepped inside. Of the three schools of magic employed by the Inquisition, she was most proficient with sorcery, using her potential to directly affect the world and, when need be, drawing upon the vast power of Volmar. Opening locked doors was little more than a trick, but she was capable of real magic when the need called.

The school of sorcery was the most diverse, with further subdivisions in elemental magic, conjuration, and alteration. Beck had found an affinity for alteration very early on in her training and had specialised in it. It was the most literal form of sorcery, the ability to change the world around her, and its uses were near endless. Of course, there were the darker sub-divisions of sorcery such as necromancy, but the Inquisition did not teach, nor condone, practitioners of those evil arts, and the eradication of those that did was one of the organisation's chief mandates.

Beck had encountered necromancers before, and their ability to breathe life into the dead was both horrifying and unforgivable. Necromancers' powers were never stronger than when they were near the Land of the Dead, and Beck had seen first-hand what such heretics were capable of when they could draw upon the power of that cursed place. She shuddered at the memory and pushed it away. That they'd recently witnessed a Drurr ship carrying a necromancer worried Beck greatly. The Drurr had always abhorred the practice as much as the Inquisition did; it was, after all, responsible for the downfall of their once great civilisation.

It occurred to Beck that Princess might not be so easily fooled by her ruse. She took a pistol from her jerkin and laid it on a nearby cabinet before approaching the window and waiting. The first mate would appear with the oil and she would instruct him to place it next to the gun to secure her alibi. As soon as he was gone, she would contact the Inquisition.

Arbiter Darkheart may have recently freed the demons of the Void from their indenture, making long-distance communication harder, but there were still ways. They were limited and draining and required absolute concentration, but the Inquisition had come up with an alternative and Beck needed to talk to Inquisitor Vance. He needed to know everything that had happened so far, and she needed new orders.

"Reparations will be made," Drake assured the skinny woman. "Store what's left in the cellar for now and come by the *Fortune* tomorrow with a number. If it's reasonable, I'll see you're paid for the inconvenience."

Tanner laughed from the other side of the table, and Drake suppressed a shudder at the noise. His recent nemesis and now ally had been a second shadow from the moment he made land, following him around and participating in his discussions with the inhabitants of New Sev'relain. It was an annoyance, but one Drake could abide, as not only did it seem to be cementing their new-found alliance, but the people of New Sev'relain could see just what kind of man Tanner was and they were quickly learning how different life would be under the blackguard's rule rather than his own.

"Still want to be king, mate?" Tanner said with a dark grin.

They were sitting either side of a table in the Righteous Indignation while a veritable celebration went on around them. Pirates from all the crews socialised together, and though there was a strained atmosphere in the air, the folk of New Sev'relain appeared to be accepting of those from Fango. Tanner was nursing a mug of ale like it was the last in the world, and Drake was already on his second and wishing it was his fourth.

"Still want to take it from me?" Drake replied with a golden-toothed grin of his own.

Tanner laughed and slapped the table hard. A couple of nearby pirates, men from Drake's crew, turned and looked, but they soon realised violence wasn't on the cards.

"Why be king though, Drake?" Tanner said. "Word as I hear it says ya got all the money of a king with none of the shit that comes with it. So why? Unless it's just to prove ya in charge."

Drake narrowed his eyes. He didn't credit Tanner with an abundance of subtlety, but neither did he trust the man, and that seemed like a decent policy given it wasn't thirty days ago that Tanner had been about to cut out Drake's tongue with a rusty knife. Drake rubbed the scab on his nose and winced.

"Legitimacy," he said, and it was almost half the truth. "I might have money, but if I sail into Sarth I'll still get my neck stretched just the same as any common criminal. If I can legitimise the Pirate Isles, make peace with Sarth, and the Five Kingdoms and Acanthia and the Dragon Empire, then I can go anywhere. We can go anywhere."

He leaned back in his chair. "Think, Tanner. No more hiding, skulking into shit hole ports to sell things at a tenth of what they're worth."

"No more piracy," Tanner rumbled, his smiles and laughter long gone.

"Nothing ever works out quite the way it's planned, Tanner. There'll still be fights to be had and ships to be robbed, but we make it so everyone wants to pass through our waters pays a tax, and we use that money to build real towns here in the isles. We won't just be pirates any more – we'll be the greatest damned navy the world has ever seen. That's real power. The power to influence the world."

"And that's why." Tanner stared at Drake, and there was real evil in his eyes. "Ya want the type of power even money can't buy, only loyalty, and those that are loyal willing to lay down their lives for ya."

Drake had to give Tanner something for being more perceptive than he would have guessed. "Aye," he said, and waited for the pirate's response.

"Ya got bigger stones than I guessed, Drake. Just remember who's helping ya get there, and know I can take away my support at a moment's notice."

Drake was about to respond to the veiled threat when the door to the tavern opened and three Riverlanders swaggered in, followed by Deun Burn himself, all of them with tattooed faces. Captain Burn snarled at the gathered crowd of drunken, celebrating pirates, before his gaze settled on Drake's table and he made his way over, his kin behind him.

"You order a Riverlander?" Drake asked Tanner.

Tanner spat. "No one ever wants to see one of those vagrant bastards."

Deun stopped at the table and made a show of standing over Drake, looking down at him. Drake took the opportunity to ignore the man and sup on his ale, which, unfortunately, was on the verge of running dry.

"Morrass," Deun hissed eventually, after it became clear to everyone that Drake wasn't willing to pay the man any attention.

"Captain Burn," Drake said with false cheer. "I didn't notice you standing there. Pull up a chair, why don't you? You know Tanner Black?"

The captain of *Rheel Toa* eyed Tanner suspiciously before looking around for a chair and finding none spare. "So it's true? Even Captain Black works for you now."

Drake smiled at Deun. "More of an alliance, really. What happened to Captain Khan? I've heard reports that he sailed away just after meeting with you, and he hasn't come back yet. I ordered him to guard New Sev'relain. I'm a little curious as to what would have made him sail off like that."

"He was betrayed," Deun said with a grim set to his skull-tattooed face. "We were all betrayed."

Drake glanced across the table to find Tanner looking right back. "Betrayed by who?"

"One of my brothers. Captain of *Berris Dey*. He tricked the big fool into sailing after a ship in our waters. It was a trap. Set by the Five Kingdoms and baited by my *hitschkk* of a brother."

Drake had no idea what the Riverlander had just said, only that the word made his ears hurt. "I'd quite like to meet this captain of *Berris Dey*," he said. He'd seen the ship floating out in the bay.

"He has been dealt with," Deun Burn said with a nod.

"How can I be sure of that?"

Deun looked at Drake. The man might have looked confused, but the skull tattoo that covered his face hid the subtleties of his expression. He quickly fiddled at his belt and retrieved a pouch, opening it and dumping a patch of leather on the table between Drake and Tanner. It was a crude thing, a circle of leather with a few holes and a pattern like scales.

"We removed his honour," Deun said, straightening up and standing to his full height.

Drake looked down at the circle of leather again, and then up to find Tanner Black grinning madly in the lantern light.

"That's his face, isn't it?" Drake said.

Deun Burn nodded.

"You people do some weird shit," Drake said, glancing at the patch of skin and trying to keep his stomach from turning. "What happened to the rest of him?"

Deun picked up the flap of skin and tucked it back into its pouch. "Dealt with."

"You ate him, didn't you?" Drake said.

Tanner Black laughed, a deep noise that somehow drowned out the din around them.

"Did you at least find out how much the owner of that face told the Five Kingdoms bastards before you filled ya bellies?"

Captain Burn's skull face frowned. "No."

"Because I reckon there's a good chance he told them where this place is. If he knew where New Sev'relain is, then now so do they." Drake slammed his fist against the table, launched to his feet, and stormed past the Riverlander, not caring if either of the other two captains followed him.

Outside the tavern, Drake stopped and stared up towards the treeline and then down towards the docks. Deun Burn burst outside after him, followed lethargically by Tanner Black, who still seemed more amused by the situation than anything else.

"We're gonna need folk in the forest, watching," Drake said, holding up his hand against the bright sunlight. "I was at Old Sev'relain, and they landed on the far side of the island, came out of the trees before any of us knew what was happening. Surprise being their best weapon, I guess."

"They would never survive the forests of the Isle of Goats," Tanner said with pride in his voice. "Fango is a safer town."

"Aye," Drake conceded. "Maybe. But this little island ain't called many deaths for nothing, Tanner. They might make it over the beaches and through the forest, but they'll pay a heavy toll. Still best to have folk out there watching though."

Looking towards the docks again, Drake saw Keelin Stillwater slogging his way up the sandy stretch. The man had that little wench of his with him and they seemed deep in conversation.

"We're gonna need weapons," Drake said. "I want every pirate armed and every spare weapon – sword, axe, or sharp stick – in the hands of the townsfolk. Prioritise those who know how to use them. We arm as many folk as possible."

He turned back to Deun and Tanner to find the two men not jumping to his commands. Tanner had stopped grinning and was regarding Drake curiously. Deun seemed caught between the two of them, waiting for Tanner to fall in line before he would himself. Drake took a step forward and stared up at Tanner. The big pirate did not look cowed.

"Ya really wanna make ya stand here, Morrass?" Tanner said slowly. "Fango is better for it. With a few bows and those who can use them we could hold Fango against an army."

Drake shook his head. "We do it here, Tanner."

"Do what here?" Stillwater said, sounding a little out of breath from the walk up the beach. The little woman beside him was staring with wide eyes at the assembled captains, and she wasn't the only one. Folk were stopping nearby and edging closer, attempting to listen in.

"Five Kingdoms are coming," Tanner said. "Drake wants to make his stand here instead of Fango."

"When are they coming?" Stillwater said.

"Don't know," Tanner replied. "Fucking Riverlanders gave us away though."

More and more folk were stopping now that some had heard Tanner speak. One man even ducked into the tavern, no doubt to spread the rumour. There was nothing for it now; soon the whole town would know.

"We dealt with the traitor," Captain Burn insisted.

"Aye, mate," Tanner said, stepping closer and towering over the Riverlander. "So ya say, and ya got a pretty little flap of skin by way of proof, but how are we to know the rest of ya ain't just as treacherous?"

"This isn't helping, Tanner," Stillwater said.

"Speaking of the treacherous, you should probably just keep that mouth of yours shut, mate," Tanner said, turning on Stillwater.

"Are they really coming for us again?" asked one of the townsfolk nearby, a woman of middling years with stained clothing and a young boy holding onto her leg.

"I didn't betray you, Tanner," Stillwater said, squaring up to the bigger pirate. "I escaped you."

"Aye," Drake roared over all of them – the pirates, the captains, and the townsfolk – then waited for them to quiet down before he continued. "They're coming for us again."

"Where do we run to now?" said one of the townsfolk.

"Fango," Tanner shouted quickly before turning his dark eyes on Drake. There was a challenge there that couldn't be ignored.

"We're not going to Fango," Drake yelled before he lost he crowd. "We're not going anywhere."

He looked around, meeting as many eyes as possible. "Aye, they're coming for us again, and they're coming hard." Drake had no idea how many ships they'd attack them with this time, but they'd escaped five during the parley at Ash. "And we'll do to them what we did to that monster." He pointed at the skeleton of the Man of War still keeled over down the beach. It was little more than the bones of a ship these days – every useful plank of wood had been salvaged to help build the town – but they kept it there as a reminder of where they came from.

"We're gonna reinforce the town. All work on homes and the like stops; anyone left homeless gets taken in somewhere." Drake pointed towards the forest. "We need to clear the trees back and build a wall. Watch towers, we'll need watch towers."

"That's a lot of work, Captain Morrass," said one of the townsfolk, a large man with more lines in his face than there were waves in the sea. "How long do we have?"

"I don't know," Drake said truthfully. "Could be weeks, could be hours."

"Hours?" one of the townsfolk cried. The crowd broke into chaos. Some folk shouted at each other, some at Drake, and others just pleaded or prayed for their lives.

Drake let out a ragged sigh and looked to his fellow captains for help. He received none.

"Fango," Tanner said, just loudly enough for Drake to hear.

"Yes, it's a lot of work," Drake roared. "And no, we don't have long to do it. But one thing is for fucking certain. They are coming. So the sooner you all stop pissing and moaning to me and get started, the better state we'll be in when they arrive, because nobody fucking leaves. Here is where we're making our stand, so anyone with a job, get to it. Anyone without a job, find one."

There was some mumbling from the crowd and some of the townsfolk wandered away, but more stayed behind, looking expectantly from Drake to Tanner to Stillwater.

"Now! Unless you all want to die when the bastards get here," Drake shouted.

Stillwater nodded. "Drake's made the choice, and here is where we fight them. Get to it, people."

The crowd began to disperse, pirates and townsfolk alike slipping away to find jobs. Drake was raging inside. The fools hadn't listened to him. They'd heard his orders and they hadn't moved until Stillwater agreed with them. He blamed Tanner – the man's claim that Fango was safer had scared the folk of New Sev'relain, and they believed him.

"Reckon they just needed someone to agree with you," Stillwater said once most of the crowd had gone. "You really think this is the best idea, Drake?"

"You questioning my orders, Stillwater?" Drake turned on the man, wondering when everyone had started doubting him.

"Good orders should always be questioned," Stillwater said. "Bad orders should always be ignored."

Tanner laughed. "So ya still remember something from aboard me ship, boy."

Stillwater shook his head at Tanner. "Oh, aye. I remember you saying it. Also remember you beating me with a bucket for questioning one of your orders."

"Never said there wasn't a price for questioning good orders." Tanner grinned and turned his attention back to Drake. "We'll stay and help ya fight, Your Majesty. I do hope we *all* get through it." The big pirate laughed and turned away, striding towards the beach and his ship.

"Bastard is going to undermine me every chance he gets," Drake said, staring after Tanner.

"He's not wrong about Fango being more defensive," Stillwater said.

"It's not about which is more defensive. It's about territory, and Fango is his. New Sev'relain has to be the seat of my power, the capital of the Pirate Isles, otherwise he has too much influence."

"What about the people?" Stillwater said. "They've a better chance of surviving at Fango."

Drake looked at him and shook his head. "They've a better chance of surviving under my boot, not his."

The Phoenix

Keelin dug his feet into the dirt and pulled hard on the rope. The woman in front and two men behind him did the same, and slowly the wooden pillar began to rise. Those attached to the other rope, opposite Keelin's team, let it out hand after hand as Keelin and his three companions pulled it in. The same thing was happening all across the treeline, the bones of a wall being erected to provide New Sev'relain better protection from the forest and anything that might come out of it.

Out of the corner of his eye he saw another pillar going up; this one only had one person pulling on the rope – Beck. Keelin had long known the woman was an Arbiter, ever since she'd used her magic on him and forced him to tell the truth, and now others were starting to suspect. No one person was strong enough to do the work of four, not without the help of magic. The problem, at least as far as Keelin saw it, was that nobody else cared.

He doubted he was the only one to have cause for grievance with the Inquisition and its murderous ways, but the other pirates and townsfolk didn't seem to mind. Beck was helping New Sev'relain, getting her hands dirty and pouring as much blood and sweat into the strengthening of its defences as the next person. Much more than some.

With every pillar the Arbiter helped to erect, with every tree felled and pit dug, with every section of wall built and every watch tower raised, the witch hunter was gaining the respect and admiration of folk who should be running her out of town. She was a murderer as sure as any other Arbiter, and Keelin couldn't forgive any of them. At least, not until he caught the Arbiter who had murdered his little sister. Not until he showed Arbiter Prin as much mercy as the bastard had shown a scared little girl whose only crime had been recurring sickness and her own intuition.

"Ease off a bit, Cap'n Stillwater," said the man behind him. "Ya pullin' too hard. This ain't no race. Slow an' steady is safest, eh?"

Keelin let out the ragged breath he'd been holding in and matched his pace to the rest of his team's, aware that his anger towards the witch hunters had got the better of him. He'd just spent so long trying to find his revenge that it often clouded his mind.

The pillar dropped the last few feet into the post-hole dug for it and they pulled it upright. A girl and her father rushed forwards with a cart full of dirt and quickly shovelled it into the hole around the pillar, and after a few minutes they were instructed to let go of the ropes. The pillar held upright, and someone patted Keelin on the back.

"Ten minutes' break, then on to the next one."

Keelin nodded to the hairy pirate coordinating the work and sank gratefully down onto the dirt. He pulled a water skin from his belt, sucking down gloriously wet sips and letting the sweat run down his face and drip from his chin. His eyes found Beck again. The Arbiter didn't bother to rest – she moved straight on to the next wooden pillar and took up the rope on her own again, working tirelessly. Keelin remembered the screams that tore from his sister's throat as the fires lit by Arbiter Prin ate her alive. Tears welled up in his eyes, but he could no longer tell if they stemmed from pain or rage.

Not two years ago Keelin had thought he was close. He'd traded with another witch hunter – passage from Larkos to Fortune's Rest in return for Arbiter Prin's location. It turned out the witch hunter had lied; the little town he directed Keelin to had never heard of an Arbiter by the name of Prin.

A few months later Keelin learned of the Observatory in the ruins of HwoyonDo, the capital city of the Forgotten Empire. There, he was assured, he would be able to find Prin and his vengeance. He paid a high price for the information, and the seller gave no reassurances.

Keelin told his crew, and they were more than happy to follow him – not for his dream of vengeance, but for the riches hidden within the lost city. Unfortunately, the waters around the Forgotten Empire were as dangerous as the jungle that covered the land, and more than a few ships had been lost sailing blind. They needed the charts of someone who had sailed through those waters before, and only one captain, and one ship, was known to have gone there and come back. Keelin looked around for Drake Morrass, but he couldn't see the infamous pirate anywhere. He'd started following Drake in the hopes of swiping the charts from him, but

somewhere along the course Keelin had found himself believing in
Drake's vision of a unified Pirate Isles. The Five Kingdoms and Sarth
were coming, and they were trying to wipe out the pirates. Keelin
couldn't allow that. The isles, and the folk who lived there, had taken
him in after he escaped his father. Tanner Black may have made Keelin a
pirate and given him a job, but it was the people of Fango and Sev'relain
and Black Sands who gave him a home. Drake wanted to protect those
same people because he wanted to wear a crown and be in charge of
them; Keelin just wanted to help them. He'd seen too many people and
cities burn in his short lifetime.

"You ready, Captain Stillwater?"

Keelin nodded to the hairy pirate and followed him to the next
pillar. He noticed Beck had finished raising another and was holding it
steady as dirt was poured into the post-hole. Keelin still didn't trust the
woman, but he had to give her some grudging respect. She was damned
useful to have around.

Aimi raised her left hand and pointed at the target, drawing back
her right hand. She took a deep breath and let it out smoothly. Throwing
her right hand forwards, she let go of the knife. The little blade spun end
over end over end before clattering against the outside wall of Keelin's
cabin and dropping to the deck. She'd missed the target by a good two
feet.

Harsh laughter sounded behind her and she cringed as she
recognised Smithe's voice. The big quartermaster was a special kind of
creepy, and Aimi knew his type . She'd spent long enough working in a
tavern in Old Sev'relain to be able to tell which pirates were to be
avoided at all costs, and Smithe was definitely one. He was the kind of
man who enjoyed the violence of the way of life over the freedom. He
lived to hurt folk and he would take his enjoyment anywhere he could get
it. She tried to avoid Smithe as much as possible, but *The Phoenix* wasn't
the largest of ships and her relationship with its captain, along with her
breasts, only served to draw the quartermaster's attention.

"Useless bitch," he said with a sneer as Aimi collected her knife.
She clenched her jaw tight; there was no point in bristling at the man's

comments. Smithe outranked her and could make her life unbearably hellish with the assignment of duties and shore leave, and that would only tempt Keelin to intervene on her behalf, which, she suspected, was exactly what the quartermaster wanted.

As Aimi bent down to collect her knife something thudded into the wall just inches from her head. She fell backwards, scrambling away on her arse, her heart pounding in her ears and her mouth suddenly as dry as a desert, all to Smithe's braying laughter.

The knife that had come so close to ending her life was still wobbling in the wall. It was a long blade with a single edge and a handle that incorporated individual finger guards all made of shiny steel. Aimi could well imagine how a punch from a man like Smithe with that knife in hand could easily do as much damage as a stab.

"You're trying to spin the blade," Smithe said as he walked over, sparing only a glance at Aimi. She sat on the deck, staring at him wild-eyed. He pulled the knife from the wall and kicked Aimi's little piece of metal towards her. "It wants to fly straight from your hand."

Smithe walked a good distance away, then turned back towards the cabin. He held his knife by the blade and pointed it at the wall, then drew back his hand until it was beside his head. In one quick motion he extended his arm and released the little knife, which flew with alarming speed towards the target Aimi had hung on the wall. It embedded itself with a solid thunk.

"Throw the blade straight and true," Smithe said, approaching the cabin and pulling his knife from the target. "Let the weight of the handle even out its flight."

Aimi gathered her legs beneath her and stood, picking up her knife as she did. Smithe sat down on a barrel, watching her with his too-intense eyes. Aimi hated how nervous the quartermaster made her feel. She walked to the spot from which Smithe had thrown and focused. First she pointed her knife at the target, then drew it back just as Smithe had, then extended her arm and released.

Her little knife hit the wall of the cabin just a foot from the target and stuck there for a moment before the weight of it dragged its point loose and it clattered to the deck. Smithe laughed again.

"I was closer," Aimi said indignantly.

"Closer don't mean shit," Smithe spat. "Ya gonna fight with the rest of the crew, then ya need to know how to stick the enemy an' not us. Not that ya throw would've done much more than piss a real man off. Throw harder or don't fucking bother."

Aimi felt her cheeks go hot. "I'll try."

Smithe leapt off his barrel and stormed over to her. She held her ground, but with the big quartermaster bearing down on her it wasn't easy. She wanted nothing so much as to run and hide in Keelin's cabin.

"Might be my life depends on your fucking trying, one day. Or maybe even the captain's." Smithe stank of stale sweat with a hint of sweet perfume, telling Aimi much about his shore leave activities. While the rest of the town was helping build defences and prepare for an attack, Smithe was visiting the brothel.

For a while Aimi just stared at the deck beneath her, desperately willing her legs not to shake. Eventually Smithe snorted and turned away.

"Either learn to throw that thing or go hide under the captain's bed," he snarled as he stalked off.

Aimi waited until Smithe had disappeared below decks, then released the breath she'd been holding. She sank down onto her arse. A laugh from above made her glance up. Looking down from just a few feet above her on the main mast was the deeply lined face of Jojo Hyrene. Aimi had spent many an hour in Jojo's company, listening to his never-ending stories, and she counted the man as a true friend.

"He works pretty damned hard to be that scary," Jojo said with a wide smile.

"It's not just me then?" Aimi said. "He scares you too?"

Jojo nodded. "Scares everyone a bit, I think, even the Cap'n, though he'd never show it. Smithe served with Tanner back when this ship belonged to his daughter. He revelled in the cruelty."

"Wait," Aimi said. "*The Phoenix* belonged to that harpy, Elaina Black?"

Jojo laughed and his head bobbed up and down again. "Mhm, before Cap'n Stillwater stole it out from under her. *The Phoenix* was to be her first ship. Anyone else and I reckon she'd have chased them to

Rin's court and back, but not the Cap'n."

Aimi looked away from Jojo, sucking on her teeth and trying not to feel the strange jealousy that bubbled up from deep down. Keelin was hers; he'd chosen Aimi over his old flame. They spent their free time together and talked about everything and nothing, often drinking cheap rum late into the night, and she spent more nights than not in his bunk these days. Still, that he had so much history with Elaina Black worried her. She only knew of the woman by reputation, but what she'd heard made her sound even scarier than Smithe.

With a noise approaching a growl, Aimi stood and collected her fallen knife. She returned to the practice spot and launched the little blade at the target again, this time imagining it was Elaina Black's smirking face.

"Another one comin' in," someone shouted from somewhere high above her.

Aimi looked upwards to see Jojo climb up the mast a few feet and look towards the bay for a moment before breaking into laughter.

"What is it?" Aimi said as she retrieved her knife from the wall.

"The name of the ship is *My Salty Wife*," Jojo said, still chuckling.

Aimi snorted out a laugh, but it was all she could manage in her dark mood. Her father used to refer to the sea as his salty wife, and used to say he often cheated on her with Aimi's mother, but the sea was a jealous bitch and if the waves ever got wind of his adultery, his salty wife would sink him with barely a thought.

The thought of her parents brought with it a pang of regret. Aimi had never told them she was leaving, nor her sister. She'd just packed her bag and gone. She wondered how they were doing now, and if they still thought of her.

A laugh bubbled up and erupted from Aimi's belly. She was halfway across the world, embroiled in a war to build a new empire, and she was fucking the man who was going to stand on the right-hand side of the throne – and she was missing her fisherman father and his wife. If she did one day return to her parents, Aimi could only wonder if they'd even believe her adventure.

Fortune

Beck stumbled over to one of the tables set out in the sand and collapsed onto the bench. The temperature had dropped considerably in the last hour as the sun sank down. A brilliant golden sunset was waning to the west.

Someone gave Beck a hearty slap on the back. Rather than bristle and threaten the offender, she accepted it as the comradery that it was. She was beyond exhausted from the labour, and there was still so much to be done. In just a few days they'd erected all of the support pillars and had started with the even lengthier process of actually building the wall plank by plank. It would never be the sturdiest of defences, but it didn't have to be. The pirates didn't intend to sit behind their wall for a lengthy siege, but rather use it to slow down any enemy who somehow made it past the flaming cliffs, sand monsters, and enchanted forest.

"Drink this," Drake said as he sat down opposite Beck, placing a tankard in front of her. "It's water."

Beck took the tankard gratefully and started sipping at it, only then realising just how thirsty she was. She'd been working for most of the day, chanting blessings of strength to do the work of four or five people at once, or blessings of stamina to keep her muscles feeling fresh and energetic. It had taken its toll, and dehydration was only one of the issues she now faced.

"You need to slow down," Drake said.

Looking up, she saw real concern on the captain's face. He was ruddy-cheeked and sticky with sweat, his hair a tousled mess, and his face seemed to have sprouted some new lines. Beck sighed and took another sip of water, her head drooping.

"I don't know what it is you think you need to prove, but folk here are impressed. You've already done more than your share of work, but I need you to slow down. I need you ready for a fight, not collapsed in a heap like Tatters."

Beck glanced sideways at Admiral Tatters. The man was an unconscious drunken mess. He'd helped a little with the defences, erecting a pole or two, but the lure of booze had quickly taken hold and before long he was more liability than asset. To think he'd once been a loyal, respectable admiral in the Sarth navy, and now he was the town drunk of a pirate colony at war with Sarth.

"I'll be fine," Beck insisted, not looking up from her tankard. She didn't want to look at Drake lest he see the guilt she was feeling. Inquisitor Vance had given her very specific orders, but for now she was to help the pirates against Sarth and the Five Kingdoms and protect Drake against any and all threats.

For a while Drake said nothing, and Beck was content to pretend he'd gone, but she knew he was still sitting there, watching her.

"Here," he said eventually, and Beck heard him drop something heavy onto the table. "We might all be working together, but you really shouldn't leave valuable things like this just lying around."

Beck looked up to see her leather jerkin on the table. She'd taken it off early in the day when the sun was high and hot and labouring in such heavy clothing became unbearable. She was more than hot enough in just a blouse and trousers.

"Looks like someone made off with one of your pistols. Might be I can ask around and find it."

Beck looked closer and saw that one of the guns usually strapped to the front of the jerkin was indeed missing. She shook her head, still refusing to meet Drake's eyes. "I think I left it in your cabin when I was cleaning it the other day."

"Maybe we should go and retrieve it then, eh?"

There was no mistaking the suggestion in Drake's voice. They'd fucked on the way back from Ash, and Beck wouldn't deny she'd both wanted and needed it, but she also couldn't deny she was getting too close to Drake. The pirate was her mission, not her friend or lover, and she didn't need the distraction. She looked up at him then.

"Sure," she said, and cursed herself for giving in so easily.

Drake grinned and disentangled himself from the bench. Beck stood slowly, finishing her tankard of water and scooping up her jerkin as she followed the pirate towards his ship. She knew she should have said no – she'd meant to say it. She'd meant to find some food and crawl into her bunk to spend the rest of the night asleep in preparation for another hard day of labour, but she wanted Drake. She wanted to taste his lips and feel him inside her. Inquisitor Vance had given her specific orders, but he hadn't forbidden her from having sex with Drake, so she was breaking no rules other than her own.

They made it all the way to the beach in silence before an interruption both saved and disappointed Beck. Captain Sienen Zhou shouted to them as he hurried over. The captain of *Freedom* was short and wiry with long hair and an even longer moustache that dropped down past his chin and towards his chest.

"What is it, Sienen?" Drake said tersely. "I've got plans." He glanced back at Beck. "Good plans."

"Some of my boys are missing," Captain Zhou said. "Light's all but gone and they should've been back long ago."

"Missing from where?" Drake said.

"Water collection out in the trees."

"They may have stumbled into one of the magic traps," Beck said with a sigh. "I can take a team to look for them." She wasn't sure if she was glad or not for a reason to be away from Drake.

"They've made the run… must be twenty times," Captain Zhou said indignantly. "They know the route."

Beck saw Drake glance towards his ship and then back up towards the town. He was obviously torn between the desire to get Beck back to his cabin and the need to take the missing pirates seriously.

"Raise the alarm, Sienen," he said. "Every man, woman, and drunk who can hold a sharp object gets one."

Beck swung her jerkin off her shoulder and pulled it on. "Drake, if you wouldn't mind doing me up," she said quietly.

"Aye, probably for the best." Drake started pulling on the laces to tightly secure the jerkin as Captain Zhou ran off towards the town, shouting for people to raise the alarm. Within a minute small bells were ringing all around New Sev'relain, the signal to warn of a possible attack.

Beck counted eight camp fires on the beach between them and the ships. They ranged from cook fires to small blazes, each one lighting only a small area in the encroaching darkness. Each ship in the bay was also lit with a number of lanterns, and Beck counted twelve vessels, all floating on water that looked almost ethereal as the light from a waning sun gave way to that of a new moon.

"There's a new ship in the bay," Beck said as Drake finished tightening up the laces and tied them off.

Moving to stand beside her, Drake stared down the beach. "That one," he said, pointing at a ship sitting at the docks between *The Phoenix* and the *Fortune*. "I don't recognise her."

An ear-splitting whistle sounded from the town and both Beck and Drake turned to see a bright light rocket upwards, leaving a trail of red behind it until it finally exploded into shards of crimson high above New Sev'relain.

"What in Volmar's name was that?" Beck said.

"Sky fire," Drake said. "The Dragon Empire use them for celebrations and for signalling armies from a distance."

Another whistle behind them turned them both back towards the bay, and the sky was lit by another small explosion a moment later, this one green. In the dim light Beck saw men dressed in armour rush down the gangplank of the new ship before forming up and spreading out along the docks while more men climbed down behind them.

"Bastards are in among us," Drake said, and started down the beach just as the unmistakeable sound of steel on steel floated down from the town.

Beck took a deep breath and banished all thoughts of sleep or sex or anything but blood and death. "Go to the town," she said coldly. "They'll need you."

"But my ship," Drake protested, caught between the docks and the town even as the pirates around the camp fires started to react to the small army gathering on their beach.

"I'll deal with them." Beck pointed towards the ship and the soldiers pouring off it. "I can fight better without you getting in my way." She didn't wait for Drake's reply. She set off down the beach and towards the ship, hoping he would survive the battle without her protection.

The Phoenix

The walls were next to useless in most places, little more than ankle-high fences. Soldiers from the forest swarmed over them in units of five or six, forgoing the usual formations for a more skirmish style of combat. Keelin had to admit it was a wise decision, given the distance between buildings in New Sev'relain and the sheer number of alleyways and cut-throughs.

The pirates and townsfolk had one thing going for them, at least – the soldiers looked weary and out of sorts. No doubt they'd landed their ships on the north-east side of the island, where the sand monsters would have caused heavy casualties to the unwary, and there was a good chance the magical traps in the forest had caused their fair share of chaos among the ranks.

Keelin leapt into the nearest fight, both cutlasses already drawn and swinging. His swords clanged off the soldier's cuirass, leaving only a scrape in the bright metal by way of damage, but the soldier retreated from the attack and Keelin pressed forwards. A second man stepped forward with a round shield, batting away Keelin's follow-up just as a spear came over the top and nearly skewered him. Ever light on his feet, Keelin danced backwards out of the way.

The pirates and townsfolk had all been armed with an assortment of swords, axes, knives, and the odd bow, but very few had been given shields. Even fewer were used to fighting well-armed, trained soldiers on a battlefield that was more stable than not. A group of ten men and women pressed the soldiers Keelin was fighting from the other side, but they were scared to get close with a spear swinging about and shields protecting the men they were trying to kill. It was the same everywhere Keelin looked; the people of New Sev'relain simply weren't ready for this type of battle. They were well and truly outmatched.

One burly pirate with a cleft chin and tattoos showing underneath his shirt and all the way down his arms ran at the group of soldiers with a howl of rage and a big wood axe swinging above his head. The pirate leapt and, with a scream, brought down his axe on the shield of one of the soldiers. The shield split and half of it fell away. A spear was thrust at the pirate, but he caught it with his right hand and launched himself backwards, away from the group of soldiers, pulling the man on the other end of the spear with him. His fellow pirates wasted no time in stabbing the unfortunate soldier before the rest of his group could rescue him.

Most of the soldiers switched their attention and moved to face the larger, more threatening group. Keelin made his move. He ran at the last man facing him, swatting aside his sword, then leapt to his left, careening into one of the soldiers watching the group of pirates. After knocking the man to the ground, Keelin found himself in among the soldiers before any of them realised what had happened. His swords moved in a blur of low and high slashes, aiming for exposed arms and legs. The soldiers went down in a flurry of blood and screams.

A shield hit Keelin in the face and he stumbled away, tripped over something, and felt the ground hit him hard. He tasted mud and blood and struggled to breathe air back into his lungs as he tried to get his hands beneath him.

Rolling onto his back and blinking away the dark spots, Keelin saw the face of the tattooed pirate staring down at him, offering him a hand. He accepted it and was quickly pulled to his feet. The rest of the pirates had surged forwards and were busy finishing off the soldiers with brutal stabs to their faces or any other unprotected areas they could get to.

"No time fer rest, Cap'n," said the tattooed pirate, thumbing towards the forest.

Keelin saw more and more troops emerging from the treeline, many looking as though they were being chased out. They were quickly forming into small groups. The pirates and townsfolk were banding together as best they could, trying to outnumber the soldiers and drive them apart, but they were fighting a losing battle and already there were more dead pirates than soldiers.

"With me," Keelin shouted over the clash of battle, hoping that the group he'd just aided would follow his orders. He charged towards a cluster of soldiers who had just cut down three men and a woman and were heading for the town.

As he sprinted closer, one of the shield-bearers detached from the tight formation and stepped into Keelin's path. It was all Keelin could do to throw himself to his left to avoid crashing into the man, but it put him directly in front of the soldiers and they stopped to confront him even as the pirates caught up and crashed into the little shield wall like sharp, pointy waves on a rock.

The first shield-bearer went down as one of the pirates got a dagger above his guard and into his neck. Before the rest of the soldiers could react, the tattooed pirate took down another with a swing of his axe that split a shield and damned near severed the arm that held it. One of the pirates took a spear to the chest and Keelin rushed forwards. Chopping the spear shaft in half with one of his cutlasses, he kept another shield-bearing soldier at bay with the other sword as the injured pirate was dragged away from the battle. Again the tattooed pirate leapt into the fray, his big axe whipping about his head and coming down hard on a shield, the force of the blow driving the soldier to his knees.

A second spear, this one still with a head, thrust out between two shields towards the tattooed pirate. Keelin could do nothing to stop it, caught up as he was with two men pressing him with shields. The big pirate screamed in pain but grabbed hold of the spear and ripped it from the soldier's grasp.

The soldiers weren't advancing; they hid behind their shields and slashed at anyone who came near. They were most likely waiting to be reinforced, but Keelin wasn't about to give them the opportunity. A roar went up from the forest, the geyser choosing a good moment to go off. Everyone from New Sev'relain was used to the noise by now, but the soldiers weren't and it caused just the distraction Keelin needed.

Advancing, he brushed away attacks then kicked hard into the shield of the soldier to his right, forcing the man back a step. Keelin stabbed at the soldier to his left, feeling his cutlass dig deep into the flesh of the man's shoulder.

With a scream of pain, the soldier to Keelin's left fell back just as the man on the right pushed forwards to protect his injured comrade. A moment later the soldier on the right fell down dead with a spear lodged firmly in his neck. Keelin glanced to his group to see the tattooed pirate grinning madly beneath his patchy beard.

With their group broken, the remaining two soldiers bolted back towards the treeline to reinforce another squad. There were battles all over the place, and the soldiers were starting to outnumber the pirates as more and more poured from the trees and more and more of the pirates fell.

"Take weapons and shields from the fallen soldiers," Keelin called to his group.

"Don't know how to use a shield," one of the men said.

"Hold it in front of you and stab around it," Keelin said. "You're better off having one than not. What's your name?" he asked the tattooed pirate.

"Ferl," the man said as he looked down at the fallen soldiers' weapons and decided to keep his axe instead.

"You're a useful man to have around, Ferl. Who's your captain?"

"Don't got one," the big man said through his beard.

Keelin grinned. "Then stick with me. All of you, with me," he shouted as he charged towards a hard-pushed knot of pirates.

Kebble knelt in the dirt, raised his rifle, and sighted down the barrel. He picked his target and held his breath. The soldier was jabbing a spear over the top of his shield-bearing comrades and he kept dancing behind those shields to stay out of harm's way, but Kebble was watching the man from the side, hidden far away from the combat.

He squeezed the trigger and braced against the recoil. The bullet impacted into the soldier's shoulder and he went careening to the ground. Kebble had been aiming for the man's chest. He hadn't taken the crosswind into full account.

With a frown, Kebble stood, shouldered his bag, and turned away from the battle, already reloading his rifle. The pirates and people of New Sev'relain were losing the fight, and if it continued the way it was going they would soon all be dead or forced to flee again, and Kebble doubted their morale would recover after another massacre. Luckily for the people of New Sev'relain, they had him. Kebble had changed the tide of battle before, and he would do it again. Perhaps if he fought for enough lost causes he might even find a way to lift his curse.

He walked through deserted dark alleyways lit only by the light of the rising moon, setting a brisk pace but refusing to rush. People who rushed forgot things, missed things, made mistakes. Kebble had lived long enough to realise that calm hurry was far more useful than a mad dash.

A building loomed up ahead, though it wasn't his destination. The warehouse would be far too obvious a hiding place. He turned left and walked past a few more dilapidated shacks until he came to a half-collapsed building that looked on the verge of total dereliction. It was, however, purposefully designed to look that way.

Kebble slung his rifle over his shoulder and pulled the door open. Inside there was barely enough room to move, and a part of the roof had fallen in, covering much of the floor with brittle palm leaves. A rolled-up shirt in the corner of the open area suggested someone had recently been camping out in the building, but they no doubt had no idea of the fortune they'd been sleeping on top of.

Kneeling down, Kebble shifted a pile of the leaves that had fallen in, scattering a variety of insects including one large, sluggish, grumpy-looking spider. Kebble had seen the pain that a spider bite could cause and he had no wish to experience it first-hand, so he calmly shooed the little beast away with one of the fallen leaves, inwardly cursing at the delay. After the spider had departed, he finished clearing away the debris and felt around for a loose floorboard, finding it in no time and quickly tearing it from its neighbours. After three more floorboards Kebble reached in and lifted out a single barrel from its hiding place.

He drew a knife from his belt and levered the lid from the barrel, revealing the black powder inside. They'd found ten kegs of the dangerous explosive after taking the Man of War. Kebble reached into his bag and pulled out a coconut, one of the few natural food supplies on the island – but this particular coconut was just a shell split in half and held together with a thin strip of cloth. Kebble unwrapped the fabric and filled the husk with black powder before placing the two halves back together and retying the cloth. He worked at a steady pace, hurrying but not rushing, all the while aware that every moment was another in which more of New Sev'relain's people were dying. He had eight more coconuts to fill, and then he needed to find a fuse.

Fortune

Drake pointed at another group of soldiers emerging from the treeline. Clearly the Five Kingdoms bastards hadn't expected much resistance. Now they'd realised their tactic of small groups of soldiers was going to cost them greatly, and they were starting to form a more cohesive mass, no doubt under the leadership of a seasoned commander.

"Tanner," Drake shouted. "Over there. They need help."

Tanner Black looked up from the soldier he'd trapped beneath his boot and followed Drake's finger. "Aye, we're on it," the big captain growled, putting his full weight on the man beneath his foot and crushing his windpipe. Tanner stormed off to rejoin the battle, leaving the soldier flailing and clawing at his own neck, trying to suck in some air. Some battles were a hopeless cause, and the man was destined to die in the mud of New Sev'relain.

The crew of *The Black Death* were efficient killers – Drake had to give them that – though they also seemed to enjoy it a bit more than he was comfortable with. Tanner's pirates were heavily armed, and even a couple of pistols. They were putting them all to good use, and many a Five Kingdoms soldier had died to their savagery. In fact, Drake was fairly certain the crew of *The Black Death* had done more for the people of New Sev'relain than the townsfolk had done for themselves.

With a joyous cry and a crash, Tanner's crew collided with a large group of soldiers and several men from both sides went down. Fresh screams filled the air, punctuated by the twang of bowstrings.

Drake stood back from the battle, sword in hand, watching the massacre unfold. His people weren't ready for this sort of fight, and because of that they were dying. The soldiers were better trained and better armed, and although the numbers seemed almost even, most of the fallen were his subjects. If he didn't do something to change the course of the battle soon, Drake knew he would be the king of bones and little else.

Something caught Drake's eye at the treeline – a new wave of soldiers marching out from the jungle in a loose formation. His heart lurched and missed a couple of beats as he realised they were no normal soldiers, but knights dressed head to toe in metal plating – helms, breastplates, vambraces, and greaves – and wielding an assortment of sharp weaponry.

Before Drake could formulate a plan to deal with the new threat, a screaming soldier came hurtling towards him. Some of the pirates had fallen and soldiers were moving through the gap, trying to give their comrades space to spread out while they attacked the remaining pirates from behind. Over the shoulder of the man rushing him, Drake saw his pirates beginning to break, some turning and running while others valiantly died standing their ground.

With a surge of strength fuelled by rage, Drake stepped into the oncoming attack, brushing the soldier's sword aside with his own and sending a thunderous fist to the side of the man's face. Drake leapt backwards, waving his left hand in the air and wondering what had possessed him to punch the man with a closed fist. The pain was intense, but thankfully short-lived. The soldier was face down on the ground and not moving, and Drake congratulated himself on a knockout punch even as another two men came at him.

The first of the new soldiers held a round shield and an axe, and the man behind him wielded a long spear with a metal tip stained red. They took no risks as they came at Drake, the spear-wielder doing all the work while the shield-bearer protected him. Drake found himself batting away the polearm with his sword and giving ground, falling back again and again and wondering where in all the Hells Stillwater had got to.

Drake stepped backwards out of the spearman's range once again and found his back against the wall of a house. Before the spear could skewer him, a man dressed in the long, faded rags of what had once been a uniform leapt onto the spearman's back and stabbed him in the neck with a knife that looked like it belonged on a dinner table. The shield-bearer turned to help his comrade, and Drake seized the opportunity and charged. He slashed first at the man's ankles before half separating the fool's head from his body with a meaty swing that ended with his sword stuck in the soldier's neck. The body collapsed into the dust, wrenching Drake's sword from his grasp.

"Good work, Tatters," Drake said as he put his boot on the soldier's corpse and pulled his blade free.

Admiral Tatters giggled to himself and collapsed onto his knees. His eyes were wild and the smell of booze coming from him overpowered the odour of death. The admiral had once claimed Drake could never make him less than a gentleman. Drake had proven that claim wrong, and Tatters was well and truly one of them now – though judging by the yellow in his eyes he wouldn't be one of them for much longer. There was only so much alcohol a body could take before it gave up for good, and Tatters had been pickling himself ever since the townsfolk had set him free.

Turning his attention back to the battle at the edge of town, Drake saw the knights cutting a swathe through his people. Tanner's black-hearted crew, always up for a fight, had moved to engage the metal-coated bastards, but even they were falling back. The knights cared little for the impotent attacks of their enemies, and though they were slow, they were backed up by soldiers carrying spears, and those did a good job of keeping the pirates at a distance to stop them aiming for the less-protected parts of the knights' armour.

Drake watched Tanner pull a pistol from his belt and fire it into the mass of flesh and metal. One of the knights stopped and wobbled a moment before collapsing to a cheer from Tanner's crew, but they had precious few pistols and no time to reload. In reply to the murder of one their steel-clad heroes, the Five Kingdoms troops pushed forwards and the crew of *The Black Death* found themselves beating a quick retreat.

Stillwater's sharpshooter, Kebble Salt, appeared from an alleyway between Drake and the battle. The man was carrying a sack in one hand and his rifle in the other, and he looked sleek with sweat in the light of the lantern hanging outside a nearby building. Drake rushed over to the man.

"Can you do something about those knights?" Drake shouted as he approached.

Kebble Salt turned towards Drake with a start. The sharpshooter was bleeding from a wound in his side. It was hard to tell how serious the injury was, but going by the amount of blood and the man's pale complexion, Drake was leaning towards serious.

"Captain Morrass," Kebble said, his voice quivering. "I will try."

Kebble carefully placed the sack on the ground and shouldered his rifle, aiming it towards the battle. The barrel swayed and wobbled, and Kebble winced in pain. Long moments passed without the sharpshooter taking a shot.

"Is there anyone around here who ain't currently useless?" Drake growled, and was greeted by a sullen giggling from Admiral Tatters, who was busy peering into the sack Kebble had been carrying.

"Away from there, fool," Kebble hissed, lowering his rifle and shooing Tatters away. "I may not be able to aim a rifle, Captain, but I do have these."

Kebble reached into the bag and pulled out a coconut.

"Wonderful, we're saved," Drake said, and started towards the battle. He had no idea how he was going to turn the tide of the slaughter.

"They are full of black powder, Captain Morrass," Kebble shouted after him. "And I have set each one with a fuse that should last no more than five counts of one."

Drake stopped mid-stride and turned back to Kebble. The man was using his rifle as a crutch and holding one of the coconuts in his hand. "They'll explode?" he said, walking back to the sharpshooter.

"Quite violently, I believe," Kebble said with a nod. "Just light the fuse at the top and throw them at your target."

Drake stormed over and looked into the sack. He counted a good number of the weapons, at least half a dozen. A grin lit his face. He picked up the sack, leaving Kebble with the one coconut still in his hand.

"Go find Stillwater," Drake said. If the tide of battle was to turn on the use of these new weapons, then Drake wanted the glory well and truly on his shoulders and no one else's.

Kebble nodded. "Where?"

"I reckon he went down to the beach. These bastards landed a ship on us and are trying to kill us from both sides."

Again Kebble nodded, then started limping towards the beach, still using his rifle as a crutch.

The sounds of battle were deafening. Steel clashing against wood and metal, punctuated by the screams of the dying. The smell was even worse, almost enough to make Drake gag.

By the time Drake reached Tanner, the crew of *The Black Death* were on the verge of quitting the fight altogether. They could do nothing against the knights and their spear-wielding lackeys, and had resorted to retreating while spitting insults.

"Time ta run back to Fango, I reckon, Ya Majesty," Tanner said with a dark sneer and a look in his eyes that convinced Drake the man was once again considering killing him.

"Not yet," Drake said with a manic grin. "Hold the damned line."

Tanner looked like he was about to argue.

"Hand me a torch."

Tanner growled, but turned and pulled a torch from the hands of one of his crew.

Drake placed the sack of coconuts behind him and pulled out one of the little weapons, grinning at the confused look on Tanner's face. With a wink, Drake held up the fuse to the torch and the little bit of rope started fizzing.

"What the fuck is that?" Tanner said, recoiling back from the coconut.

"History," Drake said. He waited another second and then rolled the coconut quickly along the ground towards the approaching knights. It bounced once, but held together and disappeared amidst the men's steel-plated legs. Drake grinned even wider. Two more seconds passed.

Boom!

The explosion was loud and violent and threw knights and soldiers alike to the ground, stunning everyone in the area. A mist of blood shot up into the air before raining down along with the odd limb. Then the screaming started.

Tanner was the quickest to recover, and he shouted at his men to push the advantage. His crew surged forwards, and as the stunned knights and soldiers struggled to recover from the blast, the pirates fell upon them, stabbing and slashing and revelling in the bloody massacre.

Drake reached into the sack for another coconut.

The soldiers fanned out, attempting to surround Beck. She let them. The two dead men at her feet and the three arrayed around her had proven how deadly an opponent she was, and no doubt the soldiers would now attempt to rush her all at once from all directions. Beck took the opportunity to reload one of her pistols and slotted it back into her jerkin. At most she had ten shots left, including those already loaded, and given that more soldiers were arriving to skew the numbers even further in their favour, it wouldn't be enough to win the fight for her.

There was fighting all along the beach as soldiers attempted to quickly best the pirates they'd found in the sand and join the fight in the town, no doubt hoping to crush the townsfolk from behind as they dealt with the force coming from the jungle. The pirates on the beach weren't inclined to let the Five Kingdoms soldiers act on their plan, however, and there were dozens of small skirmishes taking place even as Beck now held up the largest force.

Twenty men faced her, closing in slowly.

She was tired. Days of hard labour and heavy use of strength-augmenting blessings had taken their toll, but she was an Arbiter, trained by the Inquisition and made into a weapon against the heresy of the world. The men facing her might not be heretics, but nor were they righteous, and that made her worth a hundred of them. She would prove it on the beach of New Sev'relain.

Volmar's power coursed through Beck's body, and she began to chant the words of a sorcery. She knelt down and whispered the magic into the sand. It rippled around her like a pebble dropped into a still pool. The ripples spread quickly outwards until they reached the circle of soldiers, and the sand erupted upwards, engulfing some of the men while others stumbled backwards.

Beck was already moving even as the first grains shot into the air. She set off at a sprint, straight ahead towards her first target, her speed enhanced by the blessing she chanted. The first soldier, a small man with a crooked nose and hairy palms, had been one of the smarter ones, stepping backwards away from the wall of sand. Beck leapt as she neared the wall and crashed through it as the grains of sand reached their zenith and began to fall. The man recoiled, but it was too late for him. Beck whispered a blessing of strength and his helmet and skull both crumpled under the force of her pistol as she brought the butt down on his forehead. Men were already shouting, and Beck caught at least one of them screaming something about a witch. It only served to enrage her further that the fools might consider *she* was the heretic.

Wrenching her pistol free from the swaying corpse, Beck flipped it over, aimed at another soldier, and pulled the trigger. The noise rang loud in her ears, and before she could witness the result she was already racing towards another fight.

Drawing a second pistol, Beck batted away a soldier's attempt to skewer her with his sword. She thrust her first pistol into his throat and watched his eyes bulge as his windpipe collapsed. As the last of the sand fell to the ground around her, Beck launched a kick into the dying soldier's gut and he flew away from her, rolling in the sand and thrashing like a beached fish.

Two of the soldiers were fleeing from the fight while four more were down, choking on sand. The others looked panicked. One man shouted out to the others, getting them into order. Beck wasn't about to let them get organised. She slid one of her pistols back into its holster on her jerkin and pulled the much larger pistol gun from her belt holster, aimed at the soldier shouting orders, and pulled the trigger. His chest erupted in pink mist and his body crashed into the sand.

In a mixed display of cowardice and valour, some of the soldiers broke and ran while most of them charged her. Beck holstered both her pistols and whispered Volmar's power into a sorcery, and fire burst into life in her right hand. She threw the little flame up into the air above the soldiers, already knowing it would drop down on top of her target and quickly engulf the man as he attempted to flee. Into her other hand she whispered another sorcery, and thrust it into the sand.

Mimics of Beck's hand shot out of the sand in front of her, clutching and grabbing hold of anything they could find. Some soldiers tripped and others crashed to the ground. Four soldiers still came at her unimpeded, and Beck just managed to draw two of her pistols before the first man was on her.

Ducking his sword swing, Beck thrust a pistol butt into the man's gut then whipped it up, cracking his jaw and sending him stumbling backwards with a howl of pain. She trained another pistol on the second of the oncoming soldiers and pulled the trigger. The bullet ripped through the man's shield and he fell away, screaming.

Holstering the empty pistol, Beck stepped into the third soldier's attack so that it went wide, whispering a sorcery to her empty left hand while blocking the fourth soldier's attack with the pistol in her right hand. She pressed her left hand against the chest of the third soldier and he crumpled, screaming in pain as his stomach started convulsing.

The first soldier had recovered and was charging at her. Out of the corner of her eye, Beck saw yet more soldiers hacking at the sandy hands that held them. She disengaged from the fourth soldier and met the first in a blind run, and they both crashed to the ground in a tangle of limbs.

Beck was up first, already whispering to her hand again. As the first soldier gained his feet, she tapped her hand against his head. His expression went blank as his consciousness fled. She drew her last loaded pistol from her jerkin, pressed it against the soldier's neck, and fired. The bullet ripped through his flesh and buried itself in the fourth soldier as he came towards them. Both men dropped to the sand, dead.

Beck looked about for the pistol she'd dropped when she collided with the soldier, but wherever it had fallen, she couldn't see it. Some of the men delayed by her sandy hands were now free and were busy extricating the others. Beck took the opportunity to reload her large pistol as well as four of the smaller ones. It was all she had left.

Her head swam with exhaustion and the effort of channelling Volmar's power, and her legs were wobbling. But there were still seven soldiers left, three of them already free from the sand. Two of them held shields, crouching behind them as the third worked to free his comrades. Beck wished she had some runes or charms, but most of those, and everything else that would be useful, were in her Arbiter coat stashed safely in her cabin aboard the *Fortune*.

Four more soldiers rushed up, having finished cutting down a group of pirates, making Beck's tally of enemies up to eleven. She quickly gave up on the idea of using her pistols – she simply didn't have enough shots. Her sigh of pain and exhaustion turned into a manic laugh.

With all the grace of a drunken dancer, Beck dragged her left foot around in the sand, drawing a pattern in the grains and feeling the last of her strength fail her. It took all she had to turn and stagger away from the eleven soldiers as they marched towards her in a defensive formation.

Her legs decided they could walk no further, and Beck collapsed onto her knees, just managing to turn her body to watch the oncoming men. They came towards her with shields up and steel bristling. The first soldier stepped over the formation she'd drawn in the sand without disturbing it, either by sheer luck or wise decision. Beck growled out her frustration and fumbled at one of the pistols in her jerkin, determined to take as many with her as she could. She raised the pistol just as one of the soldiers stepped onto the rune she'd drawn in the sand, breaking its lines.

The Phoenix

Smithe watched the battle on the beach unfold from the safety of the shadows. If anyone looked closely at the pier they'd see him, but he doubted anyone would. And if they did, he'd just deal with them the same way he'd dealt with the gangly soldier who was floating face down in the big drink. A smile lit Smithe's face as he watched his target.

That fancy fuck, Stillwater, thought Smithe was simple, thought he was stupid. Smithe knew the truth though – he was smarter than all of them. He'd heard them talking behind their closed doors, and he knew the real reason the captain had yet to lead them to this treasure he'd promised them. A city full of gold and gems and wonders the likes of which would make them all rich and famous, that's what Keelin Stillwater had promised the crew of *The Phoenix*. And by all accounts, the man wasn't lying.

Smithe knew the city was located somewhere in the Forgotten Empire, a land south of the Dragon Empire and well known to be dangerous. Even the waters around the Forgotten Empire were legendary; all manner of ships had wrecked themselves upon the rocks and other hidden dangers. They needed charts of the waters and Stillwater knew just where to get them, but the gutless cur didn't have the stones to take them. Well, Smithe sure as all the Hells had the stones, and the Five Kingdoms bastards had just provided him with the perfect opportunity.

The last of the soldiers from their ship ran off towards Drake's little bitch. The woman was some kind of witch, Smithe reckoned, judging by the things she was doing. He'd never seen anyone throw fire before, but there she was. Smithe decided he wanted little and less to do with her or her captain. No matter how big her tits – and Smithe could tell they were on the large side – he hoped she died there on the beach.

Detaching himself from the safety of his shadowy hiding place, Smithe set off at a jog across the docks, staying just clear of the wooden pier to hide his footsteps. This wasn't his first time sneaking around.

An explosion rocked the beach, the ground shaking with the force of it, and Smithe's legs went out from under him. The sand hit him hard and forced the breath from his lungs. Gasping, he looked towards the noise and saw flames licking at the sand. Where before the big-titted member of Drake's crew had fought with a bunch of soldiers, there was now nothing but fire and bodies, and none of them looked to be moving.

Boots thundering on wood warned Smithe of someone coming, and he turned to see a soldier running towards him, shield in one hand and bared steel in the other.

Smithe got his legs beneath him and launched to his feet. The soldier was small and looked terrified. Flames danced in the boy's eyes, reflected from the fire behind Smithe. Still the lad came on.

Smithe stepped towards the soldier to meet his rush, blocking his sword with the metal knuckles on his knife and grabbing hold of the bottom edge of the round shield. It took no effort at all to turn the shield like a wheel, and the boy's arm went with it with an audible crack. Smithe grinned wide and feral.

The lad didn't scream, and Smithe almost respected him for that. With his sword hand still free, the boy tried to stab at Smithe, but he was doomed to failure – outclassed in every way, smaller, slighter, weaker, and far less experienced. Smithe grabbed hold of the boy's sword arm and punched him in the face with his metal knuckles. The lad went down hard with a spray of blood and lost teeth.

Smithe knelt down next to the soldier and punched him in the face again and again until his fist came away dripping red. The boy's arms flailed uselessly, his breath coming out of a broken face in gurgles and wheezes. Smithe reversed the grip on his knife and stabbed the blade down into the boy's skull then pulled it free, wiped it on the lad's uniform, and continued his walk to the *Fortune*.

Sounds of fighting reached him from the deck of the ship, and as Smithe got closer he saw a man thrown over the edge to land half on the pier and half in the water. His feet were nice and dry, but his back was bent painfully and his head was dangling in the bay. He was either unconscious or dead; Smithe didn't care which. Pirate the man may be, but Smithe held no loyalty to anyone but himself, and especially not anyone from a different ship.

He walked quickly up the pier and mounted the gangplank, dipping into a crouch as he reached the deck of Drake Morrass' ship. It was clear the *Fortune* was floating with a much reduced crew, most of them no doubt up in the town where they'd expected the fight to come from, or on the beach fighting with the soldiers there. There were a few men left, but they were outnumbered by soldiers. Smithe ignored them all as he made straight for the captain's cabin.

A stocky soldier stumbled backwards into Smithe's way, a sweaty grimace on his face as he regained his balance. Smithe kicked him in the back of the knee then slashed at his neck. The soldier clutched at the wound, but there was no way he would stop the flow of blood – the knife had cut far too deep. Smithe didn't even break his stride. He reached the cabin and tried the handle. Curiously, the door was unlocked. If there was anyone inside he'd have to kill them to ensure their silence. He was more than willing to do it, and he might even find some coin on the corpse. He glanced back towards the deck. Pirates and soldiers were engaged in all manner of combat – one pirate was even fighting upside down from the rigging – but none were paying any attention to a lone figure stealing onto the ship. He pushed the door open and slipped inside, closing it behind him.

It was mostly dark, lit only by the moonlight bouncing off the water and shining in through the large window at the back of the cabin. Smithe took a moment to let his eyes adjust, then carefully began his search. He'd heard plenty of stories about Drake's pets, and some said he'd rid himself of the spider and now favoured a huge, armoured snake with lots of little legs. Smithe had never heard of such a thing before, but whether or not it existed, he had no wish to meet it.

One side of the cabin was filled with a lavish bed, a wardrobe, and a chest. Luxurious living quarters for a captain while his crew no doubt lived in bunks barely large enough to lie down in. Smithe hated the captains for the luxury they lived in. That didn't mean he wouldn't take *The Phoenix* out of Stillwater's hands at the first opportunity. He'd never slept in a bed the size of the one he was looking at now, nor worn clothes as fancy as those no doubt kept in Drake's wardrobe. They all thought they were better than him. Smithe would prove just how wrong they all were.

The other side of Drake's cabin was even larger, housing a desk and a number of cabinets and chests of drawers. Smithe spied numerous bottles of booze in one of the cabinets, and had to stop himself breaking the glass to take one of the more expensive looking bottles. He wondered how that fancy rum tasted, having never tried anything but the swill most taverns sold, but that could wait. Smithe was playing the long game. His goal was the riches, the ship, the power, and the reputation. He would have them all before he was done.

He went to the first set of drawers and rifled through them quickly. All he found was blank parchments and the ink to write on them, a number of letters each signed by someone called Rei, a child's game set on a board with a number of squares and some little toy figures to go with it, and a yellow gemstone the size of the palm of his hand. The gemstone looked valuable, and Smithe pocketed it without another thought.

The next cabinet had a desk atop it, bare except for a small pistol. Smithe had never used one of the little weapons, but he'd seen them put to devastating effect. He knew how easy they were to make work, and he decided he would have one of his own some day. Smithe wrenched at the door to the cabinet, but it was stuck fast. A small gilded lock sat front and centre, mocking him.

He had no experience with picking locks, and he very much doubted the key would have been left lying around. If this cabinet contained Drake Morrass' charts then it was likely the most valuable key on the entire bloody ship, and Drake would no doubt carry it on his person at all times. Smithe pulled on the door with all the strength he could muster. It didn't give. With increasing certainty, he knew that this cabinet was his target and the charts were right in front of him.

With a growl of rage, Smithe punched the door. It hurt, but the metal knuckles on his knife did some damage to the wood. He punched it again, and again, and again. Smithe kept punching, heedless of the noise he was making, until the door splintered and split. He wrenched the lock free, throwing it into the middle of the cabin. Inside were rolls of leather-backed parchment, and plenty of them.

Smithe pulled the first roll out and opened it up, glancing over the words and pictures and calculations as he tried to find anything that indicated which area the chart depicted. He saw *New Sev'relain* written boldly on a blob that looked like an island, and tossed the chart behind him. Smithe glanced at the door to the cabin. He could still hear the sounds of battle outside, so he went back to rifling through the cabinet.

He threw away five more charts before he came to the one he was searching for. It depicted a coastline with hazards marked all over it and the words *Forgotten but not lost* written on the landmass. Smithe grinned. He'd achieved what that ponce Stillwater could not, and the crew would rally behind him for it.

"You shouldn't be here," someone said slowly.

Smithe turned his head to see a man standing just inside the doorway. He was tall and broad and thick with muscle, but his head was small, too small for the mass of his body. Smithe was tall and strong himself, but in a straight contest of strength the giant would crush him.

Without a word, Smithe grabbed the pistol from the top of the cabinet, pointed it at the big pirate, and pulled the trigger.

The giant stumbled back against the cabin door, his body slamming it closed as he fell. Thick red blood leaked from a hole in his chest, and he looked at Smithe with confusion in his eyes.

"Why does it hurt?" the pirate said, tears welling up and rolling down his face. "Make it stop."

Smithe dropped the pistol onto the cabin floor and sauntered over to the simpleton. "Hurts because I just killed you. Still need to make sure though, eh? Can't have you telling nobody what you saw."

The big pirate let out a mewling whine as Smithe closed on him.

Kebble walked onto the beach, wincing. Every step was agony lancing through his side where the soldier had cut a slice. The man had died from a point-blank rifle shot to the face, but not before he'd given Kebble what should probably have been a fatal wound.

Having given Drake the weapons he needed to fend off the soldiers in the town, Kebble had followed the man's orders and come looking for Keelin. The captain of *The Phoenix* was nowhere to be seen. Even down on the beach, where the fighting was as good as over, there was no sign of him.

Amidst the fires, the blackened sand, and the dark objects that could only be bodies spilling out their life blood, pirates were celebrating. Some looked wounded and others drunk, and there was likely still fighting taking place in the town, but the pirates were congratulating themselves on a hard-won victory – and it did look hard won.

Kebble spotted blond hair amidst burning sand and instantly recognised the crumpled body of Drake's Arbiter. Not ten feet away he saw the site of an explosion, but not one caused by black powder, the scorch marks were all wrong. Bodies lay on the sand everywhere he looked, and many of them were missing parts, or were scorched beyond recognition. All were certainly dead.

The coconut fell from Kebble's grasp, and he used his free hand to peel away the shirt stuck to his wound, gritting his teeth against the pain. He looked down; it had stopped bleeding, and was little more than a gooey red line across the left side of his abdomen. Kebble sighed. His immortality was still keeping him alive long past his time. He'd received worse wounds than a sword slash in his long years, but he'd hoped for a moment that this one might be his last.

Still using his rifle as a crutch, Kebble started towards the Arbiter's body. He could only hope Captain Stillwater wasn't one of the corpses in the sand. Kebble attempted to avoid attachments to those more short-lived than himself wherever possible, but he'd come to respect Keelin Stillwater and almost considered him a friend. It had been a long time since he'd named anyone a friend.

As Kebble drew nearer the Arbiter, he heard a scream from behind. His legs gave out as he turned, and the pain in his side was enough to blur his vision and cause a cry to escape his lips.

By the time Kebble's vision cleared it was almost too late. A crazed soldier was almost upon him, eyes wide and filled with the kind of fear that drives a man to irrational action. Kebble managed to raise his rifle to block the sword meant for his head, but the soldier didn't stop his mad charge and both men went down in a tangle of limbs, Kebble screaming in pain.

Rolling free of the soldier and clutching at his side, Kebble opened his eyes to see the man rise to his knees, his sword raised high above his head and about to remove Kebble's.

The sand around them erupted, and something shot up and crashed into the soldier, bearing him to the ground in a combination of blood-curdling screams and cracking bones. Kebble crawled away, his heart thundering in his chest.

Three pirates leapt past Kebble and began to stab their weapons down into the sand.

Ignoring the searing pain streaking through his body, Kebble got his feet beneath him and struggled upright. He looked around for his rifle. It was nowhere to be seen. The three pirates had slowed their stabbing and slicing and were busy panting and congratulating each other. As Kebble approached the men, he saw the giant form of a sand monster lying on top of the dead soldier. The creature didn't appear to be alive; its body and wings were covered in deep red cuts, and the smell that drifted up from it was almost unbearable.

"Damn, Salt," said one of the pirates, a small woman with fiery red hair and a criss-cross of scars marring her face. "If you ain't the luckiest bastard I ever seen. Must've been the last bloody sand demon on the beach. Only one we missed, just waitin' for months, an' it picks right then to have a snack."

Kebble forced a smile onto his face. "Yes," he said. "Lucky. Thank you for killing it."

The pirate grinned at Kebble and clapped him on the arm. With a nod of thanks to the rest of them, Kebble limped off towards the Arbiter.

Immortality came in many forms. He was almost completely certain a fatal wound would end his curse, and yet he'd never received one. Even at times when it seemed certain he would, something always interfered. The pirates might believe the sand monster's appearance to have been luck, but Kebble knew better.

The Arbiter looked lifeless. Her right arm was twisted beneath her body at an awkward angle and blood leaked from her nose. Her blond hair was a tangled mess, singed in places and covered in sand. Even with his eyesight, Kebble could see no rise and fall of her chest. She wasn't the first dead Arbiter he'd seen, but with their longer lives it always felt sad to see one pass, especially one so young.

Kneeling down, Kebble let out a painful sigh and placed two fingers on the woman's neck. It was somewhere beyond faint, but he felt the pulse of her heart still beating. The Arbiter survived, barely.

Kebble scooped his hands underneath her body and summoned the very last of his strength. Standing while carrying the Arbiter was a new sort of pain, and it took Kebble three attempts to get to his feet. He managed it. He wasn't sure which destination was the best. The woman needed to be tended to immediately by someone with more medical knowledge than his own, but the ship's doctors were little better than butchers and they no doubt had more than enough folk to deal with already. Setting his feet towards the town, Kebble started up the beach.

The Phoenix

Soldiers were slipping past the pirate lines and making for the town, and Keelin feared they intended to set fire to everything the folk of New Sev'relain had been building for the last year. Taking the big, axe-wielding Ferl with him, Keelin left the front lines in search of them. He was far more useful skirmishing with individual opponents than in a wall.

Keelin spotted a few men dashing through the doorway of the Righteous Indignation and set off after them. The people of New Sev'relain could probably recover from almost any tragedy, but the burning of their favourite tavern might be too much. The drinking hole had been built out of the bones of the Man of War that had destroyed Old Sev'relain, and had even been named after the ship. It was a testament to the hardiness and determination of the folk that had made their lives on the island.

An explosion echoed up from the beach; earlier, there had been a few towards the jungle end of town as well. Keelin had no idea what was happening around him, though he was fairly certain it involved plenty of death. He only hoped most of it was being served to the Five Kingdoms. It was a strange thought, given that if not for the sake of an abusive father, Keelin might have been one of the men attacking rather than the attacked.

With a worried glance at Ferl, which the big man shot right back, Keelin pushed through the doorway to the tavern and readied himself for a fight, his cutlasses already drawn and dripping blood. The tavern was dim, lit only by a single lantern behind the bar, and almost deserted. Every pirate and townsman who called New Sev'relain their home or safe harbour was outside, fighting for their lives. Keelin had never seen the tavern so empty. Even Tatters and the other drunks had left for the battle.

Three soldiers turned to face him. They'd been on their way to the stairs that led to the first floor, and now they walked nonchalantly back to the middle of the room, clearing tables and chairs out of the way with rough shoves. Two of the men wore the familiar armour of the soldiers that Keelin felt he'd been fighting forever. One of them wore no armour, only a plain yellow tabard cinched at the waist with a strip of red cloth. The man looked oddly familiar, and it took Keelin a moment to realise why.

"Derran?"

The man wearing the tabard laughed.

"You know him?" Ferl said. The man was pacing behind Keelin like a caged animal just waiting to be let free.

Keelin winced. He couldn't reveal how he knew Derran without revealing his own past. Instead, he gave a non-committal grunt, wondering how he could extricate himself from the situation. As long as his brother recognised him there was no way it would end in a fight.

"Now it makes sense, brother," Derran Fowl said, grinning. "You're Captain Stillwater, the best swordsman in the Pirate Isles. I've been looking for you."

"Brother?" said Ferl.

Keelin sighed. His secret was out now. Whatever happened from here, Keelin would just have to weather the storm somehow.

"Admiral's orders were clear, Sir Derran," said one of the soldiers next to Keelin's brother. "Morrass and Stillwater are wanted alive for punishment."

"I don't care what your admiral's orders are," said Derran. "I can't exactly test my little brother's skill if it isn't to the death."

"Little brother?" said the soldier.

Derran's sword whipped clear of its scabbard, sweeping first right and then left and then back into the scabbard all in the blink of an eye. The two soldiers flanking him swayed for a moment before dropping, blood leaking from their necks. Keelin took an involuntary step backwards and found Ferl standing next to him, looking equally as worried.

"He's fast," Ferl said with a slight tremble in his voice.

"Ever heard of the Sword of the North?" Keelin said. "Blademaster working for the Five Kingdoms who has killed more..." The sound of the door shutting behind him and the sudden lack of Fer at his side convinced him that the big pirate had indeed heard of the Sword of the

North.

"What happened to you, little brother?" Derran said. "You always wanted to help the good folk, and now you're killing them to steal from their masters."

Keelin sighed and took a step towards him. "You ran away from home when I was just ten years old, Derran. I learned some hard lessons growing up. I learned the way the world really works."

"It didn't take you long to run away as well," Derran shot back. "Burned down the family home on your way out."

"You think Father was bad before you left? I was lucky to escape a day without a beating. And those were the good days, before Mother killed herself."

Derran said nothing for a moment. "I'm sorry about Mother. But if you think the odd beating or two is a hard life, then maybe you are still the little boy I left dreaming of heroic deeds."

Keelin barked out a laugh. "The odd beating or two? What Dad did to me was nothing compared to my time on *The Black Death*."

Derran just smiled, and Keelin couldn't help but return it. They'd been apart for longer than they'd ever known each other, but they were still brothers despite it all, and a fight seemed puerile and pointless now they were reunited.

"I almost had him a couple of years back, the bastard who killed Leesa," Keelin said.

"Arbiter Prin," Derran growled. The murder of their little sister had shaped so much of their lives. It had caused Derran to run away, and it had set Keelin on a path of revenge that had driven him for over half his life. "You really think you're a match for an Arbiter, little brother?"

"For Prin I will be," Keelin said venomously. "He needs to die for Leesa."

"Then show me," Derran said with a toothy grin. "I came here to fight the best swordsman in the Pirate Isles, and I'm not leaving until I test myself against him."

"You want to spar?" Keelin said. "There's a battle going on, Derran. My people are fighting and dying out there."

"And if you want to go help them, you best beat me," Derran

growled.

Keelin realised he was still holding his cutlasses, and he remembered Derran's words from earlier – "to the death". Before he could argue any further, his brother was striding forwards, his sword flicking clear of its scabbard, and all smiles were long gone. Keelin had seen the look in his brother's eyes hundreds of times before, in men he'd fought on land and sea. Derran Fowl meant to kill him.

The first stab was slow and lazy and Keelin turned it aside easily. Instead of returning the effort, he threw himself sideways, rolling over a table and putting the slab of wood between them. Derran had always had the reach advantage, being the taller of the two, and even now that they were both adults he was still taller.

Derran didn't round the table, nor jump atop it. He locked his eyes on Keelin's and smiled. Keelin smiled back, and a moment later the table shifted as Derran kicked it, the wood connecting with Keelin's groin and sending him staggering back in pain. The distraction gave the Blademaster all the time he needed to walk around the table, and once more Keelin found himself within easy striking distance.

Again Derran flicked a lazy attack. This time Keelin turned the slash aside and returned two of his own. Derran's sword flew backwards, catching one of Keelin's then twisting almost unnaturally to snare the other. Before Keelin knew how it had happened, he found both his cutlasses crossed and against his chest with Derran's sword pressed up against them.

Keelin pushed and Derran stepped away, his blade flicking around under Keelin's guard and scoring a hit on his chin.

"You could have killed me." Keelin dabbed at the cut, and his hand came away red.

"Yes," Derran said. "I could have. Unless you start fighting seriously, little brother, the next one will."

"You want me to try to kill you?"

"Yes. There is no other way to fight. If we hold back then we will never really know who's better."

"What does it matter who's better?" Keelin remembered T'ruck Khan wanting to duel him for the same reason, and he'd beaten the giant without killing him just like he would his own brother.

"It's the only thing that matters," Derran said as he moved forwards again.

Keelin didn't give his brother a chance to attack; he leapt forwards, slashing both high and low at once. Derran stepped back out of range and Keelin kept the pressure on, reversing his swords and attacking again. Again Derran stepped away. Keelin grinned and followed up, but a quick stab from his brother's sword sent him stumbling backwards, pain coursing through his chest.

A spot of blood appeared on Keelin's shirt, and it came with agony laced with fire. Before he could form a new plan, Derran was upon him with two quick slashes that Keelin blocked with ease. A third sweep came in, and Keelin parried and returned one of his own, trying to get some distance to recover. Derran caught Keelin's arm with his free hand, twisted and stepped close. Pain exploded in Keelin's face as the pommel of Derran's sword connected with his cheek. He staggered away, amazed that he didn't taste blood.

Opening his eyes, Keelin saw Derran standing in front of him with two swords. It took him a moment to realise one was his own.

"Impressive, br…" Keelin started, but Derran didn't let up his attack.

They were well and truly in among the tables and chairs now, and Keelin found himself giving ground and struggling not to trip over any furniture. Derran seemed as adept with two swords as he had been with one, and the man gave nothing away. His guard was as flawless as his attacks, and Keelin couldn't see an opening anywhere.

Blocking a slash from his own sword, Keelin grabbed hold of a chair and flung it at Derran. Derran stepped aside and Keelin lunged towards the opening. His sword never made it.

Keelin screamed as the floor rushed up to meet him, his left leg collapsing. Looking down, he found his own sword wobbling in his thigh. With a grimace and a growl, he tried to drag himself away from his brother.

He hadn't expected Derran to be so brutal. He'd said they were fighting to the death, but Keelin had thought it just a ploy to get him to fight harder. That his older brother might truly injure him or worse had never crossed his mind. It dawned on Keelin then that he didn't really know the man in front of him, the man he hadn't seen for over fifteen years.

"Fuck, Derran," Keelin shouted as he dragged himself backwards. The sword in his leg was agony, but pulling it out now could do more damage.

Sir Derran Fowl, knight of the Five Kingdoms and world-renowned Blademaster, closed in on him, a blank expression on his face.

"I expected more from you, Keelin," Derran said. "Not just because you're known as the best in the isles, but because you're my brother. Even as a child you showed skill. Where has it gone?"

Keelin winced and glanced at the sword his leg. If Derran came just a couple of steps further he would be close enough for Keelin to stab him with it.

Derran pulled a nearby chair towards him and sat down. He let out a loud sigh.

"What now?" Keelin said, trying to buy some time. "You kill me and the rest of the town? Five Kingdoms win, and you murdered your little brother."

"I have no intention of killing anyone else here. I came to test myself against the best swordsman in the isles. Seems I've already won. Barely even a fight."

"Your king…"

"My king is a fool, Keelin. A well-informed fool, but a fool nonetheless." Derran sighed. "He knows who you are. I should have figured it out myself. There can't be that many swordsmen with your name. My king sent me to kill my own brother. What sort of man does that?"

"What sort of man follows the order?" Keelin said desperately.

Derran smiled. "I think I'm done with the Five Kingdoms and King Jackt Fucking Veritean. There must be someone in this world who can still give me a challenge."

"What?" Keelin said, wincing at the pain and still trying to drag himself backwards.

"Perhaps the Wilds." Derran grinned, fixing Keelin with a steely stare. In that moment Keelin couldn't see a drop of the boy he'd once known, only the Sword of the North.

"Do you really think you have what it takes to kill an Arbiter?" Derran said.

Keelin was shaking with pain and fear and possibly blood loss. His brother didn't seem to care. There was no emotion in Derran's eyes.

"Goodbye, little brother."

The Sword of the North stood and stepped forward. Keelin winced, but Derran stepped past him and carried on. Keelin felt the last of his strength leaving him, and the world went dark.

Fortune

A cheer went up as the last of the soldiers broke and ran for the relative safety of the trees. The pirates didn't give chase; they were more than happy to let the jungle have the bastards. The little explosive coconuts Kebble had made had done more than just turn the tide – they'd devastated the enemy forces.

The Five Kingdoms force's biggest advantage had been their training – they'd stuck together in tight formations so the pirates couldn't get close without being cut down – but that advantage had worked against them in the end. Packed as closely together as they were, the explosions ripped through their ranks and caused equal amounts of death and chaos, and the latter let the pirates cause more of the former.

They'd won the day, though the cost had been almost more than they could bear. Already the wounded were being taken indoors and given over to triage, and anyone with even the slightest experience in the healing arts was being press-ganged into looking after those who needed it. The dead were piling up too, and there were a lot of them. Drake ordered them carted down to the beach so they could set up a proper pyre. Usually he ordered his dead given to Rin, but she wouldn't accept any who had died on land, and the offering would be more likely to anger than appease the spiteful goddess.

Tanner limped towards Drake. The big pirate was bloodied and ruddy-cheeked, but there was a weariness about his eyes that Drake had never expected to see in his old nemesis. Drake's own exhaustion had fled the moment the battle was won. He was no warrior – he was a leader, and he knew this was the time he needed to be most aware. There would be plenty of opportunities to grow his legend in the time just after a battle.

"Some of my boys want to go after the fuckers, mate," Tanner growled, waving away his ship's doctor, who seemed intent on bandaging his captain's leg.

"Best not," Drake said with a shake of his head. "You think your forest is dangerous? Stragglers on Cinto Cena don't last long, Tanner.

Besides, we've got plenty of work to do here. Folk need looking to. You should let your man see to that wound."

"It's a scratch," Tanner said.

"Scratches can kill a man just as easily as a good stabbing if the wound ain't looked after." Tanner looked exhausted, and it was no surprise given how much of the battle he'd taken part in. Drake wagered if he could just get the man to sit down, he'd be free of him for a good few hours, and in those hours Drake could claim much of the glory. "Sit down and get that bandaged, Tanner. We need you. Can't have you falling foul of an infection."

Tanner growled again, but relented and let the doctor lead him away. Drake would have grinned, but he needed to keep the pained expression plastered to his face. He needed the townsfolk to see him as tired as they were and sympathetic to the losses.

"Anyone seen Stillwater?" he shouted.

"Aye," said a big pirate with plenty of tattoos. "He was in the tavern, fighting his brother."

"His brother?" Drake hated appearing to others as though he were in the dark, but at this point he well and truly was.

The pirate nodded. "Aye. Stillwater is brother to that Sword of the North."

That name attracted a good few folk, and Drake was less than surprised. He'd met the Sword of the North once, and the man had been terrifying. Drake had never met anyone so sure of their own ability to murder everyone around them. He'd also seen a Blademaster in action once, and though it hadn't been the Sword of the North, she'd been like death given form. They moved in a deadly dance, and there seemed to be very little that could stand in their way.

"Anyone carrying a shield or a bow with me, now," Drake roared, pleased to see pirates and townsfolk alike jumping to his command. "Everyone else keep helping with the wounded." As he stormed off towards the Righteous Indignation, he was happy to have a good twenty pirates backing him up and less than happy that he was at the front of them. If the Sword of the North was in a killing mood then it was likely that Drake would die first, and there would be little that could stop the

Blademaster.

Not wanting to appear hesitant, Drake pushed open the door to the tavern and strode inside, fancying that he cut a real heroic figure. As pirates and townsfolk crammed in behind Drake, it became clear that the Sword of the North had done his damage and left. Tables, chairs, and three bodies were littering the floor, and none of the latter looked to be moving.

Drake took another step into the room. The two bodies furthest away were Five Kingdoms soldiers. The third body was wearing one of the fine blue jackets that Stillwater liked so much, only it was stained with an awful lot of red.

"Check if he's alive," Drake said, pointing to Stillwater's body. He wasn't about to let his own guard down until he knew the Sword of the North was well and truly gone.

Even inside the tavern and with the noise of twenty people around him, Drake could still hear the screams of the dying outside. It was more than a little unnerving. The tavern was a mess that they'd need to clean up soon. Pirates needed a place to drink, especially after the hell they'd all just been through.

"Get these bodies out of here," he said, turning away from the soldiers' corpses.

Tanner came limping into the tavern, followed by his squat-faced first mate and his ship's doctor, who still hadn't managed to get the big pirate to stop long enough to bandage his leg.

"He's alive," called the woman tending to Stillwater. "Looks pretty badly messed up though."

If the Sword of the North really was Stillwater's brother, there appeared to be little love between them – just enough to leave the captain alive.

"Get away from me, ya fussing shrew of a man." Tanner pushed his doctor away. "Yer old friend Stillwater needs ya fuckin' poking an' proddin' more than I."

The healer shot Tanner a baleful look, then turned away and knelt next to Stillwater. Drake seethed; he wanted Tanner gone. Unfortunately, now the man was here there was little he could do.

The Oracle had been clear, and insistent. Keelin Stillwater was integral to the creation of Drake's empire, and Drake had never known his brother to be wrong. Hironous Vance had the sight, the ability to see into people's futures, and together with Drake's own gift of manipulation they'd used it to plan the birth of the pirate empire. Drake hated relying on anyone but himself to accomplish his goals, but he needed Stillwater alive.

"Well, doc?" Drake said. "Can you save him?"

The doctor mumbled something under his breath.

"Why are we saving him?" said the big pirate with the tattoos.

"Eh?" Drake turned to the man, who, despite his size, took a quick step backwards.

"He ain't one of us," said the pirate. "He's one of them. I heard him and the Sword of the North talking. They're brothers. That makes Stillwater Five Kingdoms, one of the fuckers trying to kill us."

"I heard the Sword ain't just a knight," another pirate chimed in. "He's a noble."

"Bastard was probably in on it the whole time. He brought 'em here," continued the tattooed pirate.

The others started murmuring, agreeing that the whole thing was Stillwater's fault. They were looking for someone to blame for all the death and pain, and the poor unconscious bastard who had helped saved so many of them wasn't awake to defend himself.

"You reckon he was in on it?" Drake said. "Because of who his brother might be? Seems that same brother left Stillwater skewered with his own sword and bleeding to death right here on the floor of the tavern Stillwater himself helped to build. Hells, the lad didn't just help to build this place – he helped take down the monstrous ship it was built from."

A few of those who had been muttering about Stillwater being a traitor all of a sudden found their feet more than a little interesting.

"You reckon he ain't one of us because he's from the Five Kingdoms?" Drake said. "Well, then I ain't one of us either. I'm Acanthian born."

Drake pointed at a red-haired pirate with a fiery beard. "What about you? Where are you from?"

The man looked a little embarrassed at suddenly being the centre of attention. "Korral."

"The Wilds then," Drake said. "Well, that ain't here, so you ain't one of us. What about you?" Drake picked a tall woman with hair that looked like it might have been blond had it ever been washed.

"Flinton," she said.

"Sarth," Drake cooed. "Weren't too long ago they were at our doorstep, trying to murder us."

"I ain't no traitor," the woman said quickly, trying desperately to sink back into the crowd.

"What about you, Tanner?" Drake said. "Where are you from?"

Tanner Black held Drake's gaze for a few moments, probably deciding whether or not to lie. "Larkos."

Drake smiled. "Another free city, this one in the Dragon Empire."

Tanner nodded slowly.

"There's barely a one of us can say we come from the Pirate Isles. We're an empire of vagrants. Whether you came from nothing or everything, or all that's in between, we're all in this together."

"Can ya save him?" Tanner asked the doctor.

The man grumbled something and nodded without looking up from Stillwater's motionless body.

"Then do it," Tanner snapped.

"You need any help?" Drake said quickly, desperate to regain authority.

The doctor barked out a laugh and shook his head.

"Then the rest of you get outside and let the man do his work," Drake said. "We got plenty of other wounded to tend to, and even more dead to mourn."

Drake followed them all outside; he would be better served being seen about the town in charge of the situation than locked away in the tavern worrying about one man. The night was cooling off even though there was barely a breath of breeze, and New Sev'relain was a blur of activity. Some people were tending to the wounded while others stripped the dead before carting them down to the beach. The soldiers of the Five Kingdoms were well equipped, and not a shield, sword, or breastplate would go to waste. Even the shoes were being taken from the dead to be handed out to those townsfolk in need.

Plenty of pirates were still standing guard by the half-finished wall, watching the jungle should some of the soldiers come back for a second attempt. Drake doubted they would be so foolish, but it was better to be prepared in case of fools. Drake looked down at the beach and saw a bald-headed man limping towards him. Kebble looked to be in bad shape, but far worse was the body in his arms. Beck's long blond hair hung down from her head, singed and clumped, and she had more than a few patches of dried blood on her face, jerkin, and trousers.

Drake rushed forwards, and Kebble almost collapsed as he handed the Arbiter's body over.

"Is she…" Drake started, struggling with Beck's dead weight.

"Alive," Kebble said, dropping to his knees.

Drake searched Beck's face, and saw no signs of her breathing. He tried to think what to do, but his mind came up blank.

"She needs tending to," Kebble continued.

Drake glanced at the tavern. He could storm back in and demand Tanner's doctor tend to Beck, but that could mean Stillwater's death, and he needed the man.

"Captain Morrass," someone called, and Drake turned his head to see a bedraggled woman with deep brown hair and deeper lines on her face. "This way, Captain. I can see to her."

He recognised her as the woman who ran the brothel, and hesitated. "You know what you're doing?"

The woman fixed Drake with a stony glare. "Captain, I have dealt with more banged up women than any of your doctors. I can set bones, clean wounds, and sew better than anyone in this shit hole of a town, and I'll wager my supplies are better too. If you want her to live, then heel."

The woman turned and marched away. Drake ground his teeth together, but hesitated for only a moment before hurrying after her.

The Phoenix

Keelin opened his eyes to see a familiar wooden roof. He heard the creak and moan of a ship, and footsteps on the decking. He could smell the sea, the familiar salty tang that permeated every aspect of life on the oceans. He had no idea how it had happened, but Keelin was back on board *The Phoenix* and lying in his own bed. And if he lay really still, he could even pretend he didn't hurt all over.

It was daytime; he could tell by how well his cabin was lit. Turning his head to see the window would have required a lot of effort, and all Keelin really wanted to do was drift back off to sleep. Unfortunately, his stomach wasn't so easily appeased, and it chose that moment to let out a growl that would have sent a wolf fleeing with its tail tucked firmly between its legs.

"You're awake." Aimi's voice drifted over, and Keelin lethargically rolled his head to the side. His right shoulder blazed in agony. He ignored it with only a wince to show his discomfort.

"It's not entirely by choice," he croaked, realising then how thirsty he was.

Aimi was sitting in the chair behind Keelin's desk, looking over some papers. She sprang up and grabbed a mug and a clay pitcher. She looked different somehow. Gone were her normal stitched trousers and blouse, and in their place she wore a dark red jacket, a ruffled white shirt, black leggings, and boots that reached halfway up her calf, shiny with polish.

"New clothes?" Keelin said.

Aimi stopped by the bed and poured a mug of water, holding it carefully up to Keelin's mouth for him to sip. It felt like life running down his throat, giving him new energy.

"I've had a bit of time to kill while looking after you. I bought these a while back and spent yesterday altering them to fit better. What do you think?" Aimi took the cup away and gave a twirl. The clothes suited her, and though they wouldn't be practical for ship-board use, they would certainly catch a few stares around town.

"Beautiful," Keelin said.

"I bet you say that to all your crew," Aimi said with a grin.

"How long have I been…"

"Two days." Aimi refilled the mug and held it to Keelin's lips again. "Captain Black's doctor said you would live, so we brought you here. I volunteered to look after you."

"We won?"

Aimi smiled and nodded. "The town is still standing. We lost a lot of people though."

"My brother?"

The smile slipped from Aimi's face. "So it's true. You're Five Kingdoms nobility."

Keelin froze. He had no idea how to answer. He'd kept the secret for so long he thought it was lost. Ever since leaving the Five Kingdoms he'd been pretending to be just another pirate. If his secret was now common knowledge, he could only guess how long it would be before a mutiny removed him from his ship and probably his life. The crew would never follow if they knew where he came from.

"Apparently some folk wanted to kill you. They were blaming you for all of this," Aimi said. "Drake didn't let them. He convinced them you were one of us."

"So Drake survived." Keelin was more than a little relieved.

Aimi nodded and started towards the cabin door. Keelin tried to push himself up onto his elbows and promptly collapsed. Aimi opened the door.

"He's awake," she said. "Go get Morley." Aimi returned to the bed. "He wanted to know the moment you woke up. I'll help you up."

With gentle care, Aimi helped Keelin to sit up and swing his legs over the bed. She then fetched a jacket from his wardrobe and draped it over his shoulders before pouring him another mug of water and leaving it in his left hand. She went back to the desk and back to studying the papers arrayed upon it.

"What are you looking at?" Keelin said.

"Letters from the ship *My Salty Wife*. After all the soldiers were killed, the ship was taken. Drake found these in a chest, but he doesn't have time to look them over at the moment. I volunteered for that job too, as I was going to be sitting in here waiting for you to wake up.

"There's a lot of nothing. It looks like the ship was a passenger vessel used to ferry people of importance from Sarth to the Five Kingdoms. They took her from her captain, filled her with men and pointy objects, and sent her here. There's a letter signed with King Jackt Veritean's signet."

"The king of the Five Kingdoms?" Keelin said, incredulous.

Aimi nodded. "It's a letter offering a full pardon to any pirate captain willing to turn on their brethren."

"Bastard!"

A knock sounded at the door.

"Come in," Aimi shouted before Keelin could answer. He kept his face carefully blank, but it irritated him that she assumed such authority in his cabin.

The door opened and Morley walked in, treating Keelin to a smile. "Thought we might have lost you, Captain. I wouldn't mind a cabin this big."

Keelin wheezed out a laugh, and regretted it a moment later as it set both his shoulder and his leg to hurting. Morley had been part of his crew for almost as long as Keelin had had a crew, and the man had been both an excellent quartermaster and a competent first mate as well as a loyal friend.

"How's the crew?"

"Anxious," said Morley. "We lost a lot of good people in the fighting, Captain. Got a few new members too. New ship's boy, barely ten years old."

Keelin glanced over to Aimi. "Congratulations."

Aimi grinned. "No more scrubbing shit off the side of the ship for me," she crowed. "Finally get a real share of the loot as well. Not that there is any loot right now."

"That'd be the other issue, Captain," Morley continued. "Crew want paying. More so after so many are dead. Barely enough to fill two shifts left, and that's gonna make it awful hard to take any prey. We need money and people."

"And food," Aimi put in. "I'm getting right sick of fish."

Morley sucked at his teeth and shook his head. "We all eat what we can. Be glad there's plenty of fish to be ate."

Keelin sighed. "What about the other captains?"

"All in the same boat, Captan. Everyone has lost a lot of crew. With those bastards run off though, they all think we're finally safe. Others are looking at leaving. They ain't running away, but we're pirates. We should be pirating."

Keelin nodded. "You're right. We've earned ourselves a little freedom from attacks. Paid blood and lives for it. I need to speak to Drake first, but we'll go find ourselves a ship to take."

The door crashed open and Smithe strode into the cabin, slamming the door shut behind him with just as much force. Keelin stifled a sigh and attempted to get to his feet. His left leg, however, was not accommodating, and he promptly collapsed back to a sitting position with a pained gasp. Smithe leered at him.

"Any meeting about ship's business I should be privy to," Smithe said. "Especially any that the little bitch gets to sit on."

"I don't think you'd like to sit on some of the things this bitch sits on," Aimi said with a giggle, not looking up from the papers on Keelin's desk.

Smithe looked confused for a moment, and then a longer moment after. "What?"

"You weren't missing out on anything, Smithe." Keelin tried to draw the surly quartermaster's attention away from Aimi. "Morley was just bringing me up to speed on what's been happening these last two days."

"Aye?"

Morley nodded. "Aye."

"What would the crew say to a spot of good, honest piracy, Smithe?" Keelin said.

"Reckon some money in pockets might not be a bad thing," Smithe replied, a suspicious look about his face. "Especially if it don't mean fighting. Reckon some of the boys had enough killing for now."

"Excellent," Keelin said with a smile. "We'll set off as soon as the town is back to some semblance of normalcy and find some poor fuckers to rob blind."

"Might be worth searching for those bastards over the Sea of Stars," Smithe said with a greedy grin.

Crossing the Sea of Stars to the Dragon Empire wasn't entirely what Keelin had in mind. It would take them a fair distance from the isles, and from the young, fragile alliance that Drake had set up. It would also serve to remind Keelin that he was still so far away from his vengeance.

Smithe reached into his jacket and pulled out a large wad of treated leather. "You may have forgotten ya promise to the crew," he said, crossing the room to Keelin and holding out the object. "I ain't."

Keelin had to put the mug of water down to take the piece of leather from Smithe – his right arm hurt far too much to use. It appeared to be a folded sheet of leather-backed parchment, and Keelin had some real trouble opening it out with only the one hand. All the while, Smithe stood by with a smirk on his face. Eventually Keelin placed the thing on his bed and peeled it open. It was a chart, and not one of his. After a moment he recognised the writing as Drake's, and only a moment later he realised what the chart showed.

"How did you get this?"

"How do you think?" Smithe spat. "Broke into Morrass' cabin and took it whiles no one was watching. Thought you might have forgotten about it, Captain."

"You stole it from him?"

"Ain't that what you was planning to do?" Smithe said. "You promised us riches, Captain. Right here I just delivered you the thing you claimed was stalling us. So how about we fuck off from this little war Morrass is fighting and go get ourselves nice and rich."

Morley moved over to stand beside Smithe. There was a greedy glint in his eyes that Keelin wasn't used to seeing. "You did promise the crew, Captan."

For Keelin it wasn't about the money. In the Forgotten Empire lay a way to locate Arbiter Prin, and his encounter with his brother had made the vengeance feel urgent all over again.

"I did," he said. "We sail within the week."

Fortune

Drake looked down at the body on the floor of his cabin and felt a cold rage building inside him. After two days of giving orders, helping to move the bodies of the dead, and regularly checking on Beck, he'd finally given in to the exhaustion. Twice he'd found himself asleep, startled as someone asked for an opinion or otherwise required his attention. He'd decided he needed rest, and there was only one place he was likely to get it undisturbed.

"Must've happened during the attack," Princess said, looking very much like he wanted to be somewhere else. "Fucking soldiers boarded us and we didn't have much in the way of resistance. Don't reckon we'd have pushed them off the ship if not for Rag."

The giant centipede had climbed up Drake's leg and wrapped itself around his waist almost as soon as he set foot on his ship. Knowing full well how dangerous the beast was, Drake worried about it doing that at times, and it weighed him down – but it also bolstered his courage. Rag's armour was as hard as steel, and with a venomous bite and razor-sharp pincers, it was a devastating predator of a pet.

"She killed a good three soldiers herself and scared the rest away," Princess continued into his captain's silence. "I guess one of those bastards broke in here first though."

Drake said nothing. He tore his gaze away from Byron's crumpled form. The image of the simpleton's head caved in would likely stay with him until the end of his days. Byron had never held a weapon in his life; he'd never even been involved in a fight, as far as Drake knew. Whenever the *Fortune* and her crew took a ship he always hid below decks. It made no sense that the man had come to Drake's cabin, and even less sense that whoever had broken in had not only killed him, but made such a mess of the lad as well.

The room was chaos. Drawers had been opened, their contents rifled through and thrown about the place. Drake's chart cabinet had been broken open and his charts had spilled out, unrolling across the floor. The door to his alcohol cabinet had been smashed open and the bottles broken upon his desk. The window behind his desk had been smashed, no doubt so the culprit could make their escape with Byron's substantial body blocking the door.

"At least they didn't set fire to my bed," he growled.

"I reckon Byron caught them trashing the place," Princess said. "Lad probably asked them to leave. He was likely even polite about it."

"They weren't polite," Drake said.

"No. Pyres are almost ready, Cap'n. Should we take his body down to them?"

Drake shook his head. "Byron died on the water. We'll give his body to Rin. Perhaps she'll have him spend eternity counting seashells, eh?" Drake barked out a laugh, but there was no humour behind it. They'd all lost so many people. He'd never expected to lose Byron.

"I'll get someone to help move his body," Princess said solemnly.

Drake nodded, glancing back once more at the simpleton before turning his attention to his cabin. He knew he'd get no sleep while his room was in such disarray, and especially not with the window broken. He doubted they had the glass to fix it here on Cinto Cena, so he resigned himself to boarding it up until they could find someone to repair it properly.

Drake couldn't help but feel the weight of Rag around his waist as an oppressive burden. He was already exhausted, and the creature was weighing him down. With a tap on its head, Drake ordered Rag to climb down and the beast obeyed, if a little lethargically. Once on the floor it wound its way towards Byron's corpse.

"Don't you dare," Drake hissed, fully willing to drag the beast away if he had to.

Rag paused.

"Away!"

After another moment the giant centipede turned and made for Drake's bed, crawling underneath and curling up to sleep. Drake envied the beast for that.

The door opened again and Princess walked in with a couple of the crew.

"By her teeth," Goran cursed, refusing to use Rin's name even over water. "Poor Byron. Get his shoulders, Collo. I'll get his legs."

Collo looked down at the dead pirate and paled. "You get his shoulders."

"Just bloody do as ya told."

Drake cleared his throat loudly and sent both pirates a scathing glare. They quickly decided it didn't matter who picked up which end of Byron's corpse. After a bit of struggling and a few more curses, they dragged the body from Drake's cabin.

"Reckon they're about ready to light the pyres," Princess said after Goran and Collo had gone. "Might be good for you to attend. Maybe even light them yaself."

Drake picked up one of the charts spread across the floor. One of Beck's pistols was lying beneath it. The Arbiter was still unconscious; Drake had made every doctor and every fool that called himself a healer look at her, and they all said the same thing. Her immediate injuries had been treated, but sometimes folk just didn't pull through. He tucked the little pistol into his belt and put the last of the charts into the cabinet, shutting what was left of the door and waiting to see if it stayed shut.

"Cap'n?"

"I'm coming, Princess," Drake said. "I hear Stillwater is awake. Send someone to fetch him for me. I'll meet him down on the beach."

North Storm

Fires were dancing on the shores of Cinto Cena, and the sight made T'ruck's spirits sink, something he hadn't thought possible any more. He'd known the soldiers of the Five Kingdoms were planning to attack New Sev'relain, and he'd known he was a good few days or more behind them. He'd hoped to somehow arrive in time to help with the defence. Not that he and his seven crew would have been able to do much.

Sailing a galleon with only seven sailors would have been exhausting, and the *North Storm* was certainly no galleon. She was one of the biggest ships ever built, and every member of the crew, including Lady Tsokei, had been operating on only a couple of hours' sleep a day. And each one had performed above and beyond anything T'ruck could ever have expected from them. The surviving men and women had gone from a tight crew to a much tighter family.

When T'ruck awoke after the battle he had found the bloody corpse of Yu'truda lying across him and the witch unconscious by his side. He'd been covered in Yu's blood; he could feel and smell it on his skin and he could taste it in his mouth. At first he'd been furious at Lady Tsokei. The crew explained she'd given Yu'truda's life to him, and he very nearly stamped the life out of the unconscious witch, but he was beyond tired and his crew pulled him away and convinced him that it had been Yu'truda's choice.

T'ruck fancied he could feel Yu'truda inside him. Every now and then he felt a twinge of emotion that didn't belong. When he consulted with the witch about it, she merely shrugged and pointed out that he was no longer living his life, but Yu'truda's. T'ruck wasn't about to begin to claim he understood what she meant. Yet he would be damned if he wasted the gift given to him by the last member of his old clan. He was alone now. The Five Kingdoms had taken everything from him. Every member of his clan, his family, his friends. All that was left was T'ruck and his new family. His ship and his crew.

"We could make a run for Fango," suggested Pocket. The young man had proven himself both in battle and in the sailing of the ship, and

T'ruck had been proud to name him first mate of *North Storm*. There was still a haunted look about the lad, though. Pocket had seen too much death for his short life, and had been the cause of much of it besides.

T'ruck took in a deep breath, then sighed it out with a shake of his head. "Tanner knows we have sided with Drake. He would take the ship from us and we do not have the crew to stop him."

"We have Nerine," Pocket said.

The lad had become quite close with the witch since they'd taken *North Storm*. T'ruck didn't know the extent of the relationship, but the more ties the woman had to the ship and crew, the more T'ruck trusted her.

He shook his head again. "That would serve no one, lad. If I am to waste our lives, I would do it crushing the skulls of Five Kingdoms pigs, not fighting our own. Besides, we need help clearing the bodies from the ship before the rats mutiny."

They'd been sailing ever since taking *North Storm*, and were lucky they hadn't run across another ship or foul weather in that time. The crew had had very little opportunity to clear the dead from the bowels of the ship, and while the smell had been rancid for some time, the risk of disease was becoming a real danger. T'ruck had one thing to say for the bodies that littered his new ship, though – they were keeping the rats away from the food stores. Why chew into a barrel when there was dead flesh aplenty, just lying around?

"Those are big fires," Pocket said. "Looks like the whole town is burning."

"The choice has been made," T'ruck rumbled. "If we are to die today, we will make it glorious."

"Aye, Captain."

As the ship sailed closer, the pirate taking a turn in the nest, a woman by the name of Coral, scuttled down the rigging at a dangerous pace and ran across the deck towards T'ruck. He glanced at her before turning his attention back to hauling in the front sail.

"I see four big fires and a fuck load of ships, Cap'n," Coral said, her voice whistling through a gap in her teeth.

"Ours or theirs?"

"Hard to say," Coral said easily. "It's a bit dark, Cap'n. Don't look like the fires have touched the town though. They're all on the beach."

It wasn't long before T'ruck could make out the faint shapes of ships in the bay. Between the fires and the moonlight they were well lit, and he recognised the hulls of both *The Phoenix* and the *Fortune*.

They sailed *North Storm* right into the south bay of Cinto Cena. He'd never realised how large the bay was until it swallowed up his giant of a ship. They'd been spotted, there was no mistake about that; T'ruck could see hundreds of folk scrambling about on the beach.

They lowered the anchor and then a dinghy into the water, and T'ruck ordered everyone aboard it. He would leave nobody behind for now. He set a brisk pace, rowing with the help of Pocket and Durance, and made Coral stand at the front of the dinghy and wave a white square of cloth in the air.

As the little boat drifted up alongside one of the free piers, T'ruck found a small host of bows and spears pointed towards him – but they were held by pirates, not soldiers of the Five Kingdoms. It didn't take long for the weapons to be put away as T'ruck and the few surviving members of his crew were recognised.

Amidst congratulations and cheers, T'ruck departed the dinghy with his crew behind him and they were escorted from the pier. He found Drake, Keelin, and Tanner Black crowded around a small fire.

"Captains," T'ruck said with a nod.

"T'ruck, you insane bastard," Keelin Stillwater said. "We thought you were dead."

T'ruck's gaze drifted around the fire, coming to a sudden halt on the white-skulled face of Deun Burn. "*You!*"

Drake Morrass was up from his seat in a moment, placing himself between T'ruck and the filthy Riverlander. "Calm it down, Captain Khan," Drake said, a dangerous note in his voice.

"He sent us into a trap." T'ruck could sense the remaining members of his crew at his back, and there was anger there too.

"Wasn't him," Drake said, waving his hands in front of T'ruck's face. T'ruck glanced down at him. "Was the other dumb bastard Riverlander, and he's been… dealt with."

T'ruck clenched his jaw so hard it hurt, his eyes darting from Drake to Deun Burn. "I would see his body."

"They ate it," Drake said quickly.

T'ruck stopped cold. "What?"

"Show him the face," Drake hissed to the Riverlander.

Deun reached for the bag on his belt and pulled out a patch of leather, unfolding it and holding it up to the firelight. There were tattooed scales on the leather, and T'ruck had to admit it did look a lot like the face of the Riverlander who had sent them to die. The rage drained out of him as quickly as it had appeared, and T'ruck found himself tired and in desperate need of a drink, which Tanner Black handed over. T'ruck found it hard to believe that Drake had succeeded in gaining the alliance of Captain Black, yet here the man was and, judging by the smell of burning bodies, they'd only recently fought off the Five Kingdoms invaders.

"How did you do it?" Stillwater said, his voice full of awe. "How did you take that monster fucking ship?

"With just twenty-two of us," T'ruck rumbled.

A murmur ran through the crowd, and only when T'ruck looked up did he realise how many folk had gathered. It looked like everyone. His own crew had collapsed onto the sand behind him, and even now he could tell that some of them were asleep already. Unfortunately he wagered it would be some time before he would find the sweet bliss of unconsciousness.

T'ruck told them then of how *North Gale* had been sent into a trap, and how they'd taken one of the ships before *Storm Herald* smashed into their midsection, splitting them in half and sinking them. He told them how he and his crew had been plucked from the water only to be thrown in the brig to languish until they reached the Five Kingdoms, where they were to be hanged. He told them of his escape and freeing the crew, and he told them nothing of the witch. His crew were sworn to secrecy; Lady Tsokei's powers were to be revealed to no one. T'ruck told them little of how they'd taken the ship, only that they'd moved from cabin to cabin, murdering hundreds of men.

One of the other captains laughed when T'ruck said they must have killed a thousand soldiers, but he just stared at the man and challenged him to check the ship and the bodies that were still inside it. When T'ruck was done, Drake gave his own story, spinning a tale about how they'd guessed the attack on New Sev'relain was coming and had started preparations, but the losses had still been great.

T'ruck asked about Captain Damien Poole, and a new sadness washed over the crowd. Drake claimed Poole had been a true hero, and that he'd sacrificed himself to give the others time to get away from Ash. T'ruck would have found it hard to believe the man had even a drop of courage, and even harder to believe Poole would sacrifice his own life.

"We got a bit of a problem," Drake said eventually. "People."

"Reckon we got a few problems, mate," Tanner barked.

"We need fresh blood," Drake continued, ignoring Tanner. "Not just for our ships. For the town as well. We've lost too many of us already."

"Ya want us to start breeding, do ya?"

Again Drake ignored Tanner. "We also need to start pirating again. Bastards sailing through our waters have been left too long, unharassed while we've been running and hiding. No more. From now on we travel in packs, and we take every fucking ship we can find. Merchants, navy, slavers…"

Another murmur ran through the crowd.

"There's no money to be had from slavers," Keelin said. The man's arm was in a sling, and his leg was stretched out awkwardly in front of him.

"I don't mean to take them for money," Drake said. "I want you to take them and free the poor buggers in the holds."

The crowd got louder.

"We need people more than money or food or weapons or anything else right now," Drake shouted, loudly enough to silence the folk around him. "Reckon most folk who wear a collar would welcome a chance at freedom here on the isles."

"You'll be starting a war with the slavers guild," Keelin said, quietly enough that only those nearby could hear.

"No," Drake said with a shake of his head. "We're just laying down the rules. Anyone – *anyone* – who wants to sail our waters has to pay.

Slavers have had free passage for far too fucking long. I also need someone to sail to Larkos. Talk to the guilds, ask them for help."

"I'll go," Keelin said quickly. "I have some contacts in Larkos that might be able to help."

Drake looked torn for a moment, but nodded. "Good. This war ain't won yet. Next time they come, they'll come with everything they have, and we need to be ready. We need to meet them in the water, and we need to sink every last fucking one of them."

Part 2 - All Hands on Deck

There will be a traitor in your midst said the Oracle
Who said Drake
Someone who was once an ally said the Oracle

Land's End

When the door to his cell opened, Daimen started. After days upon days upon days at sea, followed by a long stint in a gaol cell, he'd just about decided the bastards had all but forgotten about him. He fully expected them to parade him about the city before tying a rope around his neck and giving him the drop he deserved. As far as Daimen was concerned, he did deserve it.

His crew were dead. Every single one of the poor bastards, and it was all his fault. He'd led them into death, promised them a rescue that never came.

A right fancy looking man walked into the cell. He was followed by a giant of a knight dressed from the neck down in shiny steel and carrying a metal spear that looked as though it weighed as much as Daimen himself. The fancy one wore a dazzling blue suit and carried a sword at his hip, his posture suggesting he was well used to the weight of it. Daimen had seen a fair few aristocrats in his time, and he'd have happily bet his right testicle – the smaller of the two – on the man being noble born.

"Captain Daimen Poole," the fancy man said in a fancy voice. There were no chairs in Daimen's cell, only a small cot lined with straw and a bucket, so the man stayed standing. "My name is Jackt Veritean."

Daimen laughed. "Fuck off, are ya."

The man frowned, and Daimen had to admit it looked a very royal frown, but he wasn't about to believe the king of the Five Kingdoms had climbed down off his golden throne to talk to one shipless pirate.

"I assure you, Captain Poole, I am…"

"Do ya see a ship round here anywhere, mate?" Daimen said.

"Perhaps it's in me bucket sailing on a sea of my shit? No? I ain't captain of fuckin' anything no more." Daimen paused before adding, "Ya Majesty."

The man who called himself king stared on with impressive patience. Daimen had a knack for grating on folks' nerves, and he wondered how long it would take this man to learn it.

"Daimen Poole, I assure you I am Jackt Veritean…"

"Best keep ya royal distance then, mate. You're in a cell with a dangerous pirate, don't ya know?"

"I assure you, I am quite safe from any sort of attack you might be able to muster," the king said with an air of confidence. Daimen looked from the sword at the man's hip to the big knight with the spear, who looked unconcerned by the whole situation. "Believe it or not, I am trying to save your miserable life."

Daimen laughed again. "Thought ya said ya were king. Don't take much ta save my life, mate. Just don't kill me."

"If only things were so simple." The king smiled. "You're a pirate. Self-confessed and guilty of a number of crimes. I must admit, when the list was relayed to me I stopped listening after the tenth or so. Suffice to say, by Five Kingdoms law you should be hanged until you are dead."

"Best get on with it before the rats decide to steal ya chance. They keep coming back for a nibble no matter how many times I chase 'em off." It wasn't even a lie; Daimen had a number of little bites from the pests, and it was likely because he smelled like ten-day-old carrion.

The king sighed. "I'm told you sailed your ship right into mine. My captains tell me it was a suicidal manoeuvre to stop them going after Drake Morrass and the others. You sacrificed your life, your ship, and your crew, all for Captain Morrass?"

"Amazing, the sort of shit a man will do and sacrifice for his king, eh?" Daimen couldn't keep the bitter edge out.

Jackt Veritean nodded, smiling. "As are the things a king will do for his kingdom. Do you believe in Drake Morrass?"

Daimen met his eyes. "Aye, I do." It was only half a lie. Daimen had believed in Drake. He'd believed Drake was the only man the isles could unite behind. And he'd believed Drake would sail in and save him, his ship, and his crew. Instead the bastard had turned tail and left Daimen and all his men to die.

"Would it shake your belief to know that this war we are all currently fighting was by his design?"

"Eh?"

"He came to me, your *king*, with a plan to rid myself of you and all the other pirates. It was true my merchants had been requesting aid against your brethren for some time. However, I had no way to deal with you, no way to find you. Drake changed that. He came to me with charts, and upon those charts were the locations of a number of your little towns."

"Ya full of shit, mate."

"I offered him lands and a title in return for the deaths of all the pirates inhabiting your Pirate Isles, and he agreed. He told me to start with a town called Black Sands before moving on to any of the others, claiming it was some sort of lookout town. An early warning for the rest, unless it was promptly burned to the ground. My allies in Sarth jumped upon the chance.

"Of course, Drake disappeared, and I have since learned that a number of the other locations he'd noted on his chart were false. Why do you think he would do that, Captain Poole?"

Daimen bit his tongue to stop himself cursing.

"I believe Drake Morrass wanted me and my allies in Sarth to attack Black Sands. I think he wanted us to attack the Pirate Isles. I think he wanted all you pirates terrified and running to him for salvation."

"Yer a fucking liar," Daimen said, with less conviction than he would have liked.

"I don't think you believe that, Captain Poole," the king said, pacing around the cell. "If you were willing to sacrifice yourself for Drake Morrass, then you must know him fairly well. Tell me, what would he be willing to sacrifice to convince you people that he should be wearing a crown?"

Daimen thought about it. There was no way anyone should have found Black Sands unless they knew it was there; it was hidden from all directions but one, and that one was well away from any sort of safe trade route. The Five Kingdoms and Sarth ships were sailing the isles like they knew them, instead of gutting themselves on rocks or crashing into hidden sandbanks. There was little that could explain it quite like a well-maintained chart.

"He betrayed you all," the king of the Five Kingdoms continued. "You trusted him, and he betrayed you and left you for dead. You sit here rotting in a cell while he claims himself a king of the very people he plotted to murder."

"That ain't…" Daimen started. "Ya got any proof?"

King Jackt stopped pacing and shook his head. "I don't think I need any, Captain Poole. If you need to ask for proof, then I think we both already know how much you truly trust Drake Morrass. You know he's capable of the crimes I'm laying at his feet, and more than just capable – you know he committed them."

Daimen hated it, but the bastard was right. Drake was more than capable of sacrificing an entire town to his machinations, and he'd been at Black Sands just after the massacre took place. He was the first to bring news back to Old Sev'relain, and he was the first to jump on the tragedy and start gathering folk to his flag. As soon as Black Sands was destroyed, there were some folk who suspected Drake had had a hand in it, but he managed to not only allay suspicions but use them to his advantage. It turned out they should all have kept on suspecting.

"Why are ya telling me this, mate?" Daimen said. "Ya want me to repent my allegiance just before ya hang me?"

The king shook his head. "I don't want to kill you at all, Captain Poole. I want to offer you the same thing I offered to Drake. Lands and a title. I offer you legitimacy in return for helping me crush Morrass and the rest of the pirates."

"Ya want me ta help ya murder all the folk of the isles?" Damien said, caught between disgust and rage.

"Not at all. I couldn't care less about the backwards towns that infest the Pirate Isles. I have been targeting them only because I had no other course of action. If the decimation of you pirates can be achieved with minimal bloodshed of those not involved, then that would be my preferred method. Which is where you come in."

The king paused. "You know the isles, and you know the captains. I would have you help me hunt them."

"Turn on my fellow captains to save my life?"

"Save your life. Save yourself the pain of weeks of torture. Secure yourself a future, Captain Poole." The king's voice was stern. "And all you have to do is help me catch those who abandoned you. I'll give you a day to think on it."

"What happens if I say no?"

"The penalty for piracy is death by hanging, Captain Poole, and you are most certainly guilty."

Starry Dawn

Larkos wasn't just a free city; it was more like a small kingdom ruled by thirteen different sets of laws depending on which region you visited. It sat on the eastern edge of the largest, most powerful empire in the known world, and it resisted all attempts by that empire to engulf it. Elaina loved the idea of Larkos as much as she loved the look, smell, and feel of the place.

Ships nestled in the harbour like gulls fighting over a floating carcass, and Elaina spotted a fair few she recognised as belonging to known pirates. She looked out over the bay, but soon stopped counting the number of masts – there were simply too many. One of the joys of the free cities was that they didn't care whether goods were obtained illegally; the merchants of Larkos were far more interested in how cheaply they could buy the loot than where it came from.

The weather was chilly so far north, and Elaina had chosen a heavy black jacket to wear over her blouse and britches. The jacket reached almost to the deck and gave her a distinctly menacing air that she'd helped along with a touch of dark powder around her eyes and a charcoal bandana to hold her hair in place. She would walk into the city as the proud daughter of Tanner Black, looking like a true pirate lord, and demand the assistance they needed from the guilds that ran the place.

"Ready to go, Cap?" her quartermaster, Alfer Boharn, said in his gravelly voice. She'd chosen to take the old Five Kingdoms veteran ashore with her because he had a few connections within the guild of Clerics. He was also as steady as a rock no matter how dicey the situation might become. Not that Elaina expected any trouble.

"Aye," she said with a smile. "Rovel, you have the ship. See about hiring on a couple of new crew, eh?"

"Aye, Cap," Rovel said. Elaina's first mate had been outspoken of late in his desire for some good old-fashioned piracy. Unfortunately, Elaina had her orders from her father, and Tanner had decreed that she would take no ships on her diplomatic mission. Whether that was to speed her journey or ensure her arrival, Elaina didn't know, but she knew better than to disobey her father with so much at stake.

Wandering down the gangplank with Alfer just behind her, it occurred to Elaina that none of her crew had asked for shore leave. It was true enough that they had only a few bits each to their name, but she wondered if the lack of piracy in the last few months had dulled their physical desires. Perhaps she would lounge around in Larkos' port for a couple of weeks and give her crew an advance, to show them how much she appreciated their patience.

A number of merchant assistants had already crowded around the pier, and they were busy trying to get Elaina's attention, no doubt clamouring to find which goods she'd procured and how cheaply they could procure them from her. Most of the assistants were fat, well-dressed, and sweaty despite the chill in the air. Elaina ignored them all and instead looked towards the harbour master, who was lounging on a nearby stool, a small ink-tipped feather pen walking across his fingers.

"Name?" the harbour master said without looking up.

"Elaina Black."

"Odd name for a ship," he said with a chuckle that no one nearby took up. "Still the *Starry Dawn*, is it?"

"Aye."

"Do I need to ask your profession?"

"Ambassador," Elaina said.

The harbour master laughed. "I'll put that down just because of how absurd it sounds. Length of stay?"

"Couple of weeks, I reckon."

"Two silver bits now and another twenty upon departure." The man finally looked up from the pen walking across his fingers. He gave Elaina a wide grin and set about making notes in his book. He was a handsome young man, and sure of himself. Elaina considered taking him back to her cabin and convincing him he had nothing to be so sure about, but she had more pressing matters.

"Who's in charge of the docks these days?" Elaina said as she reached into her purse and pulled out a couple of silver bits.

"Still the Clerics." The harbour master stopped his jotting and leaned back in his chair, looking Elaina up and down with a grin. "At least for another couple of moons. That's why the price for docking has gone up. They're squeezing out as much coin as they can while they can. Never know where they might be next."

Elaina nodded along. Larkos had a strange set of laws designed to equalise the power of the thirteen guilds that ran it. The city was split into thirteen districts, twelve public and one central one closed to the general populous. Each of those districts was governed by one of the guilds, and every five years the whole system was shaken up. For five years the Clerics had held the docks, one of the most profitable of the districts, but in just a short time they might find themselves running the slums or the Breakers, and there was very little coin to be made in either of those.

Once a week the representatives of the guilds met in the central district and the Council of Thirteen decided upon any matters of importance. That was where Elaina would need to be heard, and the best way for her to get in would be as an invited guest of the guild that ran the central district.

"Who's in charge of central?" she said.

"The Blades," the harbour master said. "I could knock five bits off your docking fee for a couple of… favours."

Elaina looked down him. He leered back up at her. "I could cut your empty head off your fucking shoulders for free," she said with a grin.

He shrugged. "Your loss." He went back to walking his little feather pen across his fingers. Elaina conquered the urge to grab it from him and snap the stem.

The city was bustling with life. The sheer size of Larkos put most cities to shame, and even Chade was small in comparison. Slaves were everywhere, either carrying goods to or from ships or standing around as their masters haggled and secured trade. Despite the chill in the air, the poor bastards were afforded no more clothing than they were when the sun was baking down, and Elaina wagered their iron collars got right uncomfortable in the cold.

The merchants were as easy to spot as their slaves. Even those who weren't overweight and sagging were obvious in their finery. The docks were a place for sailors, and sailors rarely wore anything other than linen.

The rich folk in their silks and other expensive fabrics were somewhere beyond obvious, and that made them pretty targets.

Thievery and other criminal enterprises were as ubiquitous in Larkos as they were in any city, and the punishments for being caught ranged from severe to final. The Clerics were fairly light-handed in dealing with criminals, and often a thief could get away with a flogging and some community service. Other guilds were less forgiving, none less so than the slavers guild, who would simply slap an iron collar on a criminal no matter how severe their crime. It served them both as a method of punishment and a form of income.

"Where to, Cap?" Alfer said. "Wouldn't mind me some downtime if we find ourselves with some spare."

"Ever been to Larkos, Alfer?" Elaina asked her quartermaster, already knowing the answer.

"Aye," Alfer replied with a laugh. "Don't reckon there's many places I ain't been."

"Then you should know the chance of having time to find yaself a brothel is somewhere south of low. I've got one destination, and that would be the central district. I need to win myself an audience with the Queen of Blades."

Alfer let loose a laugh, but quickly stopped at a glare from Elaina. "Fuck. I really hoped you might be spinning a tale, Cap. That Drurr bitch don't see anyone."

"She'll see me," Elaina said, setting her jaw and starting the long walk.

The sky had turned dark, and folk were busy lighting street lamps by the time Elaina and Alfer reached the wall that separated the central district from all the others. They'd long since passed out of the docks, and though Elaina had seen a good few Clerics, she'd had no cause to talk to any of them.

A large barred gate lay in front of them, with a wall extending from it that curved around out of sight. The central district was completely separate from the rest of the city, and very few even knew what it looked like within those walls. As they'd approached, Elaina had been able to see the tops of many buildings, and the guild hall used by the Council of Thirteen was without a doubt the largest of those, but they gave little indication as to the state of the rest of the district.

There was a small guard hut nearby, with a number of shadowy figures inside. In front of the gate stood no fewer than four Blades, resplendent in sky blue steel armour and each carrying at least four swords. It was well known that the Blades were trained in a style of combat used by the Drurr, and it was strictly forbidden for those styles and techniques to be taught to outsiders. The Queen of Blades was one of the few Drurr that the Inquisition allowed to live among humans. Elaina wondered if such a privilege was due to a deal struck, or simply the Inquisition's fear of starting a war against the free city.

"Perhaps we should come back when it's light, Cap," Alfer said quietly. "Ya know, so there's a few more witnesses around."

"Scared they might kill us just for asking?" Elaina said with a grin.

"Fuck yes, I am, Cap. What's to stop them?"

Elaina thought about it for a moment, but couldn't come up with a single thing. The guilds ran Larkos how they saw fit, and she had no doubt they weren't above a spot of murder.

"They wouldn't dare," she said eventually. "Me da would tear this place down to its foundations."

Alfer snorted. "Ya da's one man. This here is… Shit, I can't count anywhere close. There must be more folk in one bloody district than the entire of the isles."

"Stop ya whining, Alfer, and look surly. Ya know, dangerous. Like ya could take 'em all if ya wanted."

Elaina strode up to the gate and the Blades guarding it, fixing a smug look on her face. A woman in sky blue steel stepped forward to meet her, one hand on the hilt of a sword and the other held out in front of her to stop Elaina's advance.

"This is the central district, ma'am," the Blade said with a kind smile. "I must ask you to turn around and leave."

"Now that'd kinda defeat the point," Elaina said, returning the smile. "I'm here to see ya Queen."

"Then I am afraid your journey has been wasted. The Queen of

Blades does not see anyone."

"Now I know that's a lie," Elaina said.

Another of the Blades stepped forward, hand on sword hilt, while a third jogged over to the guard hut. All the while the woman who had stopped Elaina remained in front of her, and her brown eyes never shifted. A few moments later three more Blades stepped out of the guard hut and approached. They were clearly well trained, taking no chances when it came to possible intruders.

"Again, I must ask you to leave," said the Blade, her hand still out in front of her to stop Elaina moving any closer.

"Don't I even get to make an appointment?" Elaina said, realising for the first time she may have gone about things the wrong way.

"The Queen of Blades does not see anyone," the woman repeated.

Elaina ground her teeth together, but getting angry wouldn't get her anywhere. She decided on a different course. "Then how about you get a message to your bloody Queen, eh? Can you do that?"

None of the Blades said anything; they all just stood still and silent.

Elaina snorted out a laugh. "Ya tell her the future queen of the Pirate Isles wants to have a word, and we'll see if she don't see anyone. She can find me on my ship."

Without waiting for a response, Elaina turned and strode away. She was beyond angry, but that rage wouldn't serve her. Right now she needed to act with diplomacy.

They passed back into the docks district a fair time later, and Elaina let Alfer lead her to a tavern he knew to be frequented by a number of Clerics. She found a secluded table and brooded over a single flagon of piss-poor ale while her quartermaster reacquainted himself with some old friends and made a few overtures towards those in higher positions.

A handsome older man with a shock of grey in his close-cropped hair and a scarred jaw that served as testament to a number of brawl participations sat down opposite Elaina. The man had a winning smile and had brought with him a bottle of rum, which he pushed towards her. She hadn't even finished her ale, but she took the rum and drained it by a mouthful. The fiery spirit did nothing to lift her own spirits, so she pushed the bottle back towards the man and glared at him.

"Beautiful women should not be forced to drink alone," he said with a smile.

Elaina snorted. The only fool who had ever called her beautiful was Keelin. Desirable was something else though. "Ain't forced if it's my choice," she said. "So fuck off."

The handsome man held up his hands, then pushed the bottle back towards Elaina. The smile never left his face.

"I will leave, and leave you the bottle, Captain Black. And also tell you that your presence has not gone unnoticed. If the Queen of Blades will not grant you an audience, then the Nightborne will. I do hope you will consider us favourably."

The man bowed his head, a sign of respect Elaina hadn't expected, and stood. She found herself in a state of confusion. The man – a Nightborne emissary, she assumed – had sounded like he was trying to curry her favour. Elaina had never been given such a reception before; in fact, she was used to operating under relative anonymity. Her name had always carried some weight, once she let people know it, but it had always been her father who had given it that weight.

"Cap," Alfer said as he wandered over, thumbing at the Nightborne, who was making towards the tavern door. "Anyone we should be worried about?"

Elaina thought about it for a moment before shaking her head. "Quite the opposite, I reckon, Alfer. He might just be our way into the Council."

"Which guild?"

"Nightborne, apparently."

Alfer sucked in a breath that whistled through a gap in his teeth. "Don't go siding jus' yet, Cap. Clerics are interested too. All ya need to do is strut up to the guild hall and knock, and Brother Hernhold will see you his own self. Ain't many get an audience with the head without even asking."

"Ain't been here a day, and I've been turned away by one guild only to have two others come sniffing around." Elaina drained her mug of ale as she tried to puzzle it all out.

"Guilds don't offer nothing for free, Cap," Alfer said. "Each one'll want a piece of ya."

Elaina sniffed, then grunted her agreement. "Might be there's others want that piece too. Grab that bottle, Alf. Reckon it's best we head on back to the ship. See who's been about."

As dawn started to peek up over the horizon, Elaina found herself standing on the docks, staring out towards the rising sun. Her feet hurt like all the Hells from the walking, but she didn't give one drop about the pain. Her ship was gone.

Elaina and Alfer had arrived to find *Starry Dawn* missing from its berth, and the harbour master – not the same man as before – had simply shrugged and told her to bugger off. Frustration and fear had made her rash, and the harbour master had found himself sprawling on the ground with a couple of loose teeth. He'd crawled away, threatening to call the Clerics, and Alfer had quickly offered to find out if their ship had simply been moved. It was pointless. Elaina didn't need Alfer to confirm the truth for her. Her ship was gone.

The rising sun set the gentle waves of the bay on fire, and the sea looked like burnished gold. On any other day Elaina might have thought the sight beautiful. Today she couldn't appreciate it. For the second time in her life she'd had a ship stolen out from under her.

"I need you to come with me, ma'am." Elaina didn't bother turning to look at the female Cleric. "You have assaulted a Larkos official, and that's a crime here."

"Whoa, whoa there," shouted Alfer. He sounded out of breath. Elaina didn't look at him either. "Just a misunderstanding, I assure you."

There was a pause. "That woman assaulted…" the Cleric started again.

"That woman is Captain Black," Alfer wheezed out. "Believe me when I tell you Brother Hernhold wouldn't look favourably on ya if ya throw her in a cell, eh?"

"Cap," shouted another voice, and a moment later Four-Eyed Pollick appeared. His cheeks were flushed and his right eye was swollen almost shut.

"Who was it?" Elaina growled. She squinted as the sun, now rising above the horizon, became so bright it hurt.

"Rovel," Pollick said. "Near as soon as you were out of eyesight, he set about a mutiny. Convinced the crew they was better off under a pirate."

Elaina turned a furious gaze on her crewman. "And what the fuck am I then?"

Pavel, the ship's priest and doctor, walked up next to Pollick. Elaina turned her stare on him as well, but he didn't look cowed. The bastard probably believed his golden god would save him from harm.

"This is all that's left?" Elaina said. "Out of my entire fucking crew, you two are the only ones that didn't mutiny?"

Pollick dropped his eyes to the deck while Pavel gave a sympathetic smile that Elaina wanted to remove with a slap.

"Cap," Alfer said quietly. "Reckon I got 'em calmed, but we need to get off the docks. They ain't happy with the scene."

Elaina turned around, and for the first time saw how big a crowd she had staring her way. Merchants, slaves, sailors, Clerics, whores, and good folk, and all of them were watching her.

"All ain't lost yet, Cap," Alfer whispered.

"But my ship is," she hissed.

"Ain't we here to convince the Council to give you more ships?"

Alfer was right. If she could get ships from the Council of Thirteen then she could go after *Starry Dawn* and take her back. She would gut Rovel and feed him to the beasties of the deep. But if she was to convince the Council, she needed to bargain from a position of strength, and having lost her own ship she was in a decidedly weak position.

"Find us an inn, Alfer," she said quietly. "We might be here a while. One way or another, I'm getting a new ship from this fucking city."

Fortune

Beck closed her eyes and let out a heavy sigh. When she opened them again, they were set with determination. She raised her right arm and aimed her pistol at the target, a splotch of paint on an empty wooden barrel.

Her arm shook. Her hand shook. Her pistol shook. She pulled the trigger.

The sand behind the barrel accepted the bullet with silent indifference.

"Shit," she said quietly. "Shit, shit, shit, shit, shit." She raised her left arm and aimed a second pistol.

The centre of the target splintered as the bullet burst through the barrel. Beck dropped both pistols onto the cloth she'd spread on the ground and spun around, dropping onto her arse in the sand and staring out at the sea. The sight of the endless blue gave her no relief, only made her homesick for the crystal clear canals of Sarth.

It had been a good two moons or more since the attack on New Sev'relain, and still Beck was feeling the injuries she'd received. Her right arm was weak and weary much of the time, and occasionally took to hurting for no reason the doctors could fathom. The bruising had faded, as had the swelling around her ribs and face, but she still had a couple of ugly burn scars on her arms. And her hair… Beck had always liked to keep her hair long, but the fire had burned much of it away and her scissors had cut away even more. What was left barely reached past her ears, and it seemed to have lost its golden shine. For a woman who liked to pride herself on her appearance, the scars and her ruined hair were almost more than she could bear. Beck knew that scars faded and hair grew back, yet it brought her no solace. To make matters worse, she had no idea whether her right arm would ever regain its strength.

A slight breeze picked up, blowing through her blouse and cooling her skin. Beck took in a deep breath and picked up a familiar scent on the wind.

"Good morning, Drake," she said without looking his way. It was strange – she couldn't look at the man without feeling guilty for something she hadn't even done. It was why she'd thrown herself so wholeheartedly into the defence of New Sev'relain, and it was why she hadn't fucked the captain since their return. Beck knew he wanted it, and she wanted it too, but the Inquisition had given her new orders, and those orders were going to cause Drake pain.

"How's the arm?" Drake said. Beck hadn't told him about her problems, but the man was too damned perceptive for his own good.

"How's the crown?" she shot back.

"Heavy," Drake conceded. "Can't really call it a crown just yet though. Any fool with a slip of land and a few mouths to feed can call himself a king. It takes recognition to really sit a throne. I need Sarth and the Five Kingdoms to recognise us as legitimate, not just a bunch of criminals to be stepped on."

Drake sat down in the sand next to Beck, and she couldn't help but notice him staring at her cleavage. The man could be subtle when he wanted to be; he could also be as blatant as an open wound, and Beck wagered that was also by design.

"Nice secluded spot you found here," Drake said.

Beck readied herself for an argument she didn't want. "Tell me about the Drurr."

Drake went from hot to cold in an instant, and Beck could feel his frustration. But some things were more important than the pirate's feelings, and she needed to know how much he knew about the Drurr.

"Ain't important," he said sullenly. "Nice way to kill the mood though, eh?"

"It is important, Drake. As far as we know, you're the only person ever to have escaped the Drurr. You've… seen things. You probably know more about the Drurr than anyone. We need to know what you know."

"*We*," Drake echoed with a bitter laugh. "You mean the Inquisition?"

"Yes."

"You have a way of contacting them?"

Beck said nothing. The Inquisition's methods of remaining in contact with their Arbiters had always been kept secret. Arbiter Darkheart severing their old lines of communication had only made the Inquisitors even more determined to secrecy with their new methods.

"Well, I don't give a fuck what your Inquisition wants, Arbiter," Drake said. "But if it's you who wants to know, then ask away."

There were a hundred questions the Inquisition wanted her to extract the answers to. There were some Beck wanted to know herself.

"The matriarch. Who is she, and why is she after you?"

"Did you know the Drurr used to rule over us like slaves?" Drake said. "At least, until the Dread Lords broke their civilisation and your Inquisition hunted them nearly to extinction. You drove them all underground, but you far from finished them off. It's fair to say they ain't too pleased about their current standing in the world. Most of them would like nothing more than to rise up and crush us all beneath their heels for a second time.

"But they can't do that. Life is hard underground in the dark places the Drurr inhabit, Arbiter. There are things down there. Monsters your Inquisition hasn't wiped out yet. They walk right out of the walls and snatch children from their beds. Some of them digest their food before eating it. Folk still alive with their skin melting…"

Beck glanced sideways at Drake. Tears were welling up in his eyes. She'd known her questions would cause him pain, but she'd never thought to see the man cry.

"They still take slaves," Drake continued. "Pretty much as many as they can. For the most part the slaves are given the worst jobs. Mining out new areas, harvesting the fungi, scouting out the darkness when new tunnels are unearthed, feeding the trolls, being fed to the trolls. Pretty much anything the Drurr don't want to do themselves, or anything deemed too dangerous to risk a Drurr life.

"The matriarch who…" Drake trailed off, and for a while said nothing. "The bitch who owned me was a sadistic fuck. She liked to pull the odd slave from the deepest, darkest of jobs and treat them with kindness. Make them grateful to her. She wanted to make them love her. Then she'd have them tortured. Nothing permanent – she wanted her pets whole."

Drake shuddered, and Beck resisted the urge to comfort him.

"She'd torture them, then save them and treat them kind, like a lover, to make them love her again. Then she'd send them back for more torture. I reckon it was some sort of game to her. See how many times she could break a person before there was nothing of them left. I saw people kill themselves by biting open their own wrists just to escape the cycle of torment. Never saw anyone try to kill the bitch though. They all loved her too much, I guess. Despite what was done." He sniffed loudly and fell silent.

"How did you escape?"

"Not all Drurr are evil fucked-up bastards bent on slaving and torturing us *lesser* folk. There's plenty of them ain't like that, and they find some of the things the others do as deplorable as we do. I managed to find one of these sympathisers and convinced them to help me escape."

"What about the other slaves?"

"What about them? This ain't like the Black Thorn's liberation of Solantis, Arbiter. I couldn't just open a few cages and tell the slaves to fight for their freedom. I sneaked out as quietly as possible and never looked back."

"What is it like underground?"

"Dark. They don't use torches. Instead they mine these crystals and infuse them with some sort of magic that makes them glow. It's a soft light, reaches a fair ways, but it's far from bright. After a few years underground the sun is… blinding. And if you ever find yourself without one of those glowy crystals…" Drake paused and let out a bitter bark of laughter. "The darkness is complete, and there's things down there that come out when it gets that dark. Things that whisper and click and purr.

"Folk are kept in pens, like sheep. They get let out when their services are needed, like mining. The trolls do the digging, but they ain't exactly suited to delicate work, so the Drurr use slaves to mine the tunnels once they're dug. They use slaves to collect the shrooms too. It's pretty much all they eat, and there's whole caverns dedicated to growing the rubbery things. Strange thing is, some of the shrooms have a glow all of their own, light up the cavern. The shroom caverns would probably be the safest place down there if not for the Choomar."

"Choomar?"

"It's a Drurr word. Doesn't really have a translation, but the Choomar are… aggressive shrooms. They're edible like the others, but the Drurr don't eat them – they try to eradicate them. The Choomar look just like dark-root shrooms, almost exactly like, but they release spores that grow inside of a person and control them. Folk start acting strange when they're infested. They walk and talk pretty much like normal, but they start doing odd things when they think no one's watching. They gnaw on their own digits and scratch themselves bloody, like they got an itch that just won't quit. Then they start to get violent. Only against the Drurr though. I never heard of a Choomar-infected slave attacking any of the others.

"I once saw one of the poor bastards leap at a passing patriarch, biting and clawing until a couple of guards pulled him away. They started beating on him, and he screamed bloody murder and then his head just popped."

Beck glanced at Drake. His expression was deadly serious. She knew just how loose the pirate liked to play with the truth, but there were some things a person couldn't fake, and reliving the horrors of his life underground seemed to be one of them for Drake.

"What about the Drurr," she said. "How do they live?"

Drake smiled. "Like kings and queens. They build great caverns underground, hundreds of feet high, and their homes are built into the very walls all the way up to the roof. The matriarchs and patriarchs live the highest, and those in favour live close to them. The closer to the ground you are, the less important you are.

"Sometimes, while she slept, I used to stare out the window at the great cavern of Bolimar spread out below me. The little lights on the cavern floor where traders made their wares, the fighting pits where slaves were fed to trolls for the amusement of their owners. From up high it was beautiful." He sighed. "Why the questions all of a sudden, Arbiter? You've been content without the answers for a good long while, yet now you've a pressing need to know."

"I believe they're here," Beck said before she could stop herself.

"The Inquisition has spies all over the world, and some have reported seeing a Drurr corsair sailing the waters of the isles."

Drake's jaw set, and he turned hostile eyes on Beck. "How long ago did you hear about this?"

"A few days," she admitted.

"And you're just telling me now." He snorted. "Only one reason the bastards would come here."

Drake launched to his feet and started walking down the beach. Beck gathered her dropped pistols and rushed after him. "Where are we going?" she said.

"To find them before they find me."

Starry Dawn

Things were moving quickly for Elaina. It had been just one week since she'd arrived in Larkos, and one week since the traitorous cur, Rovel, had stolen her ship out from under her. In that week she'd met with four of the thirteen guilds.

Brother Hernhold was first. Elaina had no wish to become his ally if she could help it. The Cleric was as pious as his guild name, as was every single one of their order. They worshipped Pelsing, the golden god of the Five Kingdoms, and every aspect of their lives was given over to worship or earning gold, which happened to be one of the forms of worship.

Hernhold had extended a gracious offer to introduce Elaina to the Council of Thirteen as his very own honoured guest, and claimed he would back her bid for aid in the form of both ships and men. The problem with men who worshipped the golden god, as far as Elaina knew them, was that everything was a business transaction and they gave nothing away for free. She had no doubt the Clerics could, and would, help her, but they would extract a hefty price for that aid sometime in the future. If there was one thing life as a pirate had impressed upon Elaina, it was that it's always best to take as much as possible without giving anything back.

Elaina's second offer of help had come from the Nightborne. Their leader was Red, an Acanthian woman with fiery hair and not an ounce of fat on her. She was slim and no taller than Elaina, but she appeared to be made all from muscle, sinew, and bone. She talked in a distant, emotionless voice, and regarded Elaina in much the same way she imagined a dragon would regard a goat. Elaina had taken an instant dislike to the woman and the guild she represented.

The Nightborne were notorious for their questionable rituals, and Elaina had even heard rumours they drained the blood of the criminals they arrested to be served instead of wine at their banquets. The Nightborne had offered Elaina a deal very similar to the Clerics', but also threw in deep connections to the Guild in Acanthia. It was a sweet deal, and no mistake. But despite their power and prestige, Elaina wanted nothing to do with the Acanthian Guild.

On the third day of her stay in Larkos the leader of the Red Hands came to her himself. Terk Ferrywold was a brute of a man who walked around topless, despite the chill, in order to show off his muscled, well-oiled chest. It wasn't a fashion Elaina found attractive. The man appeared to be all bluster. He ordered drinks for the entire tavern and a hearty meal for himself and Elaina. She'd picked at the food while Terk stuffed as much meat down his throat as he was able, all while attempting to impress upon Elaina the importance and power of his guild.

The Red Hands ran the Moon district, a large and wealthy housing area just west of central, and they were no doubt both rich and powerful, but Elaina didn't agree with their leader's need to shout about the impressiveness of his own guild. Terk had offered Elaina ships and men, and the God Emperor of Sarth's head upon a pike. He'd also suggested that he and Elaina seal their deal amidst the silken sheets of his bed. Elaina had resisted the urge to beat him senseless with her tankard and agreed to think about his proposal. In truth she would rather have sided with the pious Clerics.

The fifth day in Larkos brought with it an emissary from the slaving guild. He was a huge man, as fat as he was tall, and he was certainly tall. He waddled into the tavern surrounded by guards who were no doubt needed to protect his obvious wealth. The man wore gemstone rings on every finger and had a variety of piercings all over his face, each ring and stud sporting a hefty jewel. The fat man announced himself as Orkus Uon, ambassador and messenger of Somolous Tain, the head of the slaving guild. Elaina despised those who traded in flesh, but she couldn't afford to make any enemies among the Council of Thirteen so agreed to hear Orkus out.

The slaving guild were unique amidst the others, in that Larkos wasn't their only place of operation. They had holdings in almost every major city in the known world, except those that outlawed slavery, and the connections and manpower they could give to Elaina eclipsed those of any of the other guilds. But Orkus didn't offer to help win the pirate's war so much as make veiled threats over what would happen if Elaina picked any of the other guilds. The slavers could make for excellent allies, but they could also make for very dangerous enemies. Despite the threat, Elaina couldn't bring herself to take help from those who peddled flesh.

On the sixth day, an emissary from the Blades walked through the tavern door. The boy was tall and slim with a bald head, and had a slight chubbiness that suggested he hadn't yet finished his growth. He greeted Elaina warmly and informed her that the Queen of Blades had requested her presence. Elaina grinned at the boy and stayed in her seat, determined to make him wait while she finished her breakfast and ale. The Queen of Blades had turned her away once, and Elaina would be damned before she went running just because the bitch had changed her tune. Rather than show frustration at the delay, the emissary stood by and waited patiently.

When Elaina finally decided it was time to meet the leader of the Blades she called for her four remaining crew and sent them on their errands. Pavel would meet with the Clerics again – they paid good coin to hear sermons from a travelling priest of their golden god, and though Elaina hated to admit it, they needed the bits. She sent Alfer to the gate district to meet with the Scarred Men and broker an audience with the Scarred Man, and she had Pollick sitting on the docks to watch the ships sail in. The man had the sharpest eyes of the lot of them, and Elaina needed to know the moment anyone they knew sailed into port.

The Blades emissary had two horses waiting outside the tavern and bid Elaina mount one as he easily swung his arse up onto the other. Elaina followed suit, and before long they were moving through the streets of Larkos at a canter, heading ever more steadily towards the central district where the Queen of Blades held court.

When they arrived at the same gate Elaina had so recently been turned away from, the young emissary leapt off his horse to exchange words with the guards. Elaina didn't hear what was said, but there seemed little to no argument and this time the gates opened for her, revealing the central district for the first time.

Elaina wasn't sure what she'd expected, but the central district wasn't it. The streets were empty and clean, and most of the place appeared to be open land given over to green gardens of grass or cobbled squares built around central podiums. Of buildings she saw little other than warehouses, a few houses, and a lot of temples built tall and proud to a variety of gods. Elaina even recognised one dedicated to Rin. It was hard to miss the spectacle floating on its very own saltwater lake – to build a shrine to the sea goddess upon solid land would be an insult the bitch would likely take personally.

In the centre of the district – and indeed the centre of the city – stood the great guild hall, the meeting place of the Council of Thirteen. Elaina found herself staring up at the giant building in wonder. It was larger than the grandest temple she'd ever seen and its curved walls were supported by many stone struts, almost like legs, that peeled away from the building to plunge into the ground. At the far end, a single tower rose even higher into the sky. The tip of it was flat, and Elaina wagered the view from that point was spectacular. When viewed from a distance the great guild hall looked much like a scorpion, poised and ready to strike at the unwary. She wondered what it looked like on the inside, what sort of treasures were hidden within, ripe for a bit of plundering.

The emissary turned them away, towards a smaller structure built all of white marble. A wall surrounded the grounds of this new building, and a number of guards patrolled leisurely around the outside of that wall. As they passed through an open gate, Elaina saw the grounds were festooned with small gardens, pools of still water, and odd bird-feeding devices. Never having paid too much attention to birds, Elaina could only name a few, and there were many more she couldn't hope to identify here. Some bathed in pools while others fed, and even more flew around the building or rested upon the white stone.

Another boy, not quite as tall but obviously of a similar age and also with a bald head, rushed out of the building and took hold of the emissary's horse. Elaina leapt down from her mount and the boy led both horses back out the way they'd come.

"This way, Captain Black," the emissary said with a smile. "I believe the Queen will see you right away."

"I should hope so," Elaina said, following the lad through the arch that led into the building. "Already been turned away once, eh."

Inside, the building was white and spotless. Green plants as tall as Elaina grew in pots near almost every wall, and those not adorned with the vegetation sported benches, a few of which were occupied with folk looking so serene it sent shivers up and down Elaina's spine. A number of doorways led off to rooms on each side of the hall, and at the far end there was a pool with ten people lounging about in its crystal blue waters. The place seemed more like an upmarket pleasure house, the type a person might find in Sarth, than the hall of one of the most prestigious guilds in Larkos.

"So where is she?" Elaina said, eager to hear what the Queen of Blades had to say and just as eager to be away from the place.

"I will let her know you have arrived, Captain Black," the emissary said. "Please wait just a short while."

Elaina snorted, trying to give the impression she didn't care. She'd never felt at home in places like this, and she included the whole city in that sentiment. The Blacks were all born to be aboard a ship, and surrounded by wood holding back water was where Elaina would always be most comfortable. She loved cities like Larkos for the freedom and distractions they offered, but she loved them in small doses.

"Captain Black," said a voice that passed through Elaina like the tingle she got from a good finger of rum.

Elaina turned to find a tall woman in a green dress that hugged her figure and left nothing, not even the knives sewn into the fabric, to the imagination. Where some women might wear a fur about their shoulders, this one wore a wreath of blades all shining and, Elaina wagered, razor sharp. Even the woman's jewellery was shaped in the fashion of little knives. Elaina wondered how many people would die if she took to a dance in a crowded room.

Yet it wasn't the vast amount of weaponry – including a long, slender sword buckled around her waist as well as all the knives – that convinced Elaina this was the Queen of Blades. It was her face. Elaina had only ever met one Drurr before, but the man had left an impression – and so did this woman. She was beautiful – not just the type of beautiful that turns heads, but the type that breaks hearts with a mere glance. Elaina felt a strange sorrow simply from looking at the Queen of Blades, and she knew that if she could just get closer to the woman, if she could just earn her approval, that sorrow would turn to unbridled joy. At a closer look, the Queen of Blades' face was distinctly Drurr. Her skin was too pale and too tight across her cheeks and nose, and her mouth was too wide and contained too many teeth. Her eyes were beyond dark; they held no colour at all, only bottomless black. Her hair cascaded down her back over the wreath of blades, and seemed to change colour as Elaina stared; one moment it was almost as dark as her own, and the next it was a shining red like freshly spilled blood.

Elaina realised she hadn't spoken – she hadn't even breathed – since she'd looked upon the Drurr. She let out a ragged breath and then quickly sucked in another lungful. Her eyes felt moist, and they weren't the only part of her. Elaina's heart was racing, and she just wanted this woman to love her.

"Captain Black?" the Queen of Blades said.

"What is this?" Elaina's voice quavered, pathetic. She wanted to drop to her knees and worship the woman. Only her pride stopped her. She was the daughter of Tanner Black, and she would worship no one. Elaina clenched her fists, digging her nails into her palms, using the pain as an anchor against the wave of love that was attempting to sweep away her sanity.

"It is a glamour, and quite a powerful one," the Queen of Blades said with a wide smile that enhanced her beauty despite the wolfishness of it. "I'm impressed you are able to withstand it."

Elaina wasn't sure what a glamour was, nor was she certain she was withstanding it. Her mouth felt dry, and she couldn't even blink her eyes for the fear that she might miss a moment of the Queen's grace.

Elaina staggered and tore her eyes away from the Drurr, furiously blinking away her tears and struggling to get her breathing under control. Her heart hammered in her ears, her knees wobbled, and her stomach was ripe with the fluttery feeling she got every time she saw Keelin.

Straightening her back and taking a deep, calming breath, Elaina looked up at the Queen again. The woman was still beautiful – there could never be any doubt of that – but the crushing feeling of love was gone. Instead, Elaina felt sadness at the loss of such a deep adoration.

She had no idea how the Drurr could do such a thing, but she hated that any person could have so much power over her emotions.

"What did you do to me?" Elaina shouted, unable to control her rage. Her hand went to her sword hilt before she realised what she was doing.

"I would advise against any acts of aggression, Captain Black," the Queen of Blades purred. "I assure you, you would not survive it. It was magic both subtle and blatant all at once."

Elaina barely understood a word the woman was saying. "How dare you!"

"I dare that and much much more, Captain Black," the Queen said, her voice now cold and heartless. "It was a test, and it pleases me that you passed where countless others have failed. Now, I understand you are currently a little on edge. Would you like a moment to calm yourself? We have much to discuss."

Elaina shook the cobwebs from her head and glared at the woman. She wanted to tear the Drurr's head off and tear down her entire guild while she was at it, but common sense won out.

She shook her head. "Then we'd best get to the discussing. Don't you dare use that glamour shit on me again."

"And exactly what would you do if I did?" the Drurr said with a wide, toothy smile. "You are entirely at my mercy, Captain Black."

"I ain't at no one's mercy, and you'd do well to curry my favour rather than coerce it."

The Queen of Blades laughed. "I like your fire, Captain Black, but I negotiate how I will regardless of your preferences. Come, let us take a seat while we discuss. Would you like some wine?"

Elaina would have liked to decline the offer, but her throat was dry and she needed a drink to fortify her nerves. She nodded and followed the Drurr into one of the chambers to the side of the hall. This new room appeared to be an aviary of sorts, with birds of a hundred different kinds littered about the place, some caged and some not. A hole in the roof allowed them to fly free if they wished – at least, those not in cages – and a number of the winged beasts were sipping from a small fountain that bubbled away merrily in one corner. In the centre of the room was a low, ring-shaped bench. The Queen of Blades moved over to it and gestured for Elaina to join her.

"Birds, huh?" Elaina said, still trying to control her emotions. "My ma has monkeys. Lots and lots of monkeys. She treats them like they're all old friends."

"I like birds," the Queen said. "They have a grace and attentiveness that very few other animals do. Their variety and individuality are akin to our own and…"

"Our own?" Elaina said. "You mean Drurr or human?"

"Both," the Queen said with a smile. "We are far more alike than you realise, Captain Black. Ah, the wine is here. I own the vineyard, so I can assure you it is of excellent quality."

Elaina accepted the glass from yet another pudgy boy-like man and sipped at it. The taste was pleasant, but she wasn't the type of person who could tell the difference between good wine and poor. She preferred her drinks in the form of fiery rum or bitter ale whenever possible.

"I've been offered ships and the men to sail and fight aboard them by four other guilds," Elaina said, wishing to get right into the negotiations so she could be away from the Queen of Blades as soon as possible. The woman's beauty was a constant reminder of the false love Elaina had felt, and the absence of that love felt very much like a broken heart.

"Straight to the point. You pirates are direct. I have some questions for you first, Captain Black. When you requested an audience, you introduced yourself to my Blades as the future queen of the Pirate Isles."

"Aye," Elaina said. It had been a rash claim. The idea had grown on her since leaving Chade, and she'd decided that Rose was right; Elaina would make an excellent queen of the isles. More than that, though, Elaina had realised it was something that she wanted.

"And how can you be queen when you do not even have a ship?"

Elaina had prepared herself for the question. "My ship is away on my business. It will be back when I need it."

The Queen of Blades let out a chuckle and sipped on her wine. "That lie may convince some, Captain Black. Should I still be calling you captain? But you will not pull the blanket over my eyes. The *Starry*

Dawn did not leave Larkos by your leave and is not currently under your command."

"Just a temporary setback," Elaina said, dropping the bluff immediately. "She'll be back under my boots soon enough. It don't change my position one drop."

"Hmmm. And what of Drake Morrass? I hear he is first in line for the pirate throne."

"Morrass is dead," Elaina said quickly. "Killed on Ash. My da is ready to plant his arse on the throne, and I'm the heir."

"You are woefully misinformed, Captain. Drake not only survived your father's little trap, but also convinced him to take a knee. He has yet to officially claim a kingdom or his crown, which I must say has me a little confused."

Elaina clenched her jaw. She couldn't imagine her father kneeling to Drake, nor even working with him. If the Queen of Blades was telling the truth it meant things must have gone sideways, and she now wondered what sort of place she would be sailing back to once she reclaimed her ship.

"Do you still claim yourself to be the future queen?" the leader of the Blades said, with a slight lift of her eyebrow that only served to make her look even less human.

Elaina shifted on the bench. She could drop her claims now and look even more foolish, or she could stick to her course. Confidence had always been one of her strengths, and she refused to look weak to the Drurr bitch.

"Aye. I got the backing of the Wilds. One way or another, you're looking at the queen of the isles."

"The backing of the Wilds? I assume you are speaking of the Lord and Lady of Chade?" The Queen tilted her head, the motion sending her hair shimmering into a strange shade of blue.

Elaina nodded with a smirk.

"Quite the endorsement. The bloodeds' days are numbered, and it appears nothing will stop Rose and her Black Thorn uniting their lands. They have supplied you with sufficient leverage to take the throne beside Morrass?"

"Aye, they gave me… eh? Beside Morrass?"

"The king will need a queen, no?"

"I ain't marrying that slimy sack of rat gut," Elaina all but shouted, and then drained off the last of her wine in one angry swallow. She'd been so certain Drake was dead, so certain she'd return as Tanner Black's heir.

The Queen of Blades sipped at her wine and watched Elaina silently. She'd already decided she wanted to be queen of the Pirate Isles. Ever since Rose had suggested the possibility to her, it had been a constant desire playing on her mind. If she was queen, then her father would have to respect her, and she could order that twice-damned first mate of his hanged for his previous crimes against her. She would be able to take Keelin as her husband too, if she decided she still wanted him. Elaina knew she could have everything she wanted if she could just get her own arse on the throne. She took a deep breath and released it slowly, attempting to calm herself. She plastered a smile on her face and met the Queen of Blades' black eyes.

"It seems you have reached a decision," the Drurr said, with no small amount of amusement.

"Aye," Elaina said. "I'd fuck Morrass to sit beside him on the throne. I've already got the Wilds' support, and I want Larkos' too. So how about you go and sell yourself to me, eh? Tell me why I should pick you over the other guilds."

The Queen of Blades smiled wide, showing off far too many teeth. "I prefer to discuss what you may offer to me."

"I offer the same thing as to any of the guilds. Unhindered passage through our waters, the support and friendship of the isles in times of crisis, and first pick to your guild of any of the wares that my people bring to Larkos."

"That is no small offer," the Queen said seriously. "This is all dependent on your ascendency to the throne?"

"Aye. You'll be backing me, not the isles. So why the fuck should I choose you?"

The Queen waved to her attendant, who quickly came forward and refilled the wine glasses. "I can offer you something the other guilds cannot, Captain Black. I can offer you the support of Larkos, not just one of our guilds."

"Ain't that what they're all offering?"

"No. Make no mistake in my fellows' offers. They will give you the support of their own guilds and whatever forces they can muster – likely a single ship, or maybe two – but only two of us have the power to cajole the rest of the Council into unified action – the Scarred Man, and me."

"So what's to stop…"

"The Scarred Man will not see you. You have already sent him one request, which he has ignored, and he will continue to ignore any further attempts. More rigid than rock is that one, and often I believe him carved from it. He will, however, respond to my advances. We have an arrangement, and between us, and those allied with us, we can sway almost any vote at the Council. No other guild can claim the same."

Elaina made a show of sipping at her wine and regarding the Queen of Blades over the glass. She already knew she would choose the Blades as her ally. She'd known it from the moment she sailed into Larkos. They were powerful, they controlled the central district, and her father had specifically told her to gain the Blades' favour.

"Reckon we have an accord," she said with a grin.

"Excellent. There is a Council meeting in just a few days, as I am sure you already know, and I will escort you along as my guest and back your request. We shall see just how much support the other guilds are willing to give you, but I expect it will be more than the ten ships you secured from Rose."

"I never told you how many ships Rose offered me," Elaina said.

"No, you did not." The Queen of Blades smiled.

Elaina continued to sip at her wine as the Queen instructed her on how she should present herself to the Council of Thirteen. It dawned on her that she'd just agreed to marry Drake Morrass, before he himself knew anything about it. Worse, though, was that she'd just *agreed* to marry Drake Morrass. Still, once they were wed and her arse was well and truly polishing the pirate throne, there was nothing to stop her king from having a tragic accident.

The Phoenix

"See anyone we know?" Keelin said as they floated in the bay, waiting for a spot to open up. It seemed Larkos was in a busy period, and every berth was currently in use either for loading or unloading. They had a hold full of pirated loot and a burning need to get it sold before some of it spoiled.

"Depends on your definition, Captain," said Morley. "I see the *Bloody Bride*."

Keelin knew the ship well. It had belonged to Arip Winters until the fool docked in Solantis during the slave uprising. Nobody knew if it was angry slaves or mercenaries attempting to flee the chaos, but someone had busted their way onto Arip's ship and slaughtered him and half his crew. A couple of months later the *Bride* sailed into Fortune's Rest under the command of a drunkard and his five friends. Drake purchased the ship for just a few bits and gave command to his first mate, Zothus. Keelin wondered how much of the rigging was made from the silk spun by that horrific giant spider Zothus kept around. He shuddered just thinking about it.

A small dinghy made its way towards them, rowed by four iron-collared brutes who looked a lot like rowing was their sole purpose in life. In the back of the boat, steering it, was a bored-looking young man with a ridiculously pointed beard and the air of someone who thought he was in charge of something.

"Ho there," Keelin shouted down as the dinghy bumped against the hull of *The Phoenix*. "What can we do for you?"

The man with the pointed beard rose easily to his feet despite the rocking of the dinghy. "Are you the captain of this vessel?"

"Aye."

"We have a berth opening up soon, but I'll need to inspect your cargo before I can assign it to you."

"By all means, come aboard." Keelin turned to Smithe, who was lingering nearby. "Get the barrels of spice moved to the galley's food stores quickly, then show the leech everything in the hold."

Smithe frowned for a moment before breaking into a grin. He ran for the nearest hatch below, recruiting a few of the crew as he went. The surly quartermaster almost seemed a different man since he'd brought Keelin the chart of the seas around the Forgotten Empire. Keelin would never trust the fool, no matter how competent he became at his job, but at least Smithe was tolerable these days, and he truly did seem to have the crew's best interests at heart.

The inspection went much as Keelin had expected. First the inspector looked around the hold and noted down goods and numbers in his little book. Then he asked how *The Phoenix* had come by the goods, and Keelin took great pleasure in telling the man of the ships they'd robbed. The tax the inspector laid down on them was extortionate, but Keelin knew full well what time of the five-year cycle it was, and the Clerics were no doubt busy extracting every bit of coin they could from all those who docked at Larkos. Luckily the most valuable cargo they were carrying was the spices, and of them the inspector found not a trace.

They were promptly towed into their assigned berth, and merchants appeared to browse the pirated items before the ship was even tied off. Keelin let them all aboard and held an auction for the less valuable goods. He always found it best to let the fools bid against each other with little to no involvement from himself. After the auctions were done, he invited some of the richer merchants into his cabin to discuss the prices of his more exotic items. Aimi accompanied him, because her head for numbers was impressive, as was her attention to detail. She'd long since taken over the job of keeping the ship's books up to date.

After they'd found a buyer for the spices, Keelin gave Smithe permission to hand out the ship's pay – ten silver bits per sailor. The crew seemed more than happy, and well they should; it was almost twice as much as most pirates would have received for their part in the taking. Smithe organised which of the crew had first, second, and third chances at going ashore, and for the first time in as long as Keelin could remember, everyone seemed pleased.

Watching Aimi depart the ship with Jojo and Feather and a number of other pirates, Keelin took in a deep breath of the salty air of Larkos' bay and steeled himself for the next, and most important, job of his stay in the city. Unlike his crew, Keelin wouldn't have the luxury of relaxing ashore; he was here for work.

The day was just starting to darken when he summoned Kebble and Morley to his cabin. He had three cups of rum ready and waiting when the two men entered. Kebble had miraculously made a full recovery from his injuries at the battle for New Sev'relain, despite the doc pronouncing him dead on at least one occasion. Morley, on the other hand, wore his scars on the inside, and it was clear to Keelin that his first mate was letting doubts about his captain creep into his heart.

"Sit down and take a mug," Keelin said.

Morley glanced at Kebble suspiciously. Though the marksman wasn't a true member of the crew, undertaking none of the responsibilities or duties for sailing the ship, he'd proven himself an excellent warrior and an invaluable man to have around. Even Morley couldn't deny that.

"Drake tasked me with finding folk to sail and fight and settle on our isles," Keelin said once both men were sitting and sipping. "Now, he reckoned my best bet was to appeal to the guilds, try to make them support us. I ain't doing that."

Morley smiled. "'Bout time ya started thinking for yaself again, Captan."

Keelin let the insult slide. "I've got a better idea. I'm going to buy the people we need."

"What?" Morley snapped.

Kebble remained damningly silent.

"Captan," Morley continued once he'd glanced sideways and seen the dark expression on Kebble's face, "ya can't mean to participate in slavery. Ain't a man in the isles would forgive you for it, least of all Morrass. I may not like the man, but his policy on slavers is something we should all look up to."

"I ain't looking to turn slaver," Keelin said loudly, fixing both men with a stare. "I'm looking to turn liberator."

"Eh?" Morley said.

A sly smile spread across Kebble's face.

"I figure we buy the folk from the slavers guild, sail them down to the isles, and tell them they're free to do whatever the fuck they please. They can hop the next ship going anywhere, or they can help us build and help us fight. I'm saying we give them the chance to start life anew and build something for themselves with us."

Morley drained his mug and reached for the bottle, pouring himself a large portion that just so happened to empty the bottle. Keelin smiled as he opened his drawer and took out another. Lubrication could only serve to help his argument.

"Thoughts?" Keelin prompted when it looked like neither of the men was going to say anything.

"Slavers guild don't take kindly to folk freeing their property," Morley said.

"I intend to make them no one's property," Keelin said.

"Kind of the point, Captan. Even once they're bought, slavers don't like folk freeing slaves. Bad for business. The isles got a fuck load of freed slaves already – more might raise the bastards' ire."

"I reckon that ire is likely already raised, Morley. Drake ordered our lot to start pirating the slavers to free their cargo."

"One more reason not to visit the slavers guild, Captan."

Keelin sighed. "I'm hoping news of it hasn't reached them yet." It was a circular argument at best.

"How will we get them to the isles?" Morley continued. "You promised the crew the next stop would be riches beyond imagining. I don't think they'll take kindly to more delays."

"Next for us is the Forgotten Empire, Morley. I haven't forgotten, and nor do I intend to change that plan. I will hire ships to transport the folk we purchase to the isles. I may even be able to convince Zothus to accompany them."

Morley sat back in his chair, sipping at the rum. His face was caught between outright refusal and the need for the plan to work. He knew as well as Keelin that there was no better way to get the reinforcements they needed.

"Kebble?" Keelin said.

"A sound plan," Kebble said as he smoothed down his moustache. "Far more likely than convincing the guilds of Larkos to help. Their time of change will soon be upon them, and it is past unlikely any of them will stick their necks out for us, even should we throw Drake's name around. The slaving guild has polluted this world for far too long, and any move to undermine them should be welcomed."

Both Keelin and Morley were staring at Kebble. "Uh, right. Just what I was thinking," Keelin said. "Are we agreed then?"

"Is it required, Captain?" Morley said.

"Well, I'd like you both to come with me to the slavers guild. Backup and a united front, I reckon."

"Aye," said Kebble.

Morley chewed on his mug for a moment before nodding. "Aye, Captain."

Aimi followed along behind the crew, happy to hang at the back with Jojo. She'd been to Larkos before, but never as a woman. The last time, she'd been posing as a ship's boy, and that presented a whole different problem in the form of her crewmates buying her time with a whore and expecting her to do the deed.

Aimi had taken the woman to a room and, once the door was firmly closed, explained her situation. Luckily the whore was quite accommodating, and if anything seemed pleased that all she had to do to earn her pay was sit and do nothing. They'd chatted for quite some time until someone started hammering on the door. The whore arranged herself on the bed like she'd just received the best fuck of her life, and Aimi opened the door to find her crew cheering and whooping. She received quite the reputation after that for being hung like a particularly well-endowed horse. The memory brought a smile to her face.

The folk they passed gave the pirates a wide berth, all except those attempting to sell them junk, and plenty of stares were levelled their way. Sailors weren't uncommon on the docks of Larkos, but the crew of *The Phoenix* were new and that garnered attention. Some folk wondered if they would cause trouble, while others wondered how well they could deal with trouble. It was always the same with pirate crews in civilised ports.

"Stick with us," Jojo said quietly. "Pirates alone are easy pickings for authorities and thieves alike."

"It ain't my first time," Aimi said. She caught the eye of a tall man dressed in a robe with a heavy cudgel hanging from his belt.

"The Clerics are a lenient bunch when it comes to punishment, but not so much when it comes to crime," Jojo rasped. "They would happily arrest us all for little to no offence."

Laughter broke out from a couple of the crew ahead of them, and Feather dropped back, a wide grin on his face.

"Usually it's tradition ta buy the newest member of the group a good fuck," Feather said to Aimi. "But it's been decided that might not please the Cap'n too well, given that he seems to want you all to himself."

"It might not please me either," Aimi said with a scowl. "Any of you dumb fucks think of that?"

The laughter from up front fell silent.

"How about a tavern instead," Aimi continued. "First round is on me."

That got her crewmates cheering and laughing again, and Feather gave her a friendly punch on the arm. Aimi looked over at Jojo to find him smiling at her.

"That was well done."

The group turned towards a nearby tavern with a giant anchor resting outside the door. Aimi narrowed her eyes at Jojo. "Never seen you go ashore before," she said.

"You've not been with us for long, and never out of the isles before," Jojo countered.

"Still…" Aimi sniffed loudly. "The Cap'n send you?"

Jojo smiled.

"I don't need looking after."

"I agree," Jojo said.

"But Keelin doesn't."

Jojo shrugged as they arrived at the doorway to the Anchorage. "It's not my place to say what the captain thinks."

Aimi felt her mood sour a little. She wasn't some dainty lass who had never got her hands dirty, and she knew full well how to look after herself. She'd survived for years among pirates, first as a boy and then later as a woman, and not once had she got herself into any trouble she couldn't get herself out of. Except for that one time with Captain Ollo's left boot, but Aimi didn't truly count that one as it had only been half her doing.

The tavern was large and loud and well lit, with a crackling fire and plenty of lamps to show just what sort of clientele frequented it, and one and all they looked salty. Some looked up at the newcomers, while others were either far too occupied with their own business or far too occupied with their own unconsciousness. The bar was long and polished to a shine with a bear of man standing behind it. Behind him were row upon row and stack upon stack of kegs. Aimi had seen the inside of a fair number of taverns, but never had she seen one so well stocked. Each keg had a name scrawled upon the wood, and they ranged from the flamboyant to the downright ridiculous. She decided right there and then that she would try Yellow Maid of the Sea before the night was out.

The crew shuffled over to a couple of empty tables and claimed them for *The Phoenix*. A musician picked up a lute and started to play as the first round of drinks arrived, and before long they were all drinking and talking. Feather even gave them a taste of his dancing skills, though the man behind the bar scowled at the boy for jumping up onto the table. The conversation was free and easy, and Aimi found herself joining in more often than not. It seemed the crew of *The Phoenix* had accepted her just as she had accepted them. They worked their way through a good number of tankards, and as their purses got lighter, their voices got louder.

"Cap'n knows what he's doing," said Fremen, the navigator. By all accounts the man had been with Keelin from the very beginning and placed unlimited trust in him.

"Captain's an arse," Aimi said loudly, and waved her tankard around the room to make her point. She was angry at Keelin for sending Jojo to look after her, and finding it a little hard to shake that anger.

"You'd know," Jotin said with a wink.

"I do know," Aimi said. "I know better than anyone."

Jojo placed a hand on Aimi's arm, but she pulled away.

"We've known the Cap'n for longer," insisted Fremen. "Hells, even Feather's known him longer. Probably like to know him as well as you though."

"I do know him well," Aimi said as she slammed her almost empty tankard onto the table. "I know he's an arse."

Everyone laughed. Even Jojo joined in with a chuckle.

"All captains are arses," said a big bald man from a nearby table. "Part of the fucking job description, eh?" That earned another round of laughter.

"What ship are ya from, lads?" asked Feather of the sailors who had hijacked their conversation.

"*Barely West*," said another of the crew, this one tall and slim with sandy-coloured fluff on his chin.

"That name sound familiar to you?" Jojo asked Jotin quietly, a shadowed look on his dark face.

Aimi thought about it, but she couldn't say she'd ever heard of the ship. Though that wasn't surprising – there were plenty plus a lot more ships she'd never heard of.

"Well met ta ya, boys," Feather said loudly. "The crew of *The Phoenix* drink with you."

Feather and Fremen and most of the rest of the crew raised their tankards to their mouths and drank heavily, and, not wanting to be left out, Aimi followed their lead. She gulped down the last of her ale and slammed the mug onto the table with a refreshed sigh. It took her a moment to realise the crew from *Barely West* had risen to their feet, and there were no more smiles to go around.

"Is that meant to be some sort of joke?" the big bald man snarled.

"I assure you it isn't," Feather said, putting down his own mug and standing.

"We took their ship a year back," Jotin said, a moment before the first fist connected with Feather's face.

The Phoenix

Without horses it took a long time to walk all the way to the Stone district, and all three of them were aching and sore by the time they reached the slaving guild's hall. The district was known for its artisans, almost all of whom made wonders out of its namesake, and it was a wonder to behold. Buildings rose high and proud and were adorned with all sorts of fanciful designs, from snaking patterns climbing up walls to creatures hideous and beautiful alike perching on top of rooftops. Some were locked in an endless battle, while others watched the good folk pass below through sightless eyes. Fountains depicted monstrous serpents and gods from all over the known world. Statues of heroes long dead but not forgotten stood proud against the rigours of time and weather.

They'd already passed a number of slave pens, fenced-off enclosures open to the sky that held all manner of men, women, and children, all bearing the iron collars of slavery. The pens were extensive, and they weren't only confined to the Stone district. There were always new slaves coming in, older slaves unable to be offloaded, or those who had yet to have their wills broken to make them useful for servitude. Thousands of folk all penned up and awaiting a life of hellish toil and degradation. This was the side of humanity Keelin truly hated, and he wasn't alone in that. There wasn't a pirate in the isles who agreed with or condoned slavery, not least of all because their chosen profession could easily lead to such a fate.

Morley made his opinion on the matter known in a very vocal fashion, tutting and cursing at the conditions the people were kept in. For his part Keelin agreed with his first mate, but he remained silent on the matter. He didn't want his condemnation of the practice to be heard by the slavers guild until long after he was back at sea. Kebble also remained silent. If the man was as old as he claimed, then he had likely seen more slavery than all of them combined. Keelin still couldn't bring himself to believe that Kebble was immortal.

The slavers guild hall was an ugly building on the southern side of the district. It stood two storeys tall and had been built with orange stone, where most of the surrounding buildings were grey. Guards were out in full force, with twelve at the entrance all carrying spears, cudgels, and whips. Keelin had spotted regular groups patrolling the district as well. It all gave him a queasy feeling in his stomach.

"I'd like to see the guild master," Keelin said to the first guard outside the hall. "I plan to make a substantial purchase."

The guard looked Keelin up and down, his gaze coming to a brief rest on the twin cutlasses, then nodded and motioned for the three of them to follow. Another two of the guards fell in line behind Keelin and his crew, and they quickly found themselves penned in as they entered the hall. The inside of the building was a grand sight, with large tapestries depicting scenes of greatness or monsters of old, and statues of men of all shapes and sizes. Each statue bore a nameplate, but the significance was lost on Keelin. Servants wearing iron collars rushed here and there, and the presence of soldiers was as strong inside as it was out. One slave stopped when she saw Keelin and his escort, then rushed away into a nearby room. A good few moments later, a tall man as thin as a stick sauntered out of the same room.

"How can we help you today?" he said, with a bow of his head that set his many earrings to jingling.

"You the guild master?" Keelin said.

"No. My name is Tindon Lopor, assistant to…"

"I am Captain Keelin Stillwater, emissary to King Drake Morrass, and I am here to make a substantial purchase of your particular wares," Keelin said with a flourish. "Very substantial. So how about you scurry away and bring me the man in charge, eh?"

"King Morrass?" The man sounded rather sceptical.

"Aye," Keelin said, crossing his arms and levelling a stare at him.

Lopor shifted from one foot to another until it became apparent that Keelin would say no more. "I shall see if Master Tain is available."

"If he ain't, I suggest you tell him to be available."

Lopor hesitated for just a moment before scurrying away.

"That was brusque, Captan," Morley said, and Keelin detected a hint of approval.

"Aye. Position of strength, and all that," he said quietly. "For all the bastard's evil, Tanner taught me well on the best ways to negotiate with those that reckon they're powerful."

They were left waiting and guarded in the opulent hall for a long time. The guards watched them but didn't stop them wandering, and Keelin took the opportunity to give the statues a closer look. Each one appeared to be a life-sized depiction of the guild's masters dating back hundreds of years. He was examining one of the statues when its walking, talking counterpart strolled down a nearby staircase. Keelin quickly checked the nameplate and discovered the man's name was Somolus Tain. The statue was tall and broad, with a bald head, four bars running through its nose, and an exquisitely trimmed beard that gave it a distinguished appearance. The man looked remarkably similar, only with a lot less colour.

"Captain Stillwater," Somolus Tain said, his voice clipped. He walked with a limp that somehow managed to look sinister to Keelin's eyes. "I must apologise for your poor treatment. We were not expecting you."

"No reason you would have been," Keelin said with a predatory smile.

"Tell me, Captain Stillwater, are you here with Captain Black?"

"Eh? No. I'm here on my own."

"I see."

It seemed more than just a little odd that the man would ask if he was with Tanner. Most folk who knew anything about the pirates knew that Keelin had long ago unhitched his wagon from Tanner's horse.

"I'm told you wish to make a purchase," Somolus said. The man was just a few feet from Keelin now, and he smelled strongly of strawberries.

A memory welled up inside Keelin. A young boy's days spent in the local fields with his mother and younger sister. His mother had loved to pick fresh fruit, and Leesa had loved any opportunity to be out of bed even if she did have to be carried wherever she went. He couldn't remember their faces. No matter how hard Keelin tried, he could never remember their faces.

"Captain Stillwater?"

"Aye, a purchase." Keelin nodded. "Looking for a lot too."

"Forgive my ignorance, Captain. Traditionally you pirates do not purchase or keep slaves."

"Traditions change," Keelin said. "Especially when there's a war on."

"Indeed." Somolus gave a small bow of his head. "War is often a profitable time for my guild. I'm sure we can accommodate your needs. What exactly are you looking for?"

"Sailors, fighters, anyone with a trade."

"Expensive tastes," Somolus cooed. "Which sex would you prefer?"

"Both. A good mix would be appreciated."

"And how substantial would this purchase be?"

"At least two hundred bodies."

"Captan," Morley said, turning his back to the guild master. "That would be a lot of coin, Captan, and we have no way to transport so many back to the isles." He was whispering, but Keelin could see worry plain on his first mate's face. "At a push we could maybe take on another fifty passengers, if they don't mind sleeping on deck. We could never take two hundred."

"For an extra fee we would be able to transport your property to wherever it needs to be," Somolus Tain said with a voice like honey. "I guarantee most of the slaves would survive the trip."

Keelin thought about it for a moment, but the last thing he wanted was to condone a slaving ship entering the Pirate Isles. They were busy trying to stamp out the despicable trade in their waters, and to not only let them through, but also contract them to cross…

"I will arrange transport myself," Keelin said, pushing Morley aside. "How soon can you have them ready?"

Somolus Tain's face split into a wide grin. "I will have them ready for your inspection in just a few hours. After that I expect it will take a few days to prepare them for transport. If you wish, I can provide refreshments at our guild's local tavern while you wait. Of course, we will cover the expense."

"Aye," Keelin said. "An ale wouldn't go amiss while you sort the poor bastards out."

Keelin had to give one thing to the slavers guild – they treated their more refined slaves quite well. When Somolus Tain's assistant fetched Keelin and his two crew members from the tavern, Keelin had expected to be shown a bunch of wasted, rag-wearing, dirty men and women, all with iron collars and hollow eyes. He wasn't wrong on the last part.

They were standing inside one of the slave pens atop a raised stone platform. Keelin looked down on hundreds of faces, some of which stared back at him while others kept their eyes dutifully lowered. They were all dressed in plain grey shifts with no ornamentation other than their collars. For the most part, the slaves were clean and looked healthy. No doubt the guild kept the skilled products away from the ragtag scum they picked up off the street.

Keelin found himself wondering how these people had found their way into their current predicament. He shook his head to clear his mind, and found a pit of anger waiting for him in his stomach at seeing so many good people debased in such a tragic way. Slavery had always seemed horrific to Keelin, even when he was young and his family had owned slaves who worked the nearby mines. When he was younger he'd wanted to save them, to free them. Now he was older, and freeing slaves was exactly what he was about to do.

"As you can see," Somolus Tain started as he limped up the steps to join Keelin and his crew, "they have been treated kindly because of their skills."

"You mean their value?" Keelin said bitterly.

"Indeed. Valuable to us, but more so to yourself, it seems."

"Eh?"

"It appears you need them, therefore they have value to you." Somolus sounded smug. "If you did not, then you would not be willing to purchase them. I can tell by the way you look at them that you do not entirely agree with the lot they have been dealt. So your need must be great indeed. So their value to you is also great indeed."

"There's more than two hundred here," Keelin said, his voice grating.

"Of course," Somolus said. "You asked for at least two hundred, so I have provided more. Also, it may be that not all are to your liking. I implore you to walk among them and examine each one. I assure you it will be quite safe. If you find any you do not like the look of, I shall have them removed. There are three hundred and thirty-four slaves gathered before you."

Keelin ground his teeth at the display, and his hands clenched into fists.

"Can you break down their numbers by their skill sets and previous occupations?" Kebble said, stepping forward and gently moving Keelin aside with a hand on his shoulder. The sharpshooter gave his captain a brief glance before turning to Somolus Tain. "It would help us to decide upon the number we wish to purchase."

As the guild master began to quote numbers to Kebble, Keelin jumped off the platform and walked among the slaves. He saw men and women of all creeds and races. He saw some who were clearly from the World's Edge mountains, north of the Five Kingdoms. Not many folk grew so large, and there was a fierce pride in their eyes that no amount of whippings or beatings could tear out of them.

Keelin saw black skins from the southern Wilds and the painted faces of Riverlanders. He saw men and women with golden hair that suggested they were from Sarth, and many and more with the olive skin of those who called the Dragon Empire their home. There were folk from every kingdom arrayed before him, and all stood quietly while they awaited a decision as to their fates.

Keelin stopped in front of a tall, broad woman who had the look of someone who had once been well muscled, but poor conditions had led to some withering. Her hair was short, dark, and wiry, and her nose was bent.

"What's your name?" he said.

"Eldred," the woman said in an Acanthian accent.

"You know how to fight?" She looked up into Keelin's eyes, and there was danger there. However she might have been treated, it hadn't been enough to put out her fire.

"I do," she said.

Keelin looked back up at the platform, where Kebble was still in deep conversation with Somolus Tain. The slaver's guards were busy keeping watch on the slaves as a group, rather than Keelin's conversation with a single woman.

"How did you come to wear a collar?"

The woman glared at Keelin for a moment, then dropped her eyes. "By way of debt, sir." She spat the final word.

Keelin laughed softly. "I am no knight. I'm a pirate. You can call me Keelin, or Captain Stillwater. Whichever makes you happiest. How did debt give you a collar?"

Again the woman looked up at Keelin. This time there was suspicion in her eyes. "I was part of a mercenary company in the Dragon Empire. Small but competent. We travelled around looking for folk in trouble, and fixed that trouble so long as they could pay. We hunted foul people and creatures alike. Rarely stopped to think about the consequences.

"After one successful mission to eradicate a lair of urrlas, we ended up spending a bit more than we earned. Quite a bit more, actually." Eldred stopped and took in a ragged breath before sighing it out. "We couldn't pay the debt, and instead of allowing us to work it off the local town magistrate called on his prince.

"Before we even realised how fucked we were, we had a dragon fly down on us. Reat got ate by the fucking monster, and the rest of us threw down our weapons rather than follow his lead. Magistrate thanked the prince and sent him on his way. Then promptly called this buggering lot to come and slap collars on us. Reckon he got paid a good few bits for the trouble."

"They haven't managed to sell you yet?"

The woman gave Keelin a lopsided grin. "Folk don't tend to want to stick weapons in the hands of their slaves, and there ain't much else I'm good for than swinging a length of steel."

Keelin glanced first to his left and then to his right. There seemed to be a good number of folk who looked like they knew how to swing a sword.

"What would you give for your freedom?" he said.

"Ain't got nothing to give," she replied quickly.

"Sure ya do." Keelin smiled. "You've got your allegiance."

Eldred narrowed her eyes at him. "Well, sure. Reckon I'd give that."

"What about the others?" Keelin gestured to the rest of the slaves.

"Can't say for certain, but I reckon most would give anything they could to be out of this fucking iron." Eldred tugged on her collar to make her point.

Keelin turned and went quickly back to the stone platform, leaping up the steps to join his two crew members and Somolus Tain.

"How are the numbers, Morley?" he said.

"Pricey, but we can afford them with the money Drake gave us. How we'd get them all home, I don't know."

"I'll think of something."

"Are they all to your liking, Captain Stillwater?" Somolus Tain said, still sounding smug.

"We're about to find out." Keelin grinned and turned to address the crowd of slaves.

"My name is Keelin Stillwater, captain of *The Phoenix*, and I sail under the flag of King Drake Morrass. The Pirate Isles are at war with Sarth and the Five Kingdoms, and we are trying to build the isles into a place where folk from anywhere can live the lives they please. We're looking for men and women who can fight, who can sail, and who have a trade. What we're offering you in return is your freedom."

"Captain Stillwater…" Somolus screeched, stepping forward.

"Silence him," Keelin roared, pointing at the slaver.

Kebble stepped behind the guild master and drew a long knife from his belt, holding it to the man's neck. The guards started forwards, but stopped once they realised their master's life was in imminent danger.

"What are you doing, Captan?" Morley said quietly.

"Making a statement, Morley. Letting everyone know the isles are open to all."

"The slavers guild…"

"Fuck the guild," Keelin hissed, low enough that no one else would hear. "Drake's already declared war on them, just word hasn't reached here yet. We take what we can for as little as we can, and get the fuck out of here before they decide to stop us."

Morley looked caught between arguing further and following his captain's lead. Luckily for them both, he chose the latter and backed off a step.

Keelin raised his voice to a shout again. "So there's the deal. Anyone who wants their freedom can find it in the Pirate Isles. Ain't gonna say it'll be an easy life, but it will be whatever the fuck you want it to be." He turned to stare at Somolus Tain, Kebble's knife still at the man's throat. "I'll take them all," he shouted.

The slaves began to speak, a loud murmur rising behind Keelin. Most of it sounded excited. Keelin approached the guild master.

"Say what you will, Tain."

"We have a policy, Captain Stillwater," the slaver said, his voice calm despite the knife at his throat. "We do not release slaves, nor sell to those who offer freedom."

"You're gonna break that policy this time," Keelin growled. "I'll take all these poor bastards, and I'll even pay you full price for them. And you're going to thank me for it. If you don't, you'll have to find yourself a new shipping route, because I'll make sure we pirate every fucking slaver that passes within a hundred leagues of the Pirate Isles."

"You would start a war with us over three hundred worthless lives?"

"Let him go," Keelin said, and Kebble immediately stepped back, removing the knife from the slaver's throat. The guards started forwards again with weapons drawn. "You'd be the one starting the war, Tain. I'm just trying to buy a bit of flesh from you. How do you think the slavers in Chade or Sarth will feel when they hear you fucked up their shipping lanes over a few hundred *worthless lives*?"

Somolus Tain waved for his guards to stand down. There was rage in his expression, but it was clear he was beaten.

"Have them ready for transport in three days, Tain," Keelin said. "And no mistreatment of them. I want my product whole and intact."

Somolus Tain nodded. "You will have your slaves, but know that you have made an enemy today, Captain Stillwater. I hope your *king* appreciates that."

Starry Dawn

Elaina hadn't been expecting the news that Pollick came running with. She'd hoped that someone they knew might turn up, but never had she imagined it would be Keelin. The prospect of sailing after *Starry Dawn* and that gut-rotted weird Rovel with Keelin at her side set a fire in her blood. It would seem fitting, somehow, chasing down the bastard who had stolen her ship with the help of another bastard who had once stolen another of her ships.

She found Keelin's quartermaster, Smithe, in charge of the boat and taking every opportunity to remind the crew of his position of authority. Smithe was a dangerous man; Elaina had known that from the very start. He'd once served aboard *Icy Dream*, one of her father's ships, and Elaina had requested him when Tanner gave her *The Phoenix*. Smithe was a brutal demon in a fight and had not a drop of pity in him, and that made him an excellent tool. Elaina had planned to use Smithe to strike fear into the hearts of her prey and her brethren alike, but the bastard had fallen under Keelin's charm – or possibly his promise of better wages. Of course, Elaina knew that Smithe's relationship with his captain had long since soured.

Elaina swaggered up the gangplank with her three remaining crew members in tow, and stepped onto the deck of *The Phoenix* without any resistance. Smithe was grinning at her from the railing, and there were a number of the morning shift she didn't recognise taking the opportunity to lounge around with little to do. The morning light revealed that the ship had a few new knocks and scrapes, but she was, for the most part, in excellent condition.

"Morning, Cap'n Black," Smithe said with a nod. "Can't say I expected ta see you here."

"Just thought I'd stop by and see how my ship is doing, Smithe," Elaina replied easily.

"I meant in Larkos," Smithe said. "Don't see the *Dawn* anywhere round here."

"She's away on…" Elaina paused with a grin. "Business. Where's your crotch mould of a captain hiding?"

Smithe narrowed his eyes. "Went to see the slavers. Odd crew ya got with ya there."

Elaina glanced behind her at Pavel, Alfer, and Pollick, and shrugged as if it meant nothing.

"I think I'll wait for him here," she said. "What shit is your galley serving for breakfast?"

It was mid-morning by the time Keelin arrived, and the first Elaina knew of it was her old friend and lover barging through the door to the galley with a face like thunder and lightning mixing with fire. Elaina and her three crewmen had been happily exchanging stories with a few hands from *The Phoenix*, but the galley fell silent the moment the ship's captain arrived.

"Get the fuck off my ship, Elaina," Keelin said in a quiet voice that held back a sea of rage.

All eyes in the room turned to look at her, and Elaina responded by shooting Keelin the sweetest smile she could.

"Is that any way to treat an old lover?"

"You betrayed me. You tried to have me killed."

"No, I tried to save you and have Drake killed," Elaina countered. "Turns out it didn't work. What the fuck happened on Ash? How did Drake convince my da to sail for him?"

"Drake didn't," Keelin said, his face still an angry mask. "I did."

"Well, shit. Looks like all us Blacks still got a bit of a soft spot for ya," she said with a wink.

"You're still on my ship, Elaina."

"Aye, I am. Not planning to leave just yet. Figured we should have ourselves a little chat, captain to captain. Just like the old days, but with less of the fucking. Unless you've got rid of that squinty little waif yet…" Elaina let the suggestion hang; Keelin did not look amused.

"My cabin," he growled, and pointed towards the galley door before turning his glare on Elaina's crew. "You three can stay here."

Keelin waited for Elaina to pass him and then followed along behind her. She could almost feel the anger flowing off him, and it sent chills down her spine to leave a person that angry with her at her back, but she knew Keelin would do her no harm. No matter how furious he might be, the worst he would ever do would be to leave her in Larkos.

She quickly scaled the ladder up to the main deck, squinting at the sudden sunlight, and waited for Keelin to follow her. There were a great many folk on the deck, including a good few Clerics, but Elaina resisted the urge to take command of the situation. She doubted Keelin would take it too well.

"Captan," said Morley as soon as Keelin's head poked out of the hatch. "We have an issue."

Keelin leapt up the last few rungs of the ladder and stood quickly, giving Elaina a fleeting glare. She returned his aggression with a playful smile.

"What's going on here?" Keelin said.

A number of his crew were kneeling on the deck of *The Phoenix* with their hands tied behind their backs. Among the bound pirates was Keelin's waif. The sight of the woman humbled and restrained put a grin on Elaina's face.

"Are these people members of your crew?" said one of the Clerics, a tall, broad man with a shaved head and a braided beard. Keelin rested his hands on the hilts of his twin cutlasses. Elaina had seen him do it a hundred times before, and it always made her smile. Tanner had taught him to do it as a way of intimidating folk.

"Aye," Keelin growled. "What have they done?"

"They started a tavern brawl."

"We didn't start…"

With a rough smack to the back of the head, one of the Clerics silenced the lad who had protested his innocence. Keelin looked ready to intervene on behalf of his crew, but Elaina wagered he knew better than to anger the Clerics while his ship was docked in their district.

"What's their punishment?" Keelin said.

"One moon's community service," said the bald Cleric. "We brought them to you first in case you would like to… lighten their sentence."

"Captain," Morley said, stepping close to Keelin and whispering in his ear. Elaina couldn't hear what the first mate said, but she caught a definite shake of his head.

"We cannot afford to wait here for a month," Keelin growled at the Cleric. "Nor will we pay your bribe."

The Cleric straightened his back, his expression hardening. There were ten brothers aboard the ship, and they were all armed with heavy maces and bucklers. Elaina didn't doubt Keelin's crew could take them, but they would sustain injuries, and if any of the Clerics got away they would come back with numbers the pirates of *The Phoenix* couldn't withstand. Worse still were the repercussions a brawl here might have in her meeting with the Council of Thirteen. It dawned on Elaina that she might be able to stop a pointless altercation and get back into Keelin's good books all at once, and she needed to be in his good graces for what she was going to ask of him.

"Brother," she said, stepping forward.

"Captain Black," said the bald Cleric.

"What are you doing, Elaina?" Keelin hissed.

"You recognise me then," she said to the Cleric. "This will make things easier. I would like you to release them without punishment this once. They will, of course, be confined to the ship for the remainder of *The Phoenix*'s stay in Larkos, and you can tell Brother Hernhold that I will count it as a personal favour to me."

The bald Cleric seemed to consider the proposition for a few moments before a wide smile spread over his face.

"As you wish, Captain Black. They will remain on the ship."

"Of course," said Elaina. "We'll give them some shitty jobs too, eh?"

Keelin stepped up beside Elaina, and she could sense his impatience. She did her best to ignore her fellow captain as the Clerics untied the pirates and walked down the gangplank and away.

"What the fuck was that?" Keelin said as soon as they were out of earshot.

Elaina glanced at him, smiled, and said nothing.

"Thanks, Cap'n," said Jojo, the sentiment echoed by a few of the crew members that Elaina didn't recognise.

Keelin's little waif walked towards them. Her face was about as carefully expressionless as Elaina had ever seen, but there was a deep anger in the little bitch's eyes.

"Aimi…" Keelin started.

"I'll be in my cabin," she said, and then sent a glare in Elaina's direction. "As ordered."

"You mean my cabin?" Keelin said.

The little waif stopped for a moment and stared at Keelin. "No," she said, and then continued on her way to the captain's cabin. She opened the door, walked through, and closed it behind her. Elaina liked to think she'd heard the click of the lock afterwards.

Keelin turned to face Elaina and sighed. "What the fuck just happened?" The anger had turned to exasperation.

Elaina shrugged. While she wouldn't admit it, she enjoyed seeing Keelin struggle with the little bitch he'd chosen over her. If she could convince him to help her, there may be a chance to get between the two of them even further.

"Still need to have that chat, Keelin," she said. "Sooner would be better than later."

Keelin glanced back towards his cabin. "Let's find a tavern, eh?"

As they walked, Elaina asked what had happened in the isles during her absence. Having spent so long at sea, she could have missed the birth of a new god and not known anything about it. Keelin seemed happy to talk about how he'd convinced Tanner to join Drake, and about the recent battle at New Sev'relain. She wondered if he'd picked up a couple of injuries himself. He was trying to hide it, but Elaina knew him well enough to know when he was in pain and the limp was a dead giveaway.

Once they were well and truly settled at a table with drinks in hand, Elaina sat back and wondered how to broach the subject of the favour she needed to ask.

"What are you doing here, Elaina?" Keelin said. "And how do you have so much pull with the Clerics?"

"Tanner sent me," she said with a grimace. "First to Chade, then to Larkos. Didn't want me coming to Ash to confuse matters between you and him – and Drake.”

“Tanner was looking for allies in the free cities,” Keelin said with a sigh. “Did he get them?”

“In a way.” Elaina grinned. “Tanner sent me to Chade, but he didn’t get shit out of it. I did.”

“Huh?”

“Lord and Lady Chade are sending ships, men, and supplies to the isles. Thing is, they’re only there to sail for me. I’ve got a meeting with the Council of Thirteen in a few days to get the same deal from them, and the Queen of Blades is backing me for it.”

“Sailing for you,” Keelin said. “Why?”

“Pirates are on the verge of calling themselves a kingdom, yeah?” Elaina’s grin widened. “I’m throwing my name in for the throne, and I reckon I’m bringing more to the table than anyone else.”

“How many ships?”

“Ten from Chade. Gotta negotiate just that with the Council here.”

“I’ve just purchased three hundred slaves, Elaina,” Keelin said, his voice hushed.

“Eh? Why the fuck are you dealing with those buggering slavers?”

Keelin winced and knocked back the last of his ale, then called for another one.

“We need folk to sail, folk to fight, folk to live on the isles. I figured I’d bring them in by buying and freeing a bunch of slaves.”

“That’s a dumb fucking idea,” Elaina said with a shake of her head. “How are you gonna get ’em to the isles?”

Keelin took two mugs from the serving boy and pushed one towards Elaina. “With the ships you’re about to convince the Council to give to you.”

She smiled. “Favour, is it?”

“Aye.”

“One that I’ll get to call in soon then?”

Keelin narrowed his eyes at her. “Within reason.”

“It’s a deal then.” Elaina held up her mug, and after only a brief hesitation Keelin tapped it with his own.

“How did you convince the Queen of Blades to help you?” Keelin said.

Elaina waved away the question and took a gulp of ale. "Hey, Keelin," she said cheerfully. "Do you remember that deal we struck in that tavern in Larkos? The one where I carry your slaves to the isles with my ships as a favour and you owe me one?"

Keelin's face fell as he realised he wasn't going to like what was coming.

"Well, it just so happens I'm calling it in now." She smiled.

"Within reason, Elaina."

"Oh, it's perfectly reasonable, Keelin," she said sweetly. "I doubt it will cost you a thing."

"What is it?"

"I need passage home."

"What? Why?"

"Remember my first mate, Rovel? Well, that cock-fucking, mouldy crap-licker went and stole my ship. Leaves me a little stranded here."

"You let the *Dawn* get taken from beneath ya?" Keelin said, incredulous.

"Weren't exactly so much with the letting," Elaina growled as she felt the heat rising to her cheeks. "Bastard sailed off while I was ashore. Fucking coward. Anyway, I want passage on *The Phoenix*."

"What about the ships you're getting from the Council?" Keelin sounded hopeful.

"Could be weeks before they're ready, and I ain't got that much time to lose. I don't reckon you'll be hanging around for that long either."

Keelin winced and shook his head. "Elaina, we ain't going straight back to the isles. We're stopping off a bit south first."

"How far south?" Elaina said, suspicious.

"The Forgotten Empire."

Elaina had no idea what to say. Shocked began to explain how she felt, but it was a long way off finishing the job. No one sailed into the waters of the Forgotten Empire, and even fewer folk sailed out again.

"Uh… Why?" It wasn't the most elegant of responses, but her tone left Keelin under no confusion that she thought him mad.

"That's between me and my crew," he said.

"They know where you're headed and they ain't mutinied yet? Must mean there's something big in it for them. Must mean they think you've got a way to keep them alive." Elaina mulled it over. In all the time she'd known Keelin, he'd never once talked of the Forgotten Empire; whatever he thought he could find there, he'd kept it secret from her.

"So you see," Keelin said, "you really don't want to come with me."

"I still do though," Elaina said quickly. "Calling in a favour, remember?"

"Elaina…"

"Whatever the fuck you're about to say, Keelin, save it. I'm coming. At the very least you're gonna need someone to watch your back. I don't give a fuck what you're after. I've got my eyes set on my own prize."

"The throne?"

"Aye."

Keelin sipped at his ale. "And what if the only way to get it is to share it with Drake?"

Elaina grinned. "Then I guess I'll finally know the truth to all those rumours Drake spreads about the size of his cock."

Keelin dropped his eyes to his mug. Elaina wasn't sure what she was seeing on his face, but it looked an awful lot like her old lover was struggling with some jealousy. She hoped he'd struggle with it for a good long time.

Starry Dawn

"Do you know what you are going to say to them?" Pavel said with the tone of calm he used with his patients. If anything, it only put Elaina more on edge.

"I was gonna walk in and threaten the rich bastards with a good old stabbing unless they agree to give me both ships and the folk to sail them," she said.

Pavel sighed. "I'm not sure that would be the wisest tactic."

"Don't worry. I got a plan."

"More importantly, you have the backing of the Queen of Blades."

"Hopefully the Scarred Man too," Elaina said with a grin that only reached her lips. "Haven't had a chance to ask ya yet – what do ya think about crewing up with Stillwater for the trip home?"

Pavel made a face. Elaina couldn't be quite certain, but it looked a lot like the face of a man who didn't approve and was trying to approach the conversation with caution.

"I worry how it will look to your father if you sail back into the isles aboard Captain Stillwater's ship and without one of your own."

Elaina leaned forwards and poured herself a glass of iced wine. The antechamber they'd been instructed to wait in was lavish, with comfortable seating, large windows to allow a lot of light in, and a table full of refreshments. There were two other groups waiting to see the Council, but they kept their distance from Elaina and her priest.

"I do not want to see you hurt again, Elaina," Pavel continued.

She snorted. "I'll be bringing more ships and men to the isles than any other captain. My da wouldn't dare…"

"I meant with Captain Stillwater."

Elaina turned a dark glare on the priest, but decided to change the subject rather than berate him. "You been to your temple yet? They got one dedicated to Pelsing, don't they?"

"Yes, they do," Pavel said with a nod. "It appears the guilds of Larkos pay tribute to all of the gods. I have been, and I have prayed for the support of Pelsing."

Elaina laughed. "Fortune and gold, eh?"

"Fortune and gold," Pavel repeated the prayer.

The door opened, revealing a Blade dressed in a blue-and-white robe, her four swords dangling from her belt. Only the guards and the Council members were allowed arms inside the great guild hall, and all of the guards belonged to the Blades. Being in control of the central district was a grand position indeed, and Elaina could only hope it was grand enough for the Queen of Blades to exert that power in her favour.

"Captain Black," the Blade said. "The Council will see you now."

Elaina stood and gave Pavel a wink. Her stomach felt like it was dancing a drunken jig, but Elaina refused to show any discomfort. Her father had always said that no matter how bad the situation, a Black should always appear in complete control. They were words Elaina wanted to live by. They were also words she rarely found herself able to follow. She was too passionate and prone to rash actions. Planning was for folk like Drake Morrass. Elaina preferred to act before the other person had a chance to.

Following the Blade into the Council chamber, Elaina found it as grand as she'd expected. A circular table formed a ring around a large open area in the centre of the room. Light shone down from a glass-windowed ceiling and was complemented by a whole host of candles mounted to the pillars that stretched from the floor all the way up. There was a single break in the table that allowed folk to walk into the centre, and the centre was where the Queen of Blades was standing.

The Drurr stood tall and stunning in a figure-hugging dress of crimson. Her wreath of blades still rested upon her shoulders, and the smile she turned on Elaina was both welcoming and predatory.

Elaina gave each member of the Council of Thirteen a good long stare as she made her way into the centre of the room. For their part, the Council watched her silently, which only served to increase the prickling Elaina felt all over her skin. Once she stood in the middle of their circle alongside the Queen of Blades, the Drurr woman finally spoke.

"I introduce my guest Captain Elaina Black, daughter of Tanner Black, consort of Drake Morrass, and admiral of the pirate fleet."

Elaina almost cringed at the introduction. She'd never considered herself an admiral, no matter how many ships she commanded, and the title of consort to Drake Morrass somehow made it seem all too real. The idea that she might actually have to marry and sit beside the slimy bastard on the throne had never occurred to Elaina as anything other than another obstacle to overcome.

"Some of you have already met with Captain Black," the Queen of Blades continued. "I urge you not to be biased against her plea. We all know the way this works, after all."

There was a murmur of agreement from a few of the Council members, and Elaina couldn't help but feel the Queen's comment was directed at those who had tried to curry Elaina's favour themselves. She'd chosen the Blades as her representative among the Council, and that was likely to slight those others who had tried for the same position. The Queen of Blades had already warned Elaina of this, as well as which of the Council members would likely vote against her, and which were still undecided.

"The floor is yours, Captain Black," the Queen of Blades said as she exited the ring and moved to the only spare seat at the table.

Elaina waited for the Drurr to sit down before clearing her throat and raising her voice. "I'm here on behalf of the Pirate Isles."

"There is no need to shout, dear," said Lady Tienna Ro'lare. "Some of us may be old, but we can hear you quite well."

"Uh… right." Elaina felt her cheeks redden. She forged on regardless. "I'm, uh, here asking for help. We're at war with the Five Kingdoms and Sarth. They aim to purge us just like they've done before, but that ain't happening this time. This time we're fighting back. We're organised. We're united. We're determined…"

"You're doomed," said Blunt, guild master of the Broken Spears.

Elaina focused on the man, her dark eyes staring a hole through him. Blunt didn't so much as blink, let alone look away.

"We've beat 'em twice already," she said vehemently. "First time they sent a Man of War and we took it, turned its bones into a town." Elaina was well aware she was taking credit for something Keelin and Drake had accomplished, and she wasn't about to stop there. "Second when they sent a fleet. We crushed it and took their flagship for our own."

"Then why do you need our help?" said Somolus Tain of the slavers guild.

Elaina paused, trying to collect her thoughts; she hadn't expected to be interrupted so early into her speech.

"Wins don't come without losses, and we've suffered a good few wins. We need reinforcements. We're close to winning this once and for all. Beating back Sarth and the Five Kingdoms so they ain't got no choice but to recognise us as a kingdom of our own and pay the bloody tributes that go along with it. But we need a little bit of help from our friends to get us there. And, uh, I'm here hoping to count you lot among my friends – our friends."

Blunt leaned forwards with his hands on the table. He looked just like his name, broad and hard and… blunt. "*Or*" – he paused just long enough to stand up to address the rest of the Council – "we could join the other side and help wipe out the pirate pest problem once and for all."

A few of the other Council members made noises that seemed to be in agreement. Elaina looked first to the Queen of Blades and then to the Scarred Man, and she found them both silent and watching her intently. A test, she realised. They wanted to see if she could convince the Council without their help before they threw their support behind her as queen of the Pirate Isles.

"Once and for all, is it?" Elaina said. "Ya reckon that's likely, do ya?" She laughed. No one joined in.

"This ain't the first time other kingdoms have come for us with soldiers and fire, and it wouldn't be the first time they sailed away thinking they'd dealt with us for good an' all. We keep coming back though, don't we? The Pirate Isles are conveniently placed right in the middle of the main shipping route between Sarth, the Five Kingdoms, and all the way over here in the Dragon Empire. To go around the isles completely adds weeks to a journey. Weeks of open sea with no little islands for fresh water, and some of those stretches of open sea are far more dangerous than an encounter with some pirates."

"Yes, we're all aware of the prime location your people currently occupy, Captain," said Somolus Tain.

"Aye? Well, you drive us out and we just come on back once ya gone. Because there's no better place to pirate from in all of the known world. All a purge ever accomplishes is a few years of less pirates and less pirating."

"Captain Black makes a good point," Blunt said loudly, a wide grin on his smug, bearded face. "Perhaps occupation of the isles by a military force would secure the trade routes."

Elaina laughed to give herself a moment to think, but it came out as a nervous giggle.

"That's uh… that's exactly what I'm proposing, guild master Blunt. Thanks for bringing the subject up. Ya could send in your own military, sure, or maybe Sarth could, or the Five Kingdoms. Or maybe a combination of all three. I certainly can't see that turning violent." A couple of the Council chuckled at the notion.

"You'd have to support 'em," she continued, feeling a little emboldened. "With food, with pay, with booze. Trust me, guild master Blunt, ain't no military force sitting anywhere without a healthy supply of booze.

"They would need constant support to keep the isles free of us pirates, and the moment their discipline dropped – and it would – we'd be back. Not only that, but we displaced pirates would go elsewhere in the meantime. Pirate Isles is the best shipping route. It ain't the only one. Might be we move on over to the Passage.

"You're on the right course, guild master Blunt, but the way you suggest it is costly and dangerous. What happens if you let Sarth take control of the isles and they decide only Sarth merchants are allowed through?" Elaina shook her head solemnly. Blunt sat back down and steepled his hands.

Elaina smiled and glanced around at the rest of the Council. "There's already a military presence in the isles. We're already set up and ready, just without the incentive to protect rather than steal. All we need is a little help through a rough, uh, beginning."

Elaina swallowed and found her mouth as dry as sand. With a rough cough to clear her throat, she continued.

"If you help us protect what's ours and fight off Sarth and the Five

Kingdoms, then you'll get to sail your merchants through our waters without the threat of piracy. I ain't saying it'll be free, but anyone who helps us is gonna get to use the trade routes for a lot less than those that fight us."

A number of the Council were now talking to their neighbours. Only the Scarred Man remained silent among it all.

"You're proposing you tax us for use of the shipping lanes even after we help you protect the isles from invasion?" said Conney Markmarter of the Dragon Slayers.

"Aye," Elaina said a little too enthusiastically. "Aye. Discount rate, of course, on account of your help, but everyone gets taxed. No exceptions. You'll lose far less by a bit of tax than the loss of entire ships."

Again the Council members began to talk among themselves, and Elaina stood in the middle and watched them all. She caught a reassuring nod from the Queen of Blades, but it was fleeting; the Drurr was deep in conversation with Terk Ferrywold of the Red Hands. Elaina's legs were wobbling, and she locked her knees to stop the weakness showing.

When the Scarred Man finally spoke, his voice came out as a dry rasp and all other sound in the hall stopped. "You ask a lot of us, Captain Black." Elaina looked at the guild master of the Scarred Men, but it was impossible to see his face beneath his mask. "To whom should we entrust our ships and their crews? Many of us have had dealings with Drake Morrass before, and he is not always to be trusted."

Elaina sniffed and straightened her back. Her speech had meandered and she'd lost her place, but this was an expected question with a prepared answer.

"I ain't asking you to entrust your support to Drake. I'm telling you to entrust it to me. He's got the support of the people and of the captains, it's true. What he don't have is the backing to make the Pirate Isles a true kingdom. With your help, I will have that backing. I'll be sat there right beside Morrass on that throne, and you can trust *me*."

"Can we?" rasped the Scarred Man.

Elaina swallowed. "Aye."

The silence that greeted her statement said more than a thousands words.

"You've, uh, you've all heard of my father." It wasn't a question. "Many things can be said of Tanner Black, but none of them slate him as a liar. Well, he brought his children up the same way. I ain't a liar, and I'm telling you now you can trust me to do what's right by you. I don't forget my allies. Nor my enemies."

As the chatter began again, the Queen of Blades stood. "If there are no more questions for the captain at this time, may I suggest we move on to the vote?"

Elaina waited to hear an objection, or another question she would have to answer, but neither came. It appeared all had already decided one way or the other. Her heart was beating too fast, and she wanted nothing more than to collapse into a chair with a strong drink. Public speaking in front of a hostile crowd was not something Elaina ever wished to repeat.

"As I brought the captain to us, I believe I shall start with myself," the Queen of Blades continued. She'd told Elaina this was how it worked; the guild master in charge of the central district determined which order the other guild masters voted in. The opinions of others weren't meant to sway a vote, but with guilds as powerful as the Blades, the Scarred Men, and the slavers, it was impossible for their votes not to impact upon others.

"The Blades vote to support Captain Black and the residents of the Pirate Isles," the Queen announced. "How do the Scarred Men vote?"

Elaina turned to look at the Scarred Man, but it was pointless. With his hood up and his mask in place, Elaina couldn't even see the man's eyes, only the deep rents in the white mask that depicted the marks of the original Scarred Man.

"The Scarred Men vote in favour of the captain," he rasped. Elaina felt her heart quicken.

"How does the slaving guild vote?" said the Queen of Blades.

"We vote against the pirates," said Somolus Tain.

Elaina saw the surprise on the Queen of Blades' face, and turned to see Somolus Tain sneering at her. Considering the slavers guild had tried to curry her favour themselves, Elaina had assumed their support was without question. She wondered how much of the denial was an attempt at petty vengeance for the offence Keelin had given when he ordered a knife held to Somolus' neck.

With two of the three most powerful guilds in her favour and one against, the vote could still go either way. Elaina wagered she saw concern on the face of the Queen of Blades also.

"How do the Silken Soldiers vote?" said the Drurr.

Lady Tienna Ro'lare sat in her cocoon of silk wraps, old and shrivelled. "I vote against the captain's proposal," she said, and Elaina's heart beat faster still.

Even dressed in her finest clothes and with her face daubed with white powder, Elaina felt her cheeks reddening. To be in the middle of all these fools and have them vote against her, despite how passionately she'd made her plea. Rage and embarrassment never mixed well with Elaina.

"How do the Nightborne vote?"

Red, the guild master of the Nightborne, sat in relative darkness compared to the other guild masters. The candles behind her had been snuffed out, yet even that didn't account for the unnatural darkness around the sinewy, flame-haired woman.

"I like her," she said. "She has my vote."

"How do the Clerics vote?"

Brother Hernhold leaned forwards and nodded to Elaina. "The Clerics vote in favour of the proposal."

Elaina's heart was fair trying to hammer its way out of her chest, and she wished the Council would do their voting all at once, but traditions were traditions and the Queen of Blades had warned her how it would go.

"How does the Thirteenth vote?" the Queen continued.

Armen Vert, guild master of the Thirteenth and a royal bastard from the Five Kingdoms, looked unimpressed. "We vote in favour of Captain Black."

Elaina almost questioned the man's decision, she'd been so sure he would vote the other way, but good sense asserted itself and she kept quiet.

"How do the Fallen vote?"

Carowell stood up and fixed Elaina with a black stare, her dark hair framing her pale face in anger. "This is a mistake. They are pirates. They will…"

"The time for discussion is past, Carowell," the Queen of Blades said firmly. "How do the Fallen vote?"

"Against," Carowell snarled, and sat back down. Elaina had no idea what had caused the plump woman to bear so much anger against her. It certainly seemed possible she'd lost something at the hands of pirates.

"How do the Red Hands vote?"

Terk Ferrywold gave Elaina a sympathetic look. "You should have sided with me instead of the Drurr. I vote against."

"How do the Civil Sons vote?"

Jeneus Lo'ten yawned wide and loud. "Whichever way you vote, my dear bladed queen. For the pirate. Why not, eh?"

At the sixth vote in her favour Elaina's stomach turned over, and then over again. It felt as though her insides were dancing a nervous jig. One more would secure her support no matter how the last two guilds voted.

"How do the Broken Spears vote?"

Blunt, guild master of the Broken Spears and a man with impeccable taste in fine suits, smiled at Elaina wide and long. "I vote in favour of Captain Black," he said in his deep, rumbling voice.

A couple of the guild masters started shouting, and those who didn't all seemed to be busy in quieter discussions. Elaina wondered if major decisions made by the Council were always like this. The Queen of Blades fought for control of the situation and eventually managed to quieten her peers long enough to take the votes of the two remaining guilds. Elaina heard none of it. Her blood was rushing through her ears and a whoop of joy was threatening to escape her, but she held it in. She needed to maintain a measure of composure despite her victory.

With both Chade and Larkos behind her, there was no way anyone could dispute her claim to the throne, even if she did have to sit it beside Drake Morrass. There was also no way her father could be anything other than proud, even with the loss of her own ship. Tanner had sent her on an impossible task and she'd succeeded regardless.

"Captain Black," said the Queen of Blades, and Elaina realised the entire Council had fallen silent.

Straightening up again, she faced the Drurr. "Aye?"

"The Council has voted in favour of your proposal. What is left is a discussion on the amount of support that will be entrusted to you. If you would like to return to the antechamber – this could take some time."

Elaina nodded enthusiastically, a wild grin plastered to her face. "Aye, I can wait."

The Queen of Blades bowed her head slightly. "Congratulations, Captain."

The Phoenix

Keelin looked up at the *Bloody Bride* and felt a shiver travel up his spine, across his neck, and then back down his spine for good measure. He'd always felt the name of the ship was a bit macabre, and now the thing looked downright spooky. The majority of the rigging was no longer made from rope, as one would expect from most ships, but from the silk woven by that terrifying monster of a ship's pet that Captain Zothus kept. It made the *Bride* look like a giant floating nest of spiders.

"Can I help ya, Captain?" said a voice from behind, and Keelin turned to find the bald captain standing there, watching him with an amused expression. Zothus wore no shirt, and an extensive tattoo of a serpent wound its way all around his chest and arms.

"How can you stand it?" Keelin said.

"What's that, mate?"

"The spider."

"Rhi? She's quite friendly once ya get to know her. Reckon she'd take right to you. She loves the scared ones."

Keelin shuddered and glanced behind at the ship, his eyes darting around the rigging, looking for the cat-sized monster.

"What do ya want, Stillwater?" Zothus said with a laugh and a shake of his head.

"Do you still work for Drake?"

"I sail for Drake," Zothus said. "I work for my crew."

"Good enough," Keelin said quickly. "The whole of the Pirate Isles sails for Drake these days. I'm wondering if you're heading back there."

Zothus nodded slowly.

"And how would you like an escort?" Keelin said. "Seems Elaina's got some ships, and I have some slaves that need to find their way back to Drake."

Zothus narrowed his eyes. "Drake don't much like slavery. Neither do I."

Keelin held up his hands. "I purchased them to free them, Zothus. We need folk back in the isles. Folk to sail, fight, and work. They'll be delivered as slaves, but as soon as they're handed over, I want their collars removed."

"And you want me to direct these ships and free folk back to the Pirate Isles?" Zothus said. "Why not you?"

"I have another stop to make first. Might be a while, and the isles need reinforcements sooner than later."

"Send them my way." Zothus nodded. "I shall deliver them to Drake as safe as the sea allows."

It wasn't far to *The Phoenix* from the *Bloody Bride*, and Keelin hadn't expected any trouble, which made it all the more confusing when he realised he was sitting in a busy tavern with a drink in front of him and a man dressed in a white robe on the other side of the little table.

"How did I get here?" Keelin said as he looked about himself and recognised the tavern as one very close to the docks.

"I brought you here," said the white-robed man in a soothing voice. "I am sorry for the method, but I needed to talk to you and I did not want to rouse any attention."

"Right," Keelin said, still fighting the fuzzy feeling that clouded his head. "But how did I get here?"

"You walked, Captain Stillwater. Just not under your own volition. I suggest you drink. The feeling will fade very soon."

Keelin looked down at the mug in front of him. He smelled alcohol, and strong stuff by the whiff of it. Looking up, he found the white-robed man regarding him with deep yellow eyes. Keelin had never seen yellow eyes before, and they were unnerving to say the least. The rest of the tavern seemed to be going about its normal business as if nothing out of the ordinary had happened. Folk drinking, boasting, singing, drinking some more.

"Who are you?" Keelin said. He knew he should be angry, or worse, but something about the man set off a warning in Keelin's head and he knew without a shadow of a doubt that no matter how quickly he might draw his swords, it wouldn't be fast enough.

"I am the Oracle, Captain Stillwater."

"Drake's Oracle?" Drake had mentioned the man a few times.

"The very same. And now you know I am not without power. I hope it will go some way towards convincing you that I am no fraud."

"Right." Keelin picked up his mug and sniffed at it. "What is it you want from me?"

"Right now I wish to tell you a story. The story of this city. Did you know Larkos was once part of the Dragon Empire? Long ago it was the sister city to the capital of the Dragon Empire, Soromo."

Keelin took a sip; it was rum.

"The Dragon Empress ruled from her floating city of Soromo while the Dragon Emperor ruled equally from here. Under their combined government the Dragon Empire flourished, as did their dragons. These were true dragons, mind you, not the drakes that fly the skies these days. Pale shadows of their former selves, but I will get to that.

"This city was a happy place, and most of Larkos' citizens were content with their lot. Ruled by the fear of dragons in their skies. The authorities held little sway over the goings on in the streets; their power stemmed from the dragons, and those creatures could not traverse the intricacies of human settlement without destroying all around them. Gangs appeared, and lots of them, each carving out a portion of the city and ruling the crime within those portions.

"When the Dragon Emperor heard of these gangs, he directed his will towards crushing them, driving them out, and restoring order to his city. He succeeded only in causing chaos. The gangs lived in the streets and the underground, where the Emperor's dragons could not follow them.

"Eventually the Emperor gave up. He realised that the gangs did a better job of upholding order in the city than his guard ever could. He asked each of the twelve major gangs to send him a representative in order that he might negotiate with them. A deal was forged. The gangs would police the city for the Emperor, and they would each pay him tribute for the privilege of being allowed to exist."

The Oracle smiled, his eyes distant. "It was the Emperor's grandest folly, and it cost him both his life and the future of his beloved dragons.

"You see, dragons are strange creatures. In order to breed true dragons, there needs to be both a matriarch and a patriarch. Otherwise, all that will ever hatch will be drakes, and while drakes can breed more drakes, they can never breed a dragon.

"But I digress. The gangs were pleased for a while with their new legitimate authority, but it did not take long for them to realise they were paying the Dragon Emperor for no reason. They did not need him. He took from them and gave nothing back. But he had given them something in the beginning. He had brought them together and given them peace. He had stopped them warring among themselves over territory and prestige.

"So the gangs met in secret and devised a plan to rid themselves of the Dragon Emperor. They took the gate and the wall, and they turned the city's weapons of war inwards. They waited until the Emperor's dragon took flight, and they brought the beast down. The Dragon Emperor could not live without his dragon, and soon after he was found hanging.

"But the dragon patriarch had left no heir. No one had seen the treason coming, and all now knew that the dragons' time upon the world was ending. The Dragon Empress was enraged, and she threw her armies against the city of Larkos. Men fought and died. Dragon Princes rode their beasts into hails of ballistae, and the city held. No one thought it possible, but the gangs held the city walls and the city docks.

"Larkos was scarred, but it survived, and the Dragon Empress was forced to retreat before all of her dragons were lost.

"The gangs renamed themselves guilds, and they carved the city into new districts and laid down a series of laws to stop them clashing ever again. They had stood the test of war and dragon fire together, and they had come out the other side stronger, more resolute, and more unified than ever before. Eventually they added a thirteenth guild, so that no disputes between their council could ever be tied. Larkos survived and grew, and prospered into the city it is today."

Keelin sat still, waiting for the Oracle to signal he was finished with his story. He had no idea why the man had decided to tell him the tale, and he was just as unsure about what he truly wanted, but every one of Keelin's instincts was telling him not to anger the Oracle.

"Why tell me that?" he said eventually, when it seemed the man would say no more.

"It is an interesting story, don't you think, Captain Stillwater?"

"Uh… sure."

"The guilds owed their peace and their unity and their existence to one man, the last of the Dragon Emperors. Yet they removed him from power and killed his dragon – and, as a consequence, the Emperor himself.

"I cannot see the past, only the future, but I believe had they not rid themselves of the Emperor, they would have torn themselves apart. Or perhaps he would have torn them apart."

Keelin sighed and looked down into his mug. "What does…"

He looked up. He was standing outside the tavern, facing the docks. The Oracle was gone.

Starry Dawn

Elaina wandered up the gangplank onto *The Phoenix* and looked around at her temporary home. In the daylight it looked as clean a ship as it had ever been. She had a few more scars than when Tanner had given her to Elaina, but scars were just evidence that there were stories to be told.

"Ain't as sleek as the *Dawn*," Alfer said sadly.

"Bigger though," said Pollick.

"Needs to be, with her fat arse."

"Now now, lads," Elaina chastised. Some of the crew had gathered around, and pirates were notoriously defensive when it came to their ships. "This here's our new home for the time being. All comparisons to our *Starry Dawn* can wait 'til after we've got her back. Right now let's be appreciative that these fine folk are giving us the grace of their ship." Diplomacy seemed to be mostly about flowery words and empty compliments.

Elaina handed her pack off to Alfer. She didn't have much in the way of possessions these days – almost everything she owned had been stolen along with the *Dawn* – but she'd picked up a spare set of clothing and a few other essentials.

"Get those stowed away on a bunk, Alfer," she said.

"With the rest of us, Cap?"

"Where else would I be staying?"

"Well, with the Cap'n of this ship and you, I figured I had to ask."

Elaina gave her quartermaster a grin and a shake of her head, and the man set off with Pollick towards the nearest hatch. Pavel continued to hover nearby, his faded crimson robes making him stand out aboard the ship.

"Reckon you'll be bunking with the crew as well, priest," Elaina said.

"What in the name of Rin's leaking tits are you doing here again?"

Elaina turned to Keelin's little waif with a wide grin. "Haven't you heard? I'm ya new shipmate."

The waif's face went from anger to confusion, then back to anger. Elaina struggled to stop herself cackling at the woman.

"Keelin... uh, the captain agreed to this?"

"Aye," Elaina said cheerfully, stepping forward to look down on the smaller woman. "Jumped on the idea when I suggested it, actually. I think he wants a real woman on board, just between me and you."

To her credit, the waif didn't back down despite being horribly outmatched. A number of the crew had gathered around to watch the confrontation. She didn't care one drop for the attention herself, but the more folk Elaina could get on her side, the more likely the bitch would jump ship at her first opportunity.

"Back to work," Keelin roared. "Now! I intend to be under way before midday."

"Not everyone's had a turn ashore, Cap'n," said Smithe, appearing from the shadows of the main mast.

"Then those that ain't can blame those that have," Keelin growled. "Some have been ashore talking about our big score. We're leaving now, before folk start asking questions."

"Big score?" Elaina said with a smile, still staring at the other woman.

"I thought you didn't care," Keelin said coldly, brushing past her and steering the girl away from the confrontation.

Elaina watched the two walk away, noting that the woman looked far from happy. After a very brief conversation she pushed his hands away and leapt up onto the rigging, scurrying quickly up towards the nest. Elaina would have been impressed if she hadn't been so focused on being rid of her.

Keelin's shoulders slumped, and even from behind he looked weary. Elaina swaggered up beside him and gave him a friendly nudge with her shoulder, hoping the girl was watching from above.

"Anything I can do?" she said.

"You've done enough."

Elaina snorted. "All I did was walk aboard."

"I know." Keelin looked like he was about to say more, but he shook his head. "Don't go giving any orders aboard my ship, Elaina."

She grinned mischievously. "Wouldn't dream of it."

Part 3 - X Marks the Spot

The war will awaken old enemies said the Oracle
Got plenty of those to go around said Drake
She will come for you said the Oracle

Fortune

The ship drifted on its anchorage. Clouds covered the sky, and the moon was little more than a sliver, providing almost no light. Drake ordered every lantern on the ship doused. It wasn't the first time the crew of the *Fortune* had worked in near complete darkness, and they were brutally efficient in such circumstances.

The ship creaked and the waves lapped against her hull. Drake caught a whisper on the breeze as one of his crew relayed orders to another, but there was little other sound. Silence, or as near to it as possible, was as important as dousing the lanterns. Sound had an odd way of travelling across water, and Drake didn't want any hint of their presence reaching land.

He strained his eyes, but all he could make out of the islands was a dark blur. They were just around the headland of the bay, and the other ship was anchored close to the beach to obscure their presence. The Drurr didn't want anyone to know they were there. But Drake knew. He'd sent ships all over the isles, scouring his kingdom for their presence, and now he'd found them on Churnon.

New Sev'relain was once again under the protection of Captain Khan. Drake had wanted to bring the giant pirate along for the slaughter, but Khan's ship was a leviathan, larger than any other that had ever been built. It didn't lend itself to subtlety and stealth. Besides, Drake needed to leave someone of authority in charge, and there was no one in the isles more feared and respected these days than T'ruck Khan. The good folk of the isles, along with the pirates, had branded the captain a hero for his exploits.

Beck stood beside Drake at the railing, silent as the rest of the crew. Drake felt her presence keenly. Since their night in her cabin, which now seemed so long ago, she'd been refusing to let it happen again, and Drake couldn't figure out why. The Arbiter was mostly healed from her brush with death back at the battle for New Sev'relain. Her right hand still trembled a little, but apart from that she seemed healthy enough.

He glanced at her. With her hair cut short after the fire and squashed down under a tricorn hat, her plain brown trousers and bleached-bone blouse, and the leather jerkin holding six of her pistols, Beck looked more pirate than witch hunter. Drake felt himself stir, and had to look away lest he make an unwanted advance. The situation was even more maddening now she'd given him a taste. He wanted more, and he was fairly damned certain she did too, but the woman was holding back and he couldn't fathom why.

"Lower the boats." Drake's voice was a quiet growl. Princess scurried away to relay his orders, and the *Fortune*'s dingies were lowered into the water silently.

"Is this wise?" Beck whispered. "We don't even know why they're on this island."

"I know," Drake said. He wondered how many men he would lose to the monsters.

"As much as I enjoy your cryptic crap, Drake, would you mind filling me in?"

Drake ground his teeth together and let out a sigh. If he told his crew what they were likely to come up against, they'd be far less likely to follow his orders to go ashore, but if they didn't know how to deal with it, they would all likely die fighting it.

"When we sailed past the bay earlier, did you use one of your blessings to catch a glimpse of the ship there?" he said.

"Yes," Beck said. "I couldn't see it well though."

"Did you happen to spot the two big wheels on either side of the ship?"

Drake saw Beck's hat move up and down next to him in the darkness.

"Water wheels," he said. "The Drurr fit them to their corsairs. They use them sort of like oars when they need to chase ships down. Those wheels are lowered into the water and then turned real fast, and it speeds up the corsair a little."

"How do they turn the wheels?"

Drake sighed. "With trolls."

The silence from Beck was telling. Drake doubted anyone else on board had ever even seen a troll, let alone fought one. There was no way his crew of pirates with their cheap swords and short bows could ever kill one of the monsters.

"You have a plan?" Beck said.

"I always have a plan, Arbiter."

The Drurr camp was set up in a rocky clearing just beyond the beach. They had a fire good and going, and Drake could smell the faint odour of roasted shrooms in the air. It brought back a mess of memories that he'd rather have forgotten, and he forced them away, concentrating instead on the task at hand.

There were tents arranged around the rocky clearing, and many of the Drurr would be inside them. Most of the bastards couldn't abide the sight of the sky when they were trying to sleep. Their race had spent so long underground that there were generations born, grown old, and died without ever seeing the sun, moon, or stars.

Drake sent ten men into the water under the command of Ying. They would paddle quietly up to the corsair and wait for Drake's signal, then climb aboard and murder the crew left there as quietly as possible. Drake hoped the troll wasn't there, or those ten men were already lost. He was almost certain the monster would be on the island somewhere; it was most likely why the Drurr had stopped on Churnon. There was only so long a troll would remain cooped up aboard a ship without snapping and instigating a rampage. Every few weeks Drurr corsairs would stop at an island and let their trolls roam free for a few days to sate their natural desire for destruction.

The rest of the crew crept slowly along the treeline, keeping as low and silent as possible. Drurr vision excelled in the darkness, but if they weren't expecting an attack, they wouldn't think to look for one. The pirates moved closer, and Drake heard voices on the wind.

Thirty men had accompanied Drake and Arbiter Beck on the island assault, and he wagered the numbers would be more or less even. He hoped the element of surprise would count for another thirty.

The smell of roasting shrooms was stronger now, taking Drake back to the great caverns full of the rubbery fungus beneath Darkhold. He shuddered, and a moment later found Beck's hand on his shoulder. She gave him a reassuring nod – and he did feel reassured with an Arbiter by his side.

From what he could tell, there were few Drurr on watch. No doubt some were out foraging while others were asleep, and more still were sitting around a fire sharing stories, jokes, and songs. The Drurr were very similar to humans in that regard and, Drake had to admit, in many others too.

He nodded to Beck, and the Arbiter took a small chip of wood from her pocket and snapped it between her thumb and forefinger. Out in the bay, Ying was holding a similar chip, and that piece would respond by snapping in half to signal the attack.

Drake's group waited. It would take some time for the pirates in the water to scale the side of the Drurr corsair and start murdering any and all folk they found aboard. They waited some more. He didn't bother keeping track of time; it would only make the wait more nerve-wracking.

The sound of a warning shout cut fatally short drifted in across the water, and then they could wait no more. Drake signalled his group and the pirates emerged from the trees, moving as stealthily as possible.

Drake was at the front, with Beck just a crouched step behind him. The first of the Drurr to notice them was dozing with his back against a boulder. No doubt the fool was one of the watch and was taking the opportunity to catch up on some sleep. He woke with a start as Drake moved past him, but the shout was killed in his throat by cold steel. Drake kept moving.

They were still a good ten feet from the first tent when a warning shout went up to Drake's left – either one of the watch they'd missed or just plain bad luck. There was no sense in staying quiet any more; now they had to kill as many as they could before their enemy realised exactly what was happening.

With a roar, Drake launched into a charge, his sword drawn. He leapt over a rock and slashed at the back of the nearest tent, cutting a wide arc through the light cloth, and stumbled through only to trip over something and find himself sprawled in the sand with a rock for a pillow. Drake rolled to his feet just as Beck leapt through the slash behind him, missing both the bed that had sent Drake crashing to the ground and the Drurr lying on it. The Arbiter jumped up onto the bed and crushed the Drurr's skull with the butt of her pistol even as the man tried to rise. Something heavy crashed into Drake and he found himself flat on his back in the sand again, this time with a half-naked Drurr straddling him and aiming a punch at his face. Drake threw his head to the side and the woman punched only the well-placed rock. As she pulled back her hand with a howl, Drake snatched the dagger from his belt and thrust it into her stomach once, twice, and a third time for good luck. Hot red blood washed down upon his chest, and Drake heaved the wailing Drurr aside and snatched his sword from the sand.

By the time Drake regained his feet, Beck had a second dead Drurr on the ground and a third on its way down to join the others. A fifth Drurr turned and ran; Drake had no intention of letting any of the bastards get away, and he rushed after the woman.

The Drurr was bolting at a full sprint, and Drake was losing distance even moving as fast as he could. He passed small skirmishes and bodies lying in the bloody sand. He passed tents and cook fires and even a turagar, one of the small, blind, dog-like pets that some Drurr kept.

Slowing to a stop, Drake had to admit that he'd lost the fleeing Drurr, and he leaned forwards with his hands on his knees to catch his breath. It wasn't really his fault; Rag, the giant centipede, was wrapped around his waist like a heavy belt, and it was slowing him down. That the creature seemed unperturbed by Drake's recent rolling in the sand, and by the smell of battle and blood around him, gave him some cause for concern, but he had little time to dwell on it. Three Drurr were closing in on him fast.

Two of them fanned out to flank him, while the biggest of the three, a man wearing leather armour and wielding two curved scimitars, came straight on.

Drake held up his left hand to show an open palm. "I'm here to help," he spat in the chaotic jumble that was the Drurr language. It had the desired effect. The three Drurr faltered in their advance, obviously unsure what to think of the human who could speak their tongue. Drake capitalised on their hesitation.

Leaping at the Drurr in front of him, he aimed a sword slash at the man's face. The Drurr stumbled backwards and away, and the strike missed. Drake turned and launched himself towards one of the others.

He slashed twice at the smaller man, who had a look of rampant terror in his black eyes. The first strike crushed through the Drurr's weak defence, sending the fool's sword sailing away through the air. The second slash laid open his belly, spilling intestines onto the sand. Drake danced away, turning to get the two remaining Drurr in front of him before they attacked.

The scimitar-wielding Drurr started forwards, then stopped. Drake saw the feint coming and blocked the attack from his other enemy.

"Rag," he shouted, hoping the beasty would respond to its name.

In a flash the centipede uncoiled from around Drake's waist and struck, aiming for the attacking Drurr's sword hand and taking it off at the wrist with scythe-like pincers. The Drurr fell backwards, screaming and clutching at the stump. Rag, still anchored to Drake's waist, drew backwards and coiled back around him. The whole strike had taken less than a second, but it threw Drake so off balance he very nearly ended up face-down in the sand.

The remaining Drurr, the one with the dual scimitars, looked a lot more cautious now, and Drake decided to play on it. The sounds of battle filled the air along with the smell of blood and fire. It seemed some of the tents were burning.

"You've got no chance," Drake hissed in the Drurr language. "Your ship's been taken." He bent his knees and drew a finger through the sand. "This beach will be your grave."

There was fear in the Drurr's eyes. It didn't stop the fool rushing forwards, both his scimitars raised for a strike. Drake plucked up a handful of sand and threw it in the man's face, then stepped aside, out of the way of his wild slashes. The Drurr was thrashing about like a drowning rat. He'd already dropped one of his weapons and was busy trying to rub the sand from his eyes while flailing with his remaining sword. Drake approached slowly, cautiously. He waited until the man had swung around to face the other way, then poked him hard with his sword. The blade went deep into the Drurr's side, and he spun and swung towards Drake, but he was already back out of reach.

Drake picked up the dropped scimitar and whistled through his teeth. The Drurr turned and swung. Drake blocked the fool's strike with his own sword and stabbed the man through the neck with the scimitar. Stepping backwards, he let him collapse into the sand to lie bleeding and gasping out his last.

The clamour of battle had stopped by the time Drake got back to the camp. As he drew closer, he saw a number of his men standing around a tent, not moving. He had to shove through them, they were crowded so closely together, and not one of them seemed to notice him. As he pushed through he saw something that tugged open an old wound in his heart, one he'd thought healed a long time ago.

Standing in front of the tent, lit by the flickering light of a nearby fire, was the most beautiful woman he'd ever seen, and that beauty hadn't waned a drop in the years since he'd last seen her.

Eriatt, the Drurr matriarch who had once owned him, stood just outside the tent as naked as a person could be. Her pale, perfect skin. Her full, pear-shaped breasts. Her perfect face, framed by sunset hair. Drake felt his stomach flutter and his heart ache. Eriatt smiled, and a number of Drake's crew dropped to their knees, their weapons forgotten. They could no more attack the radiant creature in front of them than they could their own mothers. The power of a Drurr matriarch's glamour was far more than most folk could bear, and it was why scores of slaves served Eriatt willingly.

"Drake." Her voice was like a silken caress to his ears. "I have missed you."

Drake's sword dropped from his hand, and he felt his eyes grow moist. Eriatt opened her arms wide and Drake stared at her breasts. He remembered how they felt, how they smelled, how they tasted.

"Come to me, my love," Eriatt said. Even the harsh Drurr language sounded beautiful when it came from her lips.

Drake took three faltering steps forward and punched the bitch as hard as he could. Her head rocked back and blood erupted from her nose. Eriatt dropped to her knees and squealed in pain, and just like that the spell that held Drake's crew in thrall vanished. The men behind him shook themselves and drew in ragged breaths, and some even broke out in tears at the loss of the deepest love they would ever feel.

"How?" Eriatt spat along with a mouthful of blood.

"Did you really think I'd be so stupid as to risk seeing you again without being prepared?" Drake said. "I've got power of my own these days, you dumb bitch."

"Drake?" Beck's voice floated into the little clearing outside the big tent, and Drake turned to see the Arbiter bloodied and limping.

Eriatt started muttering in the Drurr language, and Drake recognised the beginning of powerful magics. He sent a kick into the woman's stomach, and the words failed her as she doubled over and fought for air.

"Beck," Drake said. "You Arbiters got some ways to bind magic, right? I reckon you'd best do it on this poisonous bitch."

"Give me your belt," Beck said to one of Drake's crew, and the man responded quickly despite the look of deep loss etched on his face. Beck hurried forwards and tied Eriatt's hands behind her back with the belt while the Drurr matriarch was still gasping for air. Beck then dipped a finger in a small pool of Eriatt's blood and proceeded to draw two symbols on her upper back, just below her neck.

"Done," Beck said, wiping the blood on her trousers. "Who is she?"

"This," Drake said, grabbing hold of the matriarch's hair and pulling her head back so Beck and all his crew could look upon her. "This is Eriatt Arandell, mistress of Darkhold and matriarch of the Irkonsole clan."

Drake wanted to punch the woman, to break her bones and burn her skin. He wanted to rip the Drurr to pieces, but he also wanted to comfort her, to console her, to set her free and to love her. He settled for giving her head a rough shove as he let go of her fiery hair.

Eriatt sputtered a curse, but there was no magic there, only a venomous insult. Drake understood it and he cared not a drop. He'd been called a thousand worse things since his time as a slave.

"This is the matriarch who…" Beck started, but Drake cut her off with a dark glare before she could say what the woman had done to him. She'd violated both his body and mind, and that was something he didn't want his crew to know.

Eriatt let out a weak laugh. Her shoulders were slumped and her head hung low. She looked a pitiful creature, with blood dripping from her face and her pale skin sweaty and waxen.

"*I* am the one who made *him* what *he* is," she said in the common tongue.

"*I* made me what I am," he roared, "from the broken pieces you left behind. You tried to destroy me again and again and again. You tried to turn me into another one of your broken slaves who can't live without your fucking love and approval."

Eriatt raised her head then, a cruel smile on her face. "And I *do* approve, my favourite."

Drake punched her on the cheek and she toppled sideways. Agony burst to life in his fist and he turned away, clutching his hand to his chest and letting loose a growl of pain.

Eriatt lay on her side in the sand, whimpering. Beck stood close by, a pistol cocked and ready.

"Cap'n," said Wes, the only one of his crew who seemed to be in full control of his faculties. "What…" The man sniffed loudly, and Drake realised there were wet streaks down his face. "Orders, Cap'n?"

Drake took in a deep breath and let it out as a sigh, trying to calm his emotions. He hated that Eriatt could still make him feel so much, and so badly.

"Check the camp over again," he said eventually. "Make sure we got them all, then signal Ying on the corsair. Oh, and watch out for the troll."

"The troll?" Wes said.

"Fuck." Drake had forgotten to tell his crew about the possibility of running into a troll. "If no one's seen it yet, it's probably off hunting in the forest. Just be careful in case it comes back, eh?"

Wes looked terrified. "Aye, Cap'n." He turned to leave, and some of the crew followed him. Three men stayed behind, their eyes still locked on the Drurr matriarch.

"All of you," Drake hissed in his angriest captain voice. "Fuck off."

Drake waited until all of his crew were wandering away before he turned back to Eriatt's prone form. Beck still stood nearby, and there was a look in her eyes that said she would be staying no matter how many orders or threats Drake threw her way. Instead he gave her a nod and a brief hint of a smile. If he couldn't get rid of her, it was best to make it look like he wanted her there.

"Are *you* going to kill *me*?" Eriatt said, her dark eyes staring up at Drake even though she was lying on her side with her head resting on the sand.

Drake didn't respond. They both knew what he was going to do.

"Drake, don't," Beck said. "We could learn so much from her."

"I've already learned far too much from her."

"I didn't mean you. The Inquisition. A live matriarch. We could make her talk, make her tell us everything."

Drake shook his head. "You don't know what you're dealing with, Beck. She would tell you things, no doubt, but she would corrupt your Inquisition from the inside out. You wouldn't be able to contain her."

"What?"

"If a demon sword can corrupt your organisation, this bitch definitely can."

"How do you know about the sword?" Drake felt Beck's compulsion wash over him, her magic finding no purchase on his will – not while there was a charm to guard against it tattooed onto his skin.

"Don't listen to *him*, Arbiter," Eriatt whispered from her place in the sand. "*Your* Inquisition is stronger than *he* knows. Think of all *you* could learn."

Drake laughed. "Tell me you don't feel it, Arbiter. The magic infused into her very words. It goes beyond the forming of spells. It's like your compulsion, only instead of forcing the truth from folk, it replaces it. Give her long enough and she'd convince you the sea is dry."

Beck frowned, the firelight dancing in her eyes. Eventually she nodded. "I feel it."

"*He's* lying," Eriatt tried again.

"I feel it," Beck repeated.

"The Inquisition is weak at the moment, Beck," Drake said. "We both know it's not prepared to deal with her insidious magic. She would tear it apart, and then who would stand against the Drurr?"

Beck nodded slowly, no longer questioning how Drake knew so much about the Inquisition.

"I'm putting an end to her," Drake said. "You should go."

Beck looked torn. Eventually she put away her pistol and turned, wandering away. Drake watched her go and waited until she was out of earshot. At some point Beck would realise she'd forgotten to ask about the necromancer, but it was clear the dark sorcerer wasn't here and Eriatt would never give up the knowledge she held.

Kneeling down in front of Eriatt, Drake took her by the shoulders and pulled her upright. He pulled a knife from his boot and turned it over in his hands. Eriatt watched him play with it. There was no fear in her dark eyes.

"See, that was something I learned from you," Drake said after a while, and he watched Eriatt's face crinkle in confusion. "What, you didn't feel it? That same magic you tried to use on her."

"What?" Eriatt said.

Drake grinned and nodded. "You used it on me enough. So much, in fact, I started to get a feel for it. Took me a fucking long time, but I got the hang of it my own self. I bet you didn't even know that was possible, eh? Do you really think your own daughter would just up and betray you, free your favourite slave, without a little bit of magical coercion?"

Drake watched the matriarch's eyes widen as she took in the possibility. Some lies were so satisfying to tell.

"But I meant what I said. I'm done learning things from you."

"There is always more to learn," Eriatt said, slipping back into Drurr now they were alone.

Drake watched her for a while, conflicting emotions warring inside of him.

"Why did you come for me?" he said. "Why not just let me go?"

"You belong to me." She smiled at him then, and he felt an ache in his chest.

Drake gave a sad shake of his head. "I belong to no one."

Eriatt laughed. "You will always belong to me, my love. Even long after you kill me here, you will be mine. I made you, moulded you…"

"You…" Drake started, the accusation dying on his lips. He couldn't say what she'd done to him, couldn't admit it even to himself. "You made me love you."

Eriatt smiled. "Yes. And you will never love another. Not a person, not your ship, not even this kingdom you hope to build. You are my masterpiece, my favourite. Never have I had anyone resist me quite like you, but every time you resisted it only bound us tighter together. You claim you have put yourself back together." Eriatt laughed. "I can see it. You are still broken. You will always be broken. You will always be mine."

Drake ground his teeth. "Aren't you gonna beg for your life? Offer to take me back if I let you go?"

Eriatt's eyes turned sad, and she smiled. "We both know you will never let me go, my favourite. You are going to kill me here, and you will try to trick yourself into believing that is the end of it. It is not. No matter how far you run, no matter how much power you garner, no matter how many women you fool into loving you – you will always wish it was me."

Drake opened his mouth to deny it, but his throat closed and no words escaped. He wiped away tears with the back of his hand and stared into the face of the one woman he could ever love.

"Do it," Eriatt said.

Almost gently, Drake reached up with the knife. He paused for just a moment. Eriatt didn't move to stop him. He drew the blade across her neck and waited as blood ran thick and the life faded from her dark eyes.

The Phoenix

"Hard to starboard," Keelin yelled as loudly as his voice could carry.

Fremen spun the wheel and a moment later the ship began to turn, slipping through the water at a new angle. Keelin leaned over the edge, trying to spot any hidden rocks on their new course while listening for the scrape and crack of the hull breaching. After a while he let out the breath he'd been holding. It was the tenth course correction in the last hour, and his nerves were frayed so thin he was about to snap.

A week out from Larkos they'd started to see evidence that they were straying into the waters surrounding the Forgotten Empire. The shoreline was now visible on their starboard side, and the trees were taller and more dense. There was a strange feeling too, almost as though the land itself didn't want them near it.

The sea near the shoreline alternated between calm as glass and rough as bark, and the rocks grew ever more frequent, sharp, and devious. Every member of the crew was on edge, and even the normally serene Kebble seemed out of sorts. He came to Keelin on the third day of their navigation through the hazardous waters and made an earnest plea for them to sail away and never return. It fell on deaf ears. The crew were close to their fortune, and their captain was close to the vessel of his vengeance.

Drake's chart was proving invaluable. It didn't map all of the hidden rocks, but it did show them the beach they were headed to and the best route for them to take. It also told them which islands off the coast they could stop at for supplies, and which of those islands no man should venture near. Keelin thought about Zothus' giant spider. Everyone knew the spider had come from one of the islands near the Forgotten Empire, and that was an island he wished to stay as far away from as possible.

Leaning over the side, Keelin could see deep into the crystal blue waters that lapped and sloshed against the ship's hull. The sea teemed with life here, despite the ominous reputation of the area, almost as if the beasts that called the water their home had never heard of the fate that had befallen the once great empire. Not that Keelin knew much about what had happened to the Forgotten Empire either, only that it had vanished overnight and no one who entered the dark forests ever returned.

"Do you see the fish?" Elaina said. Keelin wondered how long the woman had been standing behind him.

"Which ones?" His eyes were focused on his ship's path through the water, straining to see the hidden rocks before they presented a danger.

Elaina laughed. "The big ones swimming around our hull. Must be easily the size of a person, and I reckon they're playing games. Every now and then one comes closer and touches the ship with its fin, then backs off to join the others."

Keelin glanced downwards. Sure enough, there were some very large fish easily keeping pace with the slow progress of *The Phoenix*.

Keelin looked at Elaina to find her staring back at him, a wide smile on her face. She had a kind of plain beauty to her when she smiled, and right now it reminded Keelin of all sorts of things he'd thought he wanted to forget.

"Remember that time aboard the *Death* when my da stopped us for a spell off the coast of that island ring?" she said.

Keelin nodded. It was an island surrounded by water, which was in turn surrounded by a ring of land, which finally gave way to the sea. Target, Tanner had named the island, and they'd spent a good few days there exploring, hoping to find some hidden treasure in its green interior. In the end they hadn't found a single bit, but that hadn't stopped a young Keelin Stillwater and Elaina Black having fun. The waters surrounding the island were clear, clean, and free of any predators large enough to do a person harm, and they'd explored them for days.

"And why are you bringing up that little stop now, El?" Keelin said, turning his attention back to the ship's course.

"There were some pretty big fish there too. We caught a couple."

"Mhm," Keelin agreed. "And I thought you were bringing it up to remind me that we spent half of that little stop fucking on every spot of beach we could find."

Elaina laughed. "We did that."

"Cap'n." Aimi's voice sent a wave of dread up and down Keelin's spine. There was no way to tell how long she'd been there or how much she might have heard, but Keelin had a sinking feeling Elaina knew, and that was why she'd brought up their time on Target.

"Aye?" Keelin was afraid to turn and look at Aimi, so he kept his eyes on the water.

"According to the chart, we should be coming on the beach any time now. Just thought you might like to know."

Keelin sighed. Their relationship had been more than a little strained since Larkos, and Keelin could only assume it was because he'd let Elaina come aboard. Aimi still shared his cabin, but she spent almost no time there other than when she slept, and at those times Keelin's bed seemed like hostile waters teeming with sharks.

"Troubles?" Elaina said after a while.

"Leave it, El," Keelin snapped. "Hasn't Morley given you some duties to perform?"

Elaina laughed. "I do believe your first mate is a little afraid of me. Anytime I ask, he simply tells me to find something worth doing."

"And you thought distracting the captain was something worth doing?"

His question was met with silence. Elaina turned her attention to the sea and a mad grin split her face.

"So you really want to be queen of us pirates?" Keelin said. It was a question he'd wanted to ask since before they left Larkos, but he'd needed to judge his timing. Elaina could be prickly as a cactus in the wrong mood.

"I really do."

"To make Tanner proud?"

"Aye, that's a small part of it, I suppose. Ain't no way he could disapprove if I worked my own way onto the throne."

"Even if you stole the support that was meant for him?"

Elaina was silent for a few moments, and the sun seemed to darken a little with her mood. Keelin shivered.

"I didn't steal his support," she said eventually. "He sent me to

Chade and Larkos to get help. Didn't say it was help for him or the isles, just help. I went and got it for me. Besides, he went and bent a knee to Morrass, same as you. Way I see it, I'm the only one that hasn't got down on my knees to suckle on his cock, so I'm gonna sail on in at the head of a fleet as strong as all the other captains' combined and take the throne."

"And then suckle on Drake's cock as his wife and queen?" Keelin braced himself for the fury of the storm.

"Better that than as his *boy*." Keelin glanced up to find Elaina pulling a face at him. They both laughed. "Pirates might have themselves a king, and Drake might have himself a crown, but both are gonna need a queen too. And there's no other bitch of a captain in the isles worthy of that title."

Keelin thought about it. He imagined himself on the throne, and he imagined Aimi sitting beside him. She was smart as a scholar, quick as an eel, and stronger than most folk Keelin knew, but he wasn't sure the other pirates would accept her. Elaina, they would accept. She was born and raised a pirate, and she'd fought, killed, and grieved alongside many of the other captains. Keelin wondered how Drake would feel about marrying into the Black family, and the image didn't end happily.

"That our beach?" Elaina said, pointing towards the shore.

They anchored a good row away from the sandy shore, and there they floated for a while. Many of the crew had come up on deck to look out at the landing point that led to their promised fortune. What most of them would do with their share of the treasure was a question that would probably end in a few months of booze and pussy, and then it would be back to business as usual.

"We're a good ways out, Captan," Morley said, joining Keelin at the railing.

"I don't want the ship getting too close. She should be safe here, sheltered from most anything nature can throw at her."

Morley grunted and said no more. The man had been so outspoken against many of Keelin's decisions of late that it was going to be hard to leave the ship in his care. The only consolation Keelin could think of was that the rest of the crew would never let Morley leave the captain and the landing party behind when the promise of riches was so enticing.

Keelin grinned, imagining the look on Arbiter Prin's face when he realised who held the knife to his throat. He pushed away from the railing and walked to the centre of the main deck, whistling loudly to get the attention of his crew.

"Listen up," he shouted. "We wait here for now. It'll be dark in a few hours, and I want our first day on the island to be a good long one. Those coming ashore, I want you all up and ready to leave at first light. No stragglers. Good?"

There was a murmur of assent from the crew.

"I want ten volunteers to come with me," he continued. "It's gonna be…"

"Something moved!" shouted Olly. "On the shore."

Keelin sighed as everyone who had gathered around ran back to the railing to stare at the beach. Sailors were ever an easy group to distract, and pirates were no different. Keelin walked over to the railing.

"There was something on the beach, near the trees," Olly insisted.

"Ya bloody fool," said Fremen. "Ya didn't see nothing but the trees and a bit o' wind."

"No," Olly said. "It weren't no tree taking up a rustle. I was just looking about the sand and then I saw it. It was big, and standing there, from this distance it blended right in with the trees, but when it moved… It were big."

Some of the crew muttered something about giants, while others laughed off Olly's ramblings. Keelin shook his head and returned to the centre of the deck.

"As I was saying," he shouted, loudly enough to reclaim the crew's attention, "I need ten volunteers to come with me. It's gonna be tough and dangerous, but…"

"I'm going," Smithe said, standing tall among the crew with his arms crossed.

Keelin nodded to him. Smithe had been courteous and helpful of late, but Keelin knew full well the man still hated him, and he reckoned he'd rather have Smithe with him on the island than back on the ship spreading sedition.

Morley stepped forward, but Keelin shook his head. "Need you here, mate. Look after the ship."

"Aye, Captan."

"I'll come along," Feather said in a voice that made it sound like he was hoping someone would stop him. The lad may have moved on from the position of ship's boy and graduated to a proper wage, but he was still young, and the young always felt like they had something to prove.

Bronson stepped forward and nodded to Keelin. "I volunteer, Cap'n."

"Me too," called Elaina from up in the rigging. She was sitting above the gathering and grinning down at them. As soon as she spoke, discord travelled through the crew. Keelin had to put a stop to it before the mood turned.

"Elaina. What we're… This is between the crew. There ain't…"

"Save it, Stillwater." Elaina laughed. "I don't want a share of the loot. I ain't taking anything from any of you. I just wanna come along, is all. See what all the fuss is about. I promise neither me, nor any member of my crew, will claim even one bit of what's found there."

That seemed to cheer the crew up a little, and he couldn't very well argue with her. If someone else was willing to risk their life to further the wealth of the crew, Keelin wouldn't stand in their way.

"I volunteer," shouted Aimi from her place on the deck.

Keelin suppressed a sigh. "Aimi, I don't think… It's gonna be dangerous."

Aimi stood with her arms crossed and her chin raised in defiance. Keelin nodded his acceptance and wished he'd just handpicked a group instead.

"I'll come along," said Elaina's veteran quartermaster. "No share. Just as the cap said."

"You might need a healer," said the priest who was always following Elaina around.

"I volunteer," said Jotin, and he was quickly echoed by his brother, Jolan.

"One more," Keelin said with a nod. "Kebble?"

The marksman had kept quiet, and that was something Keelin

hadn't expected. He'd thought Kebble would be one of the first to step forward. A few of the crew moved aside to reveal Kebble leaning against the ship's main mast, a wistful look on his face. He nodded once, and it seemed to be all the assent he was going to give.

"Then we have our landing crew," Keelin said. "Those of you who are coming, get ready then get some sleep. Tomorrow we go find ourselves a fortune."

Starry Dawn

Rowing the dinghy over to the beach proved to be a lot more taxing than anyone had anticipated. But Keelin's decision to anchor so far from shore had been the right one, even if it did mean the trip was long, with the currents whipping first one way then the other at nightmarish speeds. Elaina put her back into the oar and her trust into those rowing alongside her. Judging by the sheen of sweat on Keelin's face, he was having just as hard a time at the tiller, and by the time the eleven-strong landing crew pulled the boat ashore, they were all aching and breathless from the exertion. It wasn't the most auspicious of starts.

Elaina knelt in the sand, her feet and legs soaked with saltwater and sweat dripping down her nose. Someone offered her a water skin and she took it gratefully, taking two short sips followed by two longer ones. She stood and looked around at the rest of the landing crew. Pavel was busy trying to wring the water out of his robes. Elaina thought him a fool for insisting on wearing the garb in such a situation, but the man was a priest above all else. Alfer was close by, staring into the ominous-looking forest, his hand resting on the hilt of the notched sword buckled at his belt.

Keelin, dressed in a faded blue suit with tasselled epaulettes, was talking to the man with the rifle. Kebble Salt was an odd one, and Elaina had yet to figure him out. The man kept his head a short shave away from bald and maintained his horseshoe moustache with almost a lover's touch. The crew of *The Phoenix* were more than just complimentary about him; they treated him as a hero, with all the awe and distance that folk afforded to such.

Elaina looked around for Keelin's waif and found her staring up the beach. The woman had insisted on taking one of the oars on the way across, and Elaina had to respect her for that. Despite her size, she didn't back down from a challenge. Taking another couple of short sips from the water skin, Elaina approached her. "Here."

The woman looked down at the offered water and then away.

"I ain't trying to poison ya," Elaina said with a sigh. "We all need to drink if we're gonna survive this. Weren't exactly an easy row over, and you did well at the oar. Reckon ya deserve a bit of hydration."

She looked at Elaina sceptically, but her thirst soon won out and she took the skin. "Thanks."

"Reckon you and me got off to a bad start," Elaina continued, staring down at the smaller woman. "So I think we should rectify that, seeing as we're gonna be around each other a bit. I ain't trying to come between you and Keelin." There was nothing quite like starting off an offer of friendship with a lie.

The woman finished gulping down the water and handed the skin back to Elaina. There was a look on her face that said she didn't quite believe the claim.

"Then what are you doing here?" she said. "Why come aboard in the first place?"

"Don't think I caught your name?"

"Aimi."

"Well, Aimi, if you can keep a secret – I came aboard *The Phoenix* because I don't have a ship of my own. Bastard of a first mate pinched it while I was ashore in Larkos. Now, you might know that me and Keelin go a long ways back. Well, I needed passage back to the isles, and he was one I knew I could trust."

"Sorry about your ship."

Elaina laughed. "Oh, don't you worry about that. I'll be getting it back soon as the fucks make port."

"Why come along for this though?" Aimi said. "It's a lot of danger for no share in the prize."

"I'd be bored sat on the ship waiting for you all to come back. Figured I might as well come along for the fun."

Aimi looked up at Elaina with an incredulous expression. "You're mad."

Elaina grinned. "Runs in the family. Reckon we're getting ready to head into the trees. Come on."

Each member of the expedition had their own pack to bear, and each of those packs contained food, water, and flint for starting a fire. There were no illusions that the food they were taking with them would be enough, so one of their duties, while looking for whatever it was they were looking for, would be to search for food and fresh water. All eleven of them were armed with both a weapon of their choice and a thick knife for cutting through the undergrowth.

"Stick close together," Keelin said as the last of the expedition drew near. His gaze stopped on Elaina and Aimi standing close to one another, and Elaina thought she saw a flash of worry pass over his face. "But not too close. Be ready to help each other, just try not to get in each other's way."

"What is it we're looking for, exactly?" Elaina called.

Her question was met with a silence that sounded suspicious at best.

"We're already here, aren't we?" she said with a laugh. "Right along with you, and still promising not to steal your treasure. I think it's about time you let us know what we've got ourselves into, eh?"

"The city of HwoyonDo," Keelin said, as though the name should mean something.

"Oh. A whole city then. Big, is it? Hard to miss?"

Keelin set to staring Elaina down, but she met his steely greys with her own bright blues.

"Actually, the city of HwoyonDo was rather small compared to some of the other cities the Empire built," said Kebble. "It was not the capital, nor a base of power, but instead the seat of religion and worship. People from all over the Empire would make a pilgrimage to the great temple, where they would offer up tributes to their god. Sorcerers would gather from the far reaches to crowd the Sky Spire and the Observatory, and watch the stars in hopes of enlightenment and to reap the rewards of the rocks that fall from the sky."

"You seem to know a lot about an empire that most folk call forgotten for a reason," Elaina said.

Kebble gave her a wistful smile.

"Do you know the way?" Keelin asked his marksman.

Kebble nodded. "More or less. The forest has likely reclaimed all the old roads though. It will not be easy."

"Nothing worth a shit ever is," Keelin growled. "Let's move out.

Kebble has the lead."

Elaina fell in beside Smithe. The man had been quiet for a while now, and that was unlike him. It was more than just quiet, though – Smithe had a haunted look in his eyes.

"You hear that, Cap?" he said, his eyes darting about as they walked past the first tree into the close, damp forest.

Elaina listened. She heard the sound of boots on earth and twigs. She heard the chirping of insects and the call of birds. She heard the wind stirring branches and leaves, and she heard the gentle slosh of the sea washing the beach away.

"Hear what, Smithe?"

"The whispers," he said. "Angry voices, like… like they don't want us here."

"Right." Elaina took a deep breath. "So, what's with your man Kebble? Seems he knows a bit about this place."

Smithe hacked at a branch that had had no intention of getting in his way. The brief act of violence seemed to embolden him a little.

"He thinks he's immortal. Real smug about it too. Acts like it's nothin'. Smug fuck-piece. Says he's even tried to get himself killed. Like being immortal is a bad thing. Dumb bastard. I'd be captain if I were immortal. Sure as hell wouldn't be in this forest with all its fucking whispering."

Elaina almost laughed. Smithe was considering the possibility of immortality, and the furthest he could set his sights was still captain of a ship. Simple men had simple desires, and Smithe appeared to be deranged as well as simple. The trees were most certainly not whispering at them all to leave. The spirits, however, were another matter altogether.

The Phoenix

Two days into their expedition and Aimi was fairly certain they were going round in circles. Kebble claimed to be leading them to HwoyonDo, but he didn't seem enthusiastic about the responsibility, and Aimi wondered whether he would soon lead them right back to the beach.

The forest was hot and damp and full of biting insects and other things that had far bigger teeth. Each night was a horror that started with a chorus of animal calls and ended in haunting wails and titanic roars that ripped through the forest like a wind, bringing the smell of death and decay. Each night Keelin set three watches, and each night Aimi found herself sitting at least two of them, wishing sleep would claim her. Her tremulous feelings were only made worse by Elaina Black's apparent ease with the situation. In fact, Captain Black seemed to be the only one in the entire expedition who wasn't worried by the forest.

Aimi knew something was wrong as soon as she was awake. Keelin was kneeling above her, his hand on her shoulder and his eyes darting around the forest. It was long past her watch, and the near-pitch darkness told her the sun had yet to rise.

"Feather is missing," Keelin whispered. He gave Aimi's shoulder a quick squeeze and stood.

Aimi lifted her head and looked around. The whole camp was in a state of disarray as some folk struggled to rise and wake up properly while others grasped swords and stared about in fear. Kebble had his rifle readied, but couldn't seem to find a target. Elaina was squatting down on her haunches, staring upwards at the canopy.

"Perhaps he's taking a shit?" said Smithe, with a yawn and a look that said he wasn't best pleased about being woken up.

"That's what I thought when I got up for the watch," Bronson said. "That was a fair while back. Don't know anyone who shits for that long."

"Fremen takes his bloody time about it," Smithe growled. "Likes to read a book while he hangs his arse over the ship."

"We need to look for him," Aimi said.

Judging by the looks sent her way, her statement was not well received. Not a single member of the expedition, not even Keelin, jumped at the prospect of forming a search party for their valued crewmate.

"First light ain't too far off," Elaina said, still staring upwards. "It'd be safer to wait."

"What if he's out there, hurt?" Aimi said.

"In this light we could walk right by him and not notice," Elaina said. "Not to mention, we can't see all the other dangers."

"We can't just leave him."

"I don't wanna go out there in the dark," Elaina's quartermaster put in.

"What if whatever got Feather is just waitin' for us too?" Jolan said, his voice quivering.

"He's right," Jotin jumped in. "It's a bloody trap, is what it is."

"Enough," Keelin growled, his voice quiet but full of command. Everyone stopped talking, and Aimi could hear the chitter of insects and the sound of something heavy moving through the leaf litter.

"Feather?" Keelin shouted. The noise almost seemed to echo around them. No answer floated back, and Aimi could hear nothing but the unseen wildlife and the crackling of their fire. It wasn't strictly cold enough to warrant a fire, but not a single member of the expedition had wanted to bed down for the night without the light, and there was plenty of fuel to be found.

After a while Keelin gave a weary sigh. "Elaina is right. It's too dangerous to go out in the dark, and we might walk right by Feather. We'll wait until first light, and we'll search for the boy then. Chances are he just got scared and decided to run back to the ship."

Aimi knew a lie when she heard one. Feather could be called many things, but coward wasn't one of them. All the same, it seemed to satisfy everyone else, and she wagered some of them needed to think Feather had simply run off.

They spent most of the morning searching in groups of three, only to find no sign of Feather. Elaina said she'd found a trail that quickly ran cold and could easily have belonged to one of the search party. As the sun drew near its zenith, Keelin called a halt to the search, stating they needed to move on while there was still enough light to make good progress. Aimi hoped Feather was alright, but there was a pit in her stomach that said otherwise.

King's Justice

"Aye, that's a fuckin' lot o' ships," Daimen said with a whistle.

Captain Rothin Wulfden winced at the curse. He was stout with a belly like an ale barrel and more knowledge of the sea than almost any man Daimen had met. The captain was also a horrendous bore who deplored the use of foul language and chastised anyone who practised it. Unfortunately for the captain, Daimen was too old to care much about what he thought.

"Thirty-eight so far," Wulfden said pompously, near bursting with pride. "Most are fully seaworthy – some are waiting for repairs."

"What about the fuckin' crew?" Daimen said. "Fully loaded, are they?"

The good captain fell silent and scratched at his belly.

"Ah, that'd explain it then," Daimen said with a grin. "With this many ships you're sure to sail on in an' crush the bloody pirates like the undisciplined fucks that they are. Not so easy to do when ya can't even crew ya ships."

"We lost a lot of men in the last attack. Well-trained sailors are not so easy to come by, and the soldiers we send must be taught to fight on unstable footing."

Daimen laughed. "Sea legs and sea gut, hardest things for the land dwellers to learn, eh?"

"Indeed. Sarth will soon be sending more ships and more men to help. We expect to sail into the Pirate Isles with over fifty fully manned ships. I'd like to see your Drake Morrass repel those numbers."

"Ah, stop with the 'my Drake Morrass', will ya? I'm one of you now, got me a pardon to prove it." It was mostly the truth. Daimen had a provisional pardon and a provisional deed to a lucrative spot of land in the south. Whether or not the king signed those documents was conditional on Daimen leading them to and helping them wipe out the pirates of the isles.

"Indeed," said Captain Wulfden, sounding anything but trusting.

The sad truth of the matter was that the good captain and his officers were as much Daimen's gaolers as they were his superiors. Rarely did Daimen find himself out of their watchful sight, and rarely while in their sight did he find himself feeling like a free man. Though they'd never believe him, the captain and his men had no need to be so strict. Daimen wouldn't flee even if the opportunity should present itself, and the way Land's End was locked down, he couldn't see an opportunity anywhere on the horizon.

He'd had plenty of time to think about his situation while he was locked up, and he'd come to the conclusion that the king was telling the truth. Drake would sacrifice anything to achieve his goals, even an entire town. The good folk of the isles were better off without a treacherous cur like that, just as they were better off without Tanner Black. And Daimen would be happy to help remove them, given the hefty reward that had been laid out in front of him.

"We should be under way before the new moon," Captain Wulfden continued as he gazed out across his fleet. It wasn't technically his fleet yet, but everyone with an ounce of say in the matter was pushing for the captain to be made admiral.

"So soon?" Daimen said. "Fuck me, a storm *is* coming."

The captain ground his teeth and scratched at his belly again. "The less time we give the pirates to prepare, the better. Your intelligence had best be right, Poole. I have the authorisation to execute you on the spot if you attempt a ruse."

It wasn't the first time the captain had made that threat, and Daimen would have put good money on it not being the last.

He opened his mouth to defend himself, only to be interrupted by a loud belch followed by a number of profound apologies from a man in a faded green suit that looked as though its better days were many years behind it.

"I do apologise, gentlefellows," the man slurred with a grin that showed at least one missing tooth. The smell of alcohol wafted off him so strongly Daimen suspected he bathed in booze. "I appear to have lost my purse. Could any of... you... How many of you are there? I count one, two, three, six, seven."

There were four of them, and apart from Daimen they were all dressed in their finest naval uniforms. Only the most dedicated of drunks would attempt to squeeze a bit out of the sailors.

"Could I borrow a bit or two? Just enough to get to an inn, I swear," the man slurred, staggering a little.

"The docks were meant to be cleared of vagrants, Barrows," Captain Wulfden growled, doing his very best to ignore the drunkard swaying back and forth in front of him. "Have him thrown in gaol."

"Whoa now." The drunkard stumbled back a step and fell on his arse in a muddy puddle. With a groan, the man got his hands beneath him and lurched back to his feet. "It's not my bloody fault I'm here. It's yours. I was out on shoe… schuuure… shore leave when you all just closed the port. My ship packed up and fucked off before you locked them down, and they went and left me here. Now, my good sir, I do not have much in the way of skills or talents. I do, however, know my way around a ship. Or at least bits of one. The good bits, mind, not the bilge."

"Just get him out of my sight," said the captain. "Let him bother the rest of the good folk and leave us be."

Two of Captain Wulfden's officers moved forwards to escort the drunkard away, forcibly if necessary. The men looked loathe to touch the poor fellow, but he didn't seem to be in any hurry to leave of his own accord.

"I can sail," he slurred as he was dragged away. "No? How about a bit? A copper?"

"Damned vagrant sailors are everywhere," Wulfden hissed. He bit his lip, but Daimen had heard the curse and grinned at him.

"Well, it is ya own damned fault, Captain. Ya shut down the largest port in these here Five Kingdoms. Those vagrants got nowhere to go until it opens up for trade again, eh?"

Wulfden shot Daimen an icy glare.

"Right y'are. Damned vagrants all over the fucking place. Quite right."

The captain muttered something under his breath. "Now, where was I. Oh, yes. I have the authority to execute you, Poole."

"So ya keep reminding me. Honestly, I think it's putting a real strain on our relationship, mate."

Captain Wulfden let slip an ugly smile. "Do not think you are the only traitor we have in the pirate ranks."

Daimen paused. He didn't want to play into the captain's hand, but his curiosity got the better of him. "Who?"

Starry Dawn

Elaina looked down at the empty bed roll. All of Bronson's supplies were still packed away in his sack, and there was no sign of a struggle. He was simply gone, as though he'd woken and walked away without so much as a sound. Not even the watch had heard or seen the big man leave the camp.

"We should go," Jotin said, chewing on his lip. He'd already made his mouth bloody, but it didn't seem to stop the fool. "Get back to the ship before any more of us go missing."

"We are closer to the city than we are to the ship," Kebble said as he knelt down on the opposite side of the bed roll to Elaina and poked around in the leaf litter. "Very close now."

"What?" Jotin's voice had risen to one drop from panic. "How do you know?"

Kebble pointed at a rock to his left. Jotin glanced at the small boulder and then away; the idiot hadn't even seen the markings on it.

"It's a fucking rock, Kebble."

"It is a marker," Kebble said. "And it says we are within a day's walk of HwoyonDo. The city should be safer than the forest." The lie was plain on his face. Whatever waited for them in HwoyonDo was anything but safe. More intriguing to Elaina was how Kebble knew what waited for them.

"Folk say you're immortal," she said quietly.

Kebble nodded.

"So if I stab you, you won't die?"

Kebble smiled. "It is more likely you will miss."

"I don't miss."

"Then try. I would welcome the death. But you would likely trip and miss, or the captain would catch your hand in time, or lightning would rip from the sky and strike you. I assure you, Captain Black, I can be killed. Just nothing and no one has managed it yet. I am cursed with life."

Elaina picked up a colourful beetle and squeezed it a little, then released it. It flew away on shimmering wings. "Does Keelin believe you?"

"I believe he is starting to."

Elaina glanced at Keelin, who was pacing back and forth at the edge of the firelight, staring out into the receding darkness. When she looked back, she found Kebble watching her intently.

"Spirits in this place are angry," Elaina said. "I can feel their rage."

"Can you?"

"Spend enough time among spirits, you learn to pick up on the way they feel," she said, thinking of the forests on the Isle of Goats. "Funny thing is, they're angry at you."

"They have every right to be. I created them."

Keelin was still pacing. Jotin was busy crying to his brother. The others in the camp were either trying to get back to sleep or watching the shrinking darkness with nervous head twitches. Kebble smiled at Elaina and nodded.

"You may ask your questions, Captain Black."

"Just one, really. What the fuck?"

"Spirits gather in places of great pain or joy. Often you may find them at sites of heroic or villainous deeds. Most people cannot see or hear them – they only know that something is there. But the spirits can see us. Some spirits are malevolent, while others are simply playful. The spirits here are definitely more malevolent."

"I know," Elaina hissed. "I know all of this. I've been seeing the bloody things most of my life. They infest the Isle of Goats and drag the unwary into the forest, and there they keep them. Pretty sure my ma and da see them too, but I ain't exactly ever discussed it with them. What did you mean when you said you created the spirits here?"

"Exactly what I said. I created them when I brought down the Empire."

"Pack up," Keelin growled. "We're leaving."

Elaina realised the first rays of sunlight were beginning to peek through the canopy. She knew Keelin was eager to not waste another day like they had searching for the boy, Feather. Bronson was gone, and the sooner they accepted that and moved on, the sooner they would get to

HwoyonDo.

Once the camp was packed and the contents of Bronson's pack divvied out between those that remained, they set off. Kebble led the way, and Elaina pushed past Keelin and Jotin to walk next to the marksman.

"How'd ya do it?" she said as she hacked at a vine stretching out in front of her. She believed Kebble's wild claim, and her curiosity was driving her to find out how the man had accomplished it. "You some sort of sorcerer? Like a witch?"

"No," Kebble said with a laugh. "I was born the second son of a patronless scholar who lived in the common section of HwoyonDo. We had next to nothing as we grew up. My father worked for whoever would hire him, most often criminals requesting forgeries. The one thing we did have was access to the great library. All those with a scholarly licence were afforded entrance, and as a scholar's son, so was I."

Kebble stopped and brushed some dirt away from a rock embedded in the ground. A smile spread across his face, twisting his moustache into an odd shape.

"Closer than I thought. We may have been able to complete our journey yesterday." He set off again on a slightly different course, and Elaina hurried to catch up, the others oblivious of the tale he was telling her.

"I learned at a ferocious rate, devouring every book, scroll, and scrap of parchment I could find. I studied astronomy, religion, science, magic. I learned to predict the weather based on signs any fool could see and feel. I learned alchemy, and how to apply it to the arts of healing and destruction both. I learned everything a book could teach me, including the subtleties of court behaviour.

"My reputation grew along with my knowledge, and soon the Neotromo asked me to become one of his advisors."

"Neotromo?"

"Chief magistrate of arcane studies. A powerful sorcerer, and second in authority to the Emperor himself. Therein lay my first mistake. I wasn't happy being advisor to the second most powerful man in the Empire. Growing up with nothing makes some men desire little, others it makes desire everything.

"While still working for the Neotromo, I sneaked off to the capital city of Tresingsare, where I worked my way into an audience with the Emperor and revealed just whom I worked for. The Emperor and the Neotromo were ever at odds, and I played them off each other."

Kebble sighed. "I wish I could say I did it for some noble reason, but the truth is I did it to further my own agenda. I played both sides into starting a war against each other, knowing full well whoever won would have me standing by their side."

"Who won?" Elaina said.

Kebble laughed. "The forest."

Elaina was about to savage the man for such a purposefully vague answer, when she realised he'd stopped and was staring at something above her.

A gigantic stone arch rose a hundred feet into the sky, the trees of the forest clinging to it and twisting around its great pillars. To either side of the arch were the crumbling remnants of an ancient wall, long since brought low by the forces of nature. Huge vines hung down from the arch, almost like a curtain, obscuring the view through it. Not that Elaina needed the view; she could already see that the forest gave way behind to powder blue skies dotted with white cloud, and above it all the sun shining down on them.

"Welcome to HwoyonDo," Kebble said. He sounded sad. "City of scholars and traitors."

Keelin rushed forwards, straight past Kebble and Elaina, and began hacking at the vines that hung down from the arch and pooled upon the floor. Smithe ran to help, and soon both men were frantically chopping their way through the natural gate while the others just stood and watched. Keelin was first through the hole they created, with Smithe only a step behind. They stopped on the other side of the arch, Elaina's view obscured by their bodies.

Kebble stepped forward and placed a hand on the stone. He dropped to his knees and began to cry. Unable to contain her curiosity any longer, Elaina strode forwards, pushing through the hacked tangle of vines and inserting herself between the two men on the other side.

The city of HwoyonDo rose up before them like the nest of some giant insect. Buildings of grey-brown stone rose higher than most had cause to be, with the smallest of them a good five or six storeys tall. Stone bridges ran across the sky from one building to another; some were no more than broken piles of rubble on the ground, but others had stood the tests and rigours of time and nature, and gave easy, quick access from one structure to the next.

The roadways between the buildings were easily large enough for ten men to walk abreast, and to either side of the roads were trenches where water rested or flowed. The forest had started to reclaim much of the city, and a lot of the buildings closest to the arch were infested with trees and vines. Some had even started to crumble beneath the strain, but it seemed there was only so much the forest could reclaim, even after such a period of time.

Elaina felt someone push against her back, and she stepped aside to let Alfer through behind her. More members of the expedition filtered in, and soon all of them were standing there, staring at the half-ruined city spread out before them. Only Kebble hadn't ventured through the arch. Elaina found herself more and more convinced that the marksman was no madman, but was in fact telling the truth about his immortality and even his origins.

"We're here," Keelin said, a look of reverence in his eyes.

"Aye," Smithe said. "Looks like you finally made good on that promise. Now, which way to the riches, Captain?"

The Phoenix

"Everything in this city is treasure, Smithe," said Keelin.

The grandeur of HwoyonDo wasn't lost on Keelin, far from it, but it was a distraction that didn't interest him. Of the eleven of them that had set out, two were lost already, and the longer they stayed, the more likely those who remained would join their missing companions. Keelin needed to find the Observatory. He didn't care even a drop for the supposed treasure the city held.

"We'll just pick up some bricks and run them back to the ship then, eh?" Smithe said with a sneer.

"I don't give a fuck what you do," Keelin snarled, barely sparing Smithe a glance. "There must be some street signs somewhere. Maybe I can see it if I get high."

"See what?" Aimi said.

Keelin ignored her, striding forwards into the city. Buildings rose up high on both sides and extended far into the distance, blocking out any chance of seeing what lay ahead. Rubble littered the ground where the forest was starting to reclaim its territory, but further in there were fewer signs of the jungle. It gave Keelin hope that the Observatory was still standing and untouched. He picked a tall structure on his left with vines growing up the walls. Much of one side of it had been knocked down by the trunk of a tree. It looked like it may have once been used as housing; a small metal stove, rusted beyond use, hung precariously out of one hole in the wall. Shards of pottery lay strewn among giant roots, and a tarnished spoon had been half absorbed by a gnarled knot of wood.

If he could climb up the vines and find a way to the rooftop, he might be able to see the layout of the city, maybe even spot the Observatory itself.

"Keelin!"

A hand appeared on Keelin's arm, but he shook it off, not caring who it belonged to, and advanced upon the nearest vine that looked sturdy enough to take his weight. Aimi slipped around him and stood between him and the building. Her brow was furrowed and her cheeks reddened.

"Stop!" she shouted.

For a moment Keelin considered shoving the little woman aside and starting the climb before any of the others could try to stop him. He glanced back to see the rest of his expedition standing just a few paces behind Aimi, sharing worried glances between their captain and each other. Even Smithe was frowning with concern.

"What?" Keelin said.

"Where are you going, Keelin?" said Elaina, hanging at the back of the group.

"I need to get to the Observatory."

"That where the best treasure is kept?" Smithe said.

"Why?" said Aimi.

Keelin felt his jaw clench. He was so close to his vengeance, only to be held back by those who were supposed to be helping him.

"My city is dead," Kebble said sadly as he walked slowly towards the others. Keelin spared the man a glance, and was shocked by what he saw. Kebble looked older, as though every line on his face was etched more deeply than before. His eyes were red from tears, and there were streaks down his face where they'd washed away the dirt and grime of the last few days.

"Eh?" Smithe grunted.

"It has been dead for over a thousand years," Kebble continued, his eyes darting around the ruined city before them. "Even the ancient wards that kept the forest at bay have started to fail. It's all my fault."

"Wonderful," Keelin growled, impatience tearing away at his last nerve. "This is all we need."

"Your city?" Smithe said. "Ya been here before, Kebble?"

Kebble nodded slowly. "Long ago. When thousands lived here and we…"

"Good stuff," Smithe said. "It's all very tragic, I'm sure. You know where we can find the gold? Or at least the stuff that's worth its weight?"

Kebble nodded slowly. "Yes. We should act quickly. The city may be dead, but it does not want us here."

Smithe opened his mouth to reply, but quickly shut it again with a shake of his head. Keelin groaned and turned back to the vine; he had no wish to indulge Kebble's delusion that he was immortal. Aimi still stood in his way, a determined look on her face.

"We're not splitting up," she said slowly.

"I have to do this alone," Keelin said. He knew that what he was about to do was dangerous, and he wanted no one else to risk themselves for his attempt at vengeance. There was something else as well. He wanted no one to see the pain and rage that he'd kept balled up inside ever since the death of his little sister, ever since he'd watched her burn and had been powerless to stop it.

"Do what?" Aimi said.

They'd been butting heads for weeks now, but there was real concern in her eyes. For a brief moment Keelin considered telling her everything. He considered telling her how his father had torn their family apart, about how Keelin had spent the last ten years hunting down the Arbiter who had murdered his sister. He couldn't though. He couldn't let her see his greatest weakness. Keelin had built his entire piratical career on secrets and lies. His identity was a lie, his life was a lie. Now he thought about it, there was very little that was true in his life.

"Keelin," Aimi said insistently. "Do what?"

Drawing in a ragged breath, Keelin composed himself. He looked down at the little woman in front of him and shook his head. "Go with the others. I will be back here by this time tomorrow."

"No."

Aimi stood her ground, her hands balled into fists at her side. Keelin was acting erratically, and the last thing she was about to do was let the fool run off on his own. Aimi wasn't the type to bandy around romantic clichés, but she was sure of one thing – she liked the captain a lot more than as a friend, and despite his recent spell of acting like an arse, she couldn't let him go off on his own. They'd already lost Feather and Bronson.

The captain fixed her with a steely glare, but Aimi held fast, though the intensity made her want to shrink away and join the others like a nice, meek crew member. It would take more than a stern eyeballing to scare her off.

"Jolan," Keelin said, his stare still on Aimi. "I have an errand to run elsewhere in the city. Make certain Aimi does not follow me."

"Fuck that!" Aimi spat.

"Smithe…" Keelin said.

"You can't just…" Aimi threw out her arms to push Keelin's chest, but he caught her hands and twisted her aside, sending her stumbling towards the others. A moment later two thick arms wrapped around her, holding tight.

"Smithe. Find us some treasure to take back," Keelin continued. "As much as we can carry."

"Damnit, Keelin," Aimi shouted, struggling against Jolan's grip only for it to tighten. "You simpering gull fart, you can't just fuck off on ya own."

Without another word, Keelin turned and leapt towards the nearest vine, climbing upwards hand over hand. Aimi struggled, but Jolan held her tight. Everyone else just watched the captain climb up and up, until he made it to the rooftop and disappeared from sight.

Aimi stopped struggling and Jolan relaxed his grip a little. The pirate smelled of sweat and fear, and it made her stomach curdle. She went limp with a heavy sigh, and Jolan loosened his grip a little more.

"Sorry, lass," he said quietly. "Captain's orders an' all."

"Uh huh," Aimi grunted, a moment before hooking her left leg around Jolan's and throwing her body back with as much force as she could muster.

Jolan stumbled and tripped, taking Aimi with him, and hit the ground. His grip released and Aimi rolled free in an instant, springing to her feet and running towards the same vine that Keelin had climbed. Someone shouted something behind her, but Aimi was no longer listening. She leapt for the vine and raced up it as fast as her hands and feet could take her. No one aboard *The Phoenix* could climb rigging even half as fast as Aimi, and it seemed climbing vines was no different.

The plant was rough and slimy to the touch, and by the time Aimi reached the rooftop her hands were stinging. She ignored the pain. The building had a flat roof, and much of it was crumbling away as the tree that had taken residence inside squeezed through the bricks. Aimi knew it took time, but she was always amazed by how destructive a simple tree could be when it really tried. It rose up behind her, providing shade from the midday sun. Before her stood a city the likes of which she'd never seen before.

The size of HwoyonDo put even Larkos to shame. The city stretched out forever, far into the horizon. Buildings rose high and then higher, and they were all interconnected with the stone bridges Aimi had seen from the ground. From her vantage point she could see that the forest was starting to reclaim the city in many places and, even further in, the buildings were coloured green by nature's advances – vines, trees, and moss all working to take back what humans had once stolen.

Aimi looked upon the wonder of HwoyonDo, and nowhere did she see Keelin. How he'd disappeared from sight she didn't know, but he was gone, and there were no tracks to be found on the rooftop.

A cooing noise caught Aimi's attention, and she turned to see a large bird sitting on a nearby roof, watching her every movement with beady black eyes. The creature was unnerving, to say the least, and not just because it was the size of a small dog. Aimi did her best to ignore the beasty as she wandered over the rooftop, looking for signs of where Keelin might have gone.

By the time Aimi descended the same vine she'd used to climb up, her hands were red, sore, and blistered. She trudged towards the group in a stupor, and could barely find the energy to apologise to Jolan.

"Bloody hurt, ya little bitch," the pirate said, looking very indignant. "I was only following orders."

"Sorry," Aimi said, collapsing into a cross-legged heap on the ground.

"Ah, it's alright. Didn't hurt that much." Jolan smiled. "You feeling alright?"

"My hands hurt," she admitted, showing her palms to the pirate.

Elaina's priest rushed forwards, tutting and fussing and demanding to have a closer look at Aimi's hands. She let him, focusing on the conversation going on between the others, led by Smithe.

"There's gotta be a palace or something. Place where all the best loot is kept," Smithe argued.

"HwoyonDo has no palace," Kebble said quietly. The marksman looked as though he were carrying the weight of the city on his shoulders. "There is the Sky Spire, but I cannot be certain the traps will have lost their potency."

"Traps?" said Alfer Boharn, Elaina's quartermaster.

"Yes," Kebble continued. "Magical in nature and designed to resist intruders and thieves. I believe we would be considered both."

"So stay away from this spire then?" said Smithe.

"I would suggest just that. The temple may have some riches remaining. Many would travel to pay tribute to the god."

Alfer sucked in a hissing breath. "Ain't wise to steal from gods. Some don't take kindly to such."

"Where's Elaina?" Aimi said as Pavel wrapped strips of cloth around her blistered hands.

"Huh?" Smithe grunted. He looked around. All seven of those who remained turned this way and that, looking for the missing captain. Elaina Black was gone.

"Cap?" Alfer shouted, his voice echoing a little in the distance but receiving no reply.

Pavel tied off the bandages and stood, nervously shifting his weight from one foot to the other as though he really needed to piss. Aimi pushed to her feet and went to stand next to Kebble. He was the only one of them who didn't look worried.

The Phoenix

Keelin passed from building to building, barely taking any notice of their contents. Rooms blurred together as he entered through one skybridge to leave across another, always towards the Observatory. His hands were blistered from the climb up the vine, but it was only a minor distraction. Up on the roof he'd seen the Observatory standing tall amidst a sea of smaller buildings. It was obvious even to his eye, with its rounded roof and the broken remains of what had once been a giant monoscope that the scholars of HwoyonDo had used to study the heavens.

Keelin raised his hand against the glare as he stepped out onto a skybridge. Inside, the light was dim and the atmosphere cloying. Outside, so high up, the air was crisp and the sun was bright.

"Shit!" The bridge that spanned from this building to the next was gone. It wasn't the first such unfortunate ruin he'd encountered; more than once already he'd had to double back to bypass a section that had fallen to rubble.

He could, of course, have continued his journey on the ground, but Keelin knew just how easy it was to get turned around in a large city. He preferred to stay near the rooftops, where he could see his destination to correct his course if need be.

Keelin glanced down. He was easily six storeys up, and any fall would result in almost certain death, smashed upon the cobbled streets below. The telltale rubble of crumbled bridges and walls littered the floor, and a small, rat-like creature scurried about from cover to cover, no doubt hiding from aerial predators.

Looking up, Keelin spotted another skybridge a good ten feet above him. It appeared to be intact for the most part, veering off at an angle to connect to a nearby building that was at least vaguely in the right direction. He heard the scuff of boot leather on stone and glanced back inside the building. It wasn't the first time, and he was now certain that someone was following him. It was probably Aimi, and the sooner she realised it was safer to go back to the rest of them, the better.

Keelin shuffled up to the edge of the broken skybridge, sending a small cascade of loose dust and rocks hurtling to the ground far below. He edged sideways, placed his left boot on a nearby window ledge, and pushed upwards, grabbing hold of a door frame and beginning the climb. It wasn't taxing – there were hand and footholds all over the outside walls in the forms of ledges or chunks of missing brick. It was, however, nerve-wracking, knowing that a fall would likely end his life as a nameless corpse in a city full of bones.

Keelin rolled onto the intact skybridge, wiped the sweat from his forehead for the hundredth time, and got his feet beneath him to move in a crouch, ready to leap for safety at the first sign of the bridge giving way beneath him. The stone held, and after only a few moments he was across, a new doorway before him leading into the next building. Keelin hesitated only a heartbeat before stepping through into the dim room beyond.

Like all those before, this one smelled stale and dusty. There was little of any real note. Over a thousand years had long since turned all but the most sturdy of items to dust. Here and there tarnished metal glinted underneath the rubble and dust; some of it might even be valuable. To Keelin it was worthless. The real treasure of HwoyonDo lay in its magical accomplishments, and there was one in particular that interested him.

Not for the first time, Keelin hoped the creature who had sold him the information had been truthful. If he'd come all this way and sacrificed so much only to be cheated of his vengeance… He let the thought hang, unsure how he would react in such a situation.

The buildings were large and spacious. With all the doors long since rotted away to nothing, he could see the next skybridge, two rooms further on, and hoped this one would correct his course. Keelin made it through the first room and into the second before he again heard the scuff of shoes behind him; this time it sounded far closer.

"Damnit, woman," Keelin growled, turning to give Aimi a shouting at that would hopefully send her back to the others.

The figure that stood at the entrance to the skybridge was definitely not Aimi. Keelin couldn't see the man properly, the light shining from behind rendering him nothing more than a large silhouette, but it was certainly a man – and a big one at that.

Keelin moved a hand to the hilt of one of his cutlasses and raised his voice. "Hello?"

The figure took a lurching step forward, and Keelin felt the tension flood out of him as he recognised Bronson. How the man had found them after disappearing the previous night was beyond him, but Keelin was glad, nonetheless, that the big pirate had survived his disappearance.

"Where have you been?" he said.

Bronson didn't answer. He took another lurching step forwards. A second figure darted in from the skybridge behind him. Keelin drew his sword in a flash and rushed forwards, only making it as far as the doorway before the second figure turned to face Bronson.

Elaina stood in front of the pirate, swaying slowly from side to side. Keelin watched as the big man mimicked her movements.

"What the fuck are you two doing?" Keelin said.

"Quiet!" Elaina hissed, holding out a hand behind her and pointing towards Keelin, all the while keeping up her steady swaying.

"What is this, Elaina?" Keelin took another step forward and froze. He could see Bronson's face now, and it was a mess of open, oozing wounds that almost looked self-inflicted, as if the big man had torn at his own face with his fingernails. One eye was missing, a gooey hole where it should have been, and the other was as black as the darkest night.

"This ain't your man no more, Keelin," Elaina said slowly, still swaying from side to side. Bronson mimicked her, as if in some sort of trance.

"Then who is he?"

"Fuck," Elaina snapped. "Would you just shut up and trust me for once?"

"Last time I trusted you it almost got me killed."

Elaina was still facing Bronson, her arms spread out as she moved, as if she were balancing on a narrow railing.

"Well, ya either trust me now, Keelin, or I can let this thing loose and we'll see how you fair."

"I've got my swords."

Elaina snorted. "Steel won't stop this. There a way out behind you?"

Keelin glanced back. The next skybridge was a room and a half away, no more than twenty feet, he guessed. "Aye."

"Then start backing towards it, slowly as ya like. Let me know when ya get there, eh?" There was a note of something in Elaina's voice, and it sounded a lot like fear. It wasn't something Keelin was used to hearing from her.

He began to walk backwards, slowly, one foot after the other after the other. His sword was still drawn, but after Elaina's claim, he was starting to doubt its usefulness. She kept up her slow swaying, Bronson – or whatever it was – still copying her. Keelin took another step, and his back bumped against the door frame, sending a chunk of brick the size of his head tumbling to the floor with a crash.

"Fuck!" Elaina shouted, and she turned towards him, the fear now plain on her face. "*Run!*"

Keelin turned and stumbled over the rubble he'd just dislodged, steadying himself with a hand to the floor. He launched into a sprint towards the skybridge, sure that both Elaina and Bronson were only steps behind him.

The room sped past in a blur of grey and brown dust, light shining in from the doorway in front of him. Keelin rushed through the portal, and it took too long for his eyes to adjust to the change in light. Too late, he realised the skybridge was down. He didn't have time to think – he barely had time to react. His foot hit the rubble that was the end of the skybridge and he pushed off, leaping forwards and at the same moment seeing just how distant the other side of the bridge was. He was already falling, and safety was so far away. He threw up his arms, hoping to catch hold of the ledge, all that was left of the far side of the bridge.

Rough stone smashed into Keelin's face, and the light went both dim and bright at the same time. He felt his sword fall from his grip to go tumbling to the ground, where he knew he would soon join it. Then his fingers hit the ledge, and he gripped instinctively, holding on with every drop of strength he could muster.

Opening his eyes, Keelin saw the drop below and a wave of vertigo swept over him, twisting his vision. He heard a grunt from above and the sound of leather boots skidding on stone. Looking up, he saw Elaina above him, her expression frantic.

Elaina's hands gripped hold of his own, and she braced and pulled. "Can't do this alone," she hissed through clenched teeth.

Keelin pulled. His fingers, hands, and arms burned from the effort. Slowly he began to rise. After a few moments his arms were above the ledge, and Elaina pulled him into the safety of the building.

Keelin rolled onto his back and sucked in lungful after lungful of air. His heart was beating loudly in his ears and he could feel every limb shaking with either exertion or fear or, more likely, both.

"Get up, Keelin," Elaina growled. The woman was already on her feet, staring out across the gap they'd just leapt.

A grim chuckle escaped Keelin's lips as he rolled onto his front and struggled to get his feet beneath him. His arms and legs ached, and his face stung like it had recently had an unfortunate meeting with a stone wall. He was fairly certain there was nothing funny about his current situation, definitely nothing worth chuckling about, but he laughed all the same. The laugh died in his throat when he looked out across the gap and saw exactly what had become of Bronson.

The pirate stood on the far side, waiting across the broken skybridge. His face was a red mask of torn flesh and muscle, with bone showing beneath. Part of his lip had been torn away to reveal teeth and gums. Bronson's hands were even worse. His fingers looked as if they'd been chewed on by animals, the flesh eaten away to show the bones, which looked like they'd been sharpened to points.

"He's only been gone a few hours," Keelin whispered. "What happened to him?"

"Spirits," Elaina said as she paced back and forth, never taking her eyes from Bronson. "They got inside of him. Infested his body and soul. Ain't nothing left of the man you sailed with, Keelin. They're all over him. In him."

Keelin shook his head. He'd seen some nasty things in his time at sea, but the idea that something had crawled inside one of his crew and turned the man into... something else – Keelin didn't feel prepared to deal with that sort of monster.

"You remember the forests on the Isle of Goats?" Elaina said. "I used to take you there from time to time. Every now and then we'd come across someone who seemed lost. They just wandered about, unaware and unresponsive."

"Aye," Keelin said. "I remember. You used to say the forest had got to them. That's what Tanner was always telling folk about. The reason he had all those wards placed."

"Well, those were spirits," Elaina continued, still watching Bronson. "Only, those ones weren't violent for the most part. They'd get stuck inside of people and couldn't find their way out."

She looked at Keelin. "There's spirits here too. All over the jungle and all over the city. But these ones ain't so placid. Don't reckon they take too kindly to us intruders. They want us good and gone, any way they can get it."

Bronson turned slowly and walked back into the dark room. Keelin took in a deep breath. He'd known they would encounter magic in HwoyonDo – he'd been counting on it – but spirits were something else entirely.

"How can you…"

"Shh," Elaina hissed.

Keelin shut his mouth and listened. He could hear a rhythmic thumping, getting faster and closer. He looked up.

Bronson reappeared out of the doorway at the other end of the broken skybridge and leapt towards them, flying through the air. Elaina reacted first, dashing forwards and jumping just as Bronson landed on their side of the bridge. She hit the big pirate with both feet and dropped to the floor, scrabbling to get away as Bronson teetered on the edge, his big arms waving back and forth.

Keelin started forwards, drawing his remaining cutlass with his left hand and passing it to his right. There was a crack, and the stone beneath Bronson fell away, taking the possessed pirate with it.

For a brief moment Keelin thought it was over, and he stopped, but Bronson caught hold of what was left of the ledge with his shredded fingers and held tight.

Keelin stepped forward, raising his cutlass and bringing it down on Bronson's left hand. The blade cut through flesh and bone and rang as it connected with the stone beneath, but failed to sever the hand. With a wild jerk of his arm, Bronson tore Keelin's cutlass from his grip and sent it sailing into the street below to join its partner.

Elaina grabbed hold of Keelin by the shoulders and turned him to face her. Fear and excitement had flushed her cheeks; it made her beautiful, and there was a wild look in her eyes that Keelin remembered well. Despite the danger, or maybe because of it, Elaina was enjoying herself.

"Run," Elaina hissed, and she turned, fleeing deeper into the building at a sprint. Keelin took one last look at the monster Bronson had become as it struggled to pull itself up from the ledge, and chased after Elaina.

The Phoenix

"How are your hands?" the Five Kingdoms priest said as they marched through the abandoned streets.

"Stinging like an arse with the shits," Aimi growled, with a bit more venom than she'd intended. The priest didn't deserve her anger. With neither Keelin nor Elaina anywhere nearby, Aimi was directing her ire at whoever would have it.

"Perhaps I should have a look at them again next time we stop. I may have an ointment that would help."

"Save it. I've had worse." Aimi fell silent and the priest followed suit, though he stayed close, sending furtive glances her way.

Kebble was in front, leading the way, with Smithe beside him. The surly quartermaster was in charge, and that worried Aimi even more than the missing captains. Smithe was no fan of Keelin, or anybody for that matter, and it was more than possible that he would try to find a way to leave the captain to rot in HwoyonDo. Aimi knew she shouldn't care. Keelin had been a fool, running off on his own, but no matter how much of an arse he might act, Aimi still cared for him.

Jotin and Jolan appeared from a nearby building, their faces betraying their unhappiness. They quickly moved to join the rest of the group, falling in just behind Smithe.

"More of nothing," Jolan said with a sigh. "Everything here is long since rotted to dust. City is fucking dead."

"That's the third time ya've come back with nothing," Smithe growled at the brothers. "Starting ta think ya ain't looking right."

"You wanna go have a fucking peek?" Jolan said. "Be my guest."

Smithe turned and gave Jolan a hard shove that unbalanced the pirate and put him on his arse. Jotin's hand moved to his sword, but one glare from Smithe convinced him not to draw the length of steel.

"Which one of us is in charge?" Smithe hissed.

Jolan let out a sigh and got his feet beneath him. "You are, Smithe. Sorry, mate."

"Damned right I am. What I say goes, and I'm sending you two cunts off to look for treasure."

"Ain't nothing here, Smithe," Jotin said. "We found a plate and a jug, and a couple of spoons, but… there ain't nothing here. Kebble said the city has been abandoned for thousands of years. Things just don't last that long."

"Metal don't rot," Smithe said. "Gold don't rot. Gems don't rot."

"There ain't none of those things here," Jotin said. "Unless ya want us to go back and get the spoons."

"It'd be something."

"At the first sign of the war starting, many people fled the city. I would assume they took anything of value with them," Kebble said without looking back. "The streets were chaos. People were trampled underfoot."

"So what the fuck are we doing here if there ain't no treasure?" Smithe snarled.

"The temple will still house its riches. The priests would not have fled. No matter how much death rained down upon them, they would stay. And they were more than capable of fighting off any looters who may have mistaken the chaos for an opportunity."

The group marched on in silence for a while. Aimi shielded her eyes and looked towards the sky. The sun was long past its zenith, and it was possible the light would start to wane soon. Being in the dead city after dark wasn't something that appealed to her, but then neither was spending another night in the forest.

"I do not believe that man is as cracked as he appears," Elaina's priest whispered to Aimi. "He may actually be as old as these ruins."

"Let's bloody well hope so," Aimi said quietly.

"Why?"

"Because if he ain't, then none of us have a clue where we're going."

She'd been right about the light. By the time they reached the temple, the last rays were disappearing over the tops of the gigantic buildings that surrounded them. Even worse were the long shadows that turned simple doorways into dark voids housing hundreds of terrors.

There was something else too. Aimi couldn't shake the nagging feeling that she was being watched.

It was a strange sensation, like insects crawling over her skin between her shoulders, and she always felt it when unknown eyes were tracking her. After years of working in a tavern, surrounded by pirates, she'd come to trust the unease.

"That it?" Smithe said, disbelief plain in his voice.

"Yes," Kebble said with a smile. "The Temple of the Grace."

"Grace? That the god's name?"

Kebble shook his head. "I will not speak his true name."

"Why not?" Pavel said.

"Because I am the only one alive who remembers it, and I would prefer it lost and forgotten." Kebble laughed. "I'm a little bitter."

The temple was squat compared to the buildings around it. It was long and wide and stood only a few storeys tall, topped with a domed roof surrounded by a wide saucer-like ledge supported by pillars that rose up out of the earth. Vines clung to the building like leeches, winding their way up the pillars and infesting the windows, yet no damage seemed to have been done to the structure.

Aimi glanced at the nearby buildings and then back to the temple. "Ain't none of the others covered in those vines," she said quietly. "Why, then, is the temple?"

The rest of the party looked equally as stumped, and even Kebble offered no answer to the question.

"I don't like this," Aimi continued, again feeling like she was being watched. "Something here ain't right."

"Stow it, bitch," Smithe growled. "Cap'n ain't here to flap ya cunt at, and I'm in charge. Treasure is in there, and that's where we're going. Ain't fucking leaving this shit hole without some sort of payoff."

Aimi looked at Kebble. The immortal merely shrugged in return. The remaining light was fading fast, and if they went inside the temple, Aimi guessed it would be well into the night by the time they came back out.

"Let's get some torches lit then," Smithe said after a few long moments of everyone standing around, clearly not wanting to go any further. "Stick close and keep ya eyes open for anything might be worth something, eh?"

"I will wait out here," Kebble said.

"Fuck that, mate," Smithe snapped, instantly squaring up to the marksman. "You the only one knows where shit is. We need ya in there."

Kebble shook his head slowly. "I will never again set a foot in the temple of that god. He's the bastard who cursed me. Besides, I'll wager you're all safer in there without me."

"What's that supposed to mean?"

"It means I will wait out here."

Smithe growled and stalked away.

"Can I wait out here too?" Jotin said, his voice quivering.

"No!" Smithe shouted. "Everyone else is coming with me. Now."

There was a small set of steps leading up to the temple entrance, only eight in total, each more foreboding than the last as Aimi mounted them. Even the flickering torch she lit did little to bolster her courage. There was simply something off about the entire city, and the feeling was stronger here. One glance at the rest of the group convinced her they all felt the same way. Even Smithe looked worried, fat drops of sweat beading on his forehead.

The door to the temple was made of stone, and it looked as pristine as the day it had been made. There was no visible lock, only a number of designs chiselled into its surface. Aimi recognised none of the symbols and had little time to study them. Smithe handed his torch to Jotin, placed his hands against the door, and pushed. The sound of stone grating against stone shattered the quiet. It seemed unnaturally loud, echoing around the city behind them.

As the door slowed to a gentle rest, every last one of the company peered inside with their emotions plain, ranging from mild distrust to outright terror. The room inside was darker than night and eerily still. For a long while they all stared, straining their eyes and ears, no one wanting to be the first to venture inside.

"Anybody else hear that scratching?" Alfer said.

"Rats," Smithe assured them in a voice that sounded far from sure.

"Riiiight," Alfer said.

"What else could it be?" Smithe said.

"Lad," said the older man, "you do not want me to answer that question."

"Ah, fuck this cowardly shit." Smithe snatched his torch back from Jotin and walked into the temple. The quartermaster took five paces forwards and waved his torch about a bit before turning to the rest of them, still crowded around the entrance. "Well, come the fuck on then. This place ain't exactly gonna loot itself."

Starry Dawn

The darkness dictated their decision to stop far more than any certainty that they'd lost Bronson and the spirits that infested him. They'd crossed skybridges, changed directions through buildings, and even leapt a few gaps of significant distance. If they hadn't lost Bronson by now, they weren't going to, so they might as well turn and fight.

They were inside a building, and it looked like it might once have been a bakery or some such. There was a large stone oven in one corner of the room, long unused, and a number of dusty stone tabletops. Elaina leaned against one of the tables and sucked in deep breaths of cool air. She was far from tired, and her blood was up. Excitement from the chase coursed through her veins. A laugh bubbled up from deep inside and burst out of her mouth.

"What are you laughing at?" Keelin said between deep breaths of his own.

"Same thing you are, I reckon," Elaina replied with a wink.

Keelin nodded, chuckling. "Just like old times, eh?"

"Never could decide if it was you or me who kept finding the trouble, but we were always both running from it."

"It was you," Keelin said with a grin.

Elaina snorted. "Well, that's a lot of shit if ever I heard it." She stood and stretched her back, bending over backwards into a handstand and then letting her momentum carry her upright. Keelin was leaning against a wall, watching her with a familiar glint in his eyes.

Elaina sauntered over to him. "I seem to remember it was you who came up with the plan to pinch ol' Farley's last bottle of brandy reserve."

Keelin grinned again. "My idea, sure. You stole it though."

Elaina moved closer still, close enough that she could smell Keelin's sweat. It wasn't a pleasant smell, and it should probably have turned her off, but it was having quite the opposite effect. There was nothing like a good heart-pounding chase or fight to get the blood up, and there was no aphrodisiac quite like danger.

"Seem to remember we both drank it," Elaina said, taking another step closer until her breasts pushed against Keelin's chest. She stared at him. His breath was coming quick and ragged.

Elaina lunged forwards, nipping at Keelin, catching his lip between her teeth and tugging gently. It appeared to be all the invitation he needed.

Keelin surged forwards, picking Elaina up and turning them both around, shoving her against the wall. A gasp escaped her lips and then Keelin's own were against them. There, staring down into his cold steel eyes, Elaina saw the ghost of the man he used to be, the man he really was but seemed to have forgotten.

The danger of the spirit-infested hunter forgotten, Elaina and Keelin raced to rid each other of their clothing, and in close to no time at all they were both as naked as they could be arsed to be.

He didn't last long, but Elaina was used to that. Keelin always finished first to begin with, but they'd never left it at just the one time before, and this was no exception.

"So why are we here, Keelin?" Elaina said, picking up her trousers and attempting to shake the dust out of them. She had a warm, flushed feeling deep inside, as she always did after an orgasm. It didn't mean she was about to ignore the big, important question that had been nagging her since they'd arrived. "Don't give me that shit about treasure. I know ya well enough to know ya don't give a fuck about gold more than keeping ya ship afloat and ya wardrobe full of fancy jackets."

Keelin sighed. He was sitting on one of the tabletops, mostly naked. Elaina felt her blood stir again when she looked at him, but she ignored it. They could fuck more later; now she wanted answers.

"I'm here for the Observatory," Keelin said. His eyes were pinned to her breasts.

Elaina placed her hands in front of her tits until Keelin met her stare. "That's suitably vague, Stillwater. Fancy filling me in on the rest?"

"Haven't I filled you enough for today?" Keelin grinned wickedly, again looking like the pirate Elaina remembered from years before.

"You reckon that's enough?" She winked at him. "Your standards must be slipping. I still want an answer."

"I'm looking for someone. Have been for a long time. I've heard the Observatory here has ways of finding them. No matter how far away they might be."

"The Arbiter?" Elaina said as she started buttoning up her blouse. "The one that killed ya sister?"

Keelin leapt off the tabletop and snatched his trousers from the dusty floor, shoving his legs into them. Anger marred his usually pretty features.

"How do you know about that, Elaina?"

"You told me a long time ago. You were pretty drunk at the time and bawling like a babe. I remember it clear as day though. You told me how ya sister had been sick since birth, had fits and was weak, barely able to stand. You also said she was smart, knew things a girl her age shouldn't.

"Your da thought it was more than just sickness though. He thought she was possessed, or a witch or something. He sent a request to the Inquisition, asking for one of their witch hunters to come and have a look at her."

Keelin pulled his jacket on over his shirt and kicked at a stone on the floor. "Bastard set fire to her. Burned her alive just for being a sick little girl."

"And you've spent all ya years since trying to find that bastard. Pin?"

"Prin. Arbiter Prin."

"And ya reckon ya can use this Observatory to find him? So we can go put him in the ground?"

Keelin was quiet for a long while. "Yeah."

"Let's get moving then, eh?" Elaina grinned.

"Why did you never tell me that you can see spirits, Elaina?" Keelin didn't look like he was in any rush to leave the comfort of the little bakery.

Elaina cackled. "Same reason you never told me you're noble born, I reckon." She winked at him. "I figured it out though."

Keelin snorted and shook his head. "No, you didn't. Someone on my ship told you."

"I've known ya for… I don't know. Since we were old enough to know each other, I guess. Ya really think I didn't figure it out?"

"Nobody else did."

"Nobody else sat and listened to ya voice for hours. Nobody else spent so long with ya they heard ya accent slip. Nobody else cared enough to figure it out, Keelin."

"Nobody else got me so fucking drunk I spilled my closest-kept secrets?"

"Aye, that too. Point is, your family were nobles from the Five Kingdoms who murdered their own daughter. My family can see spirits, and my da's an evil bastard who had me raped to teach me a lesson."

"What?"

Elaina's smile vanished. "Shit. Forgot ya didn't know that one."

"I'll kill him," Keelin hissed. He crossed the room and put his arms around Elaina, and she didn't stop him. It felt nice to be protected and supported. It felt nice not to be alone for once.

"No, you won't," she breathed into his shoulder. "The isles need Tanner Black. So do I."

"No, you don't, El. You never have."

Elaina let out a weary laugh.

"What about the… whoever did it?" Keelin said.

Elaina tensed, pushing out of his embrace. In truth she hated being reminded of it. Hated remembering the feeling of helplessness. The pain and the shame that went along with it. "Don't you worry. I'll deal with that fucker myself, just as soon as my arse touches my throne."

Keelin looked like he was about to say more, but he just sighed and nodded.

"So how about it, Stillwater? We gonna find this Arbiter of yours or not?"

The Phoenix

Aimi took a faltering step inside the temple and peered left and right, holding her torch out in front of her and praying there was nothing hiding in the deep shadows the light left behind.

"Bitch, hurry the fuck up or I swear I will fuck you with your own torch," Smithe growled, still standing a few feet ahead of her. The rest of the expedition were still outside, waiting for Aimi to move out of the way.

"Nice threat, Smithe," she said. She didn't move, nor stop waving her torch around. "The only problem is, I'm more scared of this temple than I am of you."

"Ya might wanna rethink that, bitch. I can be real scary."

"Are you a dark temple dedicated to a long-forgotten god in a ruined city that's been lost for thousands of years?" Aimi said. "No? Then I think I'll stay more scared of this place."

A hand landed on Aimi's shoulder and she damned near jumped out of her skin.

"Ignore him, lass," Alfer said calmly. "He don't wanna admit it, but he's scared as you are, as we all are. Still, job to get done, and all that."

Aimi nodded and took another step into the temple, still holding her torch in front of her like a shield. Smithe snorted out a laugh and turned away to look deeper into the building.

The first room was small, with a number of stone benches built into the floor. Three dark alcoves lined the wall to Aimi's left, and a glance right told her the same was true on the other side. The roof was high, and there were signs that it had once been marked with some sort of symbol, but most of the paint had long since been lost to time.

As the others started to file into the room behind her, Aimi approached one of the alcoves on the left, holding her torch out so that she could see what it contained. A stone box ran the entire length, its lid firmly in place, and there were symbols Aimi didn't understand etched upon the stone.

"Coffins," Pavel said, confirming Aimi's suspicion. "Six of them."

"Who do ya think is in them?"

"The six faces of the temple's god," Kebble said from outside. He was still refusing to set foot through the door. "I would not open them if I were you."

"Might be treasure in them," Smithe said. "Folk bury treasure with the dead sometimes."

"They are not buried," Kebble said, "and there is nothing inside but death. The temple kept many religious items made from gold, and metals even more precious. You will find them further in, either upon the altar or in the chests located in the cellar."

"Last chance, mate," Smithe said, looking back from the darkness, his face lit only by the flickering torch he held. "Share of the risk, share of the loot."

Kebble smiled. "Good luck," the marksman said before his face disappeared.

Smithe growled and stalked through the next doorway, disappearing from view along with the light from his torch. Aimi looked around at everybody else. She could see little of them but their faces in the flickering torchlight, and they all looked worried. Shrugging away the odd sensation that once again crawled between her shoulders, Aimi stepped over the stone bench and followed Smithe.

Arches spread the entire length of the long room, loop after loop of stone extending into the darkness. Each arch was about six feet in length, and they ran both front to back and from side to side, cutting the room into many small squares. On the floor in the middle of each square was a circle of discoloured stone.

"I believe they were for praying," Pavel said from behind as he waved his torch at the arches. "See the small holes on the underside of each one? Curtains were likely hung there so the faithful could pray in relative privacy."

Aimi looked upwards. The arches didn't extend vertically, but the roof was too high up to be seen in the scant light. She found herself wondering what the dome looked like from the inside, whether it had once been painted like some of the temples in Larkos.

"If this is the room they prayed in," Smithe said, "makes sense the altar would be at the end, right? Come on. Let's get this bitch looted."

Smithe stalked forwards and, with a shrug at Pavel, Aimi followed. Everyone else surged forwards, eager to get the job done and be away, their footsteps echoing loudly.

Aimi almost bumped into Smithe when he stopped, so closely had she been following the quartermaster. Behind her she heard the expedition slow and start to spread out. They'd left the square grids of arches, and in front of them now was what had to be the altar to the forgotten god.

A statue rose up so high it almost disappeared into the darkness above, a group of six figures standing back to back in a circle facing outwards, each one different but for their faces. One carried a shield, while another held a sword. One was dressed in robes, while another wore an apron and carried both a hammer and a shovel. The final two were hidden behind the others. At the feet of the statue lay a large bench, and upon it sat a much smaller depiction of the six figures, made of gold rather than stone. Each of the figures had small, different-coloured gemstones for eyes.

"Grab it, Jotin," Smithe ordered, already walking off around the statue.

"Stealing from a god," Jotin said hesitantly. "I ain't so sure about this."

"Just do it," Smithe hissed. "Kebble said this bloody god is as good as dead already. No power left."

"That ain't what he said," Aimi complained.

"Good as." Smithe completed his circuit around the statue. "Ain't nothing else here. Just the one fucking lump of gold."

"Your man outside said the rest might be kept in a cellar?" Alfer said. "We should look for some steps."

"Does anyone else still hear that scratching?" said Jolan.

"I told you it was rats, ya damned coward," Smithe snapped.

Jolan was looking up into the darkness. "Then why is it coming from above us?"

Starry Dawn

"Is this magical diviner of yours still gonna work?" Elaina said.

They were standing on a long skybridge that ran to the Observatory from the building closest to it. On the ground below were metal, glass, and stone remains of the largest monoscope Elaina had ever seen.

"I hope so," Keelin said, his voice barely more than a whisper in the dark.

"They must have wanted to look at some things really far away," Elaina said. The Observatory was almost twice as tall as the buildings around it, and the monoscope had once been a giant. But, like everywhere else in the city, time had brought down the mighty achievement.

"The stars," Keelin said. "It was used to look at the stars."

"Aye, but… Why?"

"Some people say you can tell the future by the stars. Probably shit. Maybe these folk believed it."

The door at the end of the skybridge was made of stone, and it stood proudly defiant despite the passing of time. Keelin put his back against it and pushed with all his strength. Nothing happened. Elaina joined him, putting her own weight to the slab, and together they shifted it. It moved slowly at first, but soon the door cleared its frame and swung open on surprisingly smooth hinges.

The air inside the Observatory was still and dry, and it felt odd against Elaina's skin. The hairs on her arms stood up, and she felt a strange energy all around her. It took her a moment to realise the Observatory wasn't dark. A dim glow reminiscent of moonlight shone down from the windows, even though the moon was well and truly obscured by cloud.

"That's eerie," she whispered.

"The windows absorb sunlight during the day and release it at night to keep the place lit. The creature who told me about this place described it in great detail."

Elaina grunted. "That'd be a real useful trick to know."

"We're not here to steal the secrets to making fancy windows, El. What we're looking for should be two floors up, in a laboratory filled with gears and cogs."

Keelin started searching for the stairs up to the next level. Elaina was far more interested in what this floor contained. A vast array of glass equipment was laid out, set up on wooden tables that somehow hadn't rotted to dust. Bookshelves stood along one wall, and each one was full of dusty tomes. A small shelf of scrolls sat alongside a cupboard containing glass vials, all of which were filled with a variety of coloured liquids. Elaina didn't know much about magic, but she guessed only sorcery could keep the place pristine through the passing of thousands of years. A thick layer of dust coated everything, but other than that, it looked like a working alchemist's laboratory.

"Here," Keelin called, one foot already on the first step.

"I'll catch you up," Elaina said. "I want to have a look around first."

"What for?"

"I don't know. It's just... maybe we'll find something valuable."

"I'm not looking to get rich here, Elaina."

"Not all fortunes are made of gold."

Keelin looked like he was about to argue, but he shook his head and turned back to the stairs.

"Here," Elaina said, pulling her sword out of its scabbard and tossing it to Keelin. "You might need a weapon, just in case."

"What if you do?"

"I have a knife. Always was better with the shorter blades. I'll catch you up soon."

Elaina wandered about the laboratory. She trailed her fingers through the layer of dust upon a table, picked up a small bottle of green liquid and shook it to no effect. Finding herself in front of a bookcase, Elaina began scanning the tomes. They were written in a language she somehow recognised despite never having seen it before, but though the characters were familiar she couldn't piece together what they said.

Moving on from the bookcase, Elaina examined the cupboard full of glass vials. The liquids they contained ranged from clear in colour to all sorts of greens and reds and yellows. Each vial was clearly labelled, but again Elaina couldn't quite read the language. She understood letters here and there, but the meanings of the words were lost to her. Elaina picked up a scroll from the nearby shelf and carefully unrolled the parchment. This time, whole words made sense. Elaina read as much as she could, and even as she was reading, more and more of the language became apparent. Before long she was able to decipher the whole scroll, even though the language was still very much alien to her. She went back to the bookshelf. The titles on the books all made sense to her now, where before they'd been undecipherable.

Elaina looked back down at the scroll in her hand and read it again, more closely this time. A grin formed unbidden across her face. She looked about for something to write with and found a lump of charcoal from some long-extinguished fire beneath a glass jar. She rolled the scroll out on a table and read for a third time the formulae it detailed, jotting down in the common tongue the ingredients and how to mix them. When she was done, she shoved the scroll into her little pack and leapt up the stairs after Keelin.

The Phoenix

Keelin looked in wonder at the construct in front of him. The room was filled with interconnecting machinery, and it all intersected here. A chair sat upon a large metal circle on the floor. The cogs and gears were silent now, the thin layer of dust a testament to their long slumber. Keelin could imagine that once they started up again, the noise would be deafening.

Looking down at the small scrap of leather in his hand, Keelin located what he hoped was the fourth interweave lower lever and pulled it upwards. A loud clunk sounded, but he couldn't locate its source.

The creature that had approached Keelin with information about HwoyonDo and the Observatory had been very specific about the city's location and the design of the Observatory, and with instructions on using the great machine. He'd also been very specific on the consequences should the instructions not be followed. Keelin imagined what his insides would look like cooked, and it wasn't a pleasant thought.

Locating the second low-polar lever, Keelin pulled it downwards. A strange humming noise started up, filling the entire room. Keelin felt his stomach turn over, and his hands shook just a little.

"This it?" Elaina said loudly as she leapt up the last two stairs. "What the fuck is that noise?"

"This is it. I think it's meant to make the noise."

"You think?"

"Aye. Think and hope. Find anything valuable down there?"

"Not a thing," Elaina said. "Lots of books and whatnot. Couldn't understand a damned word though. Bastards could have at least used the common tongue, eh?"

"Mhm," Keelin agreed, barely listening. He pulled another lever and several machines stirred to life, cogs turning and pistons pumping, and the noise quickly became oppressive. A rapid clicking sounded from somewhere, setting Keelin's nerves on edge.

"Are you sure about this, Stillwater?" Elaina all but shouted.

Keelin shrugged and moved over to the chair. It was small, metal, with some sort of machinery all around it and not a cushion in sight. Keelin lowered himself onto the uncomfortable seat and closed his eyes, taking a deep breath. Keelin had been hunting Arbiter Prin for a long time, but all he was really hunting was a name, and he needed more than that. He remembered the Arbiter as hollow-eyed and deep-voiced, but the man's face eluded him.

He changed tactics and brought back the memory of his sister's death. There was no way he could forget that; it was etched into his very being.

It was night; the moon was a sliver and the stars were out in force. Derran had gone to bed early, exhausted after his interrogation at the hands of Arbiter Prin. Keelin had been interrogated twice, and each time he'd been left shaken and weary. The pyre had been built up in such a short time. Neither Keelin nor his mother had realised it was happening until Leesa was dragged out of bed by their father.

Keelin followed after them, begging his father not to let it happen, but he was too small and his voice carried no weight. Leesa was crying. Keelin's little sister was young, but she was smarter than all of them. She knew what was happening and she didn't go quietly. She screamed and she struggled, but she was so small and so weak, and their father was tall and strong. He carried her to the pyre and let the Arbiter bind her to the stake. Keelin remembered seeing tears in his father's steel-grey eyes, the first and only time he'd ever seen the man cry.

Keelin tried to run to his sister, to free her from the stake she was tied to. A big guardsman took hold of him and held him tightly in a bear hug, dragging him away, far enough that he couldn't interfere. Not so far that he wouldn't see his little sister burn.

Derran burst out of the manor. Keelin's older brother was still growing and gangly, but he was powerful nonetheless and had their father's imposing, cold fury. Keelin remembered Derran and their father arguing while Arbiter Prin lit the pyre.

Keelin screamed for his brother to do something, and Derran grabbed hold of their father's sword and charged towards the Arbiter. Their father picked up a stone and launched it at Derran; the missile struck hard, hitting him on the back of the head, and the boy went down, unconscious before he hit the floor.

Leesa started to scream as the flames reached her, and Keelin remembered that screaming going on for a long time. His mother collapsed, sobbing and broken. His father tended to the unconscious form of his eldest son. All around Keelin, the guards and house staff moved away, unable to watch as the youngest member of the Fowl family was burned alive. Keelin couldn't turn away. The guard still held him tight, and all he could do was watch and listen to his little sister's screams.

When Leesa went quiet, they all knew it was over. Arbiter Prin approached Keelin's father and they talked for a while. Keelin had never seen his father look so deflated before. He'd brought the Arbiter upon them and he was responsible for the death of his own daughter. Keelin knew his father had never forgiven himself for that, but he couldn't bring himself to care about the man.

Keelin remembered the Arbiter looking directly at him, and the guard's grip grew tighter still. Prin walked close. Close enough for Keelin to see every pockmark on the man's face. Close enough for him to smell the vanilla on his breath…

A machine above Keelin whirred into life. He opened his eyes. Elaina was standing nearby, panic written all over her face.

"What?" Keelin said, afraid to move now that he'd finally got the machine working.

"Is it supposed to do that?"

Keelin ignored her and focused on his memory of Arbiter Prin, fixating on the man's face, the sound of his voice, the smell of his breath. The noises grew louder and louder, whirring and clunking, clicking and buzzing. The large metal circle on the floor in front of Keelin started to glow a bright gold that grew lighter and lighter until it was white and painful to look at.

Still Keelin kept his mind fixed on Arbiter Prin's face, voice, and smell.

Elaina opened her mouth and shouted, but he couldn't hear her over the sound of the machine, and soon the circle of light in front of him became so bright he had to shut his eyes for fear it might blind him.

Keelin focused on his image of Prin, trying desperately to block out everything else. He was shaking. Or perhaps it was the room shaking – he couldn't tell, only that something was definitely shaking.

A hand grabbed hold of Keelin's arm, and his eyes shot open just as Elaina pulled him out of the chair and threw him aside, jumping on top of him at the same time. They rolled together, away from the chair and the circle of light.

The floor shook and the sounds started to slow, fading away. Keelin stared into Elaina's terrified face, and she stared back. She was sweating, wide-eyed, her breath coming short and fast.

"I don't think it was meant to do that," Elaina said after the noise had quietened down enough that she could be heard.

The chair Keelin had been sitting on was gone, buried beneath a pile of cogs and metal shards. He was fairly certain he wouldn't have survived the burial.

"Thank you," he said, looking back at Elaina. Her gaze was fixed on something over Keelin's shoulder.

The light in the circle had faded to nothing, and lying in the centre of that circle was a pile of scorched bones.

"Is that…" Elaina started. "Was that him?"

Keelin rolled onto his feet and approached the bones. He shrugged.

"I thought you said this thing would find him."

"Powerful magics mixed with lost technology." He gave a bitter laugh. "Apparently it was designed to find a person and then bend the world to bring them here." Elaina hit him hard on the arm, and he hissed in pain.

"You should know better than to play with magic, Stillwater," she growled. "Was he already like this?"

Keelin nodded. "I think so. Maybe that's why the machine, um, broke. Prin was already dead."

"You sure it's him?"

With a shrug, Keelin sank down onto the floor. He stared at the bones. He'd spent almost half his life searching for Arbiter Prin. He'd dedicated so much of his time and his resources into his vengeance, and now, right at the end, it had been snatched away from him. He felt empty, hollowed out and numb. Emotions warred within him, but they were all muted by the loss he felt so strongly. He'd lost his purpose.

"Been a long time coming." Elaina sank down beside him. "Hatred of that man has kept you focused for so long. Must be like losing a friend, almost, eh?"

"He was *never* my friend."

"Wasn't talking about the man. I was talking about the hatred."

"I can still hate him."

Elaina sighed. "It'll fade. It's hard to keep a grudge against the dead. At some point you realise there ain't nothing left to hate, and then it's gone."

She was right. Keelin didn't want to admit it, but Elaina was right. He wanted to keep hating Prin, but the truth of it was, he couldn't. The moment he'd realised the Arbiter was dead, that vengeance would never be his, Keelin had nothing left to give the man.

"I've spent most of my life chasing this bastard," he said. "I hid it from everyone, but I was always searching for him. I've risked myself, my ship, and my crew, time and time again. I've lost good men in chasing down leads and they never even knew why. I've lost another two just getting here, and what for? A pile of old bones."

Keelin felt tears stinging his eyes, and he wiped them away on the sleeve of his jacket.

"I think you mean you risked my ship," Elaina said with a friendly shove.

Keelin laughed, but the mirth died in his throat.

"Ain't gonna say you've done right," Elaina said. "Mostly because you ain't done right. Folk followed you and you led them into danger, got some of them killed even. Well, fuck. You've only gone and done what every captain has. The thing is though, are you gonna sit here and whine about it? Maybe get a few others killed because of it? Or are you going to get up off your arse and get your crew out of this haunted fucking city?"

Keelin let out a bark of bitter laughter. "To what end? I've lived every day for the past... I don't know, longer than I can remember. All to the end of hunting down this... this corpse. I don't..."

"Well that's a load of shit. If all you wanted was this, you wouldn't have saved all those people from Sev'relain. You set up a new town with

Morrass."

"All to get his charts."

"What about my da? You convinced him to side with Morrass. That weren't for the charts. Probably made getting them harder. What about that stunt ya pulled with the slavers guild? Was that for the charts?"

Keelin shook his head.

"So now you have to make a decision. Sit here and wallow over the not-so-recent death of the man you hated, or pick yaself up and apply the energy ya spent hunting him into something else. It just so happens I reckon we could use that energy in making Morrass' dream for the isles work."

Elaina stood and dusted herself off.

"Thing is, Stillwater, I intend to be queen of the isles, and I'd rather have you at my side than that slimy fuck Drake."

Keelin considered the possibility. Sitting on a throne, in charge of a kingdom. Didn't sound too appealing. Though sitting next to Elaina did. There was just one problem with the picture – Keelin didn't want to betray his fellow captain. He actually quite liked Drake, and he believed in what they were trying to accomplish.

One thing was certain though – Elaina was right. Sitting around moping wasn't about to solve their most immediate problem, and that was getting back to the ship without losing anyone else. His grief could wait.

Keelin stood and picked up a large rock shaken loose by the machine's death throes. He approached the scorched remains, and for a long time he stood there, staring down at the blackened bones of the man who had been his focus for so long. Then Keelin raised the rock and brought it down on Prin's skull.

The Phoenix

Aimi squinted, holding her torch high. She still couldn't see all the way to the ceiling, and she couldn't see the source of the scratching. Smithe had insisted the noise was just rats running about in the walls. Aimi wasn't so sure. There was still that crawling feeling between her shoulders that said they were being watched.

"Found some steps," Jotin said. "They lead down."

The rest of the expedition crowded around the small doorway and peered down into the dark. Aimi kept her torch held high, determined to find the source of her discomfort.

"Go on then," Smithe said. "Down ya go."

"Fuck that, Smithe," Jotin whined.

"You forgetting who's in charge again?"

"I don't give a fuck if that bastard soul-sucker Reowyn himself is in charge. There ain't no fucking way I'm going down there. Place is creepy enough already without adding being trapped underground."

"If you're so set on seeing what's down there, why don't you go?" Jolan chimed in.

"Fine," Smithe growled. The surly quartermaster snatched a torch from Jotin and tossed it down the steps. Aimi heard it bounce once, twice, and a third time, followed by oppressive silence.

"Maybe we should get out of here," Smithe said.

"Reckon you might be right, mate," Jotin said.

Aimi glanced down the stairway. Just twelve steps down, the torched rested on level ground. At least, it looked level – it was fairly hard to tell with all the movement.

"What is that?" she said, squinting at the shifting floor.

"Bugs," Alfer said. "Might be best we give this one up. I've got a bad feeling about this."

Beside them, Jotin turned away from the stairwell. "Fuck!" he screamed.

Aimi slapped him on the arm for shrieking in her ear, then froze when she saw what Jotin was looking at. A lone figure stood in one of the praying squares, its features hidden in the darkness. Whoever it was, they were too short to be Kebble.

"Who the fuck are you?" demanded Smithe, taking a single step forward.

The figure tilted its head slightly, and Aimi caught sight of a tail of hair tied behind it. "Feather?" She stepped past Smithe. "Feather, is that you?"

The figure moved into the torchlight, its feet silent on the stone floor. Feather looked weary, his face smeared with blood and his eyes distant. His clothes were ripped in places and red gashes showed through the holes. Wherever the boy had been, he'd obviously been through a lot.

Aimi started to rush forwards but was yanked back by Smithe just as Feather leapt at her, slashing with claw-like hands. She stumbled, thrown off balance by the quartermaster, who let go of her and stepped in to meet Feather. The two grappled, and Smithe howled in pain as Feather's fingers dug into his arms.

Feather was hissing and spitting like the evil cat that lived aboard *The Phoenix*, and Smithe was struggling just to stop the smaller man clawing his eyes out. Alfer and Jolan rushed forwards and each grabbed hold of one of Feather's arms, pulling him off the quartermaster.

"Fuck!" Smithe yelled, waving his bleeding arms. "Lad, I don't know what's in your hold, but you're gonna wish ya didn't come back."

Smithe drew a long knife from his belt and stalked forwards. Before Aimi could stop him, the quartermaster stabbed Feather in the chest six times. Alfer and Jolan danced away as Feather dropped to the floor, moaning and writhing.

"Bit of overkill, don't you think, mate?" Alfer said sourly.

"Anybody else see his fingers?" Jolan said.

"I felt 'em," Smithe said, leaning in for a closer look.

Aimi held her torch close, and promptly lost her stomach. Feather's fingers had been gnawed away to the bone, leaving only sharpened claws behind. She finished throwing up, and Pavel moved to her side, muttering something low and soothing. She shrugged the priest away.

The others were crowded around Feather's wriggling form, keeping their distance as they watched the boy's death throes.

"My vote is for getting the fuck out of this place," Aimi said, spitting out the foul acidic taste in her mouth.

There was a unanimous round of agreement, and the whole expedition was soon making its way to the temple's exit, leaving the dying boy behind to bleed out his last.

"Well, at least we got something out of this shit hole," Jolan said, bringing up the rear. "That statue oughta be worth… *Fuck!*"

Aimi spun around. Feather was attached to Jolan's back, clawing at his chest and biting his face as the pirate flailed about. Aimi stumbled away, tripped, and collided with one of the arches, sinking down onto her arse.

Feather's teeth found Jolan's ear and the boy bit down, tearing a new scream from Jolan's mouth. Smithe rushed forwards, his knife back in his hand, and punched Feather hard in the face. The metal of Smithe's knuckle rings broke the boy's nose with the first hit, and the quartermaster didn't stop there. Smithe punched him again and again, until Feather lost his grip on Jolan and crashed to the floor.

"My fucking ear. My fucking *ear!* Tell me it's still there, Jotin." Jolan was shaking all over. Blood dripped steadily from the wounds on his head and chest. Pavel ran forwards to tend to him.

"Um…" Jotin shut his mouth and shrugged at his brother.

Feather was still twitching on the floor, gurgling on the blood weeping out of his ruined face. Smithe stood over the boy with his vicious knife still in hand.

"Fuck this." Smithe dropped to his knees, straddling Feather. He started punching, each strike accompanied by a sickening thump. Aimi was certain she'd have lost her stomach again if there'd been anything left to lose.

By the time Smithe had finished, he was dripping with sweat and breathing heavily. His expression had turned from rage to disgust, and blood and worse dripped from his fist onto the floor beside Feather's body. Pavel was busy wrapping a bandage around the head of a wincing Jolan, and the others were either silently watching Smithe or had turned away from the violence. Aimi huddled against the arch, her knees drawn up close.

Smithe stood and staggered away from the body, and Aimi got a good view of the wreckage the quartermaster left behind. Her stomach roiled and she dry-heaved.

There was nothing left of Feather's pretty face to recognise. The boy's head was all torn skin, smashed skull, blood, and bits of brain. Never before had Aimi seen anything so hideous, and none of the others had either, judging by their similar reactions. Even Smithe looked sickened to his soul at the carnage he'd wrought.

"Let's…" Smithe took a deep breath, and it came out ragged. "Let's go."

Alfer appeared at Aimi's side, holding out a hand to help her up. She took it gratefully and pulled herself to her feet, joining the others as they started once more towards the exit.

Aimi heard shuffling behind her, and turned to see Feather's corpse twitching on the floor. As if tugged by a puppet's strings, the headless body rose up into a crouch, facing the fleeing expedition.

"Ya gotta be fucking joking," Smithe said. "Ya don't even have a head!"

Feather's body lurched forwards a step, and Smithe grabbed the torch from Aimi's hand and flung it at the boy.

"*Run!*" the quartermaster screamed. It was all the permission they needed. As one, the group turned and sprinted for the dim rectangle of light that marked their way out.

With six people all trying to get out of the temple at the same time, it was a fair squeeze through the doorway and Aimi clipped her shoulder against the stone door. She cried out in pain as her momentum spun her around, and she tripped over her own feet, crashing to the ground. The world twisted and spun about as she rolled down the steps.

At the bottom of the stairs, Alfer stopped at Aimi's side and picked her up once again. Every limb hurt, and she was grazed and cut all over. Her knees were protesting at the beating they'd taken, but there were more important things to worry about.

"Where's Kebble?" Jotin said in a high, panic-stricken voice. The marksman was nowhere to be seen.

"Which way did we come to get here?" Smithe said.

Alfer pointed. "That way, I think."

"You think or you know?"

Feather's headless body lurched into view in the temple doorway. The vines infesting the building started to move, winding around pillars and crawling across the stone like snakes. The chittering noise was louder now, and a dark tide of legs and carapaces flooded out of the temple around Feather's feet.

"I think." Alfer said, walking backwards.

"It'll do," Smithe whispered. "Everybody, run. No stopping for anything. *Go!*"

The Phoenix

Kebble wandered alone through the ruined city that had once been his home. The figures he saw in the streets weren't spirits; they were ghosts of his past. People he'd once known, people he'd once loved. All dead and gone. All his fault. Now nothing but figments of his imagination.

There had always been a tugging. Kebble had felt it for long over a thousand years, an invisible rope always pulling him back to HwoyonDo. He'd searched for his death everywhere in the known world, but here and now, he knew why he'd never been able to find that end he longed for.

Kebble was a relic of a long-forgotten past. He neither desired nor deserved to live, and neither did he belong to the current age. His god had cursed him with long life. Now Kebble realised it was only until his return, only until his god could claim his miserable soul.

He passed the house that had once belonged to his first wife. They'd met at the library, both children of patronless scholars. The romance had been a whirlwind of passion and competition. Hiria had been as determined as Kebble, though she simply hadn't been able to keep up with the speed at which he absorbed knowledge. They married in the spring, and by the end of that winter, Hiria had given Kebble his first son.

Kebble moved on. He had no wish to dig too deep into those memories. He remembered his first son as both a babe and as an old, wrinkled man bitter at his father's permanent youth. Kebble remembered all of his children in their twilight years.

Walking past his father's ghost, Kebble averted his eyes. He had no wish to see the man beaten and bloody, clutching his right hand to his chest and praying his fingers weren't broken. It was a dangerous game his father had played with the criminals of HwoyonDo, and eventually it cost him everything.

Kebble's weary legs carried him to the great library, house of all knowledge the Forgotten Empire had ever earned. In many ways it represented the beginning of his journey, the beginning of his life. He had a feeling it would also be the end of both. Kebble wondered if any of the texts inside had survived the many years. Perhaps, before his end, he would learn something new.

Turning away from the library, Kebble set his feet back towards the temple. It was likely the others would have finished looting the place by now, and they might need help returning to the gate. Kebble would lead them to their destination. He wished to speak to Captain Stillwater once more, to thank the man and say goodbye.

A spirit drifted past Kebble. He couldn't see them, not like some could, but he could feel them. It was their hatred towards him that he sensed. It was hard not to feel that much malice emanating from something, even an ethereal whisper like the spirits that infested what had become of the empire.

Another spirit floated past, and then another, and another. Kebble found himself assaulted from all sides by the hatred flowing from the creatures. They were all going the same way, towards the temple.

Kebble broke into a run. He needed to warn the others what was coming.

Starry Dawn

They walked in silence for a long time after leaving the Observatory. Elaina could tell Keelin was deep in thought, and she could guess the subject. It wasn't every day someone asked you to betray a friend and sit your arse down on a throne. Not that the pirates had a throne. Now that Elaina thought about – and she thought about it quite a lot – she wanted one. A crown seemed a little ostentatious, but all kings and queens had thrones, and some of them were more than a little grand. Elaina imagined a nice wooden chair, tall and exquisitely carved out of driftwood salvaged from their enemies' scuttled navies. The image brought a smile to her face.

Keelin stopped and threw up a hand so suddenly that Elaina walked into it.

"What the fuck…" she started, but the complaint died in her throat.

Bronson was back, and the big pirate looked even worse than before. The roads were quite well lit, with the clouds clearing up and the moon and stars shining down upon them. Even in the dark, Elaina could see the man wasn't only infested with spirits; the vines that crawled along the walls of the buildings had taken up residence in his body as well.

Dark green cords wound up his legs, through his bloody skin, and inside his body. There was a small, wiggling end protruding from Bronson's ruined eye. The pirate's skeletal hands had been snapped away, and in their place sat Keelin's lost cutlasses, wedged into the ragged flesh of Bronson's arms and held in place by coiling vines.

"I'm starting to form a real dislike of this city," Keelin said quietly.

"You always were a bit slow, Stillwater," Elaina replied, taking a shaky step forward. If she could get close to Bronson without him attacking, it was possible she could hypnotise the spirits again. Hopefully she could distract them long enough for Keelin to deal some damage.

"We should be able to take him together," Keelin said, though he didn't sound too certain.

"Maybe you ain't noticed, Stillwater," Elaina said, already

beginning to sway from side to side as she approached the thing that had once been Bronson, "but he's pretty mangled and he ain't down. Killing these things ain't really an option."

"So what should we do?"

"Hamstring the fucker and run like all the Hells are behind us. Which is pretty close to the reality of it."

It was almost like a dance as Elaina moved step by step towards Bronson, swaying from side to side as she went. It was a trick she'd learned back on Fango, only back then she'd never thought she'd actually have a practical use for it, as none of the spirits there were homicidal.

Bronson lurched forwards. Elaina saw the cutlass coming and could do nothing to stop it, couldn't dodge it. The world seemed to slow, and then she was flung backwards past Keelin and rolling in the dust.

Elaina shook her head and looked up. Keelin was wielding her sword with a skill beyond her own, swatting away Bronson's wild slashes and scoring a number of hits on the bigger man's body. The damage didn't so much as slow him down.

Bronson brought both cutlasses over his head and down, forcing Keelin to block. Driven to his knees, there was nothing Keelin could do but yelp in surprise when a vine ripped its way out of Bronson's forearm and wrapped itself around Keelin's hands.

Elaina leapt past the restrained captain, right inside Bronson's reach, and planted her little dagger in the monster's good eye, then ripped it out and slashed at the vine holding Keelin.

Tearing himself free, Keelin shook his hands violently until the damned thing fell away. Elaina danced away from a wild swipe and crashed into him, sending them both rolling in the dirt.

Keelin was on his feet first and helped Elaina to hers. His hands were red and blisters were already beginning to show, but they had bigger concerns in the form of a mad spirit attempting to slice them in two.

Bronson was thrashing about wildly, swinging from side to side with Keelin's cutlasses. The man opened his mouth as if to scream and another vine thrust forth, ripping through his cheek and coiling about his neck.

Elaina glanced at Keelin and then nodded upwards. Keelin nodded back; he'd seen what she had – they'd switched positions with Bronson, and the big pirate was now between them and the Observatory. Elaina scooped a rock from the ground and hurled it at the spirit-infested pirate, a last distraction before she and Keelin turned and fled.

The Phoenix

Kebble watched the six figures fleeing through the streets. From his elevated position they looked so small. They ran with reckless abandon, terrified by the lone follower. Only he wasn't alone. From his vantage point, Kebble could see the ground moving with the creatures that flowed after the expedition.

It was a trick of the mind, and Kebble squinted to see past what his head was struggling to comprehend. The earth wasn't moving; it was the millions of insects crawling and scuttling along that made it look as though the ground were giving chase itself.

The six fleeing pirates probably didn't even know just how much danger they were in. Clearly the spirit that had taken and warped Feather's body was no mere angry whisper – more like a bellow of rage. Kebble hadn't realised they could grow so powerful.

Kebble leapt across a fallen skybridge and ran from rooftop to rooftop in an attempt to keep his comrades in sight. They were moving in the right direction, though he didn't think they would make it out of the city without his help. He only hoped they would be safe if they made it back to the forest.

Some of the six were starting to flag and fall behind. The priest of Pelsing was more stumbling than running, and the others weren't faring much better. The insects and Feather's body weren't moving quickly, but their pursuit was steady, relentless. Echoing shouts reached Kebble's ears and he saw the priest stagger to a halt and drop to his knees, clutching at his chest. Smithe skidded to a halt and ran back to him, shouting. The cry echoed up through the buildings, but Kebble couldn't pick out the quartermaster's words. Smithe grabbed the priest beneath his arms and hauled the smaller man to his feet, giving him a rough shove to drive him onwards.

Kebble heard another shout, and he set off at a sprint for the south side of the rooftop. There, looking down into the streets below, he saw Captains Stillwater and Black also running for their lives, chased by a figure that looked a lot like it had once been Bronson. Any vines Bronson passed came to life, wriggling and detaching themselves from the walls they infested, slithering along the ground like snakes.

Kebble ran across a skybridge and then across the next rooftop, leaping over a small gap to another new building. He could see the gate from his position, and it wouldn't be long before the expedition could too. The wards on the gate were designed to keep the forest out, but they'd long ago failed; it was unlikely they would work now to keep the forest in.

Kebble moved quickly to the east side of the rooftop and took up position, drawing his rifle from its sling and bringing it up to his shoulder. Looking down the sight helped him concentrate, helped him focus on the details.

The six members of the expedition were still running from the spirit chasing them. They were moving much more slowly now, with many of the group clearly struggling. Fear was driving them on past their own exhaustion. Kebble swept the barrel of his rifle along the street until he came to the figure chasing them.

Feather's headless body lurched along in a broken lope, trailing gore and insects behind him. With so many of the little creatures, anyone caught would soon be reduced to their bones, and the bugs might not even stop there.

Kebble steadied his breathing and took aim. He let the world recede around him as he targeted Feather's heart and slowly squeezed the trigger.

Feather's body was flung sideways, rolling to a stop in the street. The insect swarm surged around him like a protective shield, but nothing could protect the boy from Kebble.

Kebble reloaded and took aim again. His last shot had been dead on, punching through Feather's chest right where his heart would be. The boy's body was still twitching, still struggling to get to its feet. Even with no head and no heart, the spirit was still able to control the corpse. Kebble admitted then that he had no idea how to destroy the spirit, but he might be able to slow it down long enough for the others to escape.

As Feather struggled back to his feet, Kebble aimed lower and fired again.

Feather's left knee exploded and the body hit the ground once more, flailing, his limbs flinging out in every direction. Kebble reloaded again and took aim once more. Feather got his hands beneath him and crawled onto all fours, though one leg dragged uselessly behind him. The insects surged around and over him, coating the boy in thousands of little shells. His vision of the body obscured, Kebble aimed for what he hoped was the right knee.

A sharp pain flared on Kebble's neck, and he swatted at it with his hand. When he pulled it away he found a squashed beetle, its legs still twitching, and it wasn't alone. Hundreds of the little bugs were starting to crest the ledge around the rooftop, and they were swarming towards Kebble.

The Phoenix

Keelin staggered to a halt, leaning against a wall that crumbled under his weight. He was breathing hard and struggling to keep up with Elaina. Keelin hated to admit it, but the woman was in better shape than he was. She barely even seemed out of breath, though the red in her cheeks and the fire in her eyes made her beautiful.

They'd put some distance between themselves and the monstrosity that had once been Bronson. It wasn't enough. The big pirate was slow, but seemingly unstoppable, and nor did he tire. Keelin didn't even want to think about how the bastard was controlling the vines snaking their way through the ruined city.

Elaina winked at him and moved forwards to the intersection. They'd been heading north for the most part and needed to cut east if they were to meet up with the others at the gate.

A shot ripped through the air and echoed around the streets. Keelin recognised the sound of Kebble's rifle. He looked up, but he couldn't see the marksman anywhere.

"Trouble, ya think?" Elaina said.

"We're already in trouble," Keelin replied between breaths. "Not a stretch to think the others are too."

At the end of the street, six members of the expedition barrelled past. They didn't stop to look, so intent were they on their headlong flight. Keelin shared a glance with Elaina and then pushed back into a run alongside her.

Another shot echoed around them as they reached the intersection and stopped. To the right Keelin saw the six pirates running for their lives. His heart skipped a beat when he realised Aimi was among them, and a wave of relief washed over him, followed quickly by a much larger wave of guilt. Keelin looked left to see what they were running from, and his blood froze.

Scuttling up a vertical wall was a decapitated body, and from the remnants of shredded clothing it wore, Keelin could tell it was – or at least had been – Feather. It was moving like a grotesque out of the deepest nightmares. Thousands of insects flowed around the lad, far more than was worth even thinking about counting. Above, Kebble was running and leaping from rooftop to rooftop, his rifle in his hand.

"Come on," Elaina growled, grabbing hold of Keelin's hand and pulling him into a run.

They chased after the six pirates, closing on them quickly. Keelin shouted, a wordless cry intended to get their attention, and it worked. Aimi glanced behind and slowed to a stop, the others slowing with her.

Keelin collapsed to one knee, the exhaustion making him forget the peril just for a moment. He felt as though he hadn't slept, nor eaten, for days, and he had so little energy left. If it weren't for the murderous spirits trying to evict them, he was fairly certain he could collapse there and then and sleep on the street for a few days.

Aimi threw herself at Keelin and wrapped her arms around him, pulling him close. He hugged her back, vaguely aware of Elaina shaking her head and walking away.

"You scared me," Aimi said, pulling away from Keelin long enough to punch him, and then leaned into him again.

Keelin stood and pulled her into a close embrace. Aimi sobbed once against his chest and then drew in a deep breath. The little woman went rigid in his arms, and a moment later she was pushing him away, a confused look on her face.

"Wonderful little reunion, Cap'n," Smithe said. "But I reckon we stirred up a serpent's nest. Best we fuck off."

"That thing was Feather?" Keelin said, ignoring the strange look Aimi was giving him.

"Aye."

"Well, we found Bronson."

As if on cue, the big spirit-infested pirate lurched around the corner just a few hundred feet away, the vines he controlled snaking along the ground around him. Bronson wasted no time breaking into a sprint towards the expedition.

"Oh, fuck me," Smithe said, and it was clear just how tired the quartermaster was. The rings under his eyes, the slight stoop to his shoulders – he looked about ready to give up.

Another shot ripped through the air and Bronson crashed to the ground, the vines tangling around his limbs as he sprawled.

"Time to go," Keelin shouted with one last look at Bronson; he was already surging back to his feet. They ran. Keelin's feet hurt like all the Hells and his legs felt wooden, his knees barely bending. The others didn't look much better. He tried to think back to a time when he wasn't running, and the only image that came to mind was Elaina pinned up against the wall. Keelin threw a guilty look at Aimi and almost tripped over his own feet.

"Turn left," Alfer shouted from behind, and as Keelin swung around a corner the gate that led into the forest came into glorious view.

Another gun shot rang out, and Keelin slowed to a stop and turned, quickly steering Jotin around him to stop the pirate knocking him over. The others ran past as Keelin looked along the rooftops, trying to spot the marksman.

"Cap'n?" Smithe said, pulling up next to him.

"Kebble." Keelin pointed.

Kebble almost seemed to be dancing with Feather's headless corpse, dodging and twisting away from its clumsy attacks, then hitting the insect-covered boy with the butt of his rifle. Feather staggered towards the lip of the rooftop and careened over the side, falling to the ground below with a bone-shattering crash – but Kebble was still dancing, swatting at the air around his head.

"Shit," Smithe said as Bronson's wrecked, vine-covered body barrelled around the corner.

Keelin spun on his heel and ran, Smithe at his side. A moment later he heard a thud and Smithe crying out. Keelin turned to see his quartermaster on the ground, a vine wrapped around his legs, pulling him towards Bronson.

Another shot rang out and Bronson hit the street again, rolling away with the force of the bullet, but the vine around Smithe's legs didn't let go. Keelin saw Smithe's nasty little knife lying on the ground between them. Smithe saw it too.

"Cap'n," the quartermaster cried, clawing at the ground as the vine dragged him away. "Help!"

Keelin had been waiting for this chance for so long. A perfectly reasonable way to rid himself of the man who had challenged his authority for years. No one would argue that the captain was to blame if Smithe was killed in HwoyonDo by a murderous spirit that had taken over Bronson's body.

Keelin turned away.

With a growl that was frustration at himself as much as the situation, Keelin turned back and ran to his quartermaster's aid. He couldn't deny he wanted to be rid of the man, but he wasn't about to sacrifice Smithe to the evil spirits of a land *he* had led them to. Besides, no matter how much of a hateful bastard Smithe was, he was also part of Keelin's crew.

Keelin kicked Smithe's knife within the quartermaster's grasp and drew Elaina's sword from his belt, skidding to a stop by the pirate's legs and hacking at the vine that held him tight. Bronson started to rise again, and Keelin left Smithe to free himself and closed in on the monster that had once been one of his crew.

He slashed, putting his weight behind the blow, before Bronson could get his cutlass hands up to block. The sword buried itself in the big pirate's neck and damned near cut all the way through, but it was a short blade and Bronson had a lot of muscle. Vines erupted from the wound, snaking up around the almost-severed head. Keelin stumbled backwards and collided with Smithe, who was also staring in horror.

"Fuck it," Smithe said quietly.

Keelin glanced at his quartermaster and nodded. "Agreed."

They turned and ran after the rest of the group, leaving Bronson's struggling form behind them.

When they reached the gate, Keelin turned back to the ruined city of HwoyonDo. Bronson had given up the chase and joined Feather on the rooftops, charging after Kebble as the marksman leapt from roof to roof, occasionally turning to offer the monsters combat.

"We can't leave him," Keelin whispered, trying to think of a way to rescue Kebble.

"We can't help him," Elaina said. "We have no way to kill those things. Besides, I kind of think he wants us to go."

"What do you know?" Keelin snapped. "He ain't one of your crew."

One more shot rang out and something hit the gateway beside them. Keelin glanced at the stone, and then back towards the city. He couldn't make out what was happening in the dim light, but he knew Kebble couldn't keep fighting forever. Sooner or later the marksman would slip up and the spirits would take him.

"Let's move out," he said with a heavy sigh. "Stick close together and move quickly. We'll drink a toast to the fallen when we're back on the ship."

The Phoenix

Kebble staggered out of the doorway and onto the moonlit street. He was bloody and weary, limping and using his rifle as a crutch. He had nothing left, and despite his best efforts the spirits were still chasing him down. From behind came the chittering of millions of insects and the crash of Bronson searching the building. Still, he limped on, unable to simply give up and let them catch him.

Immortality, he decided, was a strange thing. He'd spent so many years searching for his death, yet now that it was stalking him and the end was near, he found he couldn't outrun it fast enough.

His strength wavered and he collapsed onto one knee. For a moment all he could do was sag against his rifle and cough. The rattle in his chest sounded wet, and he knew that was a bad sign. After a moment he looked up. The great library of HwoyonDo rose up in front of him.

"Fitting." Kebble pulled himself back to his feet and staggered onwards down the ruined street, a ruin he had caused. He mounted the library's steps slowly, twelve of them leading up to the grand doors. As a child, and even a young man, he'd climbed the stairs two or three at a time, always in a rush to get to the books, to learn. Now he struggled up each one, putting more and more weight on his rifle.

He paused at the threshold, the doors themselves having long since succumbed to time and rotted away. For just a moment Kebble considered turning back. The ghosts within the ruined library were even stronger, almost as though they were real, rather than just figments of his imagination. Kebble shook his head and staggered inside.

A thick layer of dust coated the floor, and moonlight streamed in through a hole in the roof high above. The front desk was long since gone, only dents in the stone proof that it had ever been there. To either side stood the bookshelves, row upon row of them stretching up into the darkness. But they were all empty, the books long since turned to dust. All of the knowledge the Empire had ever garnered, gone. Only Kebble remained, only his memories of those books remained; and after a thousand years he'd forgotten half of all that he'd learned.

In front of Kebble stood a statue, one of the six faces of his god. The scholar held a book in one hand and a knife in the other, a reminder that knowledge can be used as a weapon. Kebble collapsed at its feet, dropping his rifle and turning to lean against the cold stone. His breathing was painful now, a sharp stabbing in his chest with every draw.

Two figures stood at the doorway, silhouetted against the light. One was tall and broad, surrounded by a writhing mass. The other was small, made smaller still by the lack of a head, and there was a sea of insects creeping towards Kebble. Angry spirits finally come to finish the job.

Something tore inside him, and Kebble gasped, closing his eyes against the pain in his chest. When he opened them again a man was standing in front of him. He was tall and regal, with flowing brown robes and a face that was all too familiar. Kebble attempted to sit a little straighter, but his arms wouldn't respond. It seemed wrong to slouch so much in front of a god.

"I suppose…" Kebble coughed and tasted blood. "Both our times are finally over now. I'm the last one, the only one who still knows your name. We'll fade from this world together." There was a symmetry to it that brought a smile to Kebble's bloodied lips.

The scholar stared down at him, a book in one hand and in the other a gold statue of his six faces, each one with different gemstones for eyes. It was the statue that belonged in the temple – the temple his crewmates had looted. Kebble looked up, realisation dawning. His god was smiling at him.

Starry Dawn

Elaina stumbled through the trees onto the sandy beach and raised a hand to her eyes to ward off the sun. Blinking away the glare, she looked up and down the coastline.

"There," Aimi said, pointing down the beach.

Elaina squinted, and her heart started to hammer in her chest. A ship floated leisurely in its anchorage just a short way from the shore. *The Phoenix* had never been such a welcome sight, not even when Tanner had first shown it to his daughter and made her captain.

The remains of the expedition trudged one by one through the last of the trees and onto the sand. They were weary and beyond exhausted, but all eight of them had survived the trip back from HwoyonDo.

"Oh, blessed fuckin' sea," Jotin growled through a parched throat, dropping to his knees on the sand and rolling onto his back to stare up at the bright blue sky.

Pavel collapsed the moment sand was under his feet again. The priest was used to relative comfort, and Elaina wagered he'd never experienced anything like the hardship they'd all just been through. His crimson robes were ripped and stained dark with sweat and worse, and the man looked as though he'd lost every bit of fat on his body; his cheeks were gaunt and his eyes sunken.

Elaina hadn't fared much better. In truth, she'd lived as a pirate for every day of her life, and not once before had she been so dirty, dishevelled, and tired. Her clothes were little more than rags, and she couldn't decide if they smelled worse or better than her skin. Dried, stale sweat coated every bit of her, and she didn't want to know how large the bags under her eyes were.

Elaina had lost track of time since leaving HwoyonDo. They'd marched for days until they were all sore and swollen, chafed both in skin and in mood. After that they'd started resting from time to time, but none of them had been able to get much sleep no matter how exhausted they were. The spirits that had taken over Bronson and Feather were still behind them somewhere, and no one wanted to be the next victim. Those who did manage to drop off often awoke terrified by the nightmares that swirled inside their heads.

"Take a few minutes," Keelin said as he sank down onto his knees. "Then we make for the dinghy. The sooner we're back on the boat, the sooner we can all rest. Maybe try to forget…"

Nobody argued. They were all grateful for the rest, even if it was a short one. All too soon for Elaina's weary legs, they were moving again, trudging sliding footprints through the sand. As the sun reached its zenith, they found their dinghy right where they'd left it.

In silence, the group made the boat ready and pushed it out into the shallows, jumping in and settling into place for the row back to *The Phoenix*.

"What's that?" Alfer said, letting go of his oar for a moment to point at something along the treeline.

Everybody looked, and Elaina felt her skin crawling. Bronson stood between two giant trees, staring out towards them, only he was more plant than man now, his flesh nothing more than patches of skin around wriggling green tentacles. Elaina looked away and concentrated on her oar, pulling hard against the water. The others soon followed her course.

The Phoenix

"Throw me a bucket," Elaina shouted up to those on deck as the first of their expedition made the climb up to *The Phoenix*. After Pavel had disappeared over the railing, Elaina filled the bucket with seawater and started up the rope ladder. Aimi would have been impressed by the woman's strength, carrying a bucket as she climbed, but she hated Elaina too much to be impressed by anything the bitch did.

Aimi was next up, and as she climbed she watched Elaina lower a second bucket into the sea. Accepting the offer of help at the top, Aimi finally found her feet back on the wooden decking of *The Phoenix* and marvelled at just how good it felt.

Alfer followed her up the ladder, and no sooner was the old veteran aboard than Elaina handed him her pack with an instruction to keep a close eye on it. The pirate captain picked up a bucket of water in each hand and walked up the nearest set of steps onto the poop deck, where she proceeded to strip off and throw her soiled clothes to the planks. Before long Elaina was stark naked, and more than a few of *The Phoenix*'s crew were giving her the ogling of a lifetime. Elaina ignored the attention and picked up a bucket of seawater and dumped it over her head. Aimi winced at the pang of jealousy she felt; the desire to be clean and in a new set of clothes was almost painful. As Elaina dumped the second bucket of water over her head, Pavel appeared carrying a fresh set of clothing.

Aimi turned away. Most of the expedition were up and lying on the deck; Smithe appeared over the railing and then turned to give Keelin a hand. The captain staggered to the centre of the main deck and leaned against the mast, closing his eyes against the torrent of questions that were fired his way.

"Where's Feather?" Morley said, his voice booming over the din. "And Bronson, and Kebble?"

"Gone," Keelin said without opening his eyes. "We're all that made it back."

"What about the treasure?" asked another of the crew. Aimi

struggled to remember the man's name, but she was too exhausted to put much effort into it.

"Jotin," Keelin prompted.

Jotin groaned and rolled to his knees, reaching into his pack and pulling out the gold statue of Kebble's forgotten god, dumping it onto the deck and collapsing beside it.

After a few moments the angry shouts started.

"That it?"

"We paid three lives for a hunk of gold?"

"*Quiet!*" Smithe roared over the arguing pirates. "Cap'n's information was good. We found the damned city right where it was meant to be. Didn't have time to properly loot the fucking place though on account of being attacked by some fucking… things that were wearing the skins of our own mates."

Smithe pointed at the statue. "That there is all we managed to get. And be fucking glad we got that much, eh." With that the quartermaster sank down onto the deck with the others.

Aimi sighed and forced herself to her feet, aiming for the captain's cabin in the hopes of stripping out of her clothes and scrubbing her skin clean. Keelin caught up to her as she reached the door, Morley hot his heels.

"Are you aiming for sleep or a bath?" Keelin said with a weary smile.

"Both," Aimi said. "Maybe the other way around though."

"Maybe I'll join you."

"Wouldn't you rather join Captain Black?" Aimi snapped, trying the handle only to find the door locked. She ground her teeth and stepped aside as Morley handed the key to the captain.

"What's got into you lately?" Keelin said quietly. Morley stood close by, attempting to look like he wasn't eavesdropping.

"You," Aimi whispered back, "getting into her!" Aimi pointed towards Elaina, who was dumping another bucket of water over herself on the poop deck.

"What?"

"Don't bother lying, Keelin. Back in the city, after we met up. I could smell her all over you."

"Oh…" Keelin fitted the key into the lock and turned it. "I'm sorry."

Aimi snorted and pushed the door open. "You want to know the worst bit about it?"

Keelin was silent.

Aimi struggled against her better judgement, still trying to decide whether to tell him or not. Eventually her weariness won out and she decided she simply didn't care any more.

"I'm pregnant." She stepped into the cabin and slammed the door in his face.

Part 4 - Dead Men Tell No Tales

Sacrifices will need to be made said the Oracle
Aye said Drake
They will all look to you to lead them said the Oracle
Aye said Drake

Fortune

New Sev'relain had grown far beyond the hundred or so dispossessed refugees the town had started with. Drake wagered they now numbered at least ten times that. The forest had taken a beating, but there were still plenty of trees on the island and those that had been chopped down now stood tall as the framework for their home. Drake no longer bothered to count how many buildings had been erected, and more were rising up from the dirt every day.

The wall had been rebuilt and finished a good long while back, and now provided a hefty layer of protection against any who might try to come from the forest. Guard towers were set along its length, and those who manned them were well known to be crack shots with either bow or rifle – not that they had many of the latter.

The port was another matter, and they were well defended there too. Most of the work had gone into building up the piers and berths, allowing as many ships as possible at the docks. New Sev'relain was quickly becoming a thriving trade town, and they needed as much space as possible for both the merchant ships and those being outfitted for war. A number of war scorpions had been shipped off *North Storm* and sat ready, just beyond the shoreline in case of attack. The engineers had built ingenious platforms for the war machines that could be turned in a full circle, so no hostile ship intending to enter the bay would be safe.

Drake marvelled at the number of ships they'd brought together. He'd owned more at Fortune's Rest, of course, but most of those had been smaller vessels, not suited for combat at sea. The thought of the

Rest brought a bitter tang to his musings.

Ruien Portly had arrived with no more than twenty ships in total. Drake had entrusted the old pirate with repurposing the Rest into a fleet with as many combat-ready vessels as possible. Some had simply not been fit for purpose, and more were lost at sea during a particularly violent storm that the fat bastard should have seen coming. Drake would have strung Ruien up for his foolishness, but the man was a seasoned commander and right now they needed as many of those as they could get.

Not all of the vessels floating around the bay were Drake's to command, and that rankled him more than he could say. A few weeks ago ten ships had appeared on the horizon, and they claimed to be from Chade. At first Drake had been more than a little pleased that Anders had managed to convince Rose and her Thorn to help out, at least until the man in charge had informed Drake that the ships answered to Elaina Black and no one else. They were waiting in the bay for her return, and claimed they wouldn't take part in any conflict without her. Not even Tanner had been able to change their position.

To make matters even more infuriating, Zothus had finally returned home just a few days ago, and he'd brought fourteen ships and a few hundred freed slaves with him. The ex-slaves were quickly integrated into either the town or the fleet, and Zothus claimed they were courtesy of Keelin, but the ships were another matter. Much like the fleet from Chade, the ships from Larkos claimed they answered to Elaina Black and no one else.

Tanner's sea bitch of a daughter was in command of twenty-four battle-ready vessels, and she was very much in the column of missing. In truth, Drake wasn't certain he wanted her to appear. He'd agreed with Tanner to make Elaina his queen just as soon as the crown was good and certain, but it would be a marriage of necessity. Drake didn't want any of the Blacks sharing his bed, no matter how good she might look naked.

A new ship, one Drake didn't recognise, was drifting into a berth down at the docks. It would be safe; T'ruck would have made sure of that. The giant captain's behemoth floated at anchor just outside the bay. *North Storm* was almost fully manned now, and T'ruck insisted on inspecting every ship that came to New Sev'relain.

"Another one?" Beck said. Her compulsion was a comforting feeling now that Drake was so used to it. "And more sails on the horizon."

"Looks like," Drake said, turning a warm smile on the Arbiter. Beck returned the smile for a brief second before it dropped from her face, replaced by something a lot like hunger. The Arbiter was in Drake's bed almost on a nightly basis these days, and it was something he was more than a little thankful for. Beck was wild and passionate, and ever since their encounter with the Drurr, her appetite had been insatiable. She was holding something back though, and Drake yearned to find out what. He spotted a familiar figure wandering the streets of his little town. A smile stretched across his face and he waved to the man, beckoning him up to the balcony.

By the time the door opened and Anders stepped through, he was already carrying two drinks and Drake wagered the man would have had another if he could only grow a third hand. Anders may be a booze-soaked sot, but he was also one of the most reliable spies Drake had ever employed. He also owed his life to Drake more than once over, and that made him almost as loyal as family.

"Oh, fuck me," Anders said, near jumping out of his skin when he spied Beck sitting nearby. "Must you wear that coat, my dear? You damned near scared the intoxication right out of me, and believe me, you wouldn't like me when I'm sober."

"I don't like you now," Beck said flatly.

"Charming," Anders said, finding an empty table and setting his drinks down. "That's only because you don't yet know me. I'm a very amiable sort once…"

"Anders," Drake said.

"Aye, Captain." Anders snapped to mock attention. "Are you aware you have an Arbiter in your midst, Drake? She's wearing the coat and everything."

Beck had taken to wearing her coat again soon after the slaughter of the Drurr. Whether it was because she no longer cared who knew of her profession or because she needed the reminder herself, Drake was unsure. The Arbiter stood up, sauntered over to Anders, and plucked one of his mugs from the table before retreating to her seat near the door.

"Damned unnerving," Anders continued. "Did I ever tell you an Arbiter almost killed me once?"

"Heretic, are you?" Beck said.

"No," Anders said with a dramatic shiver as Beck's compulsion forced the truth from him. "By all the gods, that never gets any less unpleasant, does it? No, no heretic. I just happened to be in the way of an Arbiter looking for our good Captain Drake here."

Beck cocked an eyebrow at Drake. He shrugged.

"Got some news, have we, Anders?" Drake said. "I do hope it's good."

"Well, of course it isn't." Anders collapsed into a chair and scooped up his one remaining mug of beer. "See, the thing about good news is that it travels fast, faster indeed than should really be possible. Why, I could hear some good news and bear it here more expediently than any other, and yet somehow the word of that news would still outdistance me.

"Bad news, on the other hand, likes to hide and wait. It likely made it here a good few days ago, where it's been waiting for me to deliver it just because it hates to be its own bearer."

"Anders," Drake prompted with a growl.

"Alright. Just remember how we messengers detest getting shot." The drunkard sent a glance at Beck. "Believe me, I know from experience."

After a few moments of silence, Anders finally got around to delivering his news. "They're coming, Drake. Now. Already."

"Fuck." Drake wondered how quickly he could get the rest of the ships ready. "How many?"

"At least fifty ships. Mostly galleons. A few Man of Wars."

Drake looked out at the bay. Without the ships from Chade and Larkos they would be smashed, overrun by sheer numbers. He needed to come up with a way to convince them to fight for him rather than Elaina Black.

"How is it this is the first we're hearing of those sorts of numbers?" he said.

"That Five Kingdoms whelp of a king is a smart bastard," Anders said around a mouthful of beer. "He locked down Land's End while they made the preparations. I barely managed to get out ahead of the fleet. It was an impressive feat of ingenuity. You should have…"

"How long do we have?"

Anders sighed. "Not long. Probably not even long enough for me to make my usual escape. I tell you this so you realise the depth of my predicament in bringing you this dire news."

"Aye, you're a real hero, Anders," Drake growled. "Where in the Hells is Stillwater?"

"Who?"

"Doesn't matter."

"There's something else," Anders said with a heavy sigh. "They have a pirate directing them here, making sure they don't fall foul of your treacherous waters. A man by the name of Poole?"

"Daimen Poole?" Drake said.

"Most likely. Thick isles accent. Dirty-straw hair and a squat nose."

"Aye, that's Poole. Treasonous bastard."

"He seemed quite reluctant, if that's any consolation."

"Not really." It wasn't enough that the bastards had built a fleet the size of which hadn't been seen for hundreds of years – now they were turning Drake's own allies against him. He was starting to regret leaving Poole to die.

"Drake?" Beck's voice snapped him back to the problem at hand. "What do we do?"

Drake stormed over to Anders' table, plucked his drink from his hand and downed it, to a chorus of moans from the drunkard.

"We gather the captains and tell them to get their ships in order."

Fortune

The Righteous Indignation was cleared of stragglers, drunks, and anyone without the title of captain or first mate. By the time Anders sat down at Drake's table to tell him that his full war council had convened, there were nearly a hundred people crammed in, filling every chair, every stool, every corner, and all the bits in between. It wasn't just those who had signed on to help; even Elaina Black's recruits had turned up to hear the news, and Drake realised now was the time to convince them to fight for him whatever their orders.

Tanner Black was a dark presence in the room. He'd taken a corner for his own and had a number of folk surrounding him, including the worthless shit of a fool he called a son. Tanner brought eight ships to the table, and that was no small number. Only Drake and Elaina could claim more.

T'ruck Khan had claimed the middle table, and that, and his size, made him the centre of attention. The giant was now known as the Hero of the Isles, a title Drake had helped to secure for him, and his influence was greater than he was aware. No one but his most loyal of crew knew how they'd taken the behemoth that floated in their waters, and those crew members were saying nothing. In truth it didn't matter how the captain had accomplished the miracle, only that he had and that everyone knew it. T'ruck's voice would carry as much weight as he did in the coming storm of words.

There were plenty of others too. Deun Burn had rallied some of his Riverlanders, and had three ships following his command. It was far from a lot, but even one combat-ready boat could make all the difference. Sienen Zhou had captured a slaver with his own ship, *Freedom*, and now both crews sailed under his flag.

Never before in any sort of history, recorded or otherwise, had there been a gathering of captains quite like this. Even in the days of the old Captain Black, the tyrant had never known these sorts of numbers. Drake had accomplished so much already; he'd brought all the captains together and united them under his command, his rule. Now he needed to convince them to fight for their kingdom, because until they crushed the fleets of their enemies their waters would never be free of those who wished to oppress them.

It had taken a fair portion of the day to get word to all the captains, and some of them had been in the tavern for a lot of it. One or two were already a little pickled, and the beer was flowing freely now they were all gathered and the doors were shut.

Drake stepped up onto his chair, put two fingers in his mouth, and whistled so loudly even the rats paid him due attention. The noise died down – at least, as far as it could when there were a hundred pirates in a single room.

"Reckon you've probably all figured why I called ya here," Drake started. "There's…"

A loud banging on the door interrupted him, and a few moments later that same door opened. Keelin Stillwater stood on the other side with his first mate Morley beside him. Drake felt a grin spread across his face as Stillwater stepped into the tavern to a cheer from many of those inside. The grin dropped away a moment later, when Elaina Black came in after him.

"It's about damned time ya…" Drake started, but was interrupted by two captains who rushed to Elaina, jostling each other for the chance to speak first.

"Captain Black," said one, a tall man with dark hair braided into rows on top of his head. "The Lord and Lady of Chade send their regards." He finished with a respectful bow of his head.

"Hmph," grunted the other captain, who had been just a step behind. "As do the Council of Thirteen."

"How many?" Elaina said, sending a smug glance towards Drake before turning that same look on her father.

"Ten," said the captain from Chade.

"Fourteen," said the captain from Larkos, in a voice that dripped with victory.

"All at my command?"

"Yours and no one else's," said the captain from Larkos.

"Good," Elaina said.

"Where have you been, Stillwater?" Drake called, in an attempt to reclaim authority over the room.

"Following a lead," Keelin said, moving to Drake's table. "It didn't work out."

"I wouldn't say that, Stillwater," Elaina crowed, reclaiming the crowd's attention. The woman pulled a ragged scroll from her jacket and walked to the centre of the room. She slapped the scroll down on T'ruck's table. "Anyone here know any alchemy?"

A murmur ran through the crowd. It was Beck who spoke up. "I do."

"Good to see you again, Arbiter," Elaina said with a nod. "Fancy having a look?"

Beck stood and crossed to Elaina's table. Drake hopped down from his chair and followed quickly. He was more than a little curious as to how the two women knew each other, but questioning either of them about it right now would only make him seem weak. Besides, he was also fairly curious as to what Elaina had found.

T'ruck glanced at the scroll and then turned his full attention to Elaina, a silly grin on his face. Drake opted for quite the opposite, with a curt glare at the woman followed by his full and undivided on the parchment.

"Looks like gibberish," he said eventually. "And possibly a shopping list."

"What? You can't read it, Morrass?" Elaina grinned. "That's why I scribbled down a translation."

The woman was already starting to grate on Drake's very last nerve, and worst of all was that she was doing it in front of all the other captains. "Enlighten me," he growled.

"It's the recipe for Everfire."

There was a lot of noise as chairs were pushed away and pirates surged to their feet. Many tried to back away, as if the mere sight of the formula could set them on fire, while others pushed forwards to catch a glimpse.

Drake let out a sigh of frustration.

"Assuming you're right – and we ain't got nothing but your say so right now – where'd you find this?"

"The Forgotten Empire," Elaina said, a statement that could only add weight to her claim.

"What the fuck were you doing there?" Drake said, with a little more venom than he'd intended.

"Looking after Stillwater." Elaina narrowed her eyes. "Someone needs to keep him out of trouble."

Drake turned to Keelin. The man was staring into a mug of beer. He'd appropriated Drake's vacated chair and was doing a good job of trying to look uninterested in the situation. It seemed a little too much of a coincidence that Drake's chart of the Forgotten Empire's waters had been stolen and, just a short spell later, Stillwater had found himself in that area. Drake was starting to wonder if he could trust any of his captains.

"I can make this," Beck said. "I have no idea if it will work as Captain Black promises though."

"Get on it," Elaina said with a grin.

Beck gave the woman a long, hard stare, then turned her gaze on Drake, who made a show of thinking it over before nodding his assent. Beck rolled up the scroll and headed for the door.

"If this is real…" Drake started.

"Then I just brought one hell of a weapon to the table," Elaina finished for him. "Along with twenty-four ships. Of course, they're only here to sail for me if I'm queen." She grinned.

Drake looked at Tanner. The black-hearted bastard was just watching, apparently content to let matters proceed as they would.

"What do you say, Morrass?"

Drake almost laughed. It was obvious now that Elaina had no idea about the deal he'd struck with her father. He was getting both of their support for the same terms, and all he had to do was put up with them both for the rest of his life. It was a hefty price to pay, but one that was definitely worth the prize of a crown. Besides, there was always the chance neither of them would survive the coming battle.

"Aye," Drake said in a whisper amidst the sea of noise. "Can't do this without those ships of yours. Soon as this fight is over, you and me sit our arses on the throne together."

Elaina laughed. "Louder, Morrass."

Drake ground his teeth and stared at the woman. Elaina didn't flinch one drop.

"Listen!" Drake roared, the command in his voice forcing the tavern to quiet. "There's a fight coming. The big one. The last one. The one we've been gathering for. And it's coming soon.

"Sarth and the Five Kingdoms have sent a fleet fifty ships strong. We got them pretty equal on numbers there, but they'll have bigger ships, more men. We win this battle and there won't be another. The bastards will have no choice but to recognise us as a kingdom, right and true.

"You've all put your trust in me to gather you together and lead you to victory. That's exactly what I'm going to do. Can't do it alone though." Drake sent a long, poignant look at Elaina. "So the moment this is all over and I sit down as king, I'll be sitting down with Captain Elaina Black as queen."

"You'll marry her now," Tanner's voice was loud and clear over the pirates clamouring at Drake's announcement. "Don't want ya slipping your way out of it once the hard work is done."

Drake clenched his jaw so tightly it hurt.

"I'll even perform the ceremony myself," Tanner continued. "Elaina – daughter. Do you take our king, Drake Morrass, to be your lawfully wedded husband?"

Drake at least had the pleasure of seeing a look of panic flash over Elaina's face, but the woman recovered quickly enough.

"Aye, guess I have to."

"And Drake." Tanner grinned across the room. "Do you take Elaina Black, my daughter, to be your lawfully wedded wife?"

Some situations there was simply no escape from. Drake nodded. "Aye, I do."

"Then by my power as a captain of my own vessel and by the witness of all these good men an' women…" Tanner paused, a victorious smile spreading across his lips. "I now pronounce you man and wife."

A cheer rolled around the tavern, so loud that Drake had to wonder if the woman was really that popular or if the pirates were simply jumping upon any opportunity for celebration. There certainly hadn't been too much cause for it of late. Drake let the cheer do a few rounds before holding up his hands for quiet, desperate to get the situation back under his control.

"News worthy of celebration, no doubt, but right now we got more important things to talk about." Drake waited a few moments for the crowd to calm down. "The fleet is coming. It's on its way already and could be here any day. Truth of it is, we're not ready."

"We'll kill 'em!" shouted a swarthy old captain by the name of Twotone Elric, and a few of the others cheered their assent.

"Aye, we will," Drake said loudly. "But we ain't got no more time to dawdle and piss about. I don't want them getting here to New Sev'relain. A fight on land is a fight we don't want, and the good folk here have been through enough. They ain't fighters, and they don't deserve to be beaten into the role.

"I want us to meet these fuckers in open water with decks under our feet and Rin's blessing in our sails. So load up ya ships with supplies and get your crews back on board and as sober as you dare. In three days, we sail out of New Sev'relain to claim ourselves an empire."

The crowd cheered.

"To claim ourselves a *legacy*!"

The roar grew even louder and the thumping of feet on the floor was a thunderous accompaniment. Elaina smiled at Drake and drew close.

"To claim ourselves a crown," the woman all but whispered in his ear before turning and walking to the door. Drake watched her go, admiring her presence. Elaina was as strong and skilled as any pirate, the perfect queen for the tough life of the Pirate Isles. Drake was already wondering how easy she would be to manipulate.

Starry Dawn

Elaina sat in the sand, staring out at the bay and all the ships that crowded it. There were so many masts it reminded her of Chade, or Larkos. Her spirits were high, and with good reason. Drake had set himself up as king and now she was his wife. Elaina would be queen, even if it did mean the occasional sharing of a bed with Morrass. The very thought of his hands on her skin sent shivers coursing through her body. Drake was pretty enough, that was true, and if even half the rumours about him weren't shit, he knew his way around a woman's body. But Elaina couldn't shake her distaste for the man. He was slimy as a sea serpent and dangerous as a shark, and Elaina wanted nothing to do with him. But sacrifices sometimes had to be made, and Drake was hers. The thought of carrying Drake's child inside her sent a new set of shivers down Elaina's spine, and she decided to think about something else.

She had yet to choose a ship to take as her own. She had twenty-four vessels under her command, more than anyone else, but none of them were hers. The thought of *Starry Dawn*, and of those who had taken her from Elaina, made for a sour state of mind. She needed to pick a new ship and quickly, not dwell on the past. It would take some time to appraise the crew and familiarise herself with the quirks of a new boat, and time was something none of them had. She briefly considered strolling back aboard *The Phoenix*, if for no other reason than to piss off that pregnant waif, Aimi. It wasn't a real option though. Elaina was to be queen of the pirates and, as such, she should damned well have her own ship.

"Hi, Cap," Surge said, sitting down just out of striking distance.

Elaina did a good job of holding her surprise at the treasonous pirate's appearance. Instead of rounding on the bastard and stabbing him to death for taking part in the theft of her ship, Elaina simply offered him a cold, dead-eyed glare. Surge quickly took a particular interest in the sand.

"Look, Cap, about the whole…"

"Where's my ship?" Elaina growled.

"Out in the bay," Surge said quickly, his hands up in the air.

"I don't see her."

"There." Surge pointed to the bay. "Well, she's a little hidden behind *Ocean Deep*, I suppose, but she's there alright. Tanner, uh, Captain Black has her again."

Elaina made knuckles in the sand.

"I'm sorry, Cap," Surge offered. "We all are."

Elaina launched to her feet and strode away from the apologetic pirate. Tanner had taken up residence just a short way down the beach, setting up a large tent where he could hold his court apart from the residence of New Sev'relain, and Elaina was eager to have words with him.

Tanner was dozing in the afternoon sun just outside his tent with his feet up on a barrel. Blu sat near him, pretending to read a logbook, and a number of Tanner's crew were close by, guarding their captains.

"Da," Elaina all but shouted.

Tanner let out a startled snort and his eyes snapped open, dark fury burning behind his crystal blues. Blu was quicker to respond, throwing the logbook into the sand and jumping up to stand in his sister's way.

"Don't remember anyone requesting…" Blu started.

"Blu," Tanner said.

"Sit the fuck back down, brother," Elaina snapped. "Ya say one more fucking word to me, and I'll have that ship of yours taken away and given to a Riverlander."

Blu opened his mouth to reply, but there was fear in his eyes. He'd witnessed the marriage. He knew what it meant. Elaina had all but been declared queen, and he knew his sister would happily take away his toys. Blu turned to look at their father. Tanner shrugged, his eyes now glinting with amusement.

"Better obey the girl, lad," Tanner rumbled. "She's royalty these days."

"You got my ship over there, Da." Elaina had decided to forgo formalities and jump right in.

"Seem to remember we've had this conversation before," Tanner said. "It's my ship. They're all my ships."

Elaina drew in a sharp breath. "No. They're all *my* ships."

"Ah, I see the way of it now." Tanner stood, towering over his daughter. "I send ya away ta find me some allies, and ya go and recruit them all for yaself instead, aye? What a grand daughter you turned out ta be."

"You sent me away to *be* out of the way," Elaina growled. "Ya never expected me to find any help, and when I get back, I find ya working for the very bastard you were supposed to kill. Thanks to you, Da, I'm now married to Drake fucking Morrass."

For a moment Tanner looked as though he might strike her, and Elaina was ready for it, but he just growled and walked back to his seat. "It was the right thing ta do, lass. Ya mate, Stillwater, convinced me of that."

Blu looked set to burst with whatever it was he wanted to say. Elaina shook her head at him, and he kept silent.

"I want my ship back, Da," she pressed.

"Aye. Take it then. Ya crew are all still there. Well, all but that treacherous weird of a first mate. Bastard tried telling me ya had run afoul of a bad take. Said ya got stuck and thrown overboard."

"You didn't believe him?"

Tanner laughed. "Ya might be ungrateful, but ya still my daughter. Didn't take much for ya crew ta turn on the fool. Had him strung up in front of all of the town. Dumb bastard didn't think he'd run into me here, eh?"

"You let the rest of the crew live?"

"Aye. Can't go wasting the bodies, no matter how serious the crime. Killed the ring leader and be done with it. The rest can fight and die for your throne, Ya Majesty."

Elaina stood there for a few moments longer, unsure of what to say. "Well, uh. Thanks then, Da."

Tanner laughed. "A thank ya from a queen. Treasure that one forever, eh?"

Elaina nodded and turned away, thoroughly confused as to whether she'd just earned her father's respect or lost it.

Walking up the gangplank to *Starry Dawn*, Elaina felt a fluttering in her stomach. Despite Alfer, Pollick, and Pavel being right behind her, she was nervous. This was the crew she'd hired, built up, helped train, and led to riches a hundred times over. It was also the crew who had mutinied and sailed her ship away from port, leaving her stranded in a strange city with nothing but the clothes on her back. Elaina wondered what had happened to the rest of her clothes, and her other possessions. Had Rovel thrown them overboard, sold them on, or just left them where they were? It didn't matter, really – they were only things, and she could always get more. What did matter was that the ship was hers again, and this time she'd never let *Starry Dawn* go. She stepped up onto the main deck and felt the weight of many eyes turn her way. It was possible the crew hadn't yet heard of her return, let alone her marriage to Morrass. A few of them started to slink away while others just stared in shock. Surge was on deck, wearing a stupid grin, and he was standing next to a man Elaina recognised all too well – her father's raping son-of-a-shit first mate, Mace.

"Get the fuck off my ship," Elaina hissed. Her cheeks felt as though they were on fire, but she didn't care.

Mace looked her up and down, cautiously. Elaina felt her skin crawl.

"Ain't your ship," he said slowly. "It's ya da's."

Elaina stalked over to him, fighting to retain control of herself. Just being close to the rapist made her want to both vomit and claw his beady eyes from his skull. Her skin itched, and the shame and anger she'd been suppressing for so long raged inside her.

"*Off!*" she screamed.

Mace didn't move, or at least he didn't move fast enough for Elaina's liking, and she saw all manner of red. Lashing out with a wild fury, Elaina punched the bastard square in the face. Mace stumbled and grunted. Elaina wasn't finished. She followed up with another punch, and another, and another, and another. Each time she swung at him, Mace tried to get his hands up to block, but he was off balance and reeling, and Elaina knew full well how to throw a punch.

By the time Mace finally went down, collapsing onto the deck in a heap, Elaina was shaking and her fist was dripping blood. Judging by the stinging, she guessed not all of the blood was his, but she blocked out the pain.

"Rope," Elaina ordered, her voice breaking a little with her fury. A moment later Ed the Navigator appeared with a short length. It wasn't fit for rigging, but it was long enough and sturdy enough for the job at hand.

"Tie it off," Elaina said as she quickly knotted a noose in one end.

Mace was starting to come around, trying to get his hands beneath him to stand, so Elaina hit him again, a solid punch followed by an even more solid boot that left him spitting teeth and blood on the deck of her ship. Elaina knelt down and forced the noose over his head.

With a grunt that was all raw power, she pulled Mace over to the railing and lifted him up against it, then pushed him over the side and jumped backwards out of the way of the rope as it pulled taught.

Elaina breathed heavily, still shaking, her emotions a whirl that she was struggling to decipher. Mace was kicking against the hull of *Starry Dawn*, the rope choking the life from his filthy body.

"I'm back," she announced to the crew. "Ship is mine again."

Nobody argued.

"Good." Elaina looked over the railing. Mace was still struggling to stay alive. "Make sure this fucker is good and dead, then cut him free. I'll be in my cabin." The crew stayed silent, so Elaina nodded, more to herself than to anyone else, and made quickly for the captain's cabin. She hoped she'd get there before the tears hit.

The Phoenix

"We're not having this conversation," Keelin said.

"Why not?" Aimi said. "Seems we haven't had a conversation in months. Might as well start up again with this one."

"We're not having it because you are getting off my boat, now."

"No."

"Yes."

"No."

"Damnit, woman." Keelin threw his hands up in the air and stalked over to the window. "Why won't you just listen to me for once?"

"Why won't you stop trying to protect me? I don't need protecting. I managed just fine on my own before I met you, and I'd manage just fine on my own now."

Keelin opened his mouth to argue and quickly shut it again, taking a moment to calm down a little. "But you're not on your own, Aimi. You're pregnant. I'm moving you off the ship because I… *we* are about to sail into a battle, and I don't want you involved in it."

"Stop trying to protect me."

"No."

Aimi let out a growl that was all frustration and collapsed onto the bed with a sigh. "This isn't working, Keelin."

"It hasn't been for a while," he admitted.

"That why you fucked Captain Bitch back in HwoyonDo?"

Keelin sighed. Months at sea and months of the same arguments over and over again. Since HwoyonDo, Aimi had gone from cold to downright abrasive and nothing Keelin did seemed to make a damned difference. He couldn't blame her for being angry. Keelin had fucked Elaina, and they all knew it. Aimi had every right to be angry, but she also refused to listen to reason. Keelin only wanted what was best for her, and for their child, and what was best was not being on the ship in the middle of a war.

Aimi let out a single sob, and Keelin turned. Her head was buried in her hands and her shoulders were trembling. He left his spot at the window and went over to the bed, sitting down next to her and putting an arm around her. She shrugged it away. Keelin persisted, and the second time Aimi didn't resist.

"I shouldn't be crying," she said. "I'm angry with you."

"I know."

"This ship is my home."

"I know."

"This crew are my family. I don't want to leave."

"I know." Keelin wished he had something else to say, but he'd already made his decision and there was nothing she could say to change his mind.

They were both silent for a long time. Aimi stopped crying and seemed content to rest her head against Keelin's chest. It was nice, and far more comfortable than they'd been for a long time.

"Don't die," she said quietly.

"I don't intend to."

She pulled away from him then and gave him a strange look. He had no idea what she was thinking, but there was sadness in her eyes. Eventually, she stood and started to gather her things.

King's Justice

Daimen woke to a hammering at his door. It was a small cabin, little more than a hammock and some space to stand. He'd tried his best to make it his own, but it wasn't an easy task given that he currently owned nothing. The door wasn't locked; Admiral Wulfden had had the lock removed, so Daimen had set up a chair that provided him some measure of privacy – or at least some warning should they come for him.

"Poole," shouted someone from the other side. "Open this door now or I will break it down and nail you to the mizzenmast."

Daimen sighed. Everything was threats these days, either blatant or implied. He knew they didn't trust him, but it grated that they felt the need to remind him of it at every possible opportunity. He missed the days of being a captain. Being respected and trusted. Drake might be a lying, murderous bastard willing to slaughter women and children to further his own desires, but at least Daimen hadn't been living with a noose around his neck while sailing for him.

"I'm comin', ya ungrateful sods," he growled.

"Now, Poole."

"In a hurry ta see my cock, are ya? As ya want, mate." Daimen swung his legs onto the deck and pulled the chair away from the door, which slammed open a moment later. He made a show of stretching and scratching at his stones.

"Urgh," grunted the square-jawed officer on the other side of the door, looking away in obvious distaste. "Get some clothes on, Poole. Quickly. The admiral is eager for your advice."

"Aye?" Daimen said with a laugh. "First time for everything, I guess."

He would have liked to take his time getting dressed, if for no other reason than to annoy the admiral. Unfortunately Officer Square-Jaw was having none of it, and the man's sword looked a little loose in its scabbard. Something had got the whole ship riled up, and it wasn't until Daimen joined Admiral Wulfden on the forecastle that he saw just what it was.

"Fuck me," Daimen breathed as he looked out across the sea.

"You lied to us, Poole," Wulfden said.

"I didn't fucking lie." Daimen winced as the admiral's jaw tightened. "I didn't lie." He was very aware of the host of armed soldiers at his back.

"You said we could expect a maximum of thirty ships. You said you suspected there would, in fact, be far fewer than that."

"How many ships are there?"

"Over fifty," the admiral growled. "It's hard to form an exact count. We suspect they are dangerously close to equalling our numbers."

"Huh. I wonder where they got all those boats." Wulfden turned an angry glare on Daimen, who quickly stepped backwards, hands held up before him. "I swear, Admiral, on my dear old ma's grave, I did not see this coming."

There were ships everywhere. They were stretched out across the horizon, with equal numbers on either side of *King's Justice*. More masts than Daimen could count, and all were floating amidst the endless blue, as though none of them wanted to be the first to attack.

"Is that *Storm Herald*?" said one of the officers.

"Yes," said the admiral. "That explains why she never returned. How could the pirates manage to capture her?"

"Resourceful and resilient bastards, eh?" Daimen said with a laugh cut short when the admiral sent another glare his way.

One of the officers shoved a monoscope into Daimen's hands.

"Identify the most prominent targets please, Poole."

"Aye aye, Admiral." Daimen raised the monoscope to his eyes and scanned the horizon. "That one there is *The Black Death*, captained by Tanner Black himself. There's *The Phoenix*, captained by Drake's right hand, Keelin Stillwater. And right next to her is the *Fortune*. Ya take out those three and you'll break the back of the entire isles."

"Send the signal to attack, Commander," Admiral Wulfden said. "Raise sails and prepare the ballistae. I want as many ships sunk as possible in the first salvo. Let's hope our other turncoat is more useful than you, Poole."

Fortune

"Looks like they're coming, Cap'n," Princess said, sounding maudlin. "I reckon this'd be our last chance to turn tail and chase the horizon."

Drake plucked the monoscope from his first mate's grasp and stared at the fleet arrayed against them. They were all starting to pile on sail and the lead ships were gathering speed. Princess wasn't wrong – this was their last chance to run.

"Get us moving, Princess," he said coldly. "Right at them."

"Reckon I'm gonna die here in this nameless stretch of water," Princess mumbled.

Drake laughed. "Oracle has seen my future, and it's not today."

"Wonderful," Princess said as he stepped backwards. "Didn't happen to ask about my future, did ya? Thought not." He let out a sigh before raising his voice to a practised shout. "Sails up, lads. We're shoving it right down their throats."

A cheer went up, and before long Drake could hear it passing down the line of ships, thousands of pirates taking up the shout as they readied themselves for the bloodiest battle any of them had ever known.

"Can we expect any help from your god?" Beck said. Her voice was trembling. It didn't seem right for the Arbiter to get so scared about a bit of a fight, but then Drake had long ago learned that you just couldn't predict how folk would react when the time came. People died in wars, and no matter how strong or important you were, you had just as much chance of dying as the next poor sod.

"No more than we'll get off yours," he said with a glance backwards and a grin. "It ain't really her way."

"Sure would be nice to have one of those leviathans pop up and do the work for us." The Arbiter looked pale, almost sick. Drake pitied her for that. The fear of the fight sure explained her ferocity in bed of late though. Drake grinned as he remembered their latest encounter and how sore it had left him.

"Aye, that'd be a fine sight," he said. "Ain't likely to happen though. We're gonna have to win this one ourselves."

Next to the *Fortune*, Stillwater's boat was starting to pick up speed, straining to take the lead and meet with the enemy. It was some fine work to slow the ship down just a little to keep it in line with all the others. Drake's plan was simple. *North Storm* would lead the attack – the ship was a monster with a metal ram that would make driftwood out of any that got in her way. With Captain Khan's ship in the centre of the attack, the others would form into a wedge formation and sail right into the enemy lines. Their orders were to prioritise helping out their neighbours, two ships against one as much as possible, to keep the numbers on their side. Once the battle started, though, it was likely that any sort of tactics would go right out of the window. Ship to ship and man to man, the pirates would win. They had to win. They had so much more to lose than their enemy.

Drake looked towards the main mast and the little jar of black liquid that sat nearby, securely nestled within a padded wool cocoon. Everfire was one part alchemy, one part magic. Beck had managed to make just twelve small jars of the stuff in the three days before they left New Sev'relain, and one of those had been used to test it. Drake had never seen water set on fire before; it was a terrifying sight to behold.

They were all up to a good speed now, with *North Storm* leading the pack, breaking away to bear down on their enemies like a charging boar. Drake stared through his monoscope towards the enemy fleet. They were in a far less ordered formation, with some ships straggling behind while others surged ahead. He felt a grin stretch across his face.

"I'm sorry," Beck said.

"Eh?" Drake grunted, turning to face her.

Bang!

The first shot hit Drake in the midsection. The force knocked him against the railing, where he collapsed onto the deck, a look of utter confusion on his face. Beck wasn't sure whom she hated more – Inquisitor Vance for giving the order or herself for carrying it out.

Shouts came from nearby, and they would soon be followed by the sounds of boots on the deck. Beck needed to finish the job before the crew reached them.

Drawing a second pistol, she realised her right hand was still shaking. It was the injury she'd taken in the battle of New Sev'relain. It had to be. Her eyes started to blur a little, and she blinked away the tears.

"Why?" Drake managed to ask. He was still slumped against the railing, dark red blood leaking from his mouth and dripping from his chin. More red was soaking into his shirt. He wouldn't survive – Beck was sure of it – but Inquisitor Vance had ordered her to be certain.

"Sorry," she whispered again as she pulled the trigger on the second pistol.

Drake's body shook with the force of the impact and keeled over sideways, blood spreading out over the deck. Beck took a deep breath and sighed it out even as the first of the *Fortune*'s crew reached her.

Stepping to the side of the wild slash, Beck whispered a blessing of strength and punched the pirate in the chest. The poor man's ribs snapped loudly and he collapsed.

Beck drew another pistol, and a moment later another pirate dropped to the deck to bleed out his last. She walked towards the main mast. Inquisitor Vance had been adamant that neither Drake nor the *Fortune* could be allowed to survive to make it into the battle.

Another two pirates came for her, this time one to each side. Beck whispered the words of a sorcery and stamped a foot onto the deck. The wood warped and twisted as it rippled outwards. The pirates didn't even have time to move away as the decking rose around their feet and locked them in place. Beck moved on without so much as a glance at the two helpless men.

Just before she reached the main mast, something heavy dropped onto Beck from above, knocking her flat onto the deck and darkening her vision for a moment. It didn't take long to realise she was lying there entangled with a pirate who was struggling to remain conscious after his landing. Beck kicked the fool away and struggled to get back to her feet, shaking her head to clear away the dizziness that threatened her.

Something tugged on the bottom of her coat, and Beck turned to see the pirate who had dropped onto her clinging to a loose seam. She pulled a pistol from her jerkin, aimed, and pulled the trigger. The pirate's grip loosened in death.

There was shouting all over now as some pirates rushed to the aid of their fallen captain while others closed in on Beck. They were all too late.

She plucked her fallen hat from the deck and placed the tricorn back on her head, then picked up the jar of Everfire.

The Phoenix

"Cap'n," Smithe shouted, hysterical.

"What is it, Smithe?"

"The *Fortune*." Smithe pointed.

Drake's ship was aflame. Black fire danced over the deck, twisting in the breeze and whipping at the sails, leaving orange flames in its wake. Keelin hadn't seen the Everfire when they tested it out near New Sev'relain. He'd heard folk say it had a life of its own that not even water could extinguish; now he could see for himself that it was true. The black flames went where they would, neither growing nor diminishing, and everything they touched was set ablaze.

Keelin looked back at their own jar of Everfire and felt his stomach twist. There would be no saving a ship besieged by the black flame. There was no saving Drake's ship. The Everfire would burn until there was nothing left but ash floating on the water. Keelin turned back to the *Fortune* just as a pirate enveloped in flames careened over the side of the ship.

"What should we do, Captan?" Morley said.

Keelin watched the *Fortune* slow and drop behind; its sails were all alight now, and its crew's screams could be heard drifting across the water.

"Nothing," he said quietly, turning to look at the approaching fleet. "Keep on."

"But Drake…"

Keelin silenced his first mate with a glare then turned to Smithe. "Get that thing covered." He pointed to the jar of Everfire. "I don't want a stray arrow turning my ship into a pyre."

As they left Drake's ship behind, burning black and orange amidst the blue, Keelin realised how quickly they were coming up on their enemy. *North Storm* was out in front as planned, but not by a lot. The giant figure of T'ruck Khan was visible at the bow of his ship. The man feared nothing, and that was something Keelin wished to emulate.

"Hands on deck," he roared. "Weapons at the ready. Archers fire at will."

Closer and closer now. The enemy ships started to grow large, and the scale of the battle facing them humbled Keelin. Boats spread out across the horizon on both sides as far as he could see. He had little time to contemplate the matter.

The enemy ship facing *North Storm* started to turn, but it was too late and all it accomplished was presenting its port side to the larger vessel. A crack and crash echoed out across the water as the steel ram on the bow of *North Storm* connected with the smaller ship, splitting it in half. Keelin didn't have time to appreciate the destruction; a Five Kingdoms boat was sailing alongside them, blocking the view.

Arrows flew from the navy vessel. Some thudded into the deck while others sailed clean over to land in the deep blue beyond. At least one of the arrows found a mark, the pirate's scream loud and clear. The Five Kingdoms vessel, a galleon roughly the same size as *The Phoenix*, was too close, and their hulls crashed together, scraping across each other. Keelin almost lost his footing, grabbing a nearby railing to stay upright. The noise of the two ships colliding was a terrible groan, and Keelin could only hope it hadn't put a hole in the *The Phoenix*.

The first few Five Kingdoms men hopped aboard, and the sounds of battle quickly followed them. One brave sailor jumped from the navy yard, swinging across on a loose rope and coming to a rolling stop just a few feet away. He drew two swords and charged.

Drawing his new cutlasses, Keelin met the man steel on steel, blocking and parrying every blow. Then the soldier went rigid and started shaking, his swords dropping from his hands and his body dropping to the deck a moment later. Smithe stood above the fallen soldier, his wicked dagger bloody and a snarl on his face.

"Cut the ropes," Keelin roared as loudly as he could. "Push us away. Keep the sails up." Keelin and Smithe rushed to the aid of the crew members attempting to defend their ship from invaders. They turned the tide of one small skirmish, outnumbering the soldiers and bringing them down with well-aimed stabs and slashes that left the poor bastards bleeding out their last.

Keelin slashed at a man's leg and the soldier went down screaming, only to be stabbed in the face by Jojo's spear. Keelin kicked the corpse away and stepped past it to reach the railing. He raised his sword and brought it down hard, severing one of the ropes that held the two ships together.

"Shove off," he screamed, sheathing his swords for a moment and pushing as hard as he could against the navy ship's railing. The two vessels started to part, slowly at first, steadily moving further and further. As long as they could keep any more grapples from locking hold, they would soon be far enough away to begin gathering some speed.

Keelin opened his mouth to give his crew some encouragement and looked up just in time to see an archer on the other ship loose an arrow.

North Storm

T'ruck laughed like a man possessed as his foes drowned around his ship. The first of the enemy fleet had cracked and fallen apart like stale bread when *North Storm* hit it, and now they were free of the wreckage and on the hunt for more prey.

His ship was fast, and it suffered from a poor turning circle due to its size. They didn't want to get too far away from the fight, so T'ruck ordered the ship slowed as it turned to port. Their job was far from simple, and much of the outcome of the battle hinged on their success. They were, perhaps, the only hope now that the *Fortune* was sunk.

Everywhere boats were locked together with vicious fighting underway aboard them. T'ruck hungered to join in, to feel the thrill of combat, but he would follow the plan for now. *North Storm* was a ship like no other, with machines of war capable of tearing smaller vessels apart, and that was what they would do.

"Bring us in as close as you can," T'ruck said to his navigators, Kanon and Serar. The ship was too large for a single wheel; it had two, and they needed to be turned in tandem. Serar was just a few minutes older than her brother, and the twins worked together as one on the wheels of *North Storm*. T'ruck couldn't have asked for a better pair of navigators.

"We can cut those bastards' tails off if you want, Captain," Serar called as she turned the wheel.

"That is not your job," T'ruck said. "Just get us close and let the bastards' own war machines tear their fleet apart."

North Storm levelled off, and they were close enough to the enemy's arse that T'ruck could see the panic on the faces of some of the crew. They were engaged with *Freedom*, and the ships were locked together fast with Sienen Zhou's crew holding the deck, under strict orders not to cross onto the other vessel.

"First three scorpions, fire," T'ruck roared, and a moment later the weapons made an odd cracking sound as they released. Of the three bolts, only one hit its intended target, while one splashed harmlessly into the water and the third lodged itself into *Freedom*'s hull. T'ruck's crew were quick to cut the ropes of the two bolts that had missed.

"Brace the wheel," T'ruck called to his navigators, and then, "Second three scorpions ready for the next ship."

The crew of the navy vessel realised what was happening too late. The bolt was lodged deep into the ship's hull, and down so low it was dipping into the water. A perfect shot. As *North Wind* sailed on, the rope pulled taught and strained against the huge main mast. T'ruck heard his navigators grunt with the effort of keeping the ship sailing straight. The enemy vessel gave a visible lurch sideways just before a large section of its hull around the scorpion bolt ripped free of the surrounding wood. Water started gushing into the hole.

"Cut it free," T'ruck shouted with a wild laugh, but the order wasn't needed. His crew knew their jobs, and they were already busy setting up the next set of bolts.

They would gut as many of the enemy as possible. If they could sink them, they would; otherwise, their goal was to cripple the boats. Drake had claimed mobility would win the war as much as numbers or any magical fire, and T'ruck wagered he had the right of it. A ship without a rudder could do nothing but sit and wait for the pirates to pick them off.

King's Justice

"Uh, Admiral," Daimen said. "That big fucker is behind us and doing its very best to fuck us all in the arse."

"Poole, if you cannot keep that tongue of yours civil, I will have it cut out," Admiral Wulfden said through gritted teeth.

"In the middle of the battle? Seems like a right waste of man power, that."

The admiral sighed and signalled one of his officers. "Turn the ship starboard, Commander. Have the ballistae ready to fire. Torches lit."

"Aye aye, Admiral."

They were one of the few ships not engaged in battle with the pirates; they were sailing in close formation with two other Man of Wars, and those two seemed more than capable of dealing with the pirates that had come alongside them. Wulfden had made sure to bring the ship to a stop, though, so as not to leave the protection of its escort.

"Whatever this plan of yours is," Daimen said, "I hope it's a good one, 'cos that ship is big and…"

"Poole," Wulfden barked. "Shut up."

Daimen held up his hands and watched as the behemoth with *North Storm* written on its side sailed along behind the navy vessels. It had already ripped the arses off two ships, and any moment it would be ripping the side from *King's Justice*. Poole was fairly certain none of the crew would survive the swim back to Land's End.

"Ready," shouted the commander. "Take aim."

The bigger ship was coming into full view behind them now, and Daimen spotted a giant near its wheel. Only one pirate he knew was so large, and that meant T'ruck Khan was aboard the other vessel. Daimen imagined the big captain tearing his arms off for turning traitor and quickly slunk back behind Admiral Wulfden.

"Fire," Wulfden shouted, and torches were touched to the bolts loaded in the ballistae, making them sizzle. "Loose!"

The ship rocked with the force of the ballistae all releasing at once, and Daimen steadied himself on the admiral's shoulder, the fatter man's lower centre of gravity keeping them both upright. Four of the bolts hit home, lodging themselves in the side of the monster ship, and one splashed harmlessly into the water. Wulfden shrugged Daimen's hand away from his shoulder.

"That it?" Daimen said. "Ah, we're fucked for sure." His jaw dropped as four successive explosions ripped a massive hole in the *North Storm*.

The Phoenix

Keelin tasted blood, felt it leaking down the side of his face and dripping from his chin. The arrow had grazed his temple. It occurred to him then that if the arrow had been just a couple of fingers to the right, he would have lost an eye. Worse than that, he would probably be dead. It was a sobering thought.

Arrows were still being traded back and forth between the two ships, and many of *The Phoenix*'s crew were up and pushing against the other vessel. Keelin felt as though he were in a daze, watching the scene unfold without taking part in it.

"Get down, Cap'n," Jolan hissed, grabbing hold of Keelin's arm and pulling him down below the railing.

Keelin blinked the daze away and reached up to touch the cut on his temple. It stung like a nest of bees, but it didn't feel too serious.

"Are we free?" he shouted.

"Rigging is caught," someone shouted back.

"Cut it loose," Keelin roared, and he gave Jolan a pat on the shoulder by way of thanks for pulling him to safety.

Keelin waited for what seemed like forever. Arrows still flitted back and forth between the two ships. One enterprising soldier tried to leap across and was quickly stabbed by the pirates hiding beneath the safety of the railing.

"We're free and clear!" The shout brought a smile to Keelin's face.

"Get us some speed," he called, breaking from the cover and striding towards the main mast. An arrow flew past him and embedded itself in the wood. "Someone kill that fucking archer."

The shield that covered the Everfire had an arrow sticking out of it. Keelin pulled it away and carefully picked up the jar of death. They were moving now, gaining speed and starting to slip away from the other ship. He broke into a sprint, holding the jar securely against his chest and hoping it wouldn't spontaneously burst into flame. He mounted the stairs to the quarterdeck two at a time and slid to a stop, throwing the jar towards the other ship.

The Everfire sailed through the air, but they were simply too far away from the Five Kingdoms vessel. The jar dropped and struck the hull at the waterline, bursting into black flame only to be submerged in water the next moment.

Keelin watched as the dark fire defied the sea and began to climb the side of the ship, leaving an orange blaze in its wake. The Everfire reached the railing and climbed over. It almost looked like it was alive. The screaming started, but it was lost amidst the chorus of battle elsewhere.

Keelin glanced to starboard, then across to the port side. Everywhere he looked, ships were locked with other ships, the crashes and shouts of fighting drifting out across the water. At least five boats were already on fire, and even as he was counting them a pirate ship and a navy vessel sank down into the waves together, locked in a flame-kissed embrace.

North Storm was free from the fight, as planned, and was sailing behind the enemy, attempting to gut as many of them as possible. T'ruck would want to take the ship hunting as soon as possible, but Keelin could only hope the giant's patience won out.

"Where to, Cap'n?" said Fremen.

"Bring us about," Keelin said, crossing the deck to stand next to his navigator.

As *The Phoenix* started to turn to starboard, Keelin scanned the line and spotted *Rheel Toa* fighting an impossible battle with a Man of War. Deun Burn and his crew would be sorely outnumbered and in need of relief.

"There." Keelin pointed. "Get us in on the opposite side to Captain Burn."

Fremen nodded and barked out a laugh. "Aye aye, Cap'n. I hope the Riverlanders appreciate this."

Keelin hoped the Riverlanders were still alive.

An explosion echoed out across the water, followed by another, and then two more. *North Storm* was listing to port with smoke pouring out of her belly. So much of the battle rested on T'ruck, his ship, and his crew. So many of their best warriors were aboard the gigantic boat.

"Captan?" Morley said. "Should we help?"

"No," Keelin growled. "Stick to the plan."

"*North Storm* is the plan."

"She's not sunk yet, Morley. T'ruck will keep her afloat."

Starry Dawn

Elaina hacked at the shield in front of her again and again and again. Her sword did little damage to the wooden barrier, but it kept the soldier's guard up high. One of her crew thrust a spear past her leg and up into the man's groin. He screamed in pain and finally let his guard down. Elaina's next swipe rent a gash through his screaming face, and he went down bleeding and mewling. Elaina moved on to the next fight, letting the man die in agony.

All the soldiers were carrying shields. Elaina hated shields. Only cowards hid from a fight, and that was what they all were – nothing but cowards trying to keep her from her throne. A small group of soldiers were crowded near the bow of the ship, hiding behind their shields while her crew darted forwards, trying to land a blow on the snivelling grots. Elaina ran at the shields, screaming with murderous intent, and launched herself at the closest soldier. They both went down to the deck and Elaina found herself lying on top of the shield with the man beneath it. She dropped her sword and dragged a knife from her boot. She stabbed around the shield, feeling the blade pierce flesh again and again as she screamed into the dying man's face. Hot blood spilled out over her hand.

The other soldiers had fallen back and Elaina's crew were busy pressuring them, pushing them towards the railing. She picked up the dead soldier's shield and heaved it through the air; it banged against the hull of the other ship. She screamed a wordless cry of fury and plucked her sword from the deck, advancing towards the few soldiers who remained.

One of the men broke and ran, trying to leap back to his own ship. He failed the jump and dropped into the sea below. The other soldiers panicked, but it was too late; Elaina's crew surged forwards, kicking and stabbing, and sent the remaining three Five Kingdoms men over the side and into the blue.

"We're free," cried one of *Starry Dawn*'s pirates.

"Then get us moving," Elaina shouted. "And someone throw the bloody fire at them."

Elaina didn't wait to see her orders carried out. Wiping slick blood from her hands onto her trousers, she stalked aft towards the wheel, intending to pick a new target and get them close. She felt the need to prove her worth again, and that meant she needed to take more ships than Keelin, more than Morrass, and more than her father.

"Why isn't Blu getting into the fight?" she said, the question directed at no one.

"Looks like he's patrolling, Cap," Gurn said. "Catching any that get through, maybe?"

"Trying his best to stay out of the fight, more like," Elaina said, and spat on the deck. "Useless, cowardly rat cock."

The ship shuddered beneath their feet and Elaina looked up. Their rigging was tangled with the navy ship's, holding the two boats together. New grapples were thrown over the side and hooked onto *Starry Dawn* just as one of Elaina's crew tossed the jar of Everfire.

Elaina watched in horror as the jar flipped through the air, bounced off the navy vessel's sails, and dropped to its deck, exploding into living black flame.

"Cut us free!" she screamed as loudly as she could.

The soldiers and sailors on the navy vessel immediately set about trying to put the fire out, throwing buckets of water over the black blaze to no avail. The fire would consume everything in its path until there was nothing left, and even then it would live on for a while, scorching the sea. If *Starry Dawn* was still attached, she would go down with the other ship, if she didn't burn to ash first.

Elaina leapt over the railing onto the main deck and ran to the first grapple she saw. She chopped at it with her sword, cutting the rope clean and taking a fair chunk out of the railing as well.

The fire was spreading fast on the other vessel, black flames dancing and spinning, trailing orange and yellow in their wake. The fire grew and grew, popping and crackling, and Elaina could smell burning wood and seared flesh.

Navy soldiers and sailors alike gave up the idea of putting the blaze out and started abandoning ship, many making the jump over to *Starry Dawn*, but Elaina had no time to fight them. She needed to save her boat.

"Cut us free!" she screamed again, hacking at another grapple as a soldier landed on the deck behind her.

The hulls of the two ships bumped together, and Elaina was close enough to feel the heat of the fire. She hacked away another grapple, then put her hands against the navy ship's railing and pushed.

"Push!" she cried, closing her eyes tight and shoving with every bit of strength she could muster.

The heat was intense, uncomfortably hot on Elaina's hands and face. She opened her eyes; the orange blaze was close, far too close for comfort. The black flame, having already set most of the deck on fire, was spinning and turning as it hunted for something fresh to consume.

There were folk all over the railing now, pushing with everything they were worth, and slowly – far too slowly for Elaina's liking – the two ships started to drift apart.

The black flame shifted course and began to twist towards *Starry Dawn*, snaking its way across the blazing deck. The heat became oppressive as the other ship was turned into an inferno. The dark fire reached the railing just a few feet away and Elaina backed up a step, her eyes wide and pinned to the monster. The flame held there for a moment, and Elaina wondered if it was watching her somehow. Then it spun away to hunt for easier prey.

A scrap of burning sail floated down into the chasm between the two ships as they drifted apart, the last stretch of fire mercilessly cut away from *Starry Dawn*. Elaina took a deep breath and coughed from the smoke she inhaled.

"Good job," she managed to wheeze out. Her heart was racing and her hands were shaking a little from the excitement. She clapped the nearest man on the shoulder and gave him a wild grin. The Five Kingdoms soldier grinned back.

North Storm

T'ruck opened his eyes to deep blue smudged with black. The sky was cloudless and beautiful, marred only by scant wisps of smoke. His head rang like a bell struck too many times, and he felt sick to his stomach. He was floating, soaked through, and he tasted salt on his lips. The hulking mass of *North Storm* drifted into view on T'ruck's right. It was impossible to mistake the behemoth for anything else.

Slowly the ringing started to get quieter. There was something else, another sound, something above the lapping of waves against the creaking hull of his ship. Screaming. The screams of the dying, awash in pain, were a peculiar noise. Nothing else in the world sounded quite like a man who didn't want to die.

T'ruck breathed in deep and brought his legs down to start treading water. For a sailor and a pirate, T'ruck wasn't a good swimmer, and it took him longer than he would have liked to paddle over to *North Storm*'s hull. The ship was riding low in the water and listing over towards him, but even so there was nothing to grab hold of, no way to pull himself up out of the water.

With a growl of frustration, T'ruck dug his fingernails into the hull, trying to hook them into the little seams between the planks of wood that made up his ship. Once he deemed his fingers secure, he pulled himself upwards, scrabbling against the hull with his boots. Hand over hand, with his nails tearing and screaming in pain, T'ruck began his climb, anger fuelling every inch.

With bloody hands and fingernails ripped from their beds, T'ruck clung to the side of his ship like a determined spider. But even he had limits, and this was one of them. He screamed, raw frustration lending volume to his voice.

A face appeared over the railing, looking down. His first mate, Pocket, spotted with blood and grinning like a serpent's maw.

"Thank fuck, Captain. I ain't ready to lead this ship."

"Rope," was the only reply T'ruck could manage.

"Aye aye, Captain."

T'ruck felt another fingernail begin to rip free from its bed and he squeezed his eyes shut, trying to block out the searing pain. Something slapped against his back and he opened his eyes. A rope was dangling from above, Pocket staring down at him once more.

T'ruck pulled his remaining nails from the side of his boat and pushed off with his feet, grabbing hold of the rope as he did so. His back bumped against the hull and he started to pull, dragging himself up hand over hand.

Reaching the railing, T'ruck swung a leg over and rolled onto the deck of his ship, wasting no time in regaining his feet and taking in the damage. *North Storm* was in chaos. Whatever trickery the Five Kingdoms dung slugs had used on them had caused damage and carnage on a grand scale.

"We're fucked, Captain," Pocket said. "Boat's barely moving and we lost a lot of people, still not sure how many. Below decks is even worse." He paused. "And the cat is dead."

T'ruck glared at his first mate. Pocket backed up a step and held up his hands.

The main mast was down, the deck around it splintered and broken. The mast itself lay half across the ship and half in the water. Nearby there was a hole in the main deck, scorched wood and bits of men and women dotted all around. Injured pirates were clustered here and there, some tending to their own wounds, some in the lengthy process of dying and letting everyone nearby know about it.

"We're drifting," T'ruck rumbled. Beyond the chaos of his ship, the battle was still waging. Ships entangled with ships. Boats on fire, both black and orange. Wreckage floating on the waves. An explosion thundered across the water and one of the other pirate vessels started sinking, a section of its hull bursting outwards and upwards and smoke billowing forth. He knew that kind of explosion well; black powder was the cause, and lots of it.

One of the navy ships, a Man of War yet untouched by the battle raging around it, detached from its neighbours and turned towards *North Storm*. T'ruck judged they had very little time before they would be wading through blood, both Five Kingdoms' and their own.

"Get the mast cut away," he said to Pocket, and scanned the deck of his ship.

Lady Nerine Tsokei was standing aft, near the wheel. Her dark brown skirt was ripped in places and her green blouse could be seen through similar rents in her jerkin. The witch's hair was tousled, and her dark eyes looked like a predator's, searching for prey.

"You're alive," T'ruck said with a smile. He'd feared the witch might have been caught in one of the explosions, and not just because he needed her help.

"Alchemy is nothing but a pale mockery of magic," Lady Tsokei said through gritted teeth. "I wish to strike back, Captain." Blood was dripping from the fingers of the witch's left hand. She was wounded, but her pride would never let her admit it. T'ruck respected that stubbornness.

"There." He pointed at the approaching Man of War. "We need time to recover from the attack, time to get my ship in order. They're all yours – if you can take them."

Lady Tsokei shot a dark glance towards T'ruck, and he felt the fear she projected so intensely that he took an involuntary step backwards. The witch looked away, and T'ruck felt his courage return.

"You and you," he said, pointing to two nearby pirates, "grab a shield and protect the lady at all costs."

"I do not need protecting, Captain," the witch said.

T'ruck stepped close and looked down at the smaller woman. "You are aboard my ship, and I'll damned well protect you if I want to. No matter the magic you possess, I doubt you are immune to a well-aimed arrow."

Lady Tsokei nodded.

T'ruck grinned and turned away. "Kill them all."

Starry Dawn

The soldier went for his sword. Elaina reached down and put her hand over his, stopping him drawing the blade, her other hand going for his neck. They wrestled for a moment until the soldier grabbed hold of Elaina's tunic and pulled her close, throwing his head forwards so it connected with her chin.

Ignoring the pain, Elaina struggled to keep the man close, one hand pinning his own to his body while she pushed against his head with her other, forcing him to stare at the sky.

They growled and snarled at each other as they wrestled, each one aware that one wrong move could spell the end. The soldier was bigger than Elaina, and probably a little stronger too, but she was no weakling and had been raised fighting men larger than herself. Even so, Elaina found herself pushed backwards and felt the railing bump against her arse. The soldier managed to slip his chin beneath her hand and bit down on the flesh between her fingers. Elaina cried out in pain and threw herself backwards, over the edge of the ship, taking the soldier with her into the blue below. She let go of him as they fell. He wasn't so quick, and they both hit the water awkwardly, the impact driving the air from her lungs. Gasping in saltwater, Elaina kicked to get her head above the surface, coughing and drawing in beautiful air, but the soldier was still holding on to her tunic.

Elaina kicked and punched and managed to free herself from his grasp. She paddled away a little, giving herself some distance to face him as she began treading water. The soldier's head broke the surface and Elaina pushed herself up out of the water and towards him, landing a heavy punch across his face as he tried to blink away the water from his eyes. He reeled from the blow and kicked towards Elaina, catching her in the stomach with a steel-plated boot. Coughing and spluttering, Elaina paddled away. By the time she'd recovered, he was facing her, treading water and paddling with one hand while the other was hidden below the surface. A thin shimmer of silver betrayed the sword he was holding.

Spitting salty water out of her mouth, Elaina drew her own steel and held it in front of her. She'd never tried a sword fight underwater before, but there was a first time for everything and she'd be damned if she was going to lose to some old pig from the Five Kingdoms.

It was a strange sort of dance the two performed as they both worked at treading water while forcing the other into an opening. The battle waged on around them; Elaina could both hear and smell it, but she didn't dare take her eyes from her opponent for even a moment, despite the lumbering hulks sailing past them.

The soldier lunged, a strangely slow and exaggerated motion in the water, and Elaina parried with her own sword, then whipped the blade upwards and out of the water with a splash. It had just the desired effect, and the soldier started and thrashed, attempting to back away while still holding on to his sword.

Elaina pressed forwards and felt a sting across her belly. The soldier grinned. His wild thrashing had been a trap; he was more devious than she'd given him credit for.

Something bumped against Elaina's foot and she dared a glance into the water. Large, dark shapes were moving in the murky blue below. They were far out in the deep ocean, and the battle was making plenty of waves; anything could be coming up from the depths for a snack, and whatever the creatures were, they were likely to find plenty of morsels.

Then it dawned on Elaina that she was bleeding. Elaina dropped her sword into the depths and turned towards her ship, kicking into the fastest swim of her life. She didn't bother looking behind to see what the soldier might be doing. She didn't care.

"Cap," someone shouted down from the deck of *Starry Dawn*. Elaina could happily have kissed every one of her crew for realising she'd gone overboard and pulling the ship to a halt.

A rope ladder dropped over the side of the hull and Elaina changed her course a little, still kicking and pulling herself through the water as fast as she could. A scream echoed out from somewhere behind her, and a glance upwards revealed the look of fear on Pollick's face as he watched over the railing.

"Better hurry, Cap," the lookout yelled.

Elaina's fingers touched wood and she stopped kicking, her own momentum slamming her into the boat. She grabbed hold of the ladder and wasted no time hauling herself out of the blue, rushing upwards as quickly as her limbs would carry her. Something bumped against the hull below her, and Elaina glanced down to see grey scales and a fin disappearing under the surface. The waters were clear enough to give her an idea of the size of the beasty, and it would have been enough to strike plenty of fear into even the most courageous pirate.

Rough hands grabbed hold of hers and helped her up and over the railing. Pollick and Surge were nearby, and some of the rest of the crew were busy throwing the bodies of Five Kingdoms sailors and soldiers overboard.

"Thought we'd lost ya for a moment there, Cap," Pollick said with a wide grin.

"I need a new sword," Elaina growled, running wet, shaking hands through her hair. "Are we fit to sail?"

"Aye, Cap," said Surge.

"Then get us moving, quartermaster."

The Phoenix

Even as the first grapples were thrown, Keelin hurled himself across the watery expanse towards the Man of War. He landed heavily against the hull, fingers gripping the railing, and started to pull himself up and over. Keelin's crew were quick to follow, some leaping across after their captain's example while others swung over on ropes. Before long there were a great many pirates on board the Man of War, and the Sarth crew found themselves fighting a battle on two fronts.

Keelin couldn't see onto the Riverlanders' ship. Judging by the number of soldiers still aboard the navy vessel, Deun Burn and his crew were holding their own. Riverlanders had many a foul reputation, and some of them were well deserved – one being their renowned ferocity in a fight.

A number of the soldiers on board the Man of War turned to face the new threat. Keelin decided to give them something other than the crew of *Rheel Toa* to worry about. Drawing his cutlasses, he gave a battle cry and charged, knowing his crew would follow him in.

Keelin was the first to reach the enemy lines and he ducked under a wild swing, cutting the soldier near in half as he stood inside the man's guard. Not bothering to finish the dying man off, Keelin stepped up to his next opponent as the rest of his crew caught up, crashing into the soldiers. Chaos erupted on the deck, with steel clashing against steel and the smell of blood and fire in the air.

A block followed by a hilt to the face sent a hook-nosed soldier reeling, and Keelin followed with a powerful slash that opened him up from shoulder to hip. He kicked the man's body into his comrades behind and stabbed left, hobbling a soldier long enough for one of his pirates to deal the killing blow.

For what seemed like forever, Keelin's world became the ebb and flow of combat. Blocks and parries, slashes and stabs. Always moving, always keeping his opponents guessing. The lessons of his childhood served him well. He might never be as naturally gifted as his brother, but he wasn't known as the best swordsman in the isles for nothing.

After a while Keelin had to drop back, his arms aching from swinging his cutlasses and his hands stinging from all the impacts. The crew of the Man of War were faltering hard now that Captain Burn's Riverlanders had started to cross onto the bigger ship. Trapped between two blood-thirsty crews, the soldiers from Sarth were collapsing in upon themselves, and it was only a matter of time before the ship belonged to the pirates.

"Are you injured, Captain?" said Jojo. The man wasn't much of a fighter these days, so he tended to stay towards the back of any scrap they encountered, but he was still one hell of a sailor.

"No, just tired. Best to take a breather before jumping back in." Keelin had already killed eight men aboard the Man of War, and he'd injured a few more. Such brutal combat took its toll on both body and mind. He suspected he would need some dark rum to go with his dark thoughts once all was said and done.

"Don't think you'll need to," Jojo said with a grin. "Looks like they're surrendering."

The sailor was right. As the soldiers fell further and further back and their numbers dwindled, the two pirate crews merged together and the numbers made the victory clear. The soldiers were already starting to lay down their arms and beg for mercy. Keelin was happy to give it to them. The day was far from done, and he'd already seen too much killing. He'd already been the cause of too many deaths.

"That's enough," he roared as he strode forwards, leaving Jojo behind. "Let the bastards live."

"And why should we do that?" Captain Burn said. He had a nasty, jagged-bladed axe in his hand and a grimace on his skull face.

"Because I say so," Keelin said, grabbing hold of the Riverlander's shoulder and pulling him around. "No sense in any more killing than is needed. The cowards have surrendered, and we ain't without mercy."

"And just leave them behind to sail on and attack us again." Burn punctuated the statement with a growl. "I think not."

"We disable the ship. Cut the rudder. They'll be stuck here for hours. Far too long to be of any help with the rest of the battle."

"Safer to kill them."

"Ain't about what's safe this time, Deun," Keelin said, hoping his voice held as much steel as he knew his eyes did. "It's about what's right. Let's show them we're not savages. That we can be reasonable and merciful."

Deun held Keelin's gaze for a few moments before nodding. He turned to the cowering soldiers. "If it were up to me, I'd eat you all."

Keelin clapped his fellow captain on the shoulder before turning to the soldiers. "He's not joking. He really would eat you. We're disabling your ship, leaving you alive. Once the battle is over you will be free to return home. Just sit quiet 'til then and you'll all survive this yet. Where's your captain?"

A few of the soldiers gave each other a look and then quickly dropped their heads. A bad feeling began to creep its way through Keelin's gut.

"Where is your captain?" he said again, putting as much command into his voice as he could.

The Man of War erupted in smoke, flame, noise, and death.

North Storm

Nerine knelt upon the starboard side of the poop deck and dipped her hands into a bucket of seawater. The two pirates tasked with guarding her were nearby, fidgeting nervously and watching the approaching Man of War.

"Rin," she said, staring into the bucket. "I invoke your name and demand your attention." The water began to ripple. Nerine hated invoking gods; demons were so much more amiable.

"What's she doing?" said one of the pirates. "What are you doing?"

"This sacrifice I give to you." Nerine tore her eyes away from the bucket of water and fixed them on the pirate who had questioned her. "Grant me permission to give you more."

The pirate's face went slack and his arms dropped to his sides. His body swayed a little as Nerine dominated his will. The pirate was still inside somewhere, watching as if from very far away, but he no longer had any control of his actions. He was now her minion to do with as she pleased.

"Burton?" said the other pirate. "Burton, you alright?"

"Give yourself to Rin," Nerine said to Burton, and the man walked calmly towards the starboard railing and flung himself overboard.

"Burton!" The other pirate ran to the railing and looked down. "Man over board. Man over…" His voice trailed away and he staggered back from the railing, waving a hand in the air in a foolish attempt at a protective sign. Nerine pitied the ignorant.

"M-m-merfolk," he stuttered, his eyes wide with fear.

Nerine drew her hands from the bucket and wiped them on her trousers, then walked over to the railing and looked down. Burton was gone. Lithe shapes darted about beneath the surface, waiting for the rest of the sacrifices they'd been promised.

The Man of War flying Sarth colours was drawing close now, close enough that Nerine could make out the sailors rushing to and fro. Soldiers crowded the deck, armed with all manner of weaponry. Bows were a problem. Those with swords and axes would never get close enough to be a threat to Nerine, but those with arrows needn't get close.

"Protect me," she said to the cowering pirate. "Or join your friend in Rin's court." He inched forwards, shield and sword held in front of him.

"You won't need the weapon," Nerine said with a lopsided grin. "Just the shield. I will be the weapon."

The first of the arrows from the Man of War started to fly over as the ship sailed up from behind, attempting to run parallel to *North Storm*, where it would be easiest to board the crippled vessel. Captain Khan's crew were too busy to fight, either getting the ship back in order or tending to the dead and wounded.

Nerine began to chant and opened herself up, requesting power. Her request never reached the Void. No sooner had she made herself ready than she felt Rin rush into her, the sea goddess' power filling her.

Bits of Nerine's shadow began to peel away from the deck, slithering towards the railing and disappearing over the side. It was Rin's power inside her, and the goddess had dominion over the water and many of its more terrifying aspects, but Nerine shaped that power. She was the Keeper of Shadows, a title earned and jealously guarded.

An arrow hit the deck close by, and the pirate with the shield stepped a little closer to Nerine, his circle of wood held high. More and more shadows were detaching themselves from her now as she directed all of the power gifted to her by Rin into one sorcery. With the sun on the ship's port side, *North Storm*'s shadow became hers, a vast weapon to be used against their enemies.

"Captain," shouted one of the pirates. "Uh... the... uh... Captain!"

Nerine looked sideways to see Captain Khan rush to the railing and look down. The bronzed northerner blanched visibly; he'd seen Nerine's monster.

"Are you doing this?" Khan shouted at Nerine over the noise. She smiled back at him, still chanting the words of her sorcery, still directing the power of the sea goddess.

The captain on the Man of War saw it too, a mass of shadow bubbling and writhing at the base of *North Storm*, thrashing the water to foamy white. A few more arrows flitted across the divide; one headed straight towards Nerine but was caught in her guard's shield. The Man of War started to turn away, trying to flee the shadows. Nerine couldn't allow it; she'd promised Rin further sacrifice, and the sea goddess would have her payment one way or another.

A dark tentacle shot out from the writhing mass beneath the boat. It darted in and out of the water, as thick as a main mast and as strong as steel. Panic hit the deck of the Man of War, but it was too late for them to get out of the way and the shadowy tendril punched through the hull and started to drag the huge ship down.

With the sorcery finished, Nerine closed herself off from the power of the sea goddess. Her limbs grew heavy, exhaustion flooding her body. She wanted to rest, to close her eyes and sleep, but the battle was far from over and she had to see what her shadow monster could do. It was almost as large as the shadow she'd once defeated in order to gain its power.

Another dark tentacle shot out from *North Storm* and ripped its way into the other ship's hull, followed quickly by another. Screams floated over the water along with a final few arrows. Then the bulk of the monster detached itself from the *North Storm* and rushed across the waves. It slammed into the Man of War, sending it rocking and reeling.

The creature was far from pretty – a bloated mass, much like a tick, with dark, flailing arms that ripped at its prey. Soldiers and sailors were crushed or sent sailing through the air to land in the waves, where they were quickly plucked from the surface to be dragged below by darting figures Nerine couldn't quite see. Wood was torn free from the rest of the ship to be tossed away and forgotten. One mast was chopped down with a casual flick and another soon followed as the beast pulled its shadowy body up onto the Man of War's deck. Some of the soldiers attempted to attack the creature, but their weapons had no effect. Steel could do nothing against a shadow. They would be better served by fire, but it would have to be an inferno to scare away such a monster.

The crew of *North Storm* had all but stopped their work to get the ship under way again. They stood staring at the carnage Nerine's creation was causing. Awe had a way of distracting men.

"A kraken," said one of the crew. A misinformed opinion, but one

Nerine was happy to allow if it meant she retained some anonymity. "Never thought I'd see one."

"Aye," Captain Khan shouted. "A kraken. Guess Rin really must be looking out for us. Now get the fuck back to fixing my ship."

The Phoenix

The world was noise and bright light.

Keelin was lying on a deck, staring up at a mast as it slowly toppled away from him. The blue sky was marred by dirty clouds of rising black smoke. The air itself tasted acrid and his chest hurt when he breathed.

Rolling onto his side, Keelin started coughing. The ringing was fading a little now, and he could hear shouts and screams, and the creaking and groaning of a ship in poor health.

Strong arms grabbed hold of him and started to pull him up. With a sigh, Keelin relented and got his feet underneath him. Another coughing fit hit, and he squeezed his eyes shut against the pain. Every bit of him seemed to hurt, and none more so than the feeling of his brain trying to drill its way out of his skull.

It took a lot of effort to open his eyes again, but when he did Keelin found Smithe staring at him, waving a hand in front of his face and mumbling something under the sounds of death and fire.

"What is it, Smithe?" Keelin said as he looked around. His voice was quiet, distant.

There was a hole in the Man of War – a rather large hole – and blood and bits of people all around. Somewhere below decks a fire seemed to be raging, and smoke was rising up out of the hole. The deck shifted a little beneath Keelin's feet, a movement he knew well. The boat was taking on water fast and would be sunk in mere minutes.

Smithe shook Keelin by the shoulders, and he looked back to find a concerned expression on his quartermaster's face. Keelin had to concentrate to decipher the man's words over the din that was hammering inside his own head.

"Morley," Smithe shouted.

"What about him?" Keelin said.

Smithe pointed at the hole in the Man of War. "Don't reckon he made it, Cap'n."

"Fuck." Keelin launched into another coughing fit. The smoke was starting to get thick and his lungs were burning. "Get everyone back on board *The Phoenix*. And congratulations on making first mate."

He expected Smithe to smile or gloat. Instead, the burly pirate looked sad and tired. A moment later Smithe was storming off, shouting orders.

Nearby, Deun Burn was staring down into the hole. The ship was noticeably lower in the water. It gave an unsteady lurch; they had very little time left.

"Deun," Keelin shouted as he approached. Even with his voiced raised, he still sounded quiet to his own ears.

The Riverlander turned to look at him. His skull face was smudged with ash and he had a haunted look about him.

The Man of War gave an awkward creaking sound followed by the unmistakeable snapping of planks. Keelin glanced down at the deck, hoping he had enough time.

"Deun," Keelin repeated, stopping close to the Riverlander. "How many have you lost?"

"Too many," Burn said. "Too many lost to this war. To Morrass' war."

"Bring your crew aboard *The Phoenix*," Keelin said quickly. "We've both lost too many. Apart we will be beaten by the next boat we try to board, but together we're stronger than we were before."

"*Rheel Toa…*" Deun said.

"Will float here safe and abandoned. We'll drop you back on your ship once this fight is over." There was another creaking crack beneath them. A second mast snapped and fell, toppling over the aft railing.

"Quickly, Deun."

The Riverlander nodded slowly and turned away, barking orders to his crew in their own language. Keelin let out a deep sigh and ran towards his ship. The Riverlanders joined him, swelling the numbers of his crew.

As the Man of War finally collapsed in on itself and sank beneath the waves, leaving bits of flotsam and bad memories as the only proof it had ever existed, Keelin scanned the sea. Everywhere he looked, ships were locked together, ships were on fire, ships were stopping near wreckage to pull their comrades out of the deep blue. The sun was shining and the world somehow seemed dark.

"We've got incoming," Deun Burn said, and Keelin turned. The Riverlander was growling as he stared out to sea. Keelin followed his gaze; another ship was approaching, flying the colours of Sarth and wearing the scars of a recent battle and victory.

"Ready to repel boarders," Keelin shouted.

Starry Dawn

Elaina scrambled up the rigging as fast her hands and feet would carry her, climbing in a way that would have made her mother's monkeys proud. Reaching the yard, she grabbed hold with both hands and let go with her feet, dangling high above the deck. She turned and swung her legs up to grip around the yard and started to scurry along, upside down. By the time she reached the flaming section of sail it was long past salvageable. Elaina wrapped her legs tight and let go with her hands, pulling a dagger from her belt and cutting away at the sail with wild abandon. Before long the flaming canvas was floating harmlessly down to the deck, and Elaina had only a few minor burns to show for it. She breathed a sigh of relief.

"Cap," Alfer shouted up from the deck. Everyone down below looked so small.

"Aye?"

"*Ocean Deep* is moving up on our stern."

Elaina barked out a laugh and swung her body upwards, catching hold of the yard and turning around again, then headed back towards the mast. It was just like Blu to wait until the the fighting had thinned down a bit before joining in. No doubt the coward was looking to claim some glory. Some of Elaina's glory.

Heading upwards instead of down, Elaina raced towards the nest. She climbed in quickly, giving Four-Eyed Pollick a quick shove. Pollick screamed, turning on Elaina with a small knife. "Oh, fuck. Sorry, Cap. Thought it was… um… I dunno, really. Not you."

"We're all a little on edge, Pol…" Elaina trailed off as she took in the sight from up high. As far as she could see, ships dotted the blue water, some locked together, others sailing or sinking. One pirate ship was running – or rather limping, given the condition of its sails – back towards home. The thickest of the fighting was to the north. Man of Wars and galleons from both sides were crashing into each other, tiny specks leaping from one ship to another. Captain Khan's behemoth was over that way too. The ship was moving, but it looked in bad shape. Even from such a distance Elaina could see the holes in her side and the smoke still trailing out of her hold. *North Storm* wasn't done though. She was turning towards the fight and picking up speed.

Close to Khan's ship was an enemy Man of War swamped beneath some sort of dark mass that was tearing at the ship. At first Elaina thought it was Everfire, but it didn't appear to be burning, just ripping the ship to pieces.

The Black Death was free of enemies and sailing fast towards the fighting to the north. Elaina knew her father well enough to know the man would be itching to get into every fight he could find and sow as much chaos as possible, furthering his own dark reputation. Elaina wished she could be beside him, but she wished to be queen even more.

Ocean Deep was slowing beside them, and from up high Elaina could see Blu's crew on deck and armed, many of them looking like they were about to board an enemy. A nasty feeling started crawling its way through her gut.

Half swinging, half falling, Elaina raced down ropes and rigging to the deck of her ship. She arrived just as Blu's men starting to board. Her brother's crew were armed and fresh and ready for a fight. Elaina's crew were weary from battle and not expecting an ambush from those they considered allies.

Ocean Deep's pirates started moving forwards, overwhelming *Starry Dawn*'s crew with sheer numbers. None of Elaina's pirates fought back; they knew when they were well and truly fucked, and this was most definitely one of those times. Swords were taken, knives confiscated, and any who fought back were given an efficient beating.

As soon as Elaina's crew had not a weapon to share among them, Blu appeared. He leapt down from his bigger vessel with a cruel grin.

"What's the meaning of this, Blu?" Elaina shouted up to her brother. She was itching to get her hands on a sword. Unfortunately the traitorous pirates had taken hers, and it didn't look like they were considering giving it back.

"Ho, little sister," Blu said with a smug grin. He was wearing his finest clothing. There was a battle raging around them, and here was her brother, dressed up like a peacock, staying far clear of the fighting.

"Get off my ship, Blu," Elaina hissed.

"Um… no," Blu said, following up with a dramatic laugh that many of his crew picked up and carried on.

"Cap?" Surge said. "What do we do?"

"You do nothing," Blu shouted. "What can you do? This ship is mine now, taken in battle, and all you on board are my prisoners. I expect them back at Land's End will want a few pirates to hang once all this is over."

"You're siding with them?" Elaina said.

Blu looked at his sister and laughed. "Da said you were as good as queen already. Reckoned the only thing that'd keep ya from it is death. Time to test that."

King's Justice

"That one seems to be coming right for us," Daimen said. "Looks like Tanner ta me."

Admiral Wulfden shouldered Daimen out of the way and stared at the approaching ship. Their escorts had been forced to peel away, and now there was nothing between them and the angry pirates bearing down upon them.

"How can you be sure it's that black-hearted wretch?" Wulfden said.

"Well, mate, the first thing to give it away would be that it's his ship."

Wulfden growled and shoved past Daimen again. It appeared that no matter where he stood, it was always in the man's way. The admiral ran a hand through his perfectly groomed hair, messing it out of place, and sent a worried glance towards one of his officers, who looked nervously at one of the other officers.

They were in trouble, and no mistake. Two other Man of Wars had been assigned to escort the admiral and his ship. One of them was busy suffering at the hands of *North Storm*, and the other had been sunk by what looked like a kraken. The wind had gone right out of the admiral's sails when the beasty rose up from the water and ripped the ship to pieces.

"His ship is smaller," Wulfden said. "We will outnumber his forces."

"Aye," Daimen said. "Reckon ya will. Of course, Tanner Black ain't exactly a stranger to taking on shitty odds, mate. His men are rabid blood drinkers. Half of them ain't even rightly people. Least, not like you and me. Civilised folk, ya know. Word is he uses some dark magics too."

The admiral glared at Daimen, who almost laughed. The wind was already turning, and he was about to find himself on the wrong side of it again. He needed a way out, and it was unlikely Tanner would provide one for him. He needed to convince Wulfden to turn tail and flee.

"I've heard…" Daimen started.

"Shut up, Poole," Admiral Wulfden hissed. "Turn us into them. I want all hands armed and ready. Tanner Black in chains will be a fitting prize to present to the king."

The officers jumped to their admiral's orders while Daimen stood nearby, trying to figure out a way to get the man to change his mind.

"Battle don't look to be going too well," he ventured.

"It could still go either way," Wulfden growled. "See there." He pointed towards *North Storm* and the Man of War locked together. "We have weakened the vessel. She falls apart as my soldiers cut down her crew."

"Ya ships are burning, Admiral."

"So are yours." Wulfden glared scathingly at Daimen. "Do you really think yourself so subtle, pirate? Your loyalties are finally made clear. Don't worry, I assure you you will live to see your people die."

"My loyalties are to myself, mate. And I'm not responsible for this shit storm you think you're winning. You are."

The admiral turned and drew his sabre from its sheath.

"Ah, fuck me." Daimen backed away. "What happened to keeping me alive to witness the downfall of me people?"

"I find myself no longer able to abide your presence, Poole." Wulfden took a wild swing in Daimen's direction.

"Admiral?" shouted one of the officers.

"Just ridding myself of this pest." Wulfden took another swing.

Daimen again dodged backwards out of his reach, well aware that he would soon run out of places to run. The man led forwards with a lazy thrust and Daimen turned away from the attack, again moving out of his range. Wulfden was already starting to redden in the cheeks.

"Stand still and die," he said with another swipe.

"Aye, fuck that." Daimen stepped into the next thrust. The blade missed him by a breath and he punched the admiral hard in the face, and then again because he really wanted to.

Stunned and reeling, Wulfden was in no condition to stop Daimen as he plucked the sabre from his fat hand and spun him around. He held him tight, sword to chubby neck.

The soldiers and sailors who had rushed to their commander's aid quickly slowed when they saw shining steel threatening to murder the man in charge.

"Aye, I reckon ya all got the right of it now. Any of you fuckers take another step my way and I'll bleed this bastard like the fat fucking pig he is."

The admiral groaned.

"Ah, fuck you too. I'll curse all I fucking want."

Wulfden was starting to recover from the punches, no doubt realising exactly what was happening and how much shit he was in. "You'll hang for this, Poole."

Daimen pulled the sabre a little closer to the man's throat, pressing it tight against his skin. "Well, seeing as you were about to kill me anyway, I reckon I'll take my bloody chances. 'Sides, all I'm trying to do is save all our lives. You, ya fat fuck, should be shitting grateful, not trying to skewer me."

"Uh, Admiral…" said one of the officers, the one with the shifty eyes.

"Turn us around," Daimen shouted. "Back ta the Five Kingdoms, I reckon. Haste and all that."

"They'll broadside us."

Daimen risked a glanced behind. *The Black Death* was closer than he'd have liked and bearing down on them with speed. For a brief moment he thought he could even see Tanner Black standing on the bow, grinning with mad abandon as he came on.

"Fuck!" Daimen turned back to the crew. Wulfden was sweating and his skin was slick. The bastard was fidgeting, but was far too scared to move with a blade so close to his throat.

Daimen grabbed hold of the admiral's left arm and twisted it behind his back so that he hissed in pain. Confident that his prisoner had no chance of escape, Daimen raised his voice to a shout. "Pull in the sails and bring us to a stop. All weapons down. Any one of you fucks thinks to fight and I'll bleed this bastard."

A few of the sailors glanced at each other; the officers looked far from convinced. "If we surrender they'll kill us."

Daimen laughed. "Of course not. Tanner Black is many things, it's true, but the man's honourable as an ordained priest." Daimen had to wonder if he'd ever told a bigger lie. "We surrender the ship and he'll let ya all live. Better chance than trying to fight him. Not to mention having to explain to ya king why your admiral is missing his throat."

"Do it!" Wulfden sputtered.

Daimen had to respect the crew for their loyalty. They quickly set about taking in the canvas and all weapons were dropped to the deck. A crew of pirates would have stormed Daimen whether he held their captain or not.

The Black Death sailed up beside them in quick order, and Daimen could see Tanner and his murderous crew waiting aboard. Grapples were quickly tossed over, and a moment later pirates swarmed onto the deck of the Man of War, Tanner first among them. They paused when they saw the sailors and soldiers of the Five Kingdoms huddled at the far end of the deck, unarmed and expecting quarter. Tanner stepped forward and eyed the cowering men, then swept his gaze up to where Daimen was standing, his sword still at the admiral's neck.

"Uh…" Tanner started.

"We surrender," Wulfden said as Daimen pressed the blade a little tighter.

"Wonderful," said Tanner. "We don't."

"Prisoners, Tanner," Daimen shouted.

"Ah, you know me, Poole – I don't take any."

There was some nervous shifting on the deck where the Five Kingdoms soldiers and sailors were cowering. They had only a few weapons close by, whereas Tanner's crew were far forwards, weapons ready and menacing.

"You do now."

"You don't dictate terms to me, ya damned traitor. Especially not when I've taken your ship."

"Ya only took the fucking ship because I made them surrender."

"And we of the isles thank ya from the bottom of our hearts." Tanner mounted the steps to the forecastle. "Still going to kill you all though."

"Fuck me, Tanner. Would ya just take ya head out of ya arse for a drop and look at what I'm giving you? This fat bastard is Admiral Wulfden, commander of this here entire fleet. He's the key to winning this war right now. He can give the signal to surrender. For all of them to surrender."

"I would never…" Wulfden sputtered.

"No?" Tanner said. "I think you will."

With a wave, Tanner summoned a couple of his crew forwards to take custody of the admiral. Tanner remained behind, his sword drawn and a dark look in his eyes as he stared at Daimen.

"Don't see why we need you, mate," he said with a grin.

Daimen threw Wulfden's sabre to the deck. "I'm not the traitor, Tanner. I just did what I had to to survive. Fucking Morrass is the traitor."

"What?"

"Bastard set this entire thing up. Organised it right from the burning of Black Sands. He's the reason all this is happening. He sacrificed hundreds, thousands, just to sit his arse on a throne and have you lick his boots."

"That so?" Tanner said, advancing on Daimen. "Tell me, Poole. Have ya got any proof?"

North Storm

The clash of steel on steel rang out loud as T'ruck landed a heavy blow on the gaunt soldier. Before the man could recover, T'ruck sent another overhead swipe crashing into the bastard's sword. They weren't even from the Five Kingdoms – these men were wearing the blue-black colours of Sarth – but T'ruck didn't care. His blood was up and pumping rage-fuelled strength through his veins.

The man beside him, a charming veteran of the seas, went down with a sword in his gut, and T'ruck roared. He shoved his huge shield forwards, pushing the gaunt soldier backwards, and then swung at the soldier who had skewered the pirate. T'ruck couldn't remember the pirate's name, but it didn't matter; the man was part of his crew, and T'ruck counted his crew as family.

A woman almost as tanned as T'ruck himself stepped forward over the groaning veteran as he died, and T'ruck treated her to a toothy grin before charging into the enemy lines.

A lucky strike opened a wound on T'ruck's right leg, but it wasn't serious enough to bring him down. He swung his sword first to his left, over the top of his shield, and then to his right, causing as much chaos as he could in the enemy lines while his own crew pushed forwards. Spinning around, T'ruck brought his sword upwards in a foolish slash that left him wide open. The blow caught a Sarth soldier in the face and snapped his head backwards. It was impossible to tell which killed the soldier – the gaping, bloody gash that had once been his face, or the broken neck. It didn't really matter.

Parrying a spear thrust, T'ruck tripped over a body and stumbled. He caught himself on *North Storm*'s railing and realised for the first time just how close the two ships were. Loosely lashed together by some rope and grapples, the boats were only a man's height from each other and *North Storm* was riding low in the water. More soldiers were waiting aboard the Man of War, and T'ruck had to admit that he was once again outnumbered.

His own crew were pushing hard against the Sarth soldiers now, trying to reclaim the deck of their ship, and T'ruck loosed a battle roar to inspire them.

A soldier crashed into T'ruck's shield. The man was big and heavy and almost knocked him to the deck, but he steadied himself on one knee. His sword was gone, slipped from his grasp, so T'ruck reached forwards, grabbed hold of the soldier's head, and slammed it against his shield. After three solid blows, the soldier was bloody and stunned. T'ruck pulled him around by his head and tossed the bastard overboard between the two ships. A hand locked onto T'ruck's arm with an iron grip and tugged him half over the railing.

Dropping his shield and holding on to the railing, T'ruck struggled against the big soldier's weight. The man's face was bloody, and his snarling lips showed at least one broken tooth, but there was fear in his eyes.

The two ships were drifting closer, their hulls coming together. T'ruck tried to pull his arm back, but even his strength had limits.

"Let go!" he screamed at the soldier still gripping his arm.

T'ruck squeezed his eyes shut and pulled with every bit of strength he had as the two ships met. There was a brief scream and then he was free, stumbling backwards from the railing and colliding with someone, sending them both crashing to the deck.

When T'ruck opened his eyes he found himself lying atop a half-stunned soldier with a crooked nose and a dazed look in his eyes. T'ruck rolled off the man and back to his feet. He realised something was still attached to his wrist – an arm, severed at the shoulder, its fingers still locked in a death grip.

The soldier regained his knees and let out a shout as he thrust with his sword. T'ruck parried the blade with the severed arm then took the limb in both hands and swung hard. The bloody end crashed across the soldier's face and sent him back to the deck, but T'ruck didn't stop there. He swung again and again and again until the soldier stopped moving and the bloody limb lost its rictus grip on his wrist.

"Captain," shouted one of his crew, and T'ruck looked up to see Pocket alive and well. It brought him much joy.

"Cut the ropes and get us clear," T'ruck growled to his first mate, already looking around for his sword and shield. The two ships were close together now, and his crew had all but cleared the deck of *North Storm*. The soldiers from the Man of War were crowding their railing, still trying to stab across at the pirates.

"Captain, we can't keep her afloat much longer," Pocket said frantically. "Water's coming in faster than we can bail. She's going down."

T'ruck looked across his ship and then back to the Man of War. Pocket was right. They were sinking, and quickly.

"All hands," T'ruck roared. "Abandon ship! Let's fucking take theirs!"

T'ruck scooped up his shield and a nearby axe and ran towards the railing. He leapt across to the Man of War, leading the charge and crashing a hole through the defenders.

T'ruck laid about, swinging left and right, blocking and barrelling through his enemies. He took wounds, feeling them all and ignoring them all. The pain only helped him feel more alive, and he had to live. He was no longer just living for himself, not since taking *North Storm*. Now he was living for Yu'truda as well. Now he was living for his clan as its sole survivor.

T'ruck lost track of time. Lost track of the number of men he maimed or killed. One moment he was fighting alone amidst a sea of hostile blades, and the next he was surrounded by his crew, their ferocity bolstering him when he began to tire.

Somewhere, far away, a horn blew loudly, its cry echoing across the waters. T'ruck planted his axe in a man's skull and kicked the body away, wrenching the dinted blade from the corpse as it fell. He turned, looking for another fool to die by his hand, but the remaining crew of the Sarth Man of War were backing away and laying down arms. They were surrendering.

T'ruck stalked towards a soldier who was leaning against the main mast. The man winced and dropped to a knee, one hand held up as if to defend himself.

"Get up," T'ruck screamed. "Fight me."

"We surrender," the man cried, his eyes full of fear.

"All of you?" he roared. "There must be one among you not a coward. Come at me." He threw his shield away. "Come at me!"

None of the soldiers made a move other than to cower and look away.

With a roar, T'ruck flung his axe as hard as he could out to sea. He looked out at the battle. Ships were on fire. Ships were sunk or sinking. Ships were locked together. The sky was just beginning to darken, and not from the smoke, though there was plenty of that.

North Storm was sinking on the other side of the Man of War. T'ruck could no longer see his ship's deck, only the masts and the men and women still scrambling aboard the new boat.

The witch, Lady Tsokei, glided past him. The woman was as graceful as she was dangerous, even surrounded by armed pirates on a deck slick with blood. She looked out across the battle and then glanced back, motioning to T'ruck.

"What is it?" he growled as he joined her at the railing. He had no stomach for accepting the soldiers' surrender, instead trusting Pocket to secure the prisoners.

"Do you see the flags?" Lady Tsokei said.

The blast of a horn floated across the sea again, and T'ruck squinted against the low sun. Ships were fleeing the carnage – not pirate ships, but his enemies'. White flags were rising on those that remained.

Starry Dawn

"You mean to kill me then, brother?" Elaina said, her head held high despite the shitty situation. If she was about to die then she would bloody well go out fighting and do her best to take Blu with her, not cowering in fear and pleading for her life.

"Yes," Blu replied with a grin.

"Thought we was taking prisoners?" said one of Blu's crew, a large man with long hair tied into a braid. "To hang. A, uh… What you call it? A gift. Ain't much of a better one than the queen."

"Aye, we're taking tributes back to King Veritean. Not her though." Blu's lip curled upwards into an ugly smile, the same one their father wore when he got violent. "Too dangerous. Gotta kill her."

"What about Da?" Elaina said. "Ya think he'll just let this go?"

"No. But then, not even Tanner Black can rise from a watery grave. Old bastard ain't dead yet, then he will be soon. Doubt he'll be taken alive for hanging though, probably just gutted on his own ship."

"Nice and neat, eh? Everyone but you dead." Elaina knew she had to buy time. Blu loved the sound of his own voice, and she hoped to keep him good and talking. With any luck another ship would stop by to even the odds. "You were the traitor all along, weren't you?" A horn echoed across the water. It was far away, but some sounds carried for miles on the open ocean.

Blu laughed. "Aye. Ya nearly had me a while back, little sister. Remember that Acanthian fluyt? Captain was a Guild man through and through, spotted my ship docked up in Land's End. Luckily for me, you killed him long before he could talk."

Elaina swept her gaze over Blu's crew. They were vicious bastards one and all, and they looked like they were just waiting for an excuse for a bit of violence. They were also pirates, and pirates didn't like working for free.

"Just what are you getting out of this, Blu?"

"A pardon for my crimes. Land and a title in the Five Kingdoms. Legitimacy. No more of this risking my life to make other folk rich.

Starting myself up as a merchant in a world without pirates. Seems fairly lucrative to me."

Elaina laughed. "What about them?" she said. "What's your crew get out of this?"

"Pardons and a place on my first merchant ship. Good pay and no risk."

"And they're content with that?" Elaina was looking not at Blu, but at his crew. "Content with giving up their freedom to live off whatever scraps you throw them?"

A few of the crew started to whisper among themselves.

"They'll live, and they'll live well. Better than dying here, nothing but food for the sharks and worse. Now, if you're quite done talking, little sister, I've been wanting rid of you for a very long time."

Elaina readied herself to leap at him; she doubted the bastard would kill her himself, but if he did she'd tear out his eyes before he was done.

A second horn blasted out across the water.

Blu paused, his head cocked to the side as if he expected more, but after a moment he shrugged and turned his attention back to Elaina. He advanced upon her with two of his crew at his side.

"Cap!" Four-Eyed Pollick called down from the nest. "The bastards are turning tail."

"What?" shouted Blu, his eyes darting upwards.

Elaina grinned and punched Blu hard in the face. The bastard went down in a stunned, bleeding mess. Elaina shook the pain out of her hand. She was still faced by Blu's crew, and they were still armed.

"Navy ships are fleeing," Pollick shouted. "Those that can. White flags are rising on others."

Blu shoved away the hands that were trying to help him up. "Kill 'em all!" he sputtered, pointing with his sword in Elaina's direction.

Ocean Deep's crew hesitated. It was all the delay Elaina needed.

"Fight is done," she shouted. "Navy lost. We won. Ain't no reward waiting for you now, Blu."

"They know too much," Blu said as he struggled back to his feet, addressing his crew. "Kill 'em or we're all…"

"Pardons," Elaina said, pitching her voice louder than her

brother's. "I offer you all pardons. Amnesty for your recent traitorous transgressions."

"You…" Blu's voice cracked a little.

"Are the queen of the isles. In charge." Elaina grinned and took a step forward. Blu backed up and bumped against one of his crew. The pirate was looking from his captain to his queen, his expression intense.

"Attack us now and they'll know. The whole of the isles will know," Elaina said. "You'll be hunted everywhere you run. No safe port in the known world will harbour you. *Or* you can stand down, take your traitorous captain into custody, and live in the kingdom we've just created. No repercussions for your crimes."

"On your word?" said the big, long-haired pirate. She was negotiating with him now, Blu all but forgotten.

Elaina nodded. "As queen."

"Wait," Blu squealed. He lunged forwards with his sword, only to be dragged back by the man behind him.

The big pirate kicked Blu in the back of his knee, sending the bastard to the deck, and tore the sword from his hand. "This here is a mutiny," he growled. "Don't reckon you're fit to lead no more, Cap'n."

Blu screamed in fury and frustration, thrashing about, but more of his own crew moved forwards to restrain him. Elaina's crew had started to pick up their weapons. There was still a nervous tension aboard the ship.

"I'll fucking kill you for this, El," Blu shouted.

"Shut it, Captain," said the pirate holding Blu's sword. He raised his arm to strike.

"Don't kill him," Elaina said quickly, rushing forwards and getting in the way before the pirate could swing.

"Fuck you, bitch," Blu snapped. He tried to surge back to his feet, but his crew held him fast.

Elaina carefully reached up and took the sword from the big pirate's hand. "Don't kill him," she repeated. "You kill him, and there ain't nothing that will save you from our da. We hand him over to Tanner."

The pirate looked far from convinced, but he nodded.

Blu laughed. "You do that, El. Hand me over to Da. I'll be back on my ship in a day, and I'll string the fucking lot of ya."

Elaina's brother thrashed about some more, but he was being held down by three of his own men and they held him fast. Eventually he stopped struggling and contented himself with spitting in Elaina's direction.

"Alfer, show them to the brig," Elaina said. "Throw the whore-faced dung pile in and bring me the key. Make sure he's guarded too."

As Alfer led the crew holding Blu below decks, Elaina faced the big pirate.

"You the first mate?" she said. There were a lot of *Ocean Deep*'s crew still aboard *Starry Dawn*, and even with her own crew armed once again, a fight would end badly for them. He nodded slowly, staring down at her.

"You can read?" Elaina said. "Letters and charts?"

"Aye."

"What's your name?"

"Mobep." Judging by his skin colour and accent, he was from deep in the southern Wilds.

Elaina grinned and held out a hand. "Congratulations, mate. You just made captain. *Ocean Deep* is yours."

The Phoenix

Keelin hung from the rigging of his ship as she sailed up next to the *King's Justice*. Though, he had to admit, *The Phoenix* wasn't so much sailing as she was limping. She was taking on water, missing both rigging and sail in places, and the wheel kept getting stuck. There would be nothing for it but to beach her for a while once they were safely back at New Sev'relain.

As soon as they were close enough Keelin wrapped a rope around his hand and swung across onto the deck of the *King's Justice*. He needed to know why the navy forces had surrendered, and Tanner Black was sitting aboard the answer. A few moments later, Deun Burn landed nearby. The skull-faced Riverlander had been a pain in the arse ever since he'd come aboard Keelin's ship, demanding to share in the command of *The Phoenix* and shouting orders to his men in the harsh language only the Riverlanders knew. Unfortunately, Deun and his crew were also the only reason Keelin and his own were still alive. They'd fought side by side and back to back against superior numbers, and while Keelin doubted he would ever like the Riverlander, he was starting to respect him.

"Stillwater." Tanner Black's voice rang out deep and loud. "Just the man I was looking for."

Tanner was sitting on the poopdeck railing overlooking the quarterdeck, with a pipe in hand and the most unlikely company Keelin had expected to see.

"Socialising with traitors now, are we?" Keelin said as he drew close.

Tanner laughed. "Still better company than Riverlanders."

Deun Burn hissed a couple of words and drew his sword. Keelin held up a hand to stop him. "Let it go," he said quietly, and Deun sighed deeply. They were all exhausted.

"Good to see ya again, mate," Daimen Poole said with a grin around a pipe of his own. "Fast friends, me and Tanner these days. Plenty in common."

Tanner growled, and Daimen stopped short of patting the man's arm.

"Such as?" Keelin joined the two at the railing and looked down over the quarterdeck.

There was a fat man tied to the mast, sagging against his ropes, and a large number of sailors and soldiers wearing the colours of the Five Kingdoms being menaced by Tanner's crew. There were more soldiers being lowered to the water in a dinghy with no oars.

"A mutual disdain for Drake Morrass," Tanner said, with a dark glance in Keelin's direction.

"I'm still wondering why he's even alive," Keelin said, thumbing towards Daimen. "Shouldn't he at least be down there, tied to the mast?"

"What? With the admiral?" Poole laughed.

"Wasn't talking to you," Keelin said.

"See how quickly my good friends turn on me?"

"You turned on us." Keelin was a bare drop away from gutting the man.

"No, mate. I sacrificed myself, my ship, and my crew for you. Then I find out it was all for a lie. Drake started this war. Made a deal with that young pup of a king from the Five Kingdoms. He gave them Black Sands and was supposed to give them the rest of us too. Looks like he changed his mind though, figured he could use the war to unite us. Worked too. The bastard."

Keelin looked to Tanner, who was staring back at him. He read the question in Keelin's eyes and nodded once.

"Fuck," Keelin said, climbing over the railing and sitting down next to Tanner. "Played us all like strings on a harp."

"And what a melody he played," Tanner said.

"Anyone find themselves in the least bit surprised, though?" Daimen said.

Keelin shook his head. He'd been suspicious of Drake from the start, but the man had a charisma about him and it had sucked Keelin in and muddled him up until he found himself believing all of Morrass' shit. Worse than just believing it, he'd convinced others to believe it.

"Do we have proof?" he said.

"Do we need it?" Deun Burn hissed.

Tanner shrugged his big shoulders. "Got charts. Should match up with Drake's."

Keelin shook his head. "*Fortune* went down."

"Eh?" Tanner said. "When?"

"Before the battle even started. Black flames. Reckon someone smashed the jar of Everfire."

"With any luck the greasy rope-licker went down with his ship," Daimen said with a laugh.

"If not, we've got him." Tanner pointed with his pipe to the man tied to the mast. "Admiral of this here navy fleet. Confirmed everything Poole says."

"That's how you got them to surrender." Keelin laughed. "I'd thought the fight could still have gone either way. Seemed odd they'd just turn tail and run."

Tanner nodded. "Poole convinced the man to lay down arms."

"At the point of a sword?"

Poole shrugged. "Best way to negotiate, I've always found."

Tanner swung his legs over the railing and hopped down onto the poopdeck. "A word, Stillwater."

Keelin suppressed a sigh and followed Tanner, marvelling at how much his limbs protested at the idea of moving again. They walked towards the stern and looked out at the calm waters that had just recently been a battlefield.

Ships were everywhere, some sailing, some limping, some doing their very best not to sink. At a rough count Keelin guessed they'd lost a full half of their vessels, including *North Storm* and *Fortune*. He didn't even want to imagine how many people they'd lost.

"If Drake survived..." Keelin started.

"We'll hang him," Tanner finished.

Keelin nodded.

"It's my daughter I want to talk about. Elaina will be queen, no doubt about that now." Tanner smiled. "Without Drake around there'll be plenty of people looking to sit beside her."

"I've got..."

"I reckon it should be you, Stillwater."

Keelin laughed. "I don't think she needs anyone…"

"Don't be dense, lad. Ain't about needing a king over a queen, though Rin knows we'll need one at some point to continue the line. It's about my daughter needing someone to temper her… temper."

Tanner grimaced. "Back on Ash, Stillwater, I agreed to join you and Drake because your argument was sound. I knew the folk of the isles would never follow me, nor would half of the captains. Also knew they'd follow Drake, at least to a point. Always knew the bastard would show his true colours eventually. It's my temper, you see…"

"It's your reputation, Tanner."

"Aye, that too. A lot of that comes from my temper though. Short fuse, they call it. It's a curse of my family. Elaina has the same damned temper."

"I know."

"Aye, and I know you know. So stop fucking interrupting me. She likes you. Always has. And she's better around you. Calmer, happier. Less prone to fits of murderous rage."

"Tanner, I've got a child on the way with…"

"Aye, that little squinty bitch you let swab ya deck. I know. What of it? You really think to pick her over my daughter? Over the chance to be king?"

Keelin sighed. He really had no idea what to do. Aimi was pregnant, it was true, but they hadn't been getting along for a long time. There was friction there that went deeper than a simple misunderstanding, and it went deeper than Keelin cheating on Aimi. He also had to admit that Elaina was Elaina, and he'd loved her for as long as he'd been a pirate.

"Don't mistake me, Stillwater," Tanner continued. "I ain't promising you to my daughter. Elaina will choose herself who she wants beside her. I'm saying you should ask, and I think she'll take ya. Reckon you'll both be better off with each other than without."

Keelin stared out at the setting sun and wished he had a bottle of rum to help him drown his thoughts.

"Just remember, lad," Tanner said. "I damn near raised you. Don't ever expect me to bend a knee."

Starry Dawn

The dead were given a sea burial en masse. Every ship still floating collected the bodies, both pirate and navy, and they were identified as best was possible. Names were noted, and the families of those that had them would be informed and paid for the sacrifice. Normally the bodies would have been wrapped in canvas and weighted, the best way to ensure they reached Rin's court, but there were just too many. So many that Elaina was certain the dead outnumbered the living.

Starry Dawn's ceremony was brief. The bodies were lined up on the deck and she spoke a few words about what their sacrifice meant to the isles and how Rin was sure to take them. Then they were thrown overboard. No one stopped to watch the denizens of the deep come up to feed on the dead. Everyone heard it though.

Once the ceremony was done, they broke out the rum and everyone drank more than a few measures. Elaina left her crew singing mournful shanties as she rowed Blu over to *The Black Death*. He was sullen and spiteful and might have tried to kill Elaina, but his hands were tied and the new captain of *Ocean Deep* accompanied them. Elaina left her brother with their father, and she wagered it was the last time she would ever see Tanner's eldest son.

When the sun rose on the next morning, the real work began. The sea had gone from calm to choppy, which made the job at hand that much harder. Sailors and soldiers alike were given a choice. They could join the Pirate Isles, join the crews of those they'd fought against, or they could return to their kingdoms.

Many chose to join the pirates. They had before them a real opportunity for a new life, unfettered by their low status. In the Pirate Isles there was plenty of land and plenty of jobs, and Elaina felt her spirits soar as their ranks swelled.

Officers were taken as prisoners, to be returned to their own people upon agreement to the cessation of hostilities. Everyone else returning to their own homes was packed aboard the worst and most rickety of the vessels still floating and told to be on their way.

Elaina counted forty-four ships in her fleet by the time those wanting to return had been sent off. It was now official – the Pirate Isles had the largest and best-armed fleet of ships in the known world. There was simply nobody left to challenge them. But it wasn't over, she knew that. Her people might crown her as queen, but there would be peace talks and negotiations before Sarth and the Five Kingdoms accepted the pirates as a nation of their own. They would, though, Elaina knew. She held all the cards now. She could form blockades around ports, lock down the shipping lanes. Her enemies had no option but to agree to her demands.

Word had got around about the *Fortune* burning before the battle, and only a few of her crew had turned up. Elaina dared to hope that Drake was dead.

The trip back to New Sev'relain was long and tedious despite the fair weather. Sharks and serpents and worse trailed them for a few days, hoping they would throw some more bodies overboard. Eventually even the most persistent of scavengers lost interest. Elaina took to imagining herself on a throne, maybe even with a crown.

When their home port rose up from the horizon, it was clear they weren't the first to arrive. Some of the ships crowding the bay were new, while others were pirates who had fled the battle or left before the main force. *Starry Dawn* had kept pace with both *The Phoenix* and *The Black Death*, but the other two slowed as they approached to let Elaina make land first. It was a small sign of respect, one that put a smile on her face as her ship docked in the seat of her new empire.

Folk crowded the docks, from the piers to the sand and all the way back to the town proper. They came out in droves to see their new king and queen and hear of the battle that had finally secured their safety and freedom.

Elaina dressed for the occasion, wearing her best and smartest breeches and blouse and a long, grand coat over the top, all black. Her hair was getting long, almost down to her shoulders, so she tied it back with a bandana and applied just a touch of dark powder to make her blue eyes stand out. Feeling she looked every bit the conquering pirate queen, she strolled down the gangplank to the waiting masses.

Elaina had experienced notoriety before. This was different. The folk here didn't just know her – they cheered for her, they celebrated her return. The noise was near deafening, and some folk even tried to touch her, almost as though by the mere act some of her good fortune might rub off on them. Through it all Elaina grinned and nodded and desperately tried not to reach for a weapon.

"Where's Drake?" an older lady, plump and red-faced, said in a booming voice.

The crowd quietened to hear Elaina's answer. "We don't know," she shouted. "The *Fortune* went down in the fight. He might have drowned."

The noise started up again; this time it seemed far less happy. Folk were muttering to each other, some sending furtive glances Elaina's way. The atmosphere was changing, and she wasn't the only one to feel it. Some of her crew followed her down the gangplank and stood at her back.

Elaina took a deep breath and shouted over the crowd's rumblings. "You all have likely heard that I married Drake. Queen of you and the isles. Well, that agreement went further than just looking pretty by Morrass' side. I agreed to take on his dream should he fall in battle."

It was a bold-faced lie. Elaina had never made such an agreement with Drake, and the marriage had clearly been under some duress on both sides, but she'd see his dream through all the same, because it was the right thing to do. Besides, the good folk of the Pirate Isles wanted to hear it. They needed to hear it.

"Drake might be gone, but I remain. We've won the battle, aye, and the rest of the war needs fighting with words, not swords. As queen, I'll be visiting Sarth and the Five Kingdoms. I'll make certain they realise they're beaten and that if they ever bother us again, we'll destroy them. I'll make peace. A peace we can all prosper from."

Some of the crowd turned and walked away, looking anything but happy, but more stayed; some even began cheering again. The plump older lady stepped forward, a sceptical look on her face.

"Do you really think you can do this in his stead?"

Elaina smiled. "I've already made an alliance with the free cities, and it was my fleet, more than his, that won us our freedom. Aye, I can do it. I'll do a better damned job than he ever could."

The woman chewed her lip for a moment before nodding and holding out her hand. "Name's Breta. I sit on the council here. Brought folks' problems to Drake when it was needed. I'd happily do the same for you."

Elaina took Breta's hand and shook it. It seemed to be all the confirmation many of the crowd needed, although a few more people still slunk away. It didn't matter – it was the support of the many Elaina needed, and she'd convince the others through her actions.

The Phoenix

Keelin watched Elaina stroll up the beach towards the town, surrounded by people wanting her opinion or her orders. It wasn't too long ago that he'd been in that position, with all the folk of New Sev'relain looking to him to solve their problems. He'd hated it then. It had seemed a real imposition when all he really wanted to do was sail the seas and find a way to exact his vengeance.

It all seemed a bit foolish now. Keelin had devoted so much of his life to hunting down the Arbiter only to find he'd been dead for Rin knew how long. So much of his life wasted. Now he needed to decide what he wanted to do with however much remained. On the one hand he could pursue Elaina and the throne she now came with; on the other he could try to make things right with Aimi.

Keelin sighed and leaned on the railing. "What do you think I should do?" he asked the figurehead. She was a glorious bird with wings of flame, hatching from naught but ashes. Rebirth from fire. Seemed a fitting name when he took the ship; after all, he'd set fire to his family home and then run away to become a pirate. It had seemed a romantic notion back then. The boy he'd been would never have expected to see so much blood, so much death.

A man departing one of the nearby ships caught his eye. A man with long, lanky hair and a milky white eye. Keelin turned and ran for the gangplank.

"I'm going ashore, Smithe," he said as he ran past his new first mate, not waiting to hear a response.

Keelin launched himself down the gangplank and hit the pier running, holding onto his cutlasses so they wouldn't swing around too much and injure anyone nearby. He spotted his quarry making his way up to the town proper.

Keelin caught up to the man under the shade of a lonely palm tree that dared to call the beach its home. "Prin…" he started, doubling over as he tried to catch his breath. "Princess."

"Aye?" Princess said mournfully. He turned to Keelin with a heavy sigh. "Thought that were you, Stillwater. Nice jog?"

"Drake?" Keelin said, still breathing heavily in the close air.

Princess' shoulders slumped. He looked old and worn through. "Dead," he said.

"You're sure?"

"Bitch of an Arbiter put two shots in his chest then set fire to the ship. Most of the crew burned up. Me and Anders got a boat lowered before that damned Everfire... No idea what happened to her. Everything got a bit hectic." Princess let out a loud sigh. "I hope she drowned. Or burned. I think I'd prefer burned, actually."

"Dead," Keelin mused.

"Aye," Princess said. "Now if ya don't mind, I'm gonna go drink myself unconscious in the tavern. Got picked up by the *Freedom*, and Captain Zhou don't let a drop of booze onto his ship. Bastard."

Princess trudged away towards the town, leaving Keelin beneath the palm tree. After a few moments he realised someone was watching him, and he turned to find Aimi nearby. The bump of their child was starting to show beneath her blouse.

"Hi," Keelin said, and cursed himself for how foolish he sounded.

"I wondered if you were gonna come see me," Aimi said. "After a while I just thought, 'Fuck it, I'll take the first step.'"

"How are you?" Keelin smiled weakly. "How's the, um..."

"I'm fine. Our child is fine. At least, as far as I can tell. It wriggles and kicks occasionally, makes it uncomfortable to do anything – and nothing."

Keelin nodded. "Good. I mean, not about the discomfort, but... good."

Aimi sighed. "So I hear we have a queen now. She doesn't like me."

"It's not you she doesn't like."

"Yes, it is." Aimi shook her head. She joined Keelin underneath the palm tree and sat down on the sand.

She smelled of wood smoke and hard work. It was strange. Before, Aimi had always smelled of the sea.

"Feel free to join me," she said, a hard edge to her voice.

Keelin laughed and did as he was bid. He struggled to think of something to say. Only a few months ago they'd spent hours at a time sitting in his cabin and talking of everything and nothing, and now he couldn't think of a damned thing to say to her. He looked down at her midsection, at the bump. At his child. It was strange to think there was something living in there. Even stranger that he'd never even thought of it until now.

"Oh, for the love of Rin," Aimi said with a sigh. She reached over, grabbed hold of Keelin's hand, and placed it on her belly.

Keelin went rigid, and he wasn't even sure why. He felt nothing. Only tight skin stretched over a rounded bump where once her stomach had been flat.

"Um…"

"It's not moving at the moment," Aimi said. She took her hand away and Keelin quickly withdrew his own. "I'll let you know if it starts again."

"Good," Keelin said, and they both fell silent. "You said *her* name over land."

Aimi sighed and sent him a withering stare over her shoulder. "I'm carrying a child conceived at sea, Keelin. She's not about to smite me down for saying her name."

"That's true, I suppose." He was still trying to decide what to do, which course to take. Sometimes it was best to jump in with both feet, set your course and stick to it.

"I think you should move back onto the ship," he said, finally making a decision.

"I think that's a bad idea."

"Huh?"

"I was born at sea, Keelin, you know that. I want our child to be born at sea as well. Just not aboard *The Phoenix*. I…" Aimi paused, frowning. "I don't think we work together. If we did you wouldn't have run off and fucked Queen Bitch. I wouldn't have spent the last few months hating you."

Keelin stared towards the port, desperately trying to think of something to say. The problem was that Aimi was right, and he knew it.

Both of them knew it.

"You hate me?" he said.

"No. Yes. Not any more. Maybe a bit, still. I certainly don't love you, though." She gave him a tired smile. "I like you well enough, Keelin – most of the time. I just think we should have left it at that."

Aimi laughed bitterly. "You know what I realised recently? When you fucked the queen, I wasn't angry at her for trying to steal you. I was just angry at her for trying to steal something that was mine."

"So you were angry at her?" Keelin felt lost and confused.

"I was angry at you too, Keelin."

He let out a quick laugh and decided to change the subject. "Where will you go?"

"Point is, I was never really in it for you," Aimi continued. "Was just using you, I guess. Looks like we're both getting something out of it, at least." She placed a hand on her belly.

"I ain't leaving the isles," she said after a few moments. "Got something like a home here. Friends, at least. There's plenty of ships that take on women. Might even start seeing a few more of us as captains now, eh?"

Keelin nodded, and they were both silent for a while. "I'm sorry, Aimi," he said eventually.

"What for? If it's for fucking the queen back in HwoyonDo, then apology accepted. Anything else... Well, we both knew what we were doing, Cap'n. Nothing else to apologise for."

Keelin laughed, and a moment later Aimi joined in. For a while it was just like things were the way they used to be. Only they weren't.

"Just don't think this lets you off the hook," she said, glaring at him. "Just 'cos you and me aren't together don't mean you don't have some responsibility here. You put this child inside of me, and you're fucking well gonna help raise it."

New Sev'relain

"Drink to the fallen," Princess shouted, and not for the first time that night.

"We'll be joining them soon." A number of others took up the toast.

Daimen didn't join in the toast. It wasn't that he thought that the folk who had died didn't deserve remembering, didn't deserve being toasted. It was that he knew Princess and Zothus and all the others over on that side of the tavern were toasting to one man in particular.

"Someone should tell them bastards just why the fucker don't need toasting," he said sullenly.

He was angry, and he had every right to be. Drake was being touted as a hero, a martyr to the pirates and their cause. Morrass would forever be known as the first king of the Pirate Isles despite never having sat a throne or worn a crown. To make matters worse, those same folk who thought Drake so mighty also looked at Daimen as though he were a traitor. As though he hadn't saved them all by getting Admiral Wulfden to surrender.

"Leave it be, Poole," Tanner Black rumbled from his side of the table.

Tanner had eschewed his normal court of sycophants and not-so-subtle guards, and Daimen had chosen to sit with him. They were far from friends, but Tanner was one of the few people who knew the secrets Daimen knew. They'd all agreed to keep the truth about Drake to themselves.

"Folk deserve to know," Daimen grumbled.

"No, mate, they don't," Tanner said around a tankard of weak ale. "Bastard is dead. Something good came out of him, at least. Telling all of them now only serves to weaken the unity. Might even be enough to break us all apart again."

"When did you get so damned fucking reasonable?"

Tanner turned a dark gaze on Daimen. "The moment my daughter claimed her rightful place. She'll be queen, and I'd bet me ship that Stillwater'll be king." Tanner chuckled, and Daimen had the feeling the man was a little drunk. "I raised both of 'em myself. Taught 'em all they know."

Tanner gripped his mug of ale hard. "Drake is dead, and the kingdom he helped to build will be ruled by my descendants. Reckon that means I won, mate. And all I have to do is hold my peace. Reckon I can do that."

"Ah… fair enough." Daimen knew better than to argue with Tanner Black over his family. No one knew what had happened to Blu. Elaina had delivered her brother to their father and named him a traitor. Since then the fate of Tanner's eldest son was uncertain. Somehow Daimen doubted the man was dead. Tanner was a cruel bastard and no mistake, but even he might quibble at the act of killing his own children.

Daimen drained his tankard and slammed it down onto the table. "Reckon I might go take a piss, mate."

"Feel free to not come back," Tanner said, a dark look in his eyes that had Daimen agreeing it might be best to leave the pirate alone. Tanner might be acting civil now, but it clearly didn't sit well in his gut.

Daimen gave the man a mocking smile as he stood and started shoving his way through the dancing and cavorting pirates towards the tavern door.

"Drink to the fallen," Princess shouted.

Daimen slammed the door behind him before the others could complete their toast.

"We'll be joining them soon!" the muffled words travelled easily through the door.

It was a dark night, and a dark mood settled in upon Daimen. He'd drunk enough that he felt a little tipsy, and not even the rare cool breeze blowing through the town could lift his spirits. He felt cheated and used and angry.

Turning towards the ocean, Daimen started walking. He needed a piss, it was true, and the sound of the waves lapping against the sand had always helped him get things started, but it was more than that. Daimen needed his spirits lifting, and the sight of the sea and the boats floating in the bay might just help him with that.

The Merry Fuck, New Sev'relain's largest whore house, was just across the way from the Righteous Indignation, and it was alive with light and sound spilling out of every door and window. No doubt the whores would be making something close to a killing on a night like this, filled with the coins of the victorious. Daimen had grown up in an establishment just like it, and though he'd long ago put his past behind him, he never visited brothels.

The streets of New Sev'relain were as full of hustle and bustle as its taverns and whore houses. Daimen had rarely seen a town so drunk on its own celebration. Just a year ago he'd have been given nods of respect, maybe even the odd kind word. Now all he received were hostile stares or the quick aversion of eyes. Only Admiral Tatters stared up at him without animosity. Daimen approached the terminal drunk and flipped a bronze bit into the dirt next to him.

"Thank you, kind sir," Tatters slurred, pawing around in the dust to find the coin.

"Reckon ya might be able to go home now, Tatters," Daimen said with a smile he didn't feel.

"Home," Tatters mumbled. "I am home."

"Nah, mate. I mean ya real home. Sarth or some such, aye? Ain't you got family there, maybe waiting for ya? Parents? Wife? Kids?"

Tatters frowned and raised a mostly empty bottle to his lips. "No. Sarth not home. Nothing there. I live here. Always have. Always will."

Daimen groaned, and walked away with a shake of his head. Tatters was one more victim of Drake Morrass. The man had once been a proud admiral of Sarth. Now he lay on the streets of New Sev'relain, broken and drunk and trying desperately to forget his past.

Daimen stopped and turned back to Tatters. "That Arbiter. The one that followed Drake around. She killed him. Now, I don't know what that means exactly as it pertains to her faith and yours – what's left of it, anyways – but she killed him."

Admiral Tatters frowned, and Daimen thought he saw a tear roll down the man's face. Maybe he would sober up and return to Sarth, maybe not. Daimen hoped he could find some redemption though, if only to gain one small victory over Morrass.

Just a short way down towards the beach, Daimen spotted Elaina

Black through a window. The woman was gesticulating wildly and her mouth was moving, saying something Daimen couldn't hear. Whatever it was, she seemed animated. Then he saw Breta, the council woman, standing opposite Elaina, her arms crossed and a resolute look on her face.

Daimen almost laughed. He'd dealt with Breta and the rest of the council a few times, and he didn't envy Elaina's new position. Only Drake had ever been able to manipulate the formidable woman into anything, and even then she'd soon swung back to her own way of thinking. Breta was more responsible for the success of New Sev'relain than anyone else alive, and Elaina would need to realise that quickly if she was to survive her new crown.

The sandy beach of New Sev'relain's port was busy with drunkenness, and musical notes drifted around the sound of bonfires crackle-popping. Daimen gave them all a wide berth; he had no wish to find himself confronted by a group of hostile pirates when there was a handy fire nearby for flaming acts of punishment.

Moving a fair way into the darkness, Daimen took in a deep breath, pulled out his cock, and started to piss, staring out towards the bay. It dawned on him that he'd need a new ship. *Mary's Virtue* was long gone, another set of bones littering the waters around the island of Ash. There were plenty of available boats captured from their enemies now, though, and not nearly enough able captains for them. With Stillwater's recommendation, Daimen would be sure to secure himself a vessel. The harder job would be finding a crew who didn't know him, or finding the folk that didn't believe him a traitor. Once he'd found himself the pirates to sail the boat, he could finally get back out on the water, under his own command again.

Of course, they wouldn't be able to pirate any more, at least not like they used to. No. They would be tax collectors now; the only pirating to be done was to the ships who refused to pay to sail their waters. Daimen laughed bitterly.

"I guess the golden age of piracy is good and done now," he muttered as he tucked his cock back into his breeches.

Debilitating pain blossomed in Daimen's back, and in the same moment someone whispered "Traitor" in his ear. He staggered for a moment, and then his knees buckled, the sand rushing up to meet him. It dawned on him that he'd been stabbed, and the assassin had done a damned good job of it.

Daimen could feel the wetness spreading across his back, and the light was starting to fade. He couldn't breathe, let alone shout for help. It took all the effort he could muster to roll over, and the last thing he saw was a slim man in a faded green suit stalking away in the darkness.

North Squall

T'ruck stared out towards the bay beyond New Sev'relain, at the ships that floated there. Some were bigger than others, but *North Storm* was gone. The biggest ship ever to sail the waters of the Pirate Isles, his ship, was nothing but wreckage lying at the bottom of a nameless stretch of deep blue.

He was sitting on a bench set out on the beach, a wooden table before him with two mugs of ale atop it. One was for him, and the other was for Yu'truda. She was gone, but not really. He felt her inside somehow – not quite her presence, nor even her memories, but there was something of her inside him. It was comforting in a strange way.

Lady Tsokei seemed to glide across the sand as she approached, and she lowered herself onto the bench across the table, her dark eyes boring into T'ruck's own. He was just glad the witch was suppressing her aura of fear. He wasn't in the mood to shit his britches.

"I have spoken to your queen," Lady Tsokei said, a wry smile on her lips.

"Our queen," T'ruck rumbled. "You helped. One of us now as much as any other."

Lady Tsokei gave a short nod. "She seems to agree that given the king's death, and his murderer, the Inquisition should be looked upon unfavourably here in the isles."

"Safe harbour, is it?"

"As safe as one can be for people like me." The witch smiled. "I have decided to stay with you for a while, Captain. I quite enjoy the sea."

T'ruck shook his head. "I don't even have a boat."

"What about the Man of War we took towards the end of the battle?"

Again T'ruck shook his head. "Smaller than my last. They're all smaller than my last."

"I see." Lady Tsokei looked past T'ruck and nodded. A few moments later Pocket flopped down onto the bench next to him, dumping a small ball of mottled brown fur on the table.

T'ruck glanced first at the witch, and then at his first mate, before turning his attention back to the ball of fur. It slowly uncurled into the shape of a kitten, with paws and ears too large for its body and innocent black eyes. It stared up at T'ruck and meowed quietly.

"What's this?"

"New ship needs a cat, Captain," Pocket said with a grin.

"She is smaller than the last one," Lady Tsokei said. "But I am told the cat will be almost as large as me when fully grown."

T'ruck snorted and poked a big finger at the kitten, knocking it onto its back. The little creature rolled onto its paws and leapt at T'ruck's finger, savaging the digit with claws and teeth too small to do any damage.

"Crew is behind you, Captain," Pocket continued. "Whichever ship you choose."

T'ruck laughed as the kitten continued to attack his finger. The Five Kingdoms had beaten him and taken his entire clan away, killed them all. T'ruck Khan was the last of them. But he'd beaten the Five Kingdoms right back, and now he had a new clan. It was, now he thought about it, a far bigger clan than his last one.

Starry Dawn

Ten ships were preparing to leave, *Starry Dawn* among them. One ship was headed back to Chade, one of only two that had survived the battle. Rose might not be happy about the loss of so many of her vessels, but Elaina was sending reassurances that their agreement, and their friendship, still held. Elaina needed the alliance with Chade, and she suspected Chade needed the Pirate Isles too.

"I'll be certain to send the Black Thorn your kindest regards," a man slurred behind her. Elaina turned to see Drake Morrass' spy grinning at her.

"You work for them too?" she said.

"My loyalties are many," Anders confirmed with a deep bow. "I prefer to think I work with the Black Thorn. Though some of his people don't like me very much."

"Can't think why."

"Indeed. I'm a wonderfully amiable sort. Loved and feared by all."

"Uh huh. One less loyalty now, though, eh?"

"What's that?"

"Now Drake is gone."

"Oh, that. Of course. Gone but not forgotten. I suspect you'll build a statue of him or something."

"Aye, or something."

"Well, good luck, Your Majesty." Anders dipped into a deep, sweeping bow, before rising unsteadily and staggering off towards the gangplank. He greeted a woman waiting for him there with a drunken hug. Elaina watched him go and then looked to the ship's captain. The woman simply shrugged and followed the spy up to her ship.

Two of the ships leaving were from Larkos. A total of five vessels from the free city had survived the battle, and three of those had already gone, though with much reduced crews. Elaina had already sent a message of thanks to the Council of Thirteen, and another to the Queen of Blades.

Seven of the ships making preparations were her escort to Land's

End. It was a military force, and a substantial one. They'd already sent word to the Five Kingdoms that Elaina wanted to talk peace, but there was no way to know if they would be well received or hanged for the courtesy. Elaina intended to take enough of a naval presence that they could blockade the port if need be.

The docks were beyond busy, with supplies being loaded onto ships and pirates being roused from the town and marched onto their boats. Keelin was helping to load barrels of salted beef onto *The Phoenix*; he'd volunteered to accompany Elaina, and she'd been happy to accept.

Spotting her watching, Keelin wiped sweat from his forehead and dodged around a pirate carrying a hefty crate, launching himself down the gangplank and strolling her way. Elaina watched him with an amused grin, barely listening to Surge's report on the status of *Starry Dawn*'s own loading.

"I was hoping we could have a word before we leave," Keelin said, straightening the lapels on his jacket. Elaina liked that he was starting to take care of his appearance again; he'd even shaved recently.

"Standing right here, aren't I?" Elaina only half turned towards him, as if she were actually listening to Surge.

"Right, it's just…" Keelin drew in a deep breath, then sighed, as if he couldn't find the words.

Elaina glanced at her fellow captain. "Go on. I'm listening." She turned back towards Surge, who by now had stopped his report and was struggling not to laugh.

"Back in HwoyonDo, in the Observatory. What you said…"

"What did I say?"

"About preferring to sit beside me on the throne, instead of Morrass."

"Oh." Elaina glanced at Keelin and shrugged. "I might have. Long time ago. What of it?"

Keelin laughed. "Damnit, Elaina, you know what I mean."

"Aye," Elaina said, "I do. Still wanna hear you say it though."

"Drake's gone. I'd like it to be me who… sits beside you on the throne."

Elaina grinned at Keelin, stepped close, and kissed him. She grabbed hold of his ass, and he gripped her waist, pulling her closer. It lasted only a moment before Elaina pushed away and stepped clear of him, a grin still fixed on her face. She felt her blood racing and her heart pounding. She wanted nothing so much as to drag Keelin to her cabin and see how much punishment her little cot could take. From the bulge in his trousers, she suspected Keelin had much the same urge.

"Maybe," she said. "I have to focus on the peace talks for now. Ask me again afterwards." With that she turned and started towards *Starry Dawn*, unable to wipe away her grin.

Starry Dawn

"It itches," Keelin said, fidgeting and pulling at his collar.

"I reckon it's supposed to," Elaina said. "Something about keeping us off guard, maybe."

Keelin snorted. "No. I grew up around here, remember. This is standard formal attire for these people."

Elaina raised an eyebrow at him and turned her attention back to the dress. It was long and sleek, made from silk so it would cling to her curves and ripple as she moved. As black as her hair and name, it was cut modestly to hide her cleavage. The dress was beautiful, and Elaina had never before had a chance to wear its like. She'd rarely had a chance to wear any dress in her life. She wondered how she'd look in it, and wagered she'd be beautiful.

"I'm not wearing it," she stated firmly.

"I think you'd look good in it," Keelin said.

"I'd look fucking stunning in it." Elaina grinned for just a moment. "Still not wearing it. And take off that suit – get back into ya normal clothes."

"Gladly," Keelin said, already unbuttoning the shirt. "You know how I like my fancy jackets, but this is just stifling. I honestly don't know how folk can wear it. Damn near cuts off the airway. And these cuffs…"

"They're trying to fit us into their world," Elaina said. "Dress us up like them to… I dunno, civilise us, or something. Make us fit in with the rest of them." She sighed deeply. "But we don't fit in. That's kind of the point, ain't it."

Keelin was still stripping, throwing the uncomfortable clothes onto a nearby chair. Elaina watched him undress. She decided she'd keep the dress. She would never wear it in front of any Five Kingdoms bastards, but that didn't mean she couldn't find another time to slip into it.

"Take your time," she said playfully as Keelin pulled his old trousers up around his waist. He glanced at her over his shoulder and winked. Elaina just stared back.

Once he was dressed in his worn old suit of royal blue with gold trim, Elaina nodded at his cutlasses, discarded on a nearby couch.

Keelin laughed. "You think we're gonna need weapons?"

"I think we won the war," Elaina said. "And we've come to the seat of our enemy to demand they acquiesce to our demands. To demand peace. And I think that as we're the only two here, we should be carrying as many weapons as we can." She patted her own sword, buckled at her hip, for effect.

Once Keelin was armed again, they opened the door and signalled for the waiting attendant to lead them to his king. It wasn't a long walk, but then Land's End wasn't the capital of the Five Kingdoms, and its palace wasn't the greatest. The attendant talked as they went, and he assured Elaina that each of the six royal palaces in the capital city, Goldseat, were far grander. The man described gilded pillars of stone that took five men holding hands to circle, and a throne made entirely of gold. Elaina made sure to seem unimpressed. The truth was that she couldn't not be impressed, given the sheer extravagance of such a waste of good gold.

Eventually they arrived at a set of grand oak doors with four guards standing outside, two wearing the blue-black of Sarth and the others in the white-gold of the Five Kingdoms.

"Perhaps we should have brought T'ruck to wait outside," Keelin joked, and Elaina snorted out a laugh.

The doors were opened in short order, and Elaina and Keelin went through side by side.

"Queen Elaina Black and Captain Keelin Stillwater," their attendant announced to the room, as though everyone there didn't already know their names.

The first thing Elaina noticed was the guards. Two men and a woman dressed in plated metal armour stood near their king, and all three were well armed. One of the men was a giant, with a metal spear even taller than he was. Elaina was determined not to appear intimidated by their opposition bringing muscle to a negotiation.

"Welcome," said King Jackt Veritean. He was wearing the exact same fake smile he'd worn when they first met just two days ago. The man was young and pretty and was dressed impeccably in a white suit and a golden crown that sat lightly upon his dark hair. He beckoned to two empty seats around the circular table.

Sitting next to the king was an older man with rosy cheeks. He looked like he was related. The size of the Veritean family was almost legendary, understandable given that its kings were required to take multiple wives.

The other man at the table was tall and thin with the golden hair that was so ubiquitous in the people of Sarth. He had piercing blue eyes and a thick blond moustache. He was, if anything, even younger than the Five Kingdoms king.

"Hable Brecker," the Sarth man said, standing and giving a slight bow. "Ambassador to the God Emperor of Sarth."

"Kick his arse and burn his ships and all he sends is a boy to treat with us." Elaina grinned.

"I have full authority to make binding agreements on behalf of the God Emperor," Ambassador Brecker assured them.

Elaina nodded and looked at Keelin, who simply shrugged back. After a moment she approached the nearest chair and pulled it out, sitting her arse down and crossing her arms. Keelin pulled out the second chair and joined her.

Elaina waited for someone else to start. She'd learned a lot from her father over the years, and putting folk on edge was a lesson she'd taken to heart. For a long time everyone just stared at each other.

"Would you like…"

"Reckon we've got you over a barrel," Elaina said, interrupting the king's advisor. It was another of her father's ploys – let your opponent make the first move, but don't let them finish it.

"I was going to suggest refreshments," the advisor continued.

"You've had plenty of time to drink," Elaina snapped. "We're here to talk peace."

"We are," King Jackt said. "But talking can make one thirsty. I'll have some wine brought in."

Elaina shrugged and leaned back in her chair, her arms still crossed. "We still got you over a barrel."

The king and the ambassador shared a look.

"You defeated our latest force, it's true," King Jackt said with a forced smile. "But do not think that constitutes our entire naval presence."

"Yeah?" Elaina said. "You got anything left that can match our entire naval presence?"

Both the king and the ambassador remained silent. They could bluff and posture, but the threat the Pirate Isles now posed was too great to risk another confrontation. Elaina could now lock down trade between all the other great empires of man.

She shook her head and sighed. "I didn't come here to threaten. Nor try to take everything you got. We came here to talk peace. To figure out a way we can all live together. I ain't saying we don't want some reparations for your slaughtering of our people and burning of our towns." Elaina paused and let her words sink in. "But we're not unreasonable."

Keelin leaned forwards and took over, just as they'd planned. "We have this morning released fifty-four officers from our custody. Mostly nobles and such. Their families will be pleased to see them alive and well, I reckon. It's an act of good faith on our part. We have another fifty-five aboard our ships, including one Admiral Wulfden. Our wish is to release them all upon agreeing terms here. We don't want any more needless killing."

"Do you have any of our soldiers held captive also?" said the king's advisor.

"No," said Keelin. "Those who survived were given the choice to stay in the Pirate Isles or return home. Those who chose the latter were sent on their way. Some have likely reached you already; any that haven't aren't likely to now."

"These sound like hostages," the ambassador said, sipping at the newly arrived wine.

"Aye, they are," Keelin said. "Hostages against our safe conduct here, not bargaining chips. Whether or not we reach an agreement, the remaining hostages will be returned once we return to our ships."

"Maybe we ain't as vicious as you like to think, eh?" Elaina grinned savagely.

"Peace," King Jackt said with a smile. "And how would you propose we attain such a thing? You rob and murder our citizens for your own personal gain. It is how you exist as you do. We may have brought a war to your islands, but in truth it was started by your own hands, by your people's actions. You have been at war with us since your birth; we just finally decided to fight back."

Elaina leaned forwards, smiling at the Five Kingdoms king. "Fought back and lost."

Silence held for a good long while.

"Your numbers are too great," the king's advisor said eventually. "You take too many ships. Our merchants can no longer continue to operate at such a loss."

"We propose a different way," Keelin said. They'd discussed at length which of them should make the proposal, and Elaina had decided that it should be Keelin. They were following Drake's plan, after all, and Keelin had been with him since the beginning. No one knew Morrass' plan better.

"The truth is, the Pirate Isles are perfectly situated in the best shipping lanes between your two kingdoms, not to mention trade coming from or going to the Dragon Empire. What we propose is a tax for any and all ships wanting to sail our waters, wanting to use our islands for fresh water."

"Robbery by a different name," the Sarth ambassador exclaimed.

"Aye," Elaina said. "But it's robbery you're going to agree to. Robbery you're going to make legal."

"At the moment we take maybe one in every fourth ship that sails through our waters," Keelin said. "Far too high a number to continue, especially when we not only take the choicest goods, but we also take the ship's supplies. Often those ships don't make it to their destination because of that."

"Not to mention the ships you steal, the crews you murder," the advisor said bitterly.

"Casualties of war," Elaina said with a wink.

"You're making our point for us," Keelin said quickly. "Instead of us taking one in every four ships, we tax every ship, the same way any port does. All of the ships reach their destination. All intact. All with their entire crew alive."

"We offer protection, at a price, for sailing our waters," Elaina said.

"Protection from yourselves," said the king's advisor.

"Aye. And from any others. We'll be pretty harsh on folk who think to pirate our waters without consent."

"And anyone who doesn't pay your tax?" the ambassador said.

"Gets pirated to fuck." Elaina chuckled. "Our ships will still be sailing our waters, and they'll still stop folk and inspect them. Anyone who hasn't paid for the privilege of passing through will have their cargo taken, their ship commandeered, and their crew killed. Pretty good incentive for folk to pay, aye?"

"This is…"

"I agree to the terms," King Jackt said, interrupting his advisor. "In principle."

All eyes turned to the Sarth ambassador. The boy suddenly looked very young, chewing on his lip. Elaina fixed her mouth to a smile and watched.

"Sarth concurs," he said eventually. "In principle."

Elaina laughed. "Excellent. Seems all that's left is to talk figures. Where's that wine?"

Epilogue

Beck mounted the stairs in a rush, her new coat, a replacement for the one lost at sea, billowing behind her. She was sweating by the time she reached the top of the tower, and she took off her hat to wipe at her brow. It wasn't the first time she'd climbed the Inquisition's tower of light, but it was the first time she'd raced up the steps. She was eager to meet with Inquisitor Vance, because she needed answers.

There were no guards at the door. With the ill health of Grand Inquisitor Artur Vance, his son was now the most powerful agent the Inquisition had at its disposal. Hironous needed no one to ensure his safety.

Beck paused before knocking to straighten her coat, take a deep breath, and attempt to reign in her emotions. Getting angry wouldn't help her; the Inquisitor would likely respond better to calm. She knocked three times, and the call to enter was almost immediate. Beck opened the door and stepped inside. The room was much as she remembered. Books and scrolls lined the walls, each meticulously filed away in its own spot. A low fire crackled away in the far corner, a heavy iron grate in place to stop any stray embers escaping. A desk lay to the left of the room, and behind it sat the white-robed figure of Inquisitor Hironous Vance, eagerly scribbling away in the tome that he carried with him everywhere he went. Like his father, the only weapon Hironous ever carried was his personal book of sorceries.

"Arbiter Beck," Inquisitor Vance said without looking up. "I have heard of your success. I would like to both congratulate you on and thank you for your service. Now, what can I do for you?" Finally he glanced up from his book, and his piercing yellow eyes seemed to look straight through Beck.

"You sent me to the Pirate Isles and told me to protect Drake Morrass. I assumed it was because you had seen he would be the target of some heretic, and I suppose he was." Beck paused and let out a sigh. She'd intended to ease into the question, but now she was here all attempts at patience fled. "But once the Drurr were dead, you ordered me to kill him and burn his ship just before he led the pirates to war. Why, Inquisitor? Why did I have to kill Drake?"

Inquisitor Vance smiled sadly. "There are two answers to that question, Arbiter. First, you have heard of my gift, no doubt. Do you believe in it?"

Beck nodded. Everyone knew Hironous Vance had inherited the witch sight from his mother, the ability to see into the future.

"And did Captain Morrass ever speak to you of an oracle he visited?"

"Yes," Beck said. "It was you?"

"It was me. Captain Morrass asked me to look into the future for him. He wanted my help in building an empire out of nothing but water and criminals. I told him half of the truth. He could bring the pirates together, unite them, and win the throne he desired. What I didn't tell him was that if he ever sat upon that throne, it would all crumble around him. A good leader in times of war does not necessarily make a good leader in times of peace."

"Why not tell him the whole truth?"

"Do you believe he would have heeded my advice had I told him he would have to step down at the very moment that he acquired the throne?" Inquisitor Vance shook his head.

He was right. Beck had known Drake well by the end, and she knew there was nothing anyone could have said that would have convinced him to abdicate the throne. That knowledge didn't make her betrayal hurt any less though. Months drifting about the Pirate Isles after the battle had tempered her anger, but they'd done nothing for the guilt she felt over carrying out her orders.

"What's the second answer?" she said bitterly.

Inquisitor Vance snapped his tome shut and fixed the clasp that held it before standing and hanging the heavy book from his belt. He shuffled around the edge of his desk and approached the window that looked out over the City of Sun.

"I have seen the future of our people, Arbiter Beck. Not just our people, but all people. There is a darkness rising that has not been seen since before the Inquisition existed, and we are not prepared to face it.

"But I believe I have also seen a way for us to survive it. I need the Pirate Isles to be united, and I need them willing to fight on our side when the time comes. I am playing a long game, and Drake was but a pawn to be sacrificed for the greater good."

"What about me?" Beck wasn't sure she wanted to hear the answer. "Was I a pawn too?"

Hironous Vance glanced over his shoulder and smiled. "Yes. But I knew you would survive and return to me, Arbiter Beck. Your part is not yet done."

Books by Rob J. Hayes

The Ties that Bind
The Heresy Within
The Colour of Vengeance
The Price of Faith

Best Laid Plans
Where Loyalties Lie
The Fifth Empire of Man

It Takes a Thief...
It Takes a Thief to Catch a Sunrise
It Takes a Thief to Start a Fire

13106942R00231

Printed in Great Britain
by Amazon